# the Ironclad Exile

## Michel R. Vaillancourt

ISBN-13: 978-0-9879819-4-3

# Dedication

This novel is dedicated to my loving wife who has quietly supported me through my bouts of low confidence and worry. Thank you; most of what I make it through, I do because of you.

It also partially exists because of "Professor Elemental", whose song "Steam Powered" was entirely to blame for this "underwater colony". Thank you; your music, lyrics and wit keep telling me there is something worth doing with this thing we call Steampunk.

It is also dedicated to the entire rainbow of folks within the writing, fandom and steampunk communities. Your lives and your labours enrich the experience for everyone around you, and that needed to be reflected within this text. Representation matters. I hope that I got it right.

# Prologue

*Before I begin my story this evening, ladies and gentlemen of the Baslaurent Historical Culture Society, I would like to preface it with a few comments.*

*It might all seem far away, or long ago, but the events and more importantly, the people of this story set the stage and paved the way for the place we all know and live today. History is about people moreso than events; it is how the people of the time and place react and deal with the unfolding events that make the story of history compelling.*

*I wish to assure you that everything you are about to hear this evening is as true as I have been possibly able to ascertain. From dozens of interviews, to the review of hundreds of official transcripts, to the notes of my own journal, what you are about to hear is what happened in as much truth and detail as can be mustered.*

*I have done my best to avoid personal bias in the retelling, but as we all know of the recording and teaching of history, it is inherently a construct of the reconstructor.*

*Our story begins with our crew of heroes and their ship, returning home from a mundane foraging mission ...*

# CHAPTER ONE

## *Solitudes and Underseas*

### Cordelia
### 02h23 Standard Signal Time
### Thursday, April 7th

Cordelia ran her hand along the fresh-cut length of tree-trunk, feeling the texture of the bark under her fingers. Around her, filling the dimly lit cargo module, were rack upon rack of logs like these. Each rack contained three-and-a-half cubic metres of logs, cut in two metre lengths. All in all, there was twenty-four "cords" of wood here, filling the entire cargo module she was in from floor to ceiling, save for a narrow walkway down its length. There were four such cargo modules, equally filled with the precious cargo.

She closed her eyes as she inhaled deeply, savouring the smell of pine, of spruce, of earth, of fresh-water wet, of 'green'; smells which she had spent more than half her life thus far unable to enjoy. She sighed, her eyes still closed, and leaned forward against the logs.

A bit of sap made her fingers sticky and she giggled slightly as she played with the sensation. She glanced around in embarrassment at the noise, even though she knew she was alone.

She pushed off the log-rack and walked a few steps, until her work-booted feet made a small splash. She paused, looking down at the puddle on the deck. She set to one knee and dabbled her fingers in the water, then lifted them to her nose in the demi-gloom. Not a whiff of salt, she noted with a nod. Condensation, then, from the humidity of the tonnes of freshly cut wood in this room; chilling against the cold metal of the walls, ceiling, and floors, slowly dribbling down those surfaces, and then pooling here.

She dabbled her fingers in the small puddle again, thinking about the bizarre circumstances by which she had gotten here. Like most of the girls of her Generation, "Gen-7", in her youth Cordelia Baasch had never really thought much about the world she grew up in. It was a kilometre-wide bubble of air, glass, steel, and concrete sitting on the bottom of the sea; was not everyone's?

Her world always had dolphins that helped divers harvesting seaweed and herding fish. Her world always had tree parks that children played in, able to watch the creatures of the sea swimming past on the other side of the cerami-glass wall. Her world always had brave submarine crews that travelled far and wide, bringing back rare treasures from distant places.

Her world always had careful attention to the balance of "*green, blue and you*". Her youth was just like everyone else living in the New World, a collection of nearly two hundred seafloor towns scattered around the globe, living in harmony with the ecosystem surrounding them.

Then she grew up and learned the world was a little more complicated than all that. She turned sixteen and got her first "Precursor Studies" lecture and nearly cried. Then she turned nineteen and took her Standardised Aptitude Determination Exams, like every girl in Gen-7 did.

Her aptitudes, unlike most of the girls of Gen-7, were in breaking things, dragging things, burning things, distilling things, melting things down and blowing things up. In short order, she was assigned to the Reclamation Service and a scant three years later she had her own team. Shortly after that, she was assigned to the newly launched Reclamation Service Amphibious Vessel "*Sheerah*".

She smirked and shook her head lightly, thinking back to the day she had first boarded the *RSAV Sheerah*. "Never a dull day in the Reclamation Service, that is for sure," she chuckled in a low voice.

She stood, adjusting her blue dungarees and the tool belt that sat at her hips. She picked at a tear in the orange trim that marked one of her pockets, frowning at it. While the dungarees and the work shirt under it were a slate blue, the mouth of every pocket, the belt loops, the neckline and collar, the wrist and ankle cuffs were all a sharp orange. She wondered if they would ever change to other colours; probably not, she guessed. The Service was not big on changing things with good reason behind them that worked perfectly well.

As a minimum, she would like if they at least stopped making them in "*five standard sizes that fit no one*". She did not know a woman in the Fleet that they fit well. Cordelia was a bit taller than most women, a bit more solid than most women, and quite a bit curvier than most women. In her case, she wound up having to wear the men's "large" size to not feel like she was putting on a show every time she moved.

Not that she *minded* putting on a show, she thought with a chuckle. That was her other job, after all; but she did it on her terms and under far different circumstances than in a salvage ship, living in close quarters with more than thirty other people.

As she walked towards the door of the cargo module leading into the rest of the ship, she took another deep breath. The Spirits only knew when she might smell these scents again.

# Hal

He stared at the roof over his bunk, listening to the sounds of the ship. Sleep was not readily available tonight. In fact, it was largely absent. He rubbed at the spot between his eyes, just above his nose. He rolled over onto one elbow and his eyes sought out the clock on the wall of his cabin. A small electric light illuminated the two black hands slowly creeping across its face. He sighed at the hour.

He gave up and got up. After a moment of indecision, he relocated himself to the modest lounger-chair and picked up a book he had been meaning to read for some time. It was an account of an archaeological expedition mounted by researchers at 24N80W; a friend of his had told him it was a very engaging read.

He managed a few pages before he found himself staring at the photo on his desk. Him, in his dress uniform; a freshly made officer of the Reclamation Services. His mother and his sister, each looking resplendent in their hats and silk gowns.

Painfully absent from the photo was his father. They had not really talked much in the year from his nineteenth to his twentieth birthdays; his father had disagreed with Hal not having taken the chance to opt out of his Standardised Aptitude Determination Exams with the "Inheritance" clause and learn the Foundry business from him.

When he graduated, nearly at the top of his class, his father had not been there.

Hal closed the book quietly, setting it in the pocket on the side of the mahogany armrest of the chair. He gazed at the photo, hearing the last argument he and his father had play over again. The STADEs were there to ensure that everyone did the job to which they were best suited, to benefit everyone at Soumerville. That was their purpose.

He wanted the life that the STADE results told him he could have;

command crew of an RSAV. His life would be one of sailing beneath the seas for a thousand or more kilometres to all points of the compass. He had fancied it to be questing like a submarine knight for the crucial resources left behind by the Precursors, needed so badly now by the citizens of Soumerville. Let someone else learn to manage the Foundry; someone that the STADE results said would both enjoy it and excel at it. Soumerville needed to come before family pride.

Three years had elapsed since then. They had not spoken since.

He picked up the microphone from the intercom box near the chair and a small blue light came on under the speaker grill. As he keyed the microphone, a red light glowed beside the already illuminated blue. "Comm? Captain here. How are we?"

There was a pause and then a soft, almost smokey voice emerged. "Counsellor Koolen here, Captain. All is quiet. The vessel is progressing on autopilot. Mister Zupan laid in a four-hour course and went to get some sleep. I am on Watch while he rests."

"Thank you, Ise," Hal replied. "He does not sleep enough when we are at sea. What depth are we at?"

"Currently we are approximately in the middle of the water column, at eleven metres depth. Autopilot variance thus far has been plus or minus two metres. We are also staying within ninety metres of the centre of the track on the horizontal," Ise Koolen replied.

"All right. So, nothing to worry about then?" he asked.

"Nothing at all, Captain," came the woman's voice. She paused for a moment before continuing. "If you are feeling restless or remorseful, Captain, try some of the new 'Evening Waltzes' by Sumatrin that are part of the collection of Analog Magnetic Tape Cartridges we have in the Library for this voyage. I find them quite soothing."

Hal shook his head and laughed for a moment. She was incredibly good at what she did, he reflected. Less than a hundred words said between them in this conversation and she had him figured out, as well as having tabled a remedy.

"I think that is a very good idea, Counsellor. I will take your suggestion and do that. Call me if anything transpires up there that needs a second set of eyes."

"Of course, Captain."

# Cordelia
## 14h30 Standard Signal Time
## Thursday, April 7th
## 45.72N, 56.31W
## Temp 13c, Winds SW 40kph

"I cannot wait to get home, get these dungarees off, put on dress and silky stockings, and feel like a proper woman again," Cordelia Baasch groused from her operations position as she tousled her now-loosened blonde locks. She gave her hair another shake and put it back up into the work-kerchief. She stretched, desperately wishing for both a neck massage as well as a gin and tonic. Her crew chair, for all its supposed comfort in curved and sloped oak with goose-down-filled leather padding, felt like an ironing board to her right now.

Her eyes met those of Hal Lum, the master and commander of the *RSAV Sheerah*, who was glancing over at the woman who was his Salvage Leader. He chuckled mildly and then returned his gaze towards the modestly sized windows framed in a "mostly polished" brass that showed them the blue-green ocean ahead of them.

"I am sure the lads in the Crystal Parlour will appreciate having their favourite singing voice artfully draped over the grand piano for a few nights while we unload the harvest and then restock fuel and supplies," he commented. Even with the dim lighting of the Command Compartment, his features visibly carried a restrained amusement that was also hinted at in his voice.

She had known Hal for years; like her, he was a Gen-Seven'er. Unlike her, he had always done well in all the social places. He was a natural leader; gifted with the sort of constant, steady "we can do this" aura that persuaded everyone around him to go along with whatever harebrained schemes he had come up with. He had always had some pretty thing on his arm as they both went through their teenage years, but never long enough to really call it a commitment.

Like most of the girls of her age, she had been completely infatuated with him. Old fashioned good looks set on dark skin; courtesy and a proper gentleman; honest and charming; smart as a whip to go with all of it. There was not much to dislike. As with most of her peers, she had never screwed up the courage to even talk to him.

Then "her age" was suddenly nineteen, and there was a job that had to be done. She had thrown herself at the working adventure that was learning Salvage and Diving Operations in the Reclamation Service. Her passion for her work summarily consumed her. Hal was forgotten completely, as well as any other combination of a handsome smile and nice tush that had gotten her girlish attention. There was a community that needed her and she dove into her assigned career with gusto.

Three years later she had proudly marched aboard the *RSAV Sheerah*, in charge of her own Detail. She was ready for anything.

As small worlds go, 45N50W was smaller than most; even so, she had not been quite ready for the surprise that greeted her. In the centre seat was the youngest Captain in the fleet; Hal Lum.

She had presumed he would have gone into the family business of running the Foundry, or something of the ilk. That had apparently never been his intention. He had surprised her a few more times in the two years since then with his stubbornness, his sense of fair play and his

11

dedication to his ship and his crew.

The Navigator and Pilot, Jonas Zupan, glanced over his shoulder away from the windows and scrolling map display towards the pair. He grinned. "Aw, Skipper, you really ought to hear her. Lovely voice; it is a pity she does not grace us with it when we are out here."

She did her best to avoid an outward groan. Jonas was, by any way or mean, a womanising booze artist. Unfortunately for Cordelia, that meant a certain amount of unwelcome attention from Jonas. He had never laid a hand on her; after all, that sort of thing got you into such grief in Soumerville that she had never worried about him, or any other man, really. Still, he could be counted upon to show up intoxicated at least once to any trio of weekend performances she might sing for at the Crystal Parlour Lounge.

To add to her perceived misfortune was the fact he was a damn fine driver and navigator. He understood the way the RSAV moved at nearly instinctive level; even smelling of alcohol he was still "only" in the top half of RSAV pilot-navigators. When he was sober and determined, she trusted his abilities completely. In other words, she was ostensibly "lucky" to be on a ship with an ace captain, an ace driver and an ace engineer.

"I keep work and play firmly separated, thank-you," she snorted in mock hauteur. "If you want to hear the music or gawk the curves, gentlemen, you will simply have to drag yourselves to the 'Parlour on one of the evenings I am performing."

"Oh, you know I do, Cordie. It is well worth the walk from clear across the 'Ville," Jonas replied playfully.

"Alternately, just fail to plug your ears any time the dear lady in question is in the shower aboard this boat," the Chief Engineering Artificer, Marlon Pryce, declared as he came into the command compartment. "You manage to drown out thirty-two hundred-thousand watts of turbo-diesels as soon as the hot water hits you, my dear."

There was a moment of silence punctuated by the "clang" of the watertight door closing behind his entrance, followed by a deluge of uproarious laughter. All a completely taken aback Cordelia could manage was spluttered denials and finger-shaking.

Chief Pryce, or Marlon as he preferred, was the ace engineer she was "lucky" to be crewed with. In truth, he was a certified genius as pertained to either modern technology or Precursor relics. Many times what was simply a rusted brick to her was a "*fully articulated whirly pop with self-cleaning centi-thump bowler top*" or some similar thing to Marlon.

Of course, he had the advantage of age and experience over the rest of the crew. He was Gen-Six, which made him more than a full twenty-five years older than either Hal or herself. He had boarded his first RSAV while she was freshly into diapers. Self-described as "old and slow" or not, he was a ruthless card player, a brutal wit and a calm voice in the midst of tension.

Marlon was sort of the salt-and-peppered Uncle to the entire crew. This was why he teased her about her singing in the shower; he knew her singing voice was a point of pride to her.

"Order in the Comm, ladies and gentlemen, order in the Comm, please," Hal Lum loudly declared over the merriment.

"You, sir, may well find yourself a tad dry on 'Recreationals' the next trip out," she threatened with a wicked twinkle in her green eyes. She found it hard to be mad at Marlon. On the other hand, he was not the only one that knew a few weaknesses open to teasing.

"Now, now, hold on there dear lady! There is no reason to threaten a man's Scotch supply over a remark. Particularly a complimentary one about the clarity and extensiveness of your absolutely divine singing voice," the engineer replied, waving his hands in mock distress.

"I am sure that is exactly how you intended it, as well, sir," she retorted, drumming her fingers on the leather-padded arm of her crew chair. She was trying to maintain a healthy looking scowl of menace and doom, but suspected an amused smile was ruining the effect.

"Captain, sir, contact by passive acoustic, bearing right four-five, up two-seven" Jonas Zupan broke in. "We are running electric at seventy-five percent power; no expected tell-tale."

## Hal

He always felt an almost guilty tingle of excitement at the call of "contact" from either the Pilot at sea, or the Chief Armsman on land.

Statistically, Hal knew, it was going to be a whale. More than half the "contacts" encountered by the *Sheerah* and her sister ships were whales or sharks of some kind. If it was not a whale, then half the remaining odds said it was a false positive; a trick of water layers above them, or perhaps a defective hull microphone, or something. Beyond that point, half of those remaining odds said it was still some kind of ocean life.

It was that half-beyond-half-beyond-half, those very small but very real odds, that gave him that tingle of excitement. Perhaps they would have the ridiculous luck of finding a Precursor hulk. Of course, the last one of those recorded found was by 50N10W almost half a century ago; it was the stuff of legend.

"Thank-you, Pilot," he answered, careful to keep his voice calm and neutral. "Quiet in the Comm, please."

They had been away from home for almost ten days now and were within a day or two of another successful return. The crew would pick up on his mood; "homebound fever" would amplify it. Rocksteady.

"Quiet in the Comm, please," he repeated. "Reduce speed to forty percent, steady on the course. Your guess, Pilot?"

Zupan turned his pedestal-mounted crew chair to the left towards the engineering relay console. He then pulled two pairs of wood and brass levers back towards him to the engraved "four" mark on the side of their housing. His hand slid quickly across the polished and waxed wood surface of the control panel ahead of him, watching the corresponding four rows of twenty small electric lights. They all rapidly retreated from right to the left, until just eight bulbs in each row were still glowing softly. As they did, he flipped a trio of switches to their alternate positions and a yellow flashing light extinguished.

He turned his chair all the way to right, towards the sensor operations console there. He stared at the glowing gauges and trio of black-and-green screens. He adjusted a pair of brass dials slowly, one hand on each, first to the left and then to the right. He flipped a pair of switches upward, frowned, shook his head and then flipped one back down, clearly unsatisfied with the results he was getting.

Jonas Zupan, for the debaucherous tendencies in his personal life, was pretty much everything that a "Reclaimer"-class RSAV skipper could want in a pilot, in Hal's eyes at least. Most importantly, the debaucherous tendencies in Jonas' personal life stayed ashore.

RSAV pilots tended to be drama queens and colourful characters. It seemed to go with the territory. Some, however, did not leave that ashore. Fraternisation, wine breath and flippant disrespect were common enough to have become a stereotype of Pilot-Navigators over the history of RSAV operations.

Jonas, on the other hand, was such that when the airlocks closed and the clamps released, the man was a remarkably reliable officer. He loved his work, and Hal's impression was that it was pretty much all Jonas Zupan lived for. There were two times for Jonas, it seemed; in the pilot chair, and out of it. He all but slept at his position some days, even though gyroscopic autopilots had been available to the Mk.II Reclaimers; the *Sheerah* was a Mk.III.

Beyond the fact Jonas obviously loved his work, he was also surprisingly good at it. He could make a bottom-roll or rubble-roll feel like it was a grassy field. He always seemed to be able to keep a dead-level trim, even with a Beaufort Nine churning up the water column. He also seemed to have a knack for getting the ship where they wanted to go a little bit faster and a little bit cheaper than expected.

"Giant octopus," the Pilot-Navigator replied. "No mechanical noises, so it has to be biological. It is moving fast and it is churning a lot of water, so it is large, but I am not hearing singing. So it is not a whale. At this time of year, that means giant octopus."

"Well done, Pilot. Where are we?" Hal inquired. His eyes glanced towards the windows as though he might glimpse the beast, which was likely more than twelve hundred metres away.

"By run time from last *schnorkel* fix, estimating five hundred kilometres West-North-West of Soumerville, now making good five kilometres per hour at eighteen metres down. We have three metres below the keel wet with a sand bottom," Jonas replied.

Hal Lum looked towards Jonas Zupan. "Is our over-sized cephalopod obstruction clear of our position yet?"

"No, Sir. Still about the same relative bearing, drawing towards the bow slightly now that we have slowed down."

"Mister Olivier, ring the Bell, please. I do not want the poor creature mistaking us for a whale or something and having a bad experience with the treads or the thrusters," Lum ordered, looking towards the Chief Armsman.

"Aye-aye, Captain," came the reply.

If, once upon a time long past, it was ever considered ethically or morally acceptable to slam a several hundred-tonne steel hull into an ocean creature whose world you were visiting, simply because it was "in the way", that time was long gone. In the current day, no RSAV or MSSV skipper worth the crossed anchors on his or her lapels would even consider it. Soumerville, her RSAVs, and the population that depended on them, were now an integrated part of the same world as that giant octopus, which was somewhere out there ahead of them in the water.

Someone, a retired Gen-Five'er, had once told Hal that the Precursors had known that whales had names, and even "signed" their songs. They had known that even the smallest cephalopods would "play" and could problem solve. Orcas had been documented running "protection rackets" on northern fishing ships. Dolphins developed and taught each other new hunting techniques. Manta-rays would play "tag" with mini-subs studying them. Heaps upon scads of research pointed to the idea that the ocean was full of intelligence, and of personalities.

For some reason, the leaders and citizens of the Precursors had ignored that knowledge. In the here-and-now, every RSAV crew person knew and understood they were guests and visitors in this ocean that hid them, protected them, and provided for them. Its denizens were to be treated with respect.

Olivier keyed his intercom and a trio of chimes rung throughout the entire ship. "Attention all hands, mind your ears; Air bell. Mind your ears; Air bell."

He flipped two ebony toggle switches to the 'up' position and watched a gauge. In the bow, a piston cylinder was now pressurising with air. The piston itself was locked in place by a pair of sliding bolts, released by the third, red-painted, switch under the fingers of the Chief Armsman.

At his position, the Pilot-Navigator hastily turned his acoustic listening equipment off.

As the gauge crossed into the middle of the 'yellow zone', Olivier flipped the third switch. The bolts retracted swiftly, allowing the piston to slam forward violently into a thickened piece of the outer hull, generating a deep and eye-bulgingly loud reverberation. Effectively, the entire vessel's hull had been rung like a Precursor religious bell.

Everyone in the Comm worked their jaws and blinked to clear the ringing from their ears. "Well, Mister Zupan? Where is it?" Lum demanded.

The Pilot-Navigator turned his acoustic sensors back on and slowly rotated one of the dials in a full circle. "That did it, Skipper. It has fled. We are clear of contacts, though, everything within about thirty clicks knows pretty much where we are right now."

"Understood, Mister Zupan. Ahead all at ninety percent of cavitation threshold, initiate zig-zag advance on six-minute pacing for thirty minutes, then set power to eighty percent and best course for home," Hal ordered.

"By 'The Book', hey, Skipper?" Jonas grinned.

"Always, Mister Zupan, always. 'The Book' was written for a reason, and so far it has never been wrong," Hal chuckled in reply.

Jonas was right, of course. It was a text-book "step-aside" protocol so that any other ship that might have heard the "air bell", and was now hunting them, would have problems figuring out where they were going, as well as getting behind them.

The fact of the matter was that in the entire time he had been training for, and then actually sailing on RSAVs, Hal had never met anyone who had ever been Hunted. Nor had it ever happened to him. It was a hold-over in The Book from the period of chaos that the Generation One's had lived through, right through the years of Generation Three. However, just because it had not happened recently did not automatically mean it would never happen again.

"... And since we are discussing The Book, I note that it has been at least a full day since the last Round. Since this is as good a time as any, give me a Round, please," he ordered as his gaze moved from the piloting station to the windows ahead of them.

"Navigation, Skipper," Jonas said with a nod, "We just got out of the Great River influence zone about an hour ago. Eee-Tee-Aay, based on resumption of normal cruising at speed six is forty-eight hours; that should be on the ninth at around fourteen-thirty SST," Zupan replied.

"Very good, Pilot, that will get us home just in time for the tail of brunch," Hal grinned. "Next?"

"Engineering," Pryce began, "Right now we have about four full days of fuel, good for about twelve-fifty clicks of submerged running at full power. So, even at our current speed, we should still have plenty to get us back to the barn. All machinery is in good working order, all service and maintenance is up to date. No known issues."

Lum nodded and then looked over at Christopher Olivier, the lean and muscled Chief Armsman who had been impassively listening to the goings-on to this point. "Security?"

## Christopher

"Security: Nothing to report. The ship is currently in 'down-stations', so fore and aft deck weapons are in, caged and unmanned," Christopher replied.

"Short and to the point, Chief," Hal said with an amused smirk.

"Always, sir," was the Armsman's curt reply.

In general, he normally said little. It was intentional; his job was facts and details. His guideposts were brevity and clarity. Conjecture and opinion were not for duty hours. Small talk was for full lounges and half-litres. His job was the safety of the crew and the RSAV; if he allowed conjecture to replace facts or small-talk to muddy clarity, people in his care would die.

He had seen it happen once to another Armsman; two of Christopher's friends died in that single lapse of judgment. There would be no way he made the same mistake now that he had his own Security Detail and his own ship.

If that meant that he seemed distant or perhaps even cold to his crewmates, then so be it. He would much rather be right than nice when the safety pins got pulled and the knife switches on the weapons arming circuits got thrown. As long as his crewmates and Detail members were still around with the option to misunderstand him, he was doing his job.

Hal tried a bit too hard to be friendly, in Christopher's eyes. Hal was the Captain; not the Spirit and Morale Guide. Like Christopher, Hal's job was to be effective, not chummy. Thus far, Fate had not seen fit to bite Hal Lum in the ass, but the Armsman had a sincere sensation it was both long overdue and shortly to arrive.

Cordelia Baasch took a sip from the water flask she had at her hip belt. She recapped the flask as she began. "Salvage and Stores: Food and water for fifteen days remaining. Two hundred tonnes of cut wood logs in cargo. One Ess-and-Dee crew member in sickbay as a result of an operations accident."

Christopher glanced between Hal and Cordelia. Hal nodded at the woman as he replied.

"Your team did a banner job, Chief. Just make sure they understand that no amount of timber, scrap-steel, seaweed, venison, or whatever, is worth someone winding up in Emm-and-Que with a cracked skull, all right?"

Christopher scowled behind his mask of impassivity. Cordelia was dangerous; everything she did was flashy and on the borders of practice and protocol. If given the choice between a cutting wheel and a blast-pack, she could be counted on to reach for the blast-pack, if not two of them, every time.

Beyond that, she imparted that same sense of impatience with "good enough" or "to standard" to her own Ess-and-Ess Detail. She bred recklessness in her team from her own dissatisfaction with Fleet procedure books. Two days ago it had resulted in a badly executed tree-drop that injured one of her Detail.

Christopher considered that nearly criminal. Hal, predictably, patted her on the head and made "there-there" noises at her.

A speaker chimed softly, a blue light illuminated beneath it, and a soft, feminine voice emerged. "Spirit and Morale: Over all, positive. The Crew are fatigued but content with results of the trip so far. Some symptoms of 'homebound fever', but nothing which should cause concern."

"Thank you, Counsellor Koolen," Lum replied.

Miz Koolen, in Christopher's perspective, was one of the more redeeming features of being assigned to the *RSAV Sheerah*. He could listen to her voice over the intercoms or radios all day. She seemed to be a beacon of calm and reason in this metal-bound basin of chaos. Like himself, she used both brevity and clarity to ensure she was getting the message to her listeners.

They did what some might see as radically different jobs. However, it was his opinion that they were not entirely dissimilar. He was a guardian of the physical, and she was a guardian of the soul. To his eyes, it was evident she was as dedicated, studied and professional in her job as he was.

21

She delightfully lithe, with dark hair and dark skin. Even in the ubiquitous blue-and-orange shipboard dungarees that seemed to androgenise women as curvy as the outrageous Miz Baasch, Ise Koolen still managed to seem soft, feminine and approachable. He loved to watch her walk; when on shore Ops, he often insisted on being her dry-side escort as she visited with everyone wherever they were working. He would never tell her, of course, that beyond the importance of her personal safety was the pleasure he derived from just following her on her tasks.

"It is my pleasure to Serve and Guide, Captain," came the soft voice and then the blue light went dark, leaving only a red beside it lit. Christopher shifted at his post, wondering as he often did about what she thought of him.

Another intercom speaker behaved as the first had, permitting a cigars-and-gravel voice to emerge. "Medical and Quarantine report: Miz Klára Reed, Salvage and Dive Tech Third Class, is still recovering from her kinetic encounter with gravity propelled tree-limb to the forehead. Twelve stitches, concussion, off duties for three more days, confined to Emm-and-Que until tomorrow after breakfast. No other medical issues. Medical supplies and stores are in order."

"Thank-you, Mister Émile," Lum replied with a friendly nod in the direction of the wood-and-metal speaker box, as though the Chief Medic could see him.

To Christopher, Damiano Émile was another kindred soul. Few words, little frivolity, and genuine talent packaged in genuine professionalism. He did not babble aimlessly in some attempt to candy coat a problem. All you got with the Chief Medic was the point-blank truth, often flavoured with salt and vinegar if your circumstances were self-inflicted. Damiano visibly had the same very finite tolerance for fools and "walking ballast" that the Armsman did.

"Damiano Émile, out," came the terse reply and the blue light went out.

"We will do a weather test at twenty-hundred," Hal Lum stated, "and if the sea state has come down, we will pick up the pace with some surface cruising. Miz Baasch is correct; for a whole host of reasons, it will be good to be home."

Christopher Olivier tried very hard to not roll his eyes and allow a long-suffering sigh to escape. "Home" was merely the useless period for an RSAV like the *Sheerah*. Being parked for ten days in a "moon dock" while Ess-and-Ess techs and staff unloaded the contents of the cargo bays, while reloading the larder and storage tanks, was a waste of his time.

Sure, as with everyone else at 45N50W, he had his Second Career to keep him occupied during his "off cycle". As a mechanism to ensure that "hard skill" folks did not loose their appreciation for the need of "soft skill" people, as well as vice-versa, the "6-2-4-2 Main And Second" rule had been put in place during Gen-Two. So, if you worked six days at your Main profession, you were expected to work four days at your Secondary, with a two day break before and after your Second.

While aptitude testing chose your Main for you, it was up to the individual to pursue something they loved outside their normal scope for their Second. For example, the outrageous Miz Baasch was a "performance artist" at a gentleman's club. Ise Koolen was a park gardener, tending to a Forest Room. Christopher had heard Hal Lum was writing a social history fiction novel or something similar.

Christopher taught body fitness training. It was the least wasteful use of his time that he could come up with. Ultimately, that was the best he could say about his time not aboard the *RSAV Sheerah*.

Maybe he would use some of his wasted time thinking about how to arrange for Cordelia and Hal to get the lessons they both seemed to sorely need on the next voyage.  That would be well worth his time.

# CHAPTER TWO
## *Of Motors and Men*

**Marlon**
**13h51 Standard Signal Time**
**Friday, April 8th**
**45.34N,53.26W**
**Temp 9C, Winds S 6kph**

He had just gotten his bread down in the infernal device everyone else called a toaster when the aluminium-bound, cherry-wood-boxed wall speaker wailed for attention. He, as well as everyone else in the "O-Room", tensed and looked at the intercom box. A yellow light illuminated beneath it and then the words he dreaded reached his ears, delivered in Miz Baasch's clear voice.

"Engine Room emergency, Engine Room emergency. SEE-EEE-AY to the Engine Room. Engine Room emergency, Engine Room emergency. SEE-EEE-AY to the Engine Room. Captain to the Bridge, please."

Breakfast was immediately forgotten. He was out the door and swiftly moving down the central spinal corridor, or the "Salt Flats" as they were known, even before the yellow light had gone out once again. As he pulled open the watertight door that lead into the Engine Room, he sensed two immediate changes in the Old Girl's demeanour; she was angling upwards sharply and she was falling silent.

*"Like any woman,"* Marlon Pryce thought to himself amusedly, *"when she turns her nose up and stops talking to you, then you are in trouble. Quite likely a lot of it."*

"Chief!" Thilo Darzi bellowed from his position in front of the main control board. "Both seawater cooling pumps have failed and we have high-temperature alarms on both the mag-drives and the gearbox. I have advised the Comm and they have ordered all stop and blown all but the reserve tank."

"Good work, Mister Darzi. What are you doing about the pumps?" Marlon questioned as he made his way over to where the other man was.

"Lagounov and Davis are already on it. One is checking the breakers, the other is checking the intake manifold," Darzi replied.

The intercom box near the control station glowed yellow and then Hal Lum's voice emerged. "Engine Room, this the Comm. Update, please."

Marlon leaned over and pressed the "Talk" button and a lamp glowed red. "Preliminary is that we have lost cooling flow. We are investigating probable causes right now. You are fully restricted from anything but emergency electric motor operation and turbo-diesel operations are fully restricted with no exceptions."

There was a pause and then Hal replied. "Understood, Chief. We are coming to periscope depth as a precaution. Let me know as soon as you get a diagnosis and an ETA."

"Aye-Aye, Skipper. Engine room, out," Marlon answered. He flipped the "Talk" switch the other way and looked over at Darzi.

"I am taking over the watch keeping station. I want you to go check with Miz Lagounov and find out what progress she is making. When

26

Chamberlin gets down here, I will get him working with Mister Davis. Let me know if you need anything," Marlon ordered.

"Yes, Chief!" Darzi replied. He grabbed a work-bag of common tools and related items, then headed towards the breaker panels at the rear of the engine room.

Marlon slid into the watch keeper's chair and updated the log book to reflect the hand-over as well as note the current status. He glanced at the dials and gauges with an expert eye, then made a quick set of notes in the log book.

All in all, Marlon reflected, Hal Lum was not a bad skipper given his relative youth. Pryce had sailed with some notably worse and few better. However, one of those things about Hal that Marlon particularly liked was the captain's ability to trust his department heads to get the job done.

He might be sitting in the Big Chair mentally chewing his finger nails right now, but he would never show it. More importantly, Hal could be counted on to patiently wait for Marlon and his team to get on top of the problem.

To Marlon Pryce, that was worth its weight in nickel ingots. Marlon was not one of "those" engineers that forbade anyone not part of the Engineering Detail from stopping by to visit. To the contrary, he actually liked everyone he worked with to understand the value of what his Detail did and the less-than-glamorous conditions under which they served. On the other hand, having a nervous or micro-managing ship-boss pacing behind him and demanding progress reports every four-point-seven minutes was exactly the sort of thing that drove Marlon batty.

A bit less than three-quarters of an hour later, Marlon toggled the "Talk" switch on the intercom box for the Command Compartment. "Comm, this is Engines. We have a status update," he said as he wiped his hands on a rag. His team was clustered around where he sat at the watch-keeping station to listen in. All of them were covered in noticeable quantities of fresh grime and sweat.

"Engine room, go ahead with your report," Hal replied.

"This one goes under the heading of 'just stupid circumstances', Skipper," Marlon began, shaking his head and casting his eyes towards the deck-head. "We had the primary saltwater cooling pump fail on us as a result of something gone wrong inside the pump. What should have happened at that point is the pressure drop on the plumbing should have had an automatic gate-valve isolate the primary and open flow to the secondary, except that valve was seized shut from disuse. No flow to the secondary meant that it could not and would not spin up safely. That is when the alarms went off as temperatures started climbing."

"So we have a dead pump and a dead by-pass valve. What else?" Hal asked, his voice sounding slightly metallic over the intercom.

"That seems to be the extent of damage at this time. The duty Engineering team managed the situation properly and we seem to be in good shape," the aged chief engineer responded.

"Good. Well done to your Detail, Chief. What is involved in the repairs and how long will they take?"

"We are going to replace the faulty by-pass valve first and then restore cooling on the secondary pump. That will take about an hour. Once that is done, you will have both the Mags and the Tee-Dees available at thirty percent power," Marlon said, glancing for confirmation at some notes written in a scrawl worthy of a surgeon.

"All right. Thirty percent is more than enough for sea-keeping and avoidance. How long to get restrictions lifted?"

"At least four hours, Skipper. We will have to remove the primary pump, determine what is actually damaged with it, get it fixed if possible, then put it back into place and test it. That is a non-trivial tasking, Skipper," Marlon stated, running a hand through his greying hair.

"Understood, Chief. Current sea-surface conditions are light and favourable, so we are going to stay at periscope depth until the issue is resolved. We will message Dockyard Operations to push our Eee-Tee-Aay back by four hours and let them know that we are suffering a mechanical issue. I expect an update in four hours at the latest."

"Understood, Skipper. We will be busting our tails down here to get this fixed."

"I know, Chief. Your team are some of the best people in the Fleet. I have every confidence you will get us out of restrictions as fast as is reasonably possible. I will let you get to the work at hand. Comm, out."

# Hal

Hal Lum sat back in the teak-inlaid, brass-trimmed, oak chair at the centre of the Command Compartment and rubbed at his forehead in a moment of relative silence. Sometimes, he reflected, this chair felt far too big to him to be comfortable. This was currently one of those times.

He was in command of what was now a functionally crippled vessel. Weighing down on him was the distinct possibility that the Engineering Detail would not be able to actually repair the defective primary cooling pump. If they had to limp home on the secondary pump under thirty percent restrictions, it would add almost three days onto their trip time. The problem, of course, was that they did not have three extra days fuel left in their tanks.

He looked over at the leader of his Salvage and Dive Detail, who was currently watching him quietly. "Miz Baasch, prep a RATT-net message and inform 45N50W Dockyard Ops of our current position, situation and revised Eee-Tee-Aay at Soumerville. Work with Mister Zupan as you require for information. While we are on-Net, please get our message pointers up to date; we might as well get caught up on the news while we get repairs made."

"Aye-Aye, Captain," she replied, turning to the Radio Automatic Teletype Terminal controls beside her, starting the warm-up procedure.

Hal looked at the Pilot-Navigator and gestured towards Cordelia as he spoke. "Mister Zupan, keep us at periscope depth until Miz Baasch is done with the streaming antenna. Once she has the RATT traffic transacted and the antenna reeled in, take us back down to one-third depth. Keep speed and power requests within restrictions at all times."

"Aye-aye, Skipper," Jonas replied.

"Call me if you need me, I will be in my cabin writing up an incident report."

# Cordelia

She was not particularly thrilled with the notion of having to work closely with Jonas for anything, but on the other hand, it was hardly like she had to sit in his lap and ignore inappropriate commentary.

"Mister Zupan," she started, looking over towards where Jonas sat, "I am going to start unreeling the floating antenna array as soon as you give me the all-clear. I will get us signed into the network and start the system on collecting our incoming traffic while I work on the outgoing message. Does that sound reasonable?"

"Yep, Miz Baasch, makes smart sense to me. We are clear on acoustic and when we got up to 'scope depth, I took a look around. There was nothing for kilometres that I could see. Take your time and I will keep the Old Girl right where you need her to be while you work."

"Thank-you, Jonas. You are good to work with for stuff like this," she answered with a slight smile towards the Pilot-Navigator.

"Likewise and same, Cordie," Jonas replied, a warm grin alighting his features.

Working with the RATT equipment was one of the more technical aspects of being the Salvage Leader for an RSAV. Essentially, Radio Automatic Teletype Terminal systems used an electromechanical keyboard to encode a message on an Analog Magnetic Tape Cartridges, or AMTAC. The message was recorded as a combination of five high and low tones representing each letter, number, or punctuation. The ship then connected to the RATT network which operated on 45N50W's local frequency using a unique identifier and time-dictated passcode. Then the message recorded to the AMTAC would be played and transmitted to the network.

Once each of the messages that the *Sheerah* had stored were sent out, then the Message Centre at Soumerville would transmit any traffic destined for the at-sea RSAV. The messages were accumulated on AMTACs at the Message Centre, one or two per RSAV so that it was easy to keep track of who had gotten what traffic. Once the *Sheerah* had downloaded all of the message traffic addressed to her from the Message Centre, they would log out of the network and shut the radio off.

Then, the messages were printed off and distributed as needed within the *Sheerah*. When the RSAV got back to Soumerville, the used paper would be shredded and recycled into new paper ready for the next use.

Given that one of the primary jobs of the Reclamation Service was finding out what was going on in the world while looking for natural resources with which to feed Soumerville-style towns, it was decided that the Salvage Leader was most in need of up-to-the-day information after the vessel captain. So, RATT-net operations were made part of the Salvage and Dive Detail's responsibilities by late in the Gen-Two period.

Cordelia worked steadily and quietly to get the antenna itself deployed. All in total, it was about twenty-five metres in length, in metre-long flexible segments that had small floats attached at each joint. When unrolled, the antenna naturally floated to the surface, trailing along behind the RSAV. With even half its' length on the surface, they could easily transmit and receive over distances of a few hundred kilometres while on the move.

The only "catch" to the floating antenna was that it was somewhat fragile; the RSAV had to stay within fifteen metres of the surface, and keep its speed below five kilometres per hour at all times when it was deployed. The current situation meant there was no danger of exceeding the speed limitation, Cordelia thought ruefully.

She flipped a series of switches and then turned a trio of dials to tune the set until a familiar high-frequency squeal emerged from the monitor speaker beside her. She pressed the "connect" button, which resulted in a red lamp glowing and the squealing from the speaker getting louder. Then the speaker went silent and the red lamp extinguished itself as a yellow and blue pair began blinking in alternation.

She then flipped open a passcode book, looked up the correct code for the current four-hour period and keyed it in. The yellow and blue lights flickered back and forth a few times and then the yellow went out, to be replaced with a green.

"Got it on the first try, Cordie?" Zupan asked from where he had been watching her work.

She grinned and nodded. "Yeah, I am getting better at this. Well, that, and the upgrades they did on the digipeaters last time we had a Work Period has made a huge difference. The tuning controls work a lot better now."

"That is good to hear. That thing is pretty much our life-line while we are out here," the Pilot-Navigator said, turning back to his own consoles.

She keyed in the request for a message update and pushed an AMTAC into one of the three slots available. She then flipped a switch and started recording the incoming message traffic.

# Ise

Ise Koolen opened her eyes from where she sat cross-legged on the floor. She pulled the hood she wore back and brushed a long lock of milk-chocolate coloured hair away from the dark-chocolate skin of her face. She leaned forward and extinguished a single candle that had been burning with a sweet scent as she meditated. Wax had spilt when the *Sheerah* had surged for the surface.

She stood up, flexed and then stretched. She wondered silently exactly what the details of their current situation were. As the "Spirit and Morale" counsellor for the ship, hers was far less of an immediate operational involvement than that of, say, the Chief Engineering Artificer.

The intercom box chimed softly, a blue light illuminated beneath it and even before a voice emerged, she smiled to herself. That, she guessed, would be Hal Lum giving her a "courtesy call".

"Yes, Captain?" she queried as she moved the chair in front of her desk out of its usual position, and sat "side saddle" on the hardwood surface. She then leaned towards the intercom and rested her chin on a palm.

"How...?" came Hal's startled voice. There was a pause, followed by an amused chuckle and then he continued. "Always at the top of your game, Counsellor. I was just ringing to let you know that in spite of the excitement earlier, we are in no immediate danger. A worst-case scenario is a four or five day delay getting home, after meeting a replenishment vessel."

She nodded to herself before answering, considering the impacts this would have on the crew. "I do not foresee this to be a concern, Captain. While several would be disappointed, we have all weathered worse. My only concern would be Bambang Martinsson; I know he and his wife are expecting the arrival of their newborn any day now."

"Ah, yes. I can completely understand that he would be anxious about being at home soon," Hal answered, thoughtfully.

"Perhaps if we are to AR-VEE with a replenishment vessel, he could be transferred to that vessel for the return trip?" Ise suggested.

There was a pause before Hal Lum replied. "That is an excellent solution to the problem, Ise. I do not think anyone would begrudge him that privilege, given the circumstances. If Chief Pryce cannot get us back to relative normal, then that is how we will handle it. Thank-you, Counsellor."

"It is my pleasure to Serve and Guide, Captain," she replied, a slight smile playing at her lips, unseen by her conversational companion. The blue light went dark, leaving only the red beside it lit. She flipped the privacy switch on her side and the red light went out as well.

She turned a carousel of hanging folders that was at the side of her desk, watching the names on the ends of the folders go by. She stopped and then slid a folder with Martinsson's name on it out from the carrier which held it. She turned on a small electric lamp that cast a pool of yellow-white light over the desk and she picked up a pencil. She made a note of the conversation, skimmed a few prior notes to ensure she was perfectly familiar with the subject's circumstances and then nodded to herself.

She returned the folder to its space of origin on the carousel and then fluidly moved into her chair, and shimmied it back to its usual spot at the desk. She steepled her fingers before her with her elbows on the cloth-covered armrests of the chair, her face partially shadowed by the contrasting light sources. Her training as a Spirit and Morale Counsellor, plus her own nature and gifts, gave her tremendous insights into the people around her aboard the *Sheerah*.

There were tensions throughout the crew which concerned her. Her delicate brow furrowed for a moment and then she pulled the left and right-most bottom drawers of her desk out one-third of their length. She then pulled the centre desk drawer out about one-eighth of its length. She detached two silvered keys from a likewise silvered chain around her neck, and placed one into each of the keyholes above the left and right columns of drawers that formed the desk's 'legs'. She turned both keys together and a metallic 'click' was heard, then the blotter on the desk lifted upwards barely more than the thickness of her fingers. She lifted the front of the blotter upwards a couple of hand-spans to reveal a small, hidden compartment within the desk.

From inside the compartment, she withdrew a folder wrapped in a red leather sleeve. She removed the contents of the folder and pressed the blotter back down until it had clicked back into place securely. She took a pen, then dipped it and began writing.

*As I have noted in previous correspondence, many conversations with the crew of late have revolved around a concern about the 'luck' of the Sheerah and her Captain. Hal Lum's notable position as the youngest and least experienced captain in the fleet and the Sheerah herself being the newest RSAV in the fleet, weighs heavily on the minds of the non-commissioned crew.*

*A notable number of members of the crew have confided to me that they are worried that the string of successful missions will come to an abrupt end when the 'good fortune' of the Sheerah and her Captain runs out. Naturally, I have done what I can to persuade and suggest that Hal Lum is a product of hard work and good training and the 'luck' we are experiencing is a reflection of that. In essence, there is nothing to worry about, since there is no luck to run out of. Most of the individuals in question have given this thought and accepted the reasoning.*

*However, there are a few members of the crew who are proving intractable or implacable on this matter.*

*I am recommending the following six individuals be transferred for Invisible Reasons to other commands:*

> *1. Huey Davis*
>
> *2. Christopher Olivier ...*

# Marlon
## 20h38 Standard Signal Time
## Friday, April 8th

Marlon Pryce closed the hatch behind him as he entered the Command Compartment. He was quite aware everyone present was hoping he had good news, but were expecting bad. It was the nature of failures in Engineering, really. Most of the time, nothing went wrong. When they did, however, things could go remarkably wrong with astonishing swiftness.

"Well, Skipper," he began, "repairs are complete. Ready for the work-through?"

Hal Lum turned slightly to face him and nodded. "Let us hear it. How are we?"

"Well, Captain, in better condition than I expected, to be up front with you. So, per the update three hours ago ..."

"'*When we last left our heroes*'..." the Pilot-Navigator, Jonas Zupan, interrupted with a dramatically intoned quip and a swift grin. Marlon laughed involuntarily and a ripple of chuckles spread throughout the Comm. Marlon liked Jonas. He was a good kid that tried hard and did his best to fit in.

As a Pilot-Navigator, that was hard. That was not sympathetic conjecture on Marlon's part either; in the entire time he had been sailing MSSVs and RSAVs, he had never met one that had not been "broken" in some way, socially. Marlon was of the opinion that it was the most extreme example of Universal Balance he had seen passed out at the individual level.

Only one applicant in ten could actually get through the training required to become an RSAV pilot, regardless of what the STADEs said. They seemed to be a breed apart, gifted with some quirk that let them make a few hundred tons of metal drive a jig or swim a waltz. That same quirk, however, seemed to be the reason that none of them seemed quite able to fit into modern society.

Jonas' only real two 'problems', fortunately for Marlon's opinion of him, were a tendency to play the joker at any turn of a card, and to moon hopelessly for Cordelia Baasch. One of these days, Marlon had decided, he was going to have to take the girl aside and tell her to open her eyes.

Marlon shook his head in amusement as Hal Lum shot his Pilot-Navigator a reproachful look. "Carry on, Chief," Hal requested.

"Right-o, Skipper. So, as I was saying ... per the update three hours ago, the problem was a salt water leak into the bearing raceway for the primary seawater pump. Once a few drops of water got in, the lube started to go out, and then friction heating made a mess. We were able to get the pump out and tear it down on the bench. With some spare parts that Miz Baasch is so meticulous about ensuring we carry, whether we have ever historically needed them or not, we were able to remove the damaged bearing assembly and fashion a replacement. We also took the time to give the entire pump system a careful going over and noted some damage on the impeller blades, and replaced those."

Marlon paused, giving Hal a chance to mentally get caught up before he continued. He took a mouthful of water from the bottle he carried at his waist, like everyone else aboard the ship. He returned the bottle to its carrier and resumed speaking. "So, the forcibly refurbished pump is in place and in operation. Restrictions are seventy percent maximum power for Tee-Dees and Mags for walking, but you can sprint to one-hundred percent for no more than ten minutes an hour."

Hal Lum broke into a grin at his Chief Engineering Artificer's announcement. "Seventy percent for cruising speed? Good work, Chief! That is great news. That will only add a handful of hours onto our trip time, not entire days. We should still be able to make home for the weekend, right Pilot?" Hal asked, turning to Jonas.

Zupan furrowed his brow and looked towards the deck-head for a moment, doing the math in his head. "Aye, Skipper. Without working it out long-hand, I am guessing sometime around twenty-three hundred Saturday, Standard. We might get lucky with currents, though."

"Mister Zupan, ahead seventy percent power, please. Head for home," Hal ordered with a smile.

"Happy to oblige, Skipper."

"Mister Pryce?" Hal questioned, turning towards Marlon.

"Aye, Skipper?"

"Great job. Please thank your team for me. That is outstanding work. Your and your Detail are a credit to the Fleet," Hal stated firmly.

"Very kind of you, Skipper. I will let the boys and girls know. It is good to be appreciated."

A few moments later, as Marlon walked down Salt Flats surrounded by the thrum and rumble of the RSAV in normal cruising, he reflected that Hal was probably one of the most forthcoming Captains he had met thus far, at least when it came to praise and thanks. Hal seemed to go out of his way to make sure everyone heard a lot of positive in the course of a hard day.

It had to be earned, mind you, as Hal did not seem to be one for passing out meaningless cookies, but if you worked hard and you did well, you heard about it. That made him a pretty good Skipper to work for, all in all.

# CHAPTER THREE

*Homecoming*

## Cordelia
## 13h07 Standard Signal Time
## Saturday, April 9th
## Temp 6C, Winds SE 8kph

Most of the command crew were sitting in their lounge, the "O-Room", talking as they finished up breakfast. The lounge was comfortable and homey, with walls covered in a wainscoted northern softwood that had been oiled and polished.

Electric lights, set to look like gas lamps in wall sconces, chased the gloom away. An opened iris valve in the ceiling exposed an armoured window, which was nearly a metre across, to the sunlight streaming down through the relatively shallow waters.

Pictures of Soumerville in the early days, as well as key figures from each of the seven generations who had lived there, were about the compartment. As well, other pictures that were clearly newer showed various highlights of the past three years of missions for the *RSAV Sheerah* and her crew.

The two hexagonal tables of polished hardwood were surrounded by similar chairs with thick pillows on their seat and backs for comfort. The tables and chairs were handcrafted and unique in detail to the *Sheerah*.

A small vent kept a mild breeze blowing through the compartment, to be drawn out another similar vent on the other side of the space. The air smelled vaguely of salt, herbs and spices; a carefully selected mixture designed to keep senses from dulling as well as to keep pests from taking roost in the air system.

There was a small refrigerator that kept some sweets available and a hot-water dispenser to make either tea or coffee. It was a very comfortable sort of place and everyone who made use of it certainly valued it.

Cordelia had a favourite chair, which left her with an easy view of the whole room. As well, it was easy to recline, gaze out the ceiling viewport while day-dreaming and relax. Or, as she often preferred, to curl up with a book and read.

Normally, when you ate breakfast was entirely based on when your sleep rotation had you getting up. Supper was the meal everyone was expected to be present for, by default. Keeping supper as the "common" meal of the day meant that everyone saw everyone at least once a day and had a chance to be social.

However, amongst RSAV crews, for the last in-the-morning breakfast before arrival in Soumerville it was always a tradition to have steak, eggs, as well as a glass of bubbly mixed half-and-half with fruit juice. Everyone in the crew made an effort to be there and take part in the happy atmosphere.

RSAV crews did ten to twelve days out, followed by usually an equal number of days docked. As a result, the "Six-Two-Four-Two Rule" that everyone in Soumerville lived by simply did not work well for the RSAV crews. It worked even less well for the few MSSV crews who could be gone for twenty to forty days at a time.

For the RSAV crews, the schedule instead tended to be more akin to ten days out, followed by three days off. The crew would then spend four to six days Secondary, finishing with three more days off. Then it was time to be back out again on the next mission. The last breakfast before home port, therefore, was a chance to part ways for ten to twelve days with the crew on a good note. It had been a tradition that had been imported from Precursor fleets into the Gen-One RSAV crews and it had been whole-heartily embraced through to the current day.

The latest bit of conversation over the O-Room breakfast tables had been something that was in the "advisory" level message traffic that had come in during the last RATT message download.

"So they have closed down the Rafts entirely?" Cordelia asked, blinking in shock at the news. She was not entirely sure she had heard correctly.

Marlon, who had read the announcement aloud from the message paper he was holding, nodded at her silently even as Hal spoke up. "The Surface Condition Early Warning buoys detected a Green Fog two days ago," Lum said while rubbing at the back of his neck, "and it has been lingering around the Rafts since then. They have closed down all the pumps and pipes for fresh air and they are running the Crackers and mixing in reserve air."

"So this is the third day? But, it has been windy for three days out here. That cloud must be massive!" Zupan blinked.

"Well, if they have to keep the pipes and pumps closed until noon today SST, it will be an unfortunate new record. Keep in mind that even trace amounts of that stuff are damn deadly, so 'any' on a detector is 'too much'."

"It is a good thing we were able to get a RATT message connection before midnight," Marlon said as he sipped his tea. He paused, adding a bit more stevia to sweeten it further. "There is no point surface cruising with a Green Fog, since we cannot run the Tee-Dees. So, as you said on the First Watch Skipper, we might as well head back down and start Saturation."

"Tee-Dees" were the "turbo-diesels", Cordelia knew. They were air-hungry beasts which required running completely on the surface for top performance. Alternately, but less efficiently, they could stay within fifteen metres of the surface and use a *schnorkel* on a tether-hose. A certain amount of compressed air was kept in tanks to allow the "Tee-Dees" to be run for a short time if the vessel had to stay deep.

"Saturation" was the process of steadily increasing the air pressure inside the RSAV and altering the mixture of gasses within it to match the seafloor conditions inside of Soumerville. Which meant, of course, that Cordelia had been trying to ignore a sinus headache for the past three hours.

In a few more hours, they would be rolling up the ramp for the moon pool of one of Soumerville's three docks. She was so very looking forward to a hot bath, a stiff drink and some real clothes.

She looked over at Hal as she took a sip from her tea. "It is kind of nightmarish to consider a cloud that large. Are they sure it is not an instrument issue?" she asked.

Hal shook his head. "I do not know personally, but I cannot imagine three or four of the Soo-Soo buoys all malfunctioning at the same time, as well as the detectors on the Rafts themselves. No, I fear that the trend we have been seeing over the past decade is just getting worse," he said sombrely.

# Hal
## 23h20 Standard Signal Time
## Saturday, April 9th

Hal took the centre seat in the currently otherwise empty command compartment. The *Sheerah* was running on gyroscopic autopilot while the human pilot, Jonas Zupan, was finishing his evening meal. The safeties on the autopilot were extremely conservative, so while operating on a known-safe sea bottom like the area within a couple of hours of 45N50W, it could be trusted alone for thirty minutes or so.

Right now, the *Sheerah* was currently driving along the ocean floor, using her six massive caterpillar belts to move. "Bottom Rolling", as it was called, was the most common way for the RSAVs to move around. While the RSAVs could use underwater vectored thrust motors to move through the water column, generally speaking the RSAV moved like a lobster. It spent as much of its time crawling along as it could, with short hops up off the bottom to clear obstacles. It was slower, but far more energy efficient when travelling long distances.

Hal looked around the compartment, surrounded by the innumerable little mechanical noises of the RSAV. Ahead, past the windows and through the water column beyond, was the bulk of Soumerville. The area around Soumerville nearly had "roads" along the seafloor now, where seven generations of voyages had passed. At just about two kilometres distant on the western side of the "Northwest Highway", some enterprising crew during the Generation Two period had built an *Inukshuk*, nearly four metres tall. It was still there today, if shrouded beyond recognition by sea life.

He never tired of this moment; the first real view of home after a successful mission. Soumerville was massive, raised up a full eighteen metres from the sea floor on pilings. She was eight decks thick at the edges of the main circle, sharply increasing to twenty-three decks thick at her centre. She was an oval-shaped structure, a bit less than half of a kilometre long and somewhat more than a third of a kilometre wide. The outer edge of the main oval had eight equally sized semi-circles that jutted out, each two decks in height, called the 'Gallery Decks'.

During the day, even with the sun's light streaming down as glowing ribbons through the water, the lights of the underwater city could be made out from more than two kilometres away. Now, in the late-night darkness, it was striking constellation of white, blue and green at even twice that distance.

Windows all over the structure shone light out into the sea at night and gladly welcomed sunlight shafts from the ocean above during daylight hours. In the day time, each pane was like a gemstone set into a green and red velvet display. When viewed at night, as Hal was doing now, it was more like stars on a rich night sky.

Curtains of bio-luminescent diamonds rose from the seafloor all around the central structure of the undersea town. Each one was a fence of a sort; three pipes laid side-by-side with bleeder holes in them along their length, streaming air bubbles from the bottom to the surface. Each fenced in area contained a sizeable school of fish, being "farmed". The schools of fish disliked the turbulence caused by the sheets of bubbles, and thus stayed to the middle of their pens.

The odd ones that escaped were happily eaten by the dolphins who had taken up residence around Soumerville since early in Generation Two. The descendants of those first dolphins were now active assistants in the sea-bottom farming and work that went on each day.

Air; the one commodity that Soumerville could not endure a prolonged famine of. He glanced upwards towards the less-dark of the night time ocean surface, as though he might see the menace that lurked above. Not that he could, of course. Regardless that it was colloquially called a "Green Fog" or "Milk Sea" by everyone that had to deal with the stuff, hydrogen sulphide gas was invisible. Worse, it was both explosive and neurotoxic.

Given its importance, the production, purification and recycling of Soumerville's air was something a lot of design and infrastructure had been dedicated to. Firstly, Mother Nature was the major tool in the kit.

A combination of substantial "green spaces" within the habitation zones of the town and high-density agriculture systems elsewhere provided a noticeable part of the budget. Every apartment had two or three "quartets" of plants colloquially known as Mother-in-Law's Tongue, Money Plant, Peace Lily and Bamboo Palm growing in them, for localised air quality improvement.

Then, of course, were the Rafts. These floating structures over the town, connected by tethers, had solar-thermal collectors as well as air pumps aboard them. These used wave action to push pressurised air down into the depths for use by the undersea town.

Lastly the good news was that as long as Soumerville could generate electricity, they could "crack" air from the seawater around them. This would let them operate for several days under conditions where fresh air could not just be pumped in from the surface. It may well start to be a be sour to the nose after a few days, but no one would be turning an unpleasant shade of "asphyxiation blue".

Out here, in the shallow waters of the continental shelf, Soumerville was awash in an embarrassment of riches when it came to generating electricity. The main source of power was a set of sea-current powered "windmills", standing on the ocean floor.

Each one was a vertical, T-shaped pylon that held a nacelle at each of the ends of the crossbar. A five-bladed, fan-like propeller turned a substantial generator inside the nacelle. A cable ran from the base of the pylon along the ocean floor back to Soumerville. Given that there was forty times as much energy in an ocean current than in a wind of the same speed, it was relatively easy to satisfy the undersea town's power needs, both personal and industrial.

Given the importance of power to a functioning civilisation, however, Soumerville did have back-up systems, which in turn had back-up systems. There were four strings of buoys that used the peak-and-trough action of waves to drive air-pumps to spin pressurised-air turbo-generators. As well, within the bulk of Soumerville herself was the option of using methane gas or wood burners driving steam turbo-generators. These were a last resort, however, because they consumed precious air.

As the *Sheerah* rumbled steadily along the "Homeward Highway", Hal found himself not-quite staring at one of the Gallery Decks on the north-east "Octant" of Soumerville. Each of the Gallery Decks was primarily for some sort of social purpose; bars, lounges, art galleries, performance halls, and the like. These common spaces were crucial to the good working order of society in Soumerville, or so was the thinking. It forced people to mix, mingle and be more in touch with the other citizens they shared the town with.

The particular Gallery Deck that Hal was currently looking at was barely visible from their position. It contained the Crystal Parlour Lounge that his Salvage Leader Cordelia Baasch performed at on her Secondary. One of these days, he mused, he was going to have to go there on a night she was performing.

He was not that interested in either her preferred style of music, nor the style of venue itself, if the truth was to be told. However, as the Captain he felt it was part of his job to stay in touch with his crew and have something to talk to them about beyond "work". Life on the RSAV was not always the most pleasant, after all. He had been told once, by a more senior captain in the Fleet, that simply having something to talk about other than life onboard was remarkably valuable sometimes. So, he had always made a point of dropping in on each of his crew at some time during their Secondaries.

For some reason, though, he had never managed to get to the Crystal Parlour Lounge in the past three years. He was not entirely sure why. Maybe this time while they were in port.

His eyes went back to his more immediate surroundings. Dotting the sea floor around Soumerville, out to the distance they were now, were the sea farms and associated work-shacks. Sustainable aquaculture of all varieties such as seaweeds, molluscs, crustaceans, and fish, were a primary food provider for Soumerville. Each work-shack was connected by a seafloor tether that ran back to the main structure of the town itself, which provided air, power, and communications. He could see the lights of several of them, as well as the bio-luminescent streams of bubbles that marked workers at their labours outside, even at this hour.

A trio of dolphins swam past, towing a train of three cylinders tethered together. A "milk run" of product from one of the work-shacks, destined for Soumerville proper. Once the dolphins delivered the goods to the dock, they would be "paid" with a healthy share of fish as well as other rich fats and proteins. The dolphins were a bit unpredictable; there were times they just seemed to take the day off, regardless of what the humans wanted. Regardless of that foible, the long-term relationship had proven beneficial to both sides.

For example, under so-called "Green Fog" conditions like today, it was not uncommon for one or two of the moon-pool docks to be closed to vessel traffic to allow the dolphins a place to get a non-lethal breath. This was almost invariably accompanied by every child who was done their schooling for the day going for a swim with them, or throwing food to them.

A clunk and clang signalled Zupan coming onto the bridge. "Heya, Skipper!" the pilot-navigator said with a grin and a half-salute.

Hal grinned back at him. "'Heya', yourself, Pilot. It looks like we are almost home," he said, gesturing at the view beyond the brass-framed windows. Hal knew that he should likely take the Pilot quietly to task over the casual attitude, but where it was just the two of them and with the good mood at almost being home, he opted to leave it alone.

"Yessir ... aaaaaaaand based on the look of the track, we are rolling right down the middle of the traffic lane. So the autopilot is dead-on, which is good to know," Jonas replied with a pleased nod of his head.

Hal nodded in agreement. "All right, Pilot, please sound the bells and whistles for Special Conditions Cruising. It is time to bring this girl home."

Within a few minutes of the signal being passed through-out the ship, every position in the Comm was manned.

"Captain," began the Chief Armsman, "I have contact with Traffic Control via underwater telephone; we are directed to North Bay, Dock Three. We are to stay to the main traffic lane, right hand turn at the circumferential track. Speed restrictions are in effect, as usual; top speed is five."

"Thank you, Chief. Pilot, you heard the man. Bring us in," Hal ordered.

Chief Armsman Christopher Olivier was not exactly Hal Lum's favourite person. Olivier's service and dedication were without question; professionally, there was little more Hal could likely ask for in someone whose job was to make kill-now decisions at the snap of fingers.

However, the man was nearly unapproachably chilly; any time Hal tried to engage him in conversation that was more personal than a status report, all he got were one-phrase answers. Hal had always been of the opinion that if your crew liked you, they would go the extra kilometre for you without hesitating. While he fully understood that he needed to be a friend to his crew and not a "pal", Christopher Olivier was clearly disinterested in even that notion.

Hal had no idea what the source of friction was, but it was a point of concern. Thus far in the past three years, they had been spared any serious security concerns. However, if things continued to worsen on the surface as they seemed likely to, Hal knew that this would not last forever. He would personally feel a whole lot better if he knew his Chief Armsman, the man guarding his back with a Variable Rifle, at least liked him.

## Jonas

Jonas Zupan nodded to the Captain and turned his chair towards his controls. He flipped a series of switches, unlocking the controls from the gyroscopic autopilot. He then turned the small steering wheel, shaped like a sideways "X" with the ends closed by semi-circles, first to the left and then to the right to confirm that horizontal steering was working as expected. He then pulled the steering column back towards himself slowly.

Outside, he knew, each of the six vectored thrust motors were now illuminated in a soft blue glow that was easily visible to the human eye for a dozen metres in every direction. It was a safety feature, so that a diver around the RSAV knew to steer clear of both ends of the thruster. The *Sheerah* gently but firmly lifted off the sea bottom, leaving a plume of churned mud and silt below them. He kept the ship flat, even as it moved equally both forward and upwards. He then pushed the steering column slowly forwards, bringing the ship back to the sea bottom with a mild thud that was felt through the vessel as much as it was heard.

"Pilot confirms that the helm and navigation are ready for Special Conditions Cruising, Skipper," he announced.

"Very good, Pilot, thank-you," the Captain replied.

Jonas glanced at a set of gauges that told him how fast each of the six caterpillar treads were turning. Another set of gauges directly beneath the first told him how much ground resistance each was encountering.

The two outermost tread belts were experiencing nearly zero resistance; they were positioned on the sloped sides of the bottom hull, designed to work like "bumpers". Since they were not touching anything but water right now, they had almost no effective resistance. Thus, the complicated mess of linkages and hydraulics that Marlon Pryce kept working did not push anything beyond a minimum level of power to those treads. Underwater, as they were, the resistance of the water itself was enough keep those treads moving at around ten RPM. If they were out of the water, they would not be moving at all.

The other four tread belts, which ran the length of the belly of the RSAV in nose-to-tail pairs, were dividing the lion's share of the power between them. The treads with the best grip on the rolling surface got the most power, keeping the massive machine moving forward.

Of course, that piece of electro-mechanical wizardry was a mixed blessing. It was possible to have an RSAV suddenly and sharply veer to one side or another if one tread suddenly got far better traction, and thus more power, than the others.

Jonas Zupan shifted his gaze from the gauges, to the window showing the way ahead, then to the scrolling map view. He endlessly compared what he saw to be happening with what experience had taught him should be happening. The difference between the two was where the dangers lurked.

Driving an RSAV was a Faustian delight. There was no other easy way to explain his love-hate relationship with the *Sheerah* at times like this.

He loved the feel of how the big machine responded to his careful adjustments of the helm controls. He hated the sense that if he missed something, the people around him that he knew and respected might get hurt, or worse. He loved knowing that he was part of a fraternity of uncommon individuals, as an RSAV pilot. He hated the sense that some people just expected the worst of him anywhere but in the pilot seat because of that fraternity. He loved being the one that brought his shipmates home to their well-deserved rest and Seconds. He hated that it meant he had to leave his friends and team, and embark on a week or so of relative loneliness.

On and on the contrasts went. As far as his mind could rejoice and his heart could ache, contrast upon contrast.

"Skipper," he began as the model of the *Sheerah* moved past a way-marker on the scrolling map, "we have just passed the warning marker for the approach to the circumferential track. I am starting to drop speed to match restrictions."

"Very good, Pilot," came Hal Lum's reply. "All outside lights to full bright, please."

"Aye-aye, Skipper," Jonas replied. "Cordie, if you please?"

"Outside lights for search, service, navigation, and warning ... now on ... and at full brilliance, Pilot", Cordelia replied, flipping the switches and twisting the knobs at her station that handled those tasks. The *Sheerah* now lit the sea around her in all directions with almost twenty-thousand watts of lighting in five different colours.

As he turned to the controls that communicated his requirements to the Engineering Detail, it crossed his mind that he had gotten very fortunate when he had been posted from the *Archimedes* to the *Sheerah*. Firstly, less than five weeks after he had moved his trio of steamer trunks to his new posting, the *Archimedes* had suffered a terrible engine room explosion and onboard fire. Secondly, Hal Lum was a lot less of a whip-snapper than Captain Grover Gartner had been.

There were days, in fact, that Jonas wondered exactly why Hal and Ise put up with him. He had a quick mouth, he knew. It was a quick mouth which periodically outran his brain, unfortunately; particularly where Cordelia Baasch was concerned.

Even when she was not involved in the matter at hand, he had a predilection socially towards quipping first and thinking second. Sometimes that sounded like disrespect to those around him. He tried to apologise any time he realised he had over stepped that line that everyone else seemed to be able to see so clearly. Once in an unkind while, however, said was said and there was not a thing to be done but shrug and move on. Fortunately, there seemed to be an expectation for RSAV Pilot-Navigators to be drama queens, so more often than not he mostly got away with it.

He glanced over at where Cordelia sat, her features focused on the paperwork she was signing off on, prior to arrival. They were both Gen-Seven, but she was a year older than he was. In spite of that, somehow, he had never laid eyes on her before the day they had met for the first time in the O-Room. The ship-suits were notorious for androgenising women, but even so, she had a pretty smile, nice eyes, and was visibly curvy, which were all things that Jonas liked in a woman.

When she had made mention of her Secondary as a torch singer at the Crystal Parlour Lounge, he had made the arguably worst mistake of his life to date and gone for one of the shows. When he had seen her in the low front, lower back, red and silver dress that was slit on both sides to mid-thigh and dotted with sparkles and sequins, sitting with her legs crossed on the edge of the grand piano, all he could do was stare. When she started singing, it felt electric.

For all the cavalier attitude and show that he put forward, he had never quite managed to screw up the nerve to ask her out on a date in the two years he had known her. He had tried, so many times he had tried, but for some agonising reason the words never came out. Eventually he had resigned himself to watching from a distance, hoping one day that somehow something someway might change. So far, it had not.

He shook his head, going back to the game he was actually good at, that of juggling five different sets of information streams, interpreting them, and steering the vessel safely and surely towards the place everyone around him called home.

A few minutes of continued "bottom rolling" later, they arrived at the "circumferential track" which was a road of sorts that ran around the outside edge of Soumerville at one hundred metres distance. It had been "paved" with stones that had been moved from around the place as the site had been constructed, with more brought in as fish pens and work-shacks had been continuously added. Seven generations of RSAVs had packed those layers of stones upon stones into a surface easily as hard and solid at the concrete which the seafloor town at 45N50W was made of.

The *Sheerah* crawled along the road anti-clockwise, her lights shining off the massive bulk of Soumerville to her left. A trio of dolphins swimming along in front of them were visible through the windows. The mammals were dancing and doing loops playfully, as though they were welcoming the *Sheerah* home. Of course, Jonas thought, it was entirely possible they were. Dolphins were like that.

In the seven generations that Soumerville had stood here, she had become a living reef. Glittering clouds of fish played amongst the kelp fronds and seaweeds that had anchored themselves to the structure. In fact, it took daily maintenance by a dedicated team to make sure windows, inlets and outports were kept clear. Otherwise, nature was allowed to do as it pleased on the exterior of the underwater town.

At the northern point of the compass rose that Soumerville described with her construction, they turned south, driving now beneath the structure itself. The massive "legs" that Soumerville rested upon were lit on all six sides with flood lights, so that they were clearly visible at all times. Ahead, lights blinked in a double row to each side of a road and ramp that led up to the interior of 45N50W.

"Ramp in one minute, Skipper", Jonas announced.

"Very good, Pilot. Great work so far, Jonas; you make this look easy."

"Thanks, Skipper," he replied.

Hal Lum picked up the microphone at his station, and keyed it. Chimes sounded from all the intercom boxes throughout the ship. "Attention all hands, stand by for Ramp, Rise and Dock. Ensure all loose items are secured," he ordered.

That was one of those announcements which was almost a formality these days, Jonas thought. After you had gone *down* the Ramp in an RSAV and saw what happened to everything not put away properly, you learned in a hurry to make a habit of stowing everything in closable drawers, boxes and lockers. When the nose of a machine this big suddenly dropped twenty-two and then forty-five degrees, anything that could move, did.

Jonas eased back on the power settings, coaxing the *Sheerah* onto the base of the ramp and then up. Around the vessel, the double row of flashing lights painted the hull in a Yule scheme; the outside row of lights were a sharp blue, and the inside row on the right were red while the inside row on the left were green. The rows flashed in alternation; both outside rows lit for one second, then both of the inside rows shone for two seconds.

The nose of the *Sheerah* broke the surface in the moon-pool, and water sloughed off her curves in foamy curls as she rose up the ramp. Her outer hull lights extinguished, but the bright electric lights of the Dock made her wet skin glisten and glimmer. The cluster of Service and Supply techs, yard workers, and family members waiting at the dock all cheered at the sight of an RSAV coming home.

Inside the RSAV, the rapidly brightening glow of the windows, which was being muted less and less by the swiftly thinning water, was now a sudden dazzle as the command compartment cleared the surface. The ramp shallowed in angle, exposing more of the vessel as it continued to slowly rumble forward.

In a few more moments, the *Sheerah* was sitting flat with her deck above water level. Hatches opened and crew members emerged onto the still-glistening deck. They started preparing the forward and aft areas to secure the gangplanks and lines. She rumbled forward a few more metres and then slowly turned in place until she was parallel with the dock whose crane had a clearly visible "03" painted on the side. She then gingerly nosed ahead, until a series of lights on the dock directly at the level of the Command Compartment windows went from green, to yellow and then to red. The *Sheerah* came to a full stop, with less than a two metre gap between the edge of the dock and both her side and bow.

Inside, as he stood from his command chair, Hal Lum applauded. "Another damn fine parking job, Pilot. In the slot, on the first attempt, Jonas. Bravo!"

Jonas glanced momentarily at Cordelia as she stood and stretched, and then immediately gave Hal his full attention. "Glad to be your driver, Skipper," he grinned happily.

One of the intercom boxes buzzed and Marlon Pryce's voice emerged. "Comm, this is Eng. We have received 'all stop' and 'shut down' from Helm, and we are preparing to do so. Please confirm."

Hal looked towards the box and replied. "Order is confirmed. We are home. Thank your Detail for me, Chief; another good trip and they played a valuable part in it."

"Roger, thank-you, Wilco, Eng Out," came the reply and the lights changed under the intercom. Everyone in the Command Compartment finished their various procedures for being "parked" a few days and left, chatting and smiling.

Everyone but Jonas, who was the last out of the compartment. He quietly made his way to his cabin and started packing up his things to take ashore. Almost everyone else did this sort of thing the night before. He never did; there was no particular rush for him since there was no one waiting for him on the dock.

# Cordelia
## 01h34 Standard Signal Time
## Sunday, April 10th
## 45.00N,50.00W
## Temp 8C, Winds SW 22kph

A couple of busy hours of hard work later, Cordelia walked down and across the slightly bouncy gangway from the stern of the *Sheerah* onto the jetty. She shifted the weight of the two canvas duffle bags, slung one per shoulder.

As the leader of the Salvage and Dive Detail, as with any other Detail Leader, really, she was one of the last crew members off the ship. Her wrap-up work was also added to by her other hat as the officer-in-charge of the Stewards.

Around her, bustle and buzz was everywhere with the last remaining crew meeting family and friends. At the same time, a much greater number of Operational Support techs, as well as dock crews, were getting started on their job of turning around an RSAV for its next mission. While her crew might not be aboard for the next ten days, the *Sheerah* would be far from unoccupied in the interim.

Currently the *Sheerah's* future destination was unknown, but there was no question she would sailing again within a fortnight. RSAVs and MSSVs were simply too expensive and too vital to be left sitting idle. In addition, there was entirely no way that Soumerville could have her entire brood of nine RSAVs and four MSSVs home at the same time. There just was not enough dock space.

As she made her way along the jetty towards the opened two-story doors that lead into the heart of the town, Cordelia reflected that while she loved her work and her life aboard the *Sheerah*, she was never sad to be off and away for a ten-day or so. It was possible to have too much of a good thing, and familiarity bred contempt.

Once Cordelia was through the doors, she caught the next cable-tram heading to the central hub for this deck. She could have walked, really; it was not all that far, but it was her "little girl indulgence". She absolutely loved riding on the trams; she had spent hours just sitting on any one of the middle-deck circumferential trams riding around in a circle, people watching and relishing in the feel of the entire thing.

Once she was at the hub, it was onto one of the lifts heading upwards into the living areas of the seafloor town. For a whole host of good reasons, living and recreation areas were at the top of the Soumerville layer-cake, with trade and commerce below that, then industrial endeavours, then the town's engineering systems. At the very bottom were the docks and warehouses. Some citizens of Soumerville spent their entire lives exclusively in the top third of the town's structure. Most never left the top half.

Another tram ride coupled with a short walk got her to the door of her apartment. She turned the two keys required to unlock the metal-bound wooden door and went inside, giving the door a curt mule-kick closed. She flipped the electric lights on as she entered, dropping her two bags in the foyer.

The apartment was roughly shaped like a four-leaf clover, with the foyer being the stem. It was a standard configuration for a "*single person, away often*" home with a sitting room, a bathroom, a bedroom, a small kitchenette, and a multi-purpose room. She noted with some chagrin that her multi-purpose room still looked like a costume factory had been violently murdered in a boudoir. She resolved — yet again — that she would take on the herculean task of cleaning it up during this layover. Besides, she thought, she wanted to get her new performance dress finished before she was on stage at the Parlour again.

She went into her sitting room, and flipped through her selection of music AMTACs and shoved a well-loved cartridge into the slot, pressing the "Play" switch down. Bluesy, sexy, jazz music filled the air, and she did a little twirl, sashay and quick-step towards her bedroom. She wanted out of this ship-smelling outfit right now.

# CHAPTER FOUR

## *Life At A Hundred Below*

### Hal
**13h22 Standard Signal Time**
**Monday, April 11th**
**Soumerville**
**Temp 3C, Winds N 7kph**

Hal set his pen down atop his notebook, and leaned back in his chair. The room around him was a soft murmur of discussion and movement. Words were not coming easily today, he thought. It was not surprising, of course. It was less than a day of being back in Soumerville, and he was still mentally in the space of "captain aboard". He lifted the pilsner glass from the wooden coaster on the table and brought it to his lips. A very good lager, he decided. It was well worth the time to relax with.

A waiter drifted past quietly to see if there was anything Hal needed; no intrusion, just a quick moment of eye contact and a check to see if a beckoning gesture was made by Hal. Seeing none, the tallish and mutton-chopped fellow continued on his way.

Hal enjoyed coming here. He spent most of his time not aboard the *Sheerah* here, in fact. Even if he did not particularly feel social, all he had to do was pick one of the many single armchair, small table and lamp

59

spots and everyone just understood he was here, like others in the same kind of chairs, for some scholarly or literary pursuit. If you wanted to talk or debate, there was the bar, there were the trio of snooker tables, plus the handful of backgammon and chess tables. It was most certainly a far healthier environment for him than being alone in his apartment.

The decor was distinctly erudite, he thought amusedly. Heavy oak and cherry wood panels adorned the walls. Various pieces of furniture were made of the same materials. Fabrics for cushions were burgundies or navy in hue. Brass wall lamps plus a pair of simple but elegant glass chandeliers illuminated the place with a modest glow, while individual brass and ceramic lamps at tables or gaming areas shone brighter light in the places it was needed.

A sizeable mirror behind the bar reflected the place upon itself, giving an illusory sense of greater space. The floor was a somewhat lighter tone of polished wood, perhaps a birds-eye maple, with area rugs beneath each gathering place.

All through-out the club were bookcases, standing in pairs back to back, either three or five shelves tall. The pairs had a sign atop them indicating which undersea town had contributed them, and what general classes of literature they contained.

He had another sip of his lager while looking at the shelf of contributed works from Soumerville. He would love nothing more than his first novel to be good enough to sit upon that shelf here. Writing was something he loved to do, but not something he was naturally gifted at the way that C.A.Ryan, D.Dawson, or newer voices like A.Goff and D.Swensen seemed to be. However, this is what he wanted for his Second; the life of a novelist.

He picked up one of the three history books he had stacked on the table beside his pen, paper and pilsner glass. He flipped it open to where he had left the knitted book mark "scarf" his mother had made him when he had first started reading for pleasure as a young boy. Someone had once told him that writing a novel, fact or fiction, was a process of "research, research, research, write, write, write, edit, edit, edit". He had been blending the first two phases in equal measure as he went, simply because it felt more comfortable to him

He was currently reading through an account of the Battle of Aquarius Reach, near 25N80W, during the Generation Two period. A pair of the much more battle-worthy Reclaimer Mark-I's were famously attacked on the surface by a "pirate" flotilla. The *Sheerah*, by comparison to the *Artemis* and *Anyigba* carried thirty percent fewer crew and had thirty percent more cargo space with ten percent more range. The differences were entirely Armsmen and armaments.

At the Battle of Aquarius Reach, the two vessels had played a cat-and-mouse game for nearly twenty hours, all the time leading their pursuers away from their seafloor home town of Aquarius Rise. At the end, fourteen surface vessels and the *Artemis* had been sent to the bottom. Most importantly, the location of Aquarius Rise remained undiscovered by the "pirates". The *Anyigba* was able to limp home, with almost two-thirds of her crew injured or dead. She was removed from active service, and had the distinction of now being the only historically preserved RSAV in the world.

What Hal very much wanted to write was a book about the aftermath of that battle. Not the battle itself, that had been done many times, including a screenplay. Instead, he wanted his focus to be upon the spouses of the officers of the *Artemis*, and coping with the personal cost of a loved one's heroism to the point of self-sacrifice.

The problem, of course, was that Hal really did not personally know much about having a spouse, or even a love interest of any kind. He had dated in his teen years, of course … but that had always been because a pretty girl had taken the initiative and asked him out. It would last for two or three months, and then his preference for intellectual pursuits over making out would put an end to it.  Then the door would revolve again.

Many times, other authors he had spoken to here at the Literary Lounge had told him to "write what you know, it is what you can make believe most with".  However, he did not see much challenge in that. Maybe what he needed to do was spend some time with Marlon and his wife Annabelle and interview them, after a fashion.  See what their thoughts would be on that sort of loss.

"'Research, research, research', indeed," he said with a sigh as he picked up his glass again.

# Cordelia

Cordelia scowled at the letter in her hand as she leaned back in the claw-foot tub.  The tub was full of milky, steaming water and crowned with perfumed bubbles.  Her favourite music was playing, her favourite gin and tonic was in a glass over ice on a stool beside the tub, and she had a silly adventure-romance to read after she was done her tub time.

She should have been enjoying her second luxury-grade bath since she had gotten home.  Unfortunately, that was not the case.  All had been just fine until she had impulsively decided to open one of the pieces of mail, clearly marked as being from the Governance.  That had turned out to be a poor choice of action.

It was not just "a letter", but rather "The Letter" that she had been vaguely excited and vaguely dreading receiving for two years now.  She was now twenty-five years old, which meant it was time to start thinking about her children, and who she would like to father them.  Like many other aspects of life in Soumerville, the needs of the many outweighed the needs of the few.

The *"Letter Of Approved and Sanctioned Child-Rearing Pairings"* contained a list of twenty-eight young men who were the best possible sires for her offspring.  The selection was based on avoiding inbreeding as well as things like hereditary disease in the family tree. Other factors, such as success in their careers and the careers of their respective families, relative to the STADE predictions, were also part of the arcane process of officially sanctioned match making.

Of course, it did not mean that she had to marry any of them. She could opt to go the artificial route for getting started, as other women had in the past. However, she really did want a proper father figure for her children. She picked up her drink and had a sip, thinking about that statement.

"Her children"; what a remarkable idea that was. Her career would go on hold for five years, at least while she brought her children into the world. Then, she would be able to go back to her life on the RSAVs if she chose.

But no matter which way she went onwards with her own life, she would have brought two or three new lives into this world. She would have been responsible for ensuring they had the best possible chances at a fulfilling and contributing life in Soumerville. Perhaps, if the rumours were to be believed, they would be part of the Generation that saw Soumerville create another undersea colony a couple of thousand kilometres away. It would be a historic moment that defined a Generation, no matter when it happened.

Part of all of that, of course, would be who she chose as a father. Perhaps if they hit it off, it would be a real "happily ever after" like her own parents, or Marlon and his wife. That was what she wanted, really, if she admitted it to herself. She was a bit old fashioned that way.

Of course, anyone who wanted into her life in a permanent way was going to have to understand she had no plans of stopping either sailing or singing. That was who she was at the core of her being. They could take it or leave it. Once her five years of maternity time were done, she currently had every intention of getting right back to what she loved doing. Being a mother was supposed to add to who she was, not take away from it. Her own mother, a Stores and Supplies tech, had gone back to her career when Cordelia was six.

She knew that none of the gentlemen on this list had any way of finding out that they were an eligible pairing for her. Thus, there was no pressure or social issues weighing on her, supposedly. She knew, they did not, and how she handled the situation was up to her. There were more than just a few steamy romance novel scenes that started in a place like the Crystal Parlour with the liberated heroine walking up to some handsome buck and whispering in his ear *"So, you are on my List. Care to dance?"*. Cordelia could not imagine being nearly that forward.

Another trio of sips of her gin and another sigh passed her lips. Reasonably, she had a year or so to date her way through the list and decide who it was she liked most. The Letter was almost ten pages in total, between cover matter, closing matter and the biographical summaries of four of her approved matches per page. She flipped through, wondering if anyone else was in the Reclamation Service; it would be an interesting life, she thought, if her husband and she shared the love and life of the adventures of being RSAV crews.

Of the 28 gentlemen on the list, she readily found two in the first few pages. An Engineering Assistant and an Armsman; she wrinkled her nose slightly. Those would be the two professions most likely to leave widows, naturally. She flipped a few more pages, skimming the trio of "name, occupation, STADE score".

She nearly dropped her drink. She carefully set it down on the stool, and then looked at the last page of the list again. There, at number twenty-six, was RSAV Pilot "Zupan, Jonas Clark".

"You have got to be kidding me," she said aloud. He had apparently had one of the highest STADE scores in a Generation, she noted. It was a pity he was a drunken jerk, she thought sourly.

# Christopher

"Faster! Come on, come on, come on! You can do this! Harder!" Christopher Olivier shouted at the group of thirty individuals in the room with him. They were working in pairs, doing a simple drill: throw a medicine ball to your partner, have them hold it outwards, you step forward three paces and then throw five punches at the ball. The partner would then retreat three or four paces, throw the ball back, and the cycle would repeat.

With the medicine balls weighing around nine kilograms each, this was a gruelling exercise. He pushed his classes hard, but to Christopher, a pursuit of excellence started with your own health and your own body. If you were not willing to push hard here, you were unlikely to do so anywhere else.

"That is it! Step in, lead with the shoulder... right, left, right, left, left! Good! Good!" he bellowed in encouragement. Once this afternoon's class was over, he was going for a nine kilometre run, followed by a practice session at the gun range. With the autumn venison harvest long behind them, it had been a while since any of the Armsmen aboard the *Sheerah* had flipped the safety of either a longarm or sidearm while on duty. He personally considered that a potential problem; skills dulled with disuse. He made sure he got to the practice range every time they were parked at Soumerville. He encouraged the rest of his Detail to do the same.

He had not yet decided what his evening would be; likely a good meal at one of the lounges on the South side, and perhaps a few drinks with a pretty smile if any were favouring him. That was certainly one of the more enjoyable benefits from being an Armsman that kept himself in a fighting trim. He was rarely wanting for a pretty face for company when he was out.

"All right! Balls down! Walk the room for two minutes to cool down, and drink two-fifty. Next exercise is kettles and squats!" he called out, answered by a chorus of good-natured groans. He checked the clock on the wall, even as he tipped his own water bottle to his mouth. Two-hundred and fifty millilitres of water between each burst of exercise was something he insisted on. Dehydration was an enemy of good fitness, and sapped people of their ability to perform to their best. For every five minutes of intense exercise, he mandated a two-minute drink break.

He re-capped his drink bottle and glanced at the clock. He carried his own medicine ball over to the shelf it was usually stored on, and then moved to the rack that had the kettlebells.

"Grab a twelve-kilo kettlebell in each hand! Come on, come on! Time is not waiting for you! Your classmates should not have to either! A twelve in each hand. That is right, now balance them against your hips, and sloooowwwwly lower yourself down, straight down, straight down, until you are in a squatting position. Hold here for a count of five and then sloooowwwwly come back up, with your backs straight! Keep your backs straight! That is it! Good, good!" he called out.

He did the first few reps with everyone else, and then set his own weights down. He moved around the class correcting posture, giving encouragement, and reminding everyone of the benefits of building core body strength.

"This should not hurt. This should not be painful. If it is, set one kettlebell down and lift the remaining one with both hands. We want a burn, but not an injury. Uncomfortable is construction, pain is destruction. We want to be building up here!" he said as he moved back to the front of the room and picked up his own weights again.

That phrase was really a way of looking at life for Christopher. Comfort was stagnation. Discomfort was progress. Pain was the way the world told you that you had not prepared for the challenges ahead. As an Armsman, his job was to be prepared, to always have that slight edge of discomfort so that he was always ready to do his job to the best that could be done. Embrace the discomfort to avoid the painful alternative.

In here, or out there, the mission was the same. The weapons could be slug-throwers or barbells, but the mission was to make sure that those he worked with and lived with were protected. Beyond the security of Soumerville was a hostile world that, in his own estimation, clearly had enough of a prior civilisation that had grown soft, comfortable and complacent. When the roof had finally come crashing down on the two-hundred-year party of the Precursors, the evidence suggested that most of the revellers had been unable to take care of themselves.

Seven Generations later, the people of Soumerville and her sister towns were still living with the aftermath. This was why there were Armsman's positions on board RSAVs and MSSVs at all. Christopher was on a personal crusade to make sure everyone he knew was fit and able to take care of themselves.

"All right! Good work out everyone! That is the hour! Finish off your water, walk to cool down, and hit the showers! I will see you again in two days!" he shouted. A round of applause, thanks and congratulatory noises rang through-out the training room.

He glanced at the clock, and wondered if Ise Koolen was working in her beloved park today or not. His running route carried him through most of the park spaces in Soumerville. Each one was a literal and figurative breath of fresh air in comparison to the stroll ways and corridors of the rest of the undersea town. A lap around the circumference was around one-and-a-half kilometres; six laps was a full nine kilometres.

He used "Ise's Park" as his water break spot. If she was there, he would say hello and enjoy a few minutes of her company before setting off again on his next lap. Perhaps he could persuade her to join him for lunch. That would be a fine finish to his morning.

# Marlon
## 20h37 Standard Signal Time
## Monday, April 11th

"So when did you say you would be going back to sea, you surly thing?" Annabelle asked with a teasing grin.

"Clearly not soon enough," Marlon responded with an overly dramatized roll of his eyes.

"Marlon Andrew Pryce, there are days when you manage to make twenty years feel like a life-time," she scolded as she picked up the emptied dinner plate in front of him.

"Well, then you are better at this than I am, since you manage eternity," he replied mildly.

Her response was to hit him in the face with her expertly thrown dish cloth. They looked at each other as the damp cloth slid cartoonishly down his face and landed on the table.

"I do hope you have a better offering for dessert than that. I was hoping for cookies!" he deadpanned.

The two erupted into laughter and met halfway between their original positions in a spinning embrace with a kiss. "I swear, Marlon, you are incorrigible" she laughed.

"By the time I am done spending ten days in a sausage can with a bunch of *wunderkinder*, I am completely out of corrige. You cannot fault me that," he laughed.

She groaned good naturally at his humour and gave him a swat on the arm. "Unhand me you cad! The cookies are going to burn," she ordered imperiously.

Marlon quickly complied, giving her an equal swat on the tush to propel her over to the small electric range. "That would be a crime I refuse to be complicit in. Quickly woman, move!"

The two laughed at each other as she opened the small oven door and took out the single tray of a dozen treats. He poured each of them a cup of tea and they moved towards the modestly appointed sitting room. They sat together on the love seat and said nothing further for a few moments as the first bites of dessert were happily dispatched.

"Oh! Did I tell you yesterday that Clarissa got her Letter?" Annabelle asked him, clearly excited. Clarissa was their eldest of three children, and the only girl of the trio.

"Letter? What letter?" Marlon asked, puzzled.

Annabelle shook her head at him. "The Letter. *That* Letter. You know?"

He looked at her blankly over the rim of his suspended tea cup.

"Men," she sighed in amused frustration. "The most important letter that a woman will get at age twenty-five, Marlon? The one responsible for me being here to make your cookies for you?"

Marlon blinked and blinked again. "Are you telling me our baby got her '28-List'? We cannot possibly be that old, can we?"

"Our 'baby', my dear husband, celebrated her twenty-fifth birthday a month ago," she reminded him.

"So I suppose continuing to tell everyone I am twenty-nine is out of the question, then," he sighed.

She swatted him playfully. "Yes, you lout, just as it was ten years ago. Now are you going to listen or continue carrying on irreverently?"

"Oh, I am listening, dear heart, I am listening. I am in shock and feeling every grey hair I have, but I am listening," he replied with a sigh.

"She called as soon as she opened it. She is beside herself, of course.

So we talked for almost an hour. It turns out she knows two or three on the list already and rather likes one of them."

"Well, that will make her life a bit easier, then," Marlon nodded.

Annabelle nodded as well, her blue eyes twinkling. "Mmm. Going the route of a bunch of blind dates like I did to finally get to you is nothing I would wish on any woman. Of course, women are a bit more confident about themselves in this day and age."

"Well, and I recall you as being somewhat shy with a penchant for being a wallflower when we first met. I have no idea what happened since then," he said with a martyred sigh.

She scowled at him even as he grinned at her. "I hang around with far too many sailors, I think," she said primly.

"You have to admit it has worked out all fairly well in the end, my dear?"

"No," she said firmly. "I do not." There was a pause where they looked at each other, both desperately trying not to smile before they both fell to snickering uncontrollably. "Oh, fine," she said with the same tone he had used a moment before, "perhaps it has turned out for the better."

They laughed and she leaned her head on his shoulder. There was a moment of companionable silence broken by nothing beyond the sound of the clock on the wall and their own being.

"I am so glad you are home, Marlon," she sighed. "Every time you sail, it seems to be longer and longer these days."

"I know, darling," he said, putting an arm around her. "However, by this time next year, I am done and that will be that. I am getting too old for this foolishness, anyway. Going to sea and shore on RSAVs is a young man's job."

"I know how much you love it," she said quietly.

"Less so now. There are many good memories, and a lot of good done, but it is time to put it down."

She nodded at him. "Are you teaching tomorrow?" she asked.

"Yes. Both the beginner and advanced classes for my Precursor Archeology course. I will be up to my elbows in class planning when you get home, I expect. What about you? You are on your Second as well, right?" he asked.

She nodded. "The daycare is so much more enjoyable than the accounting office. I should be home by the middle of the afternoon, though."

"Shall we head out to catch the news and a show? Neither of us have too stressful a day tomorrow, so a bit of an outing tonight should not be too hard on us."

"That is a wonderful notion, Marlon. Let me go get changed into something presentable."

# Ise

Ise Koolen sat cross-legged beneath the curving branches of an oak tree. She had a small blanket spread out, in the space between two of the three bushes planted around the tree. A small woven basket was filled with an assortment of fruits, nuts and other just-picked delights. A bottle of water sat beside the work belt of assorted tools that were needed for working in a garden.

She sliced a piece off an apple with her work knife, and took a bite. She really should go get some supper, but neither cooking for herself right now nor the buzz of a meal-lounge appealed to her. She was in a contented state of tired and in no particular hurry to change that.

It had been a very good day of working in this Forest Room. She looked up through the branches and leaves towards the cerami-glass ceiling beyond. The last rays of the above-water sunset left a mild glow to filter down here. The rows of "sun lights" that were spaced at regular intervals were also substantially dimmed, running on a timer to nearly match the daylight cycles of the natural world. Winter days in Soumerville had longer light in them than the world above the waves, but otherwise they were close.

Her eyes moved from tree to tree around her, marvelling yet again at the simple sense that the Founders had when they designed and created Soumerville and her sister towns. Every tree in this Forest Room produced a fruit or nut that was edible by people. The oak's acorns, for example, were good for flour as well as other things. Walnuts, pecans, apples, peaches, cherries, pears, bamboo, and honey locust were here in this one forest room alone. The bushes planted around each tree were also food-bearing. Even most of the "decorative" flower beds were full of edibles. It was a place of abundant beauty.

The food from the trees was free to anyone who happened by. Gluttony, naturally, was severely frowned upon, but otherwise no one batted an eye if a family of four came here to have a picnic lunch or supper entirely from what the Forest Room provided.

Ise munched happily, watching a couple strolling arm-in-arm along a walking path. She smiled at the entirety of the moment, immensely thankful for the fortune she had to live when she did.

She pulled a book out from her hip bag, and opened it to her marked page. The topic of the text in hand was on synergistic planting for the development of self-sustaining food-forests. This was part of how Soumerville and her sister towns fed themselves, of course. Every year, at least one RSAV mission in the early spring was to change thirty or so hectares of river-accessible wilderness into another permanent food forest. Other RSAV missions would be to visit the existing planted areas for a harvest.

In seven generations of doing this, Soumerville was responsible for converting over three thousand hectares of depleted wilderness that had been sucked dry by the Precursors into teeming, bountiful landscapes again. Almost another thousand hectares of landscape which had been planted for conversion had failed due to a myriad of reasons from natural fires to hurricanes to other events. However, while those landscapes were "failed" for the purposes of feeding Soumerville, Ise knew that they had all become natural habitats that still helped heal the scars of the Precursor's practices.

The successful plantations were left to run by themselves; a combination of earthworks, water management techniques, and plant selections meant that, generally speaking, Mother Nature was the chief gardener at each of these locations. The RSAV crews that visited periodically to harvest also lent a helping hand in keeping the landscape moving in a way that was desirable. Otherwise, no one lived there.

They could not, of course. No one lived above the waves any more. Three Generations had gone by since the last immigrant from the shore-world had come to Soumerville. The combination of Green Fog events, severe weather, drowned coasts and toxic Precursor areas had simply made the surface world uninhabitable for humans. For the thousand or so kilometres in any compass direction that the *Sheerah* and her sisters roamed, they had never met another person up there.

Ise frowned, looking up towards the darkening waters beyond the glass. She wondered what it would be like, if the world were a kinder place, to be able to have a city like Soumerville sitting on dry land? At the head of a bay perhaps? What would it be like to live in a world where sealed walls against a lethally hostile environment were optional? To see the glory of a sunrise every day outside the city's glass? To be able to feel the frozen fury of a winter snowstorm any time it happened, instead of by random chance on a mission location?

She sighed. She would never know that world, of course. Still, dreaming and wondering were healthy pursuits for an active mind and spirit. *"Desire drives development"*, as the saying went. Alternately, *"Imagination inspires innovation"* was another variation. Two hundred years ago, Soumerville and her kind of town-states were deemed "impossible". Yet, here she was now, and the nay-sayers were long gone, lost to the tides of catastrophe, change, and can-do.

She stretched her legs out and shifted around to lean with her back against the trunk of the oak. She picked up an oak leaf and twirled it, smiling. Tomorrow, she had new seedlings to plant. Just thinking about it made her happy.

# Jonas
## 02h42 Standard Signal Time
## Tuesday, April 12th

*"We don't need to go far;*

*Beneath a tree in a forest room.*

*Look up through the glass;*

*Hope to see a star.*

*Just you and me,*

*a picnic basket,*

*and my*

*outta tune guitar,"*

Jonas sang as he chorded on the guitar. He stopped with a frown and looked at his finger positioning. That was the right chord for the fingers, but it suddenly it was not the right sound for the lyrics.

He tried three different chord progressions, until he found one that seemed to suit the sad romance he was trying to hide in a dance hall tune.

He took the pencil from behind his ear and marked the sheet of music on the stand with his changes.

He sighed, looking at the glass door of the music room he was in. Song writing was a sort of sweet torture for him, he reflected. He loved the creation process;  coaxing music out of whatever melancholy muse was visiting him for this session.  Divining halves of lyrics, quarters of chords, hints of moods as they drifted by him;  doing his utmost to capture and preserve them on paper.

Of course, beyond the music room, no one ever heard him sing what he wrote.  He was never happy with how it sounded in his own voice.  He wrote his music, two or three songs a year, under a *nom de plume* of "the Jay Zee Clark Project" and was content to take pleasure at hearing someone else record it to AMTAC and have it do well in dance halls.

Mostly, he wrote dance music.  While there were many purists that would frown and say if it was not "serious listening music" it was a waste of his talents, few things were more powerful and social than a dance hall of happy people living in the moment and being swept along by the music.  Or that was Jonas' opinion anyway.

So, that was the music he wrote.  Music that was supposed to soak into your heart and mind, and make it obvious that you should be moving. It was hard work.  He drove himself crazy some times, trying to get the sound in his head to come out through his fingers faithfully in their journey to paper.

There was a double-knock at the glass door and he looked up.  "Oh, hi, Kim.  Closing time already?" he asked the older woman peeking in at him.

Kimberly Cannes was the recording suites manager.  She loved music and loved helping others find their love of music.  She handled the administration of trying to keep the various music rooms and supporting equipment as busy and productive as possible.  From time to time, she was even invited to add her own whiskey-sand voice to the background of some recordings as a "doo-wop" singer.

It was a topic amongst many of the artists that there was no shortage of Gen-Seven men that would be very happy to spend time with the Gen-Six Miz Cannes; making "music", of course.

Kim, as she preferred to be called, nodded at him. "Yeah, I am sorry to spoil your groove, Zee," she said apologetically. She flicked a grey-blonde lock back from her face.

"Naw, that is ok, Kim. I was starting to spin my wheels anyway. Can I book a room for tomorrow?" he asked.

She grinned brightly at him. "Already done; same room. I was listening on the monitors, and I think you have another winner. I cannot wait to hear the finished version before you put it in the Library. So no problems, you can leave all your stuff right where you are and just pick up tomorrow if you like."

"Aw, thanks, Kim. You are the best," he said as he set the guitar down. He stretched, suddenly very aware that he had been hunched over since lunch time and it was after supper. A meal, he now realised, that he had missed.

"It is a pleasure to have you in here, Zee," the petite blonde smiled. "You seemed to be really fussing the lyrics and meter … Is this going to be The One? Are you going record it yourself?" she asked him, looking hopeful.

"Naw, I just do not have the voice for it, Kim. I am a writer, not a singer. I will let someone else make it sound good."

She arched an eyebrow and planted a fist on a willow hip. "Pipe sludge," she said flatly. "You sound great on monitors or AMTAC. I could listen to you all day. You need to believe in yourself more. I think you would do just fine recording this one yourself. Hell, I will help you get it done, if you want."

He blinked at her in surprise. "Naw, Kim, I … just … it… no, ok? I mean, I appreciate your offer, and I know you are really good at what you do on that recording board. But, " he trailed off, unable to match words to emotions.

She gave him a sympathetic smile and patted him on the arm. "I get it. Not everyone is cut out for performing. But, for Spirits' Sake Zee, please, please, please do not live in a world where you do not record your own stuff because you think you are not good enough, okay? You are. If you are not comfortable with it, that is okay. Just make it a choice, not a doom, all right?"

# CHAPTER FIVE

## *To the Sea, Return*

**Ise**
**12h19 SST**
**Monday, April 18th**

Ise Koolen opened her eyes to a remarkably irritating noise that claimed to be gentle ringing. A glance at her alarm clock exonerated it from her immediate blame. The only other thing that made that sort of racket would be the telephone. A second glance at the supposedly innocent alarm clock resulted in her moving as quickly as she could manage in the demi-gloom of her apartment, still nude, to the sitting room.

Naturally, the phone stopped its demented clatter a full stride before she reached it. She waited, knowing very well that the only people who would call her this early would be a representative of the Council of Seven. A handful of seconds went past, during which she sat on the arm of the easy-chair closest to the rosewood table that held the telephone. As predicted, it rang again.

"Counsellor Koolen," the dark-skinned woman replied, trying not to sound as regrettably hung-over as she was.

"Good morning, Counsellor. This is Trevon Marshan of the Council's RSAV Planning Service. I do apologise for the hour of the call," came a delightfully upbeat voice.

Ise smiled at the speaker's tone. "Oh, it is quite all right. Duty does not wait for convenient timing. I am Summoned, then?" she enquired, shifting her position slightly and reaching to turn the small lamp over the phone on, chasing away some of the gloom.

"Yes, Counsellor. You have been requested to meet with Captain Lum and the Mission Office staff today at seventeen-hundred, please," Trevon replied.

"It is my pleasure to Serve and Guide. I will be there," she answered, nodding slightly in spite of the knowledge the gentleman on the other end of the line could not see her. Which, given her usual desire for modesty, was entirely just as well.

"Very well. I will let the Mission Office know to expect you. Have a good morning!"

"You as well," Ise replied, doing her best to mask her dry throat. She then replaced the receiver in its cradle. She managed something akin to grace as she moved to her kitchen and set the water heating for her tea, before returning to her bedroom. She turned on a pair of lamps so that she could see what she was doing before opening her wardrobe.

She pulled on her "morning clothes", which was a set of loose-fitting soft-cotton pants and shirt in muted colours. Her mind returned to the prior night's amusements at the "Emerald of the Sea" dance hall. She really did know better than to have that much to drink, but the brunette had been remarkably charming and a delightfully good dancer. Ise had made the conscious decision to ignore responsible behaviour and common sense for the night. Even though it was not her usual style to indulge in one night stands, a certain part of her was vaguely disappointed the entirely random encounter had gone no farther than dancing, drinks and laughter.

From the kitchen, the kettle began to whistle. The agenda for the day, then, was tea and breakfast, yoga, a swim, and then getting changed into "work clothes" for the meeting at the Mission Office. She wondered where the winds of Fate were preparing to now blow the *RSAV Sheerah* and her crew.

# Hal
## 12h26 SST
## Monday, April 18th

Hal had just finished wiping his face with a towel and then applying a thick lather with his shaving brush when the phone in his sitting room began ringing. He said something curt and coarse, and then shook his head. If it was important, they would call back, he reasoned. If it was not important enough to call back, it was not important enough to warrant ruining a perfectly good shave over.

It was thus about thirty minutes later, while he was sitting with a cup of tea in hand, that the phone rang again for the third time since he had gotten out of bed. He reached over and picked up the receiver.

"Hal Lum," he offered.

"Good morning, Captain Lum," came a low but pleasant voice. "its Margret Aethelsdottir calling from the Council's RSAV Planning Service. You are required at the Mission Office today at seventeen-hundred hours."

"Good morning, Margret. Thank-you very much for the call. Please let The Brass know I will be there."

"Very good, Captain. I will let them know. Have a good morning," Margret offered.

"You as well, Margret," he replied. He returned the receiver to its usual resting place, without his eyes leaving the phone. He continued looking thoughtfully at the phone for a few moments, then flipped through the card-roller beside it until he found Counsellor Koolen's name and number presented. He dialled her six-digit number in pairs, mumbling the numbers aloud as he did.

She answered on the third ring of the phone with her usual soft and warm tone. "Counsellor Koolen here. Good morning, Captain Lum," she said.

Hal chuckled aloud and then smiled as he replied. "Good morning, Counsellor. How did you know it was me?"

"Deduction," she offered in reply. "The Mission Office called me recently this morning, and thus I can presume they have done the same with you. I know that you are perpetually concerned with your command team being as well informed as possible, and you also specifically go out of your way to ensure myself and Detail Leader Baasch have heard directly from you on matters that affect our Details, our Departments or our personal affairs.

"Very few people actually have my telephone number, and fewer of those actually call me. You are one of the few that do. Thus, I could guess you would be the one calling me," she explained.

Hal laughed again and shook his head before continuing the conversation further. "A perpetual presence of mind that is truly remarkable, Counsellor. I note you said that you received a call from the Mission Office; you have been told about the briefing today at seventeen-hundred Signal, then?"

"I have, yes."

"Very good. That is all I wanted to make sure of. Would you like to meet at the *Whale's Breach Bistro* at sixteen-hundred Signal, and then we can take the tram together from there?" Hal asked, shifting the handset to the other ear.

"That would be very pleasant, Captain. I think I would like that a good deal. I shall see you then and there," Ise replied.

"Very well. Until then, Counsellor," Hal said, and then ended the call.

## Cordelia
## 14h03 SST
## Monday, April 18th

She was in no mood for company when Marlon found her at the dock, sitting on a couple of old wooden crates, staring at the *Sheerah*. "I rather imagine I owe you an apology," he said at a level that was barely audible above the din of the dockyard.

She said nothing in reply, hoping the stony silence would persuade him to leave her be. She likely should have known better, she supposed; the older Engineer was a stubborn coot when he chose to be. She merely sighed in annoyance when Marlon moved to sit on an adjacent crate.

A lengthy and pointed silence passed before she finally looked at him and spoke with a hurt and bitter tone. "You at least owe me a bloody explanation. What the Green-Fog-Hell was that all about? I feel like an absolutely heartless bitch and I do not even know *why*, and I know I have managed to do something awful and I do not even know *what*!"

Marlon blinked at her, surprise clear upon his features. "Pardon?" he asked, taken aback.

"You bloody heard me, Marlon!" she exploded. "What the hell happened at the Parlour the other night? I was trying to have a bit of good-natured fun with the Captain, everyone's favourite conservative stuff-shirt, and the next thing I know Jonas is bolting from the place with tears in his eyes and you are chasing him out telling him not to do anything rash! The next morning, I hear that Jonas was in the drunk-tank and Christopher Oliver is 'kindly declining' to press charges over the black-eye that Jonas gave him," she roared at the Chief Engineer beside her. "What. The. Hell. Happened?"

Pryce weathered the storm with a suitably pained look on his face, and then pinched the bridge of his nose for a moment with his eyes closed. He sighed, opened his eyes, and looked at her.

"Wake up, lass," Marlon began patiently. "The lad is dolphin-flippy, bow-over-stern in-love with you."

Whatever list of answers Cordelia had been expecting from Marlon, this particular response was not on said list. In fact, it was not even on an *adjacent* list. "What? Hal is in love with me?" she gaped, looking stunned.

Pryce clapped a hand to his forehead in exasperation. "No, you silly girl!" Marlon answered. "Jonas. Our Pilot. The lad most recently who has taken up bare-knuckle boxing with our Chief Armsman. Jonas Zupan. Do you follow me?"

The utterly astonished look on her face turned to one of shocked dismay. "Oh, Spirits bright ..." she trailed off. This was beginning to sound like a horror novel to her.

"You had no clue, did you?" the older Engineer asked.

Cordelia shook her head, speechless. A flash of the name of candidate number twenty-six of her "Twenty-Eight List" appeared in her mind's eye. The *Sheerah*'s womanising booze artist was in love with her? What Hurricane-Force-Hell was this?

"I thought not," he said with a sigh that nearly got him slugged. "You poor blind fool," he continued after a moment. "Why did you think he never misses a show of yours at the Parlour? Why do you think he is always trying to get your attention on board the *Sheerah*? The lad bloody *glows* when you compliment him on his work.  What did you *think* all of that was about?"

"I … I … I just thought he was a womanising drunkard that wanted a cheap throw," she confessed, her voice sounding progressively closer and closer to tears.  "I did not mean to hurt him!  I was just trying to have some fun at Lum's expense!  It is not my fault!"

When she had seen the trio of Hal, Marlon and Jonas a few tables back from the grand piano, she had impishly decided to try to bring a blush to her other-life Captain's face.  Any malice on her part was entirely playful in intent.

She had gotten the nine-piece band to quick-change songs to a *double-entendre* laced number that was ostensibly about the rigours of working in an iron foundry.  She had launched into the number and lazily made her way over to their table and dropped into Hal's lap, arms around his neck, for the closing verse.  It was just supposed to be some sexy fun at Hal's expense.  No one was supposed to get hurt.

"No," Marlon replied, running a hand through his greying hair.  "It is not entirely your fault.  Like most things like this, it is *everyone's* fault.  The only one possibly innocent was Hal.  Everyone else involved was either being dishonest or playing a game." He sighed and looked towards the much younger woman beside him.

She returned his gaze with a sullen look, but did not argue with him.  A few moments of silence passed before she spoke.  "So now what do we do?" she asked quietly, her prior bluster and indignation completely absent.

"We learn, we live, we carry on as though normal," the older Engineering Chief replied.  "Hopefully, everyone has learned something about themselves and their shipmates.  Now, the only issue is what the individuals in question do with the lesson, I suppose.  For myself, I am going to take my darling wife's advice and leave match-making to those

84

much more gifted at it."

"Match-making?"

"Yes, match-making. I was hoping if I could keep young Zupan from letting his anxiety drive him to drink again, that perhaps he would be able to talk to you and say something about how he feels. So when Lum called me about going to see one of your shows for the first time, I invited Jonas along."

Cordelia blinked. "I am not sure where to start with that entire sentence," she replied slowly. "So, I suppose I will start with the part that makes me angry. Do not meddle in my personal affairs, Pryce. Do you hear me? Do. Not. I am a grown woman, and I do not need nor want anyone else to sort out what I do in my life off-ship!"

It was bad enough that she was still trying to sort out the idea that Jonas was "Mister Twenty-Six", without Marlon "helping". She was already dealing with no small measure of emotional confusion at the fall-out of this well-intentioned disaster.

"Understood. You have my apologies. It will not happen a first time," Marlon replied tersely, sounding irritable. "I say 'first time' because this was not about your personal affairs, Cordelia. This was about trying to help Jonas."

"Perhaps it was, but the collateral damage landed on me," she said with a scowl. Collateral damage, indeed, she thought sourly. How was she going to deal with having a love-sick crew-mate? Particularly one she had just managed to accidentally crucify with her antics.

There was another long silence. "So, what do I have to do with his drinking?" she asked awkwardly, suddenly yet again feeling very responsible.

"Directly, not much. Indirectly, a great deal."

"That is a piss-poor answer and you know it, Pryce," she interrupted irritably.

"Indeed it is. And if you had let me finish, you would have gotten enough of the rest of it to make it a reasonable reply," he answered crossly. "Just because you are feeling confused or whatever it is does not mean this is a free-fire zone."

"Sorry."

"Mmmmph. What I was about to say was that Jonas, our charming and gifted RSAV pilot, is as badly broken as I have met in almost thirty years of knowing RSAV pilots. He is an utter genius, both in and out of the driver's chair.

"Except, of course, when it comes to dealing with people. From the conversations I have had with the lad, some sober, some significantly less so, people just do not make sense to him. So, he has a sort of set of rules in his head that he uses to navigate people, the way he would navigate an unknown harbour."

Cordelia tilted her head and looked at him in disbelief. "How the Watered-Diesel-Hell does he manage to make it through a day then?"

"By avoiding the rocks with jokes and covering up the mistakes with laughter," Marlon replied. "He is a joker and clown-show by nervous necessity, from what I can tell. His other coping mechanism is to kill the nervousness and second-guessing with a stiff drink. Or three."

The Salvage and Dive Leader rolled her eyes. "That is such an *excellent* choice of coping mechanisms. You would think that Ise or one of her ilk would have problems with that."

"Counsellor Koolen hates the taste of Rye-Whiskey. She prefers 'fancy' drinks that have fizzes, mixes and umbrellas," Marlon stated in a flat tone.

"What does that have to do with anything? Besides, you have to be mistaken; Koolen always has her 'Recreationals' slotted with one bottle of," she trailed off. "Are you telling me she gives half her on-board booze supply to Jonas?"

Marlon merely replied with a nod and an infuriating smile.

She teetered on the edge of glaring at him for a long moment before an unexpected and somewhat unwelcome conclusion interrupted her. "Wait a moment. That means he drinks partly because of me. That is not fair! It is not fair to him, and it is not fair to me!"

Marlon raised a hand. "No, and no. Well, more like, 'yes, no and no', really. He very much cares about what you think of him, of course, so yes, that does make him anxious around you. Particularly when you are 'artfully draped' over the grand piano in the Parlour. However, it is not your problem nor responsibility, young lady, as to how he deals with it. Unless you decide you wish to *make* it your responsibility, it is not your responsibility."

"I feel like giving him such a piece of my mind over this," she said, suddenly feeling very angry at everyone else for the position they had left her in.

"For what? Being an insecure and very smitten young man that has never fit in anywhere well? I have my reservations about the wisdom of that."

"That is *not* what I meant, and you know it, Marlon Pryce," Cordelia growled. She was rapidly running out of tolerance for the older Engineer's "good natured" advice.

"Oh, yes it is, and you know it, Miz Baasch," Marlon countered, somehow managing to avoid sounding smug or adversarial. "Knowing a shipmate's behaviour and poor choices is partially dependent on yourself is the sort of thing that will frustrate and upset. However, yelling at him, or whatever else you intend, will not help. All it will do is make things more awkward. If you would like to make things easier for him and you, try treating him less as a poisonous lush and more like someone possibly worthy of your friendship."

# Christopher

Christopher Olivier got out of the shower, and wrapped a towel around his waist. He paused to examine the two marks on his face with some amusement via the mirror. He turned a bit to each side and audibly chuckled; left eye and right jaw. The entire situation was so ridiculous that he was having difficulty being anything other than amused.

The phone rang from his sitting room, and he moved purposefully to answer it. "Hello, Christopher Olivier here."

"Good morning, Chief Armsman. This is Public Services and Security calling, Officer Manawata speaking. Do you have a few minutes?"

"Yes, but I am not sure what you might want to speak to me about," Christopher replied with all the welcome of a granite boulder sitting on a northern shoreline in November.

"You were assaulted by crew-mate Jonas Zupan last evening, were you not?"

"It is a Community Service Record offence if he did, is it not?"

"That is correct, which is why we need to establish what happened," the Pee-Ess-Ess officer on the other end of the phone replied in a firm tone.

"Then what happened is that I walked into a door. I do not recall seeing Jonas Zupan all evening. Any other questions?" Christopher continued on in the same chilly tone.

There was dead silence for a moment. "Pardon? I mean, you must be joking?" Officer Manawata began. "He did actually assau …"

"Are you accusing me of lying, Officer?" Christopher interrupted in a now lethally cold voice.

"Well, no … no, of course not. I mean …"

"Then you have my official account on paper once, and as of the end of this call, twice verbally. Good-day, sir."

"Wait! It is imp …"

"I said 'good-day, sir'," the Armsman barked, and hung up. He shook his head in irritation and went to his kitchen and poured himself a glass of fruit juice. He went to his bedroom to get dressed.

If he reported the brief exchange of blows to Pee-Ess-Ess officially then Zupan, the stupid fool, was likely to get himself pulled off the ship. That meant another RSAV pilot, almost by definition, one less competent than Zupan, would replace him. That would just make Christopher's life more dangerous.

It also very much served the Armsman's purpose to have Jonas Zupan an available problem to Hal and Cordelia. Eventually that duo of flashy, flailing incompetence would cause its own comeuppance, and removing the Pilot-Navigator from the mixture prematurely would just slow that process down. By contrast, it was Christopher's opinion that the sooner it came to pass, the better.

Besides, the punk threw a respectable punch, Christopher thought amusedly as he had a mouthful of juice. As well, to Jonas' credit, instead of victimising someone at random and causing a problem outside the ship, he took whatever it was that was infuriating him out on the one crew-mate whose proverbial job was taking hits for the team. Christopher considered that a reasonable way of the Pilot dealing with his anger. From his perspective, if you were going to throw punches in a fury regardless of common sense, then going after someone like your Chief Armsman was a far better alternative than most.

It was not a free service, of course; he suspected the little twerp would be waking up with a bruised set of ribs, a sore shoulder and something very close to a concussion. He chuckled to himself in a minor measure of malice; a concussion *and* a hang-over at the same time were an excellent pairing to avoid. Hopefully Jonas would learn something.

He rubbed thoughtfully at a bruise on his arm where he had blocked two blows before ending the foolish affair. The dolt threw a pretty good punch. He had clearly been paying attention at the infrequent crew hand-to-hand training refreshers, contrary to what Christopher had previously thought.

# Hal
## 17h02 SST
## Monday, April 18th

"Thank you both for coming in on short notice," Alodia Holt said in a friendly tone. She was the Mission Services Mistress for the Council's RSAV Planning Service.

Like Marlon Pryce, she was from Gen-Six with the greying hair to show for it. She had been one of the finest RSAV Salvage and Dive Detail Leaders in the Fleet of her Generation. When it came time to retire from the life of an RSAV crew member, the Council had offered her the very prestigious and responsible position she now held.

She was, both in theory and practice, the most powerful person in the RSAV fleet. A Precursor navy more worried about titles might have called her the Admiral. Regardless of what her title was or might have been, for as long as either Hal and Ise had been at sea, the name on the orders sheets had been Alodia Holt's.

Hal bowed formally before replying. "It is no problem at all, Miz. It was not entirely unexpected, given the amount of time the *Sheerah* has been alongside."

Ise bowed as well, plus a polite nod. "As the Captain says," she answered in her cool, smoky voice.

"Very well, then. As you can see from this map," Alodia said, gesturing at the substantial table covered in RSAV models, sea-surface condition markers and other props, "most of the fleet is currently out. The *RSAV Emilia Lanier* is on her way home from 42.40N,71.10W. She has sent in a RATT-net message indicating that she found a substantial supply of steel-rich concrete in Precursor ruins there. Now, of course, we have been to that location a dozen times in half as many years, but a recent trio of Saffir-Simpson 'fives' has dramatically carved up the coastline in that area. That seems to have exposed some new resources."

"Well, that is very good news," commented Hal.

Ise nodded in agreement. "I would imagine the crew of the *Lanier* are feeling very fortunate."

"I would imagine you are right, Counsellor," Holt said with a smile and a nod that bounced her shoulder-length blonde-grey ponytail. "Also in the RATT-net message from the *Lanier* was a reference to an 'intermittent radio anomaly'. Unfortunately, the *Lanier* is having AMTAC transceiver issues, which means there is not much detail due to imposed message length restraints."

Ise frowned. "That could mean almost anything, unfortunately," she said, sounding thoughtful. "However, it does present an excellent opportunity for some scientific investigation."

"Agreed," Hal said with a nod to the Spirit and Morale Counsellor.

"That is what we are hoping. So, the *RSAV Sheerah* and her crew are to depart in three days, thirteen hundred SST, for 42.40N,71.10W. You will rendezvous with the *RSAV Emilia Lanier* seventy-two hours after departure, here," the Mission Services Mistress said, using a pointer to indicate a model of an RSAV on the map. "The captain of the *Lanier* will provide you with updated coastal and bottom profiles, as well as further information on the 'radio anomaly'."

Hal nodded, glancing up from where he had been scribbling on a notepad he had brought with him for the briefing. He habitually brought it with him to every briefing he attended. "Any embarked equipment?"

"Yes, you will be sailing with two 'radio environment recorders'. You will set them up at a set of coordinates that the Science and Research Centre will provide you. The locations are within a few kilometres of each other. The Arr-Eee-Arrs will run for a month, recording everything they hear, and another RSAV will recover them later for analysis."

"In addition," Holt continued, "your vessel will have two tonnes of dry goods and three tonnes of dairy embarked as cargo to transfer to the *Lanier*. She suffered a minor incident of some kind and had some supplies ruined, so we are ensuring she has more than enough on board for the trip home."

Ise held a slender finger up to ensure she had Alodia's attention. "Since we do not know the exact nature of the anomaly, I must presume a measure of risk to the vessel and crew. Also, given the severity of the geographic changes, there is additional risk."

"I would agree with that assessment, Counsellor," the Mission Services Mistress replied with an acknowledging tilt of her head.

"I would thus request a Grade-One upgrade of food supplies, as well as a likewise upgrade of entertainment materials," Ise suggested with a hint of firmness in her usually relaxed tone.

Hal glanced between the two women. He did not disagree with Ise's suggestion, better stores would mean that the crew would ostensibly be in a better mental state to deal with a potentially more stressful or dangerous situation, he was just surprised how quickly the Counsellor had made the request. Most RSAVs sailed on "Grade Three" stores and supplies; the best stuff at "Grade One" was saved for the civilian service industries of the seafloor town.

Hal would have likely submitted a request from the ship tomorrow for a "Grade Two" supplies and entertainment sheet. But here was the *Sheerah's* Spirit and Morale Counsellor lunging straight for Grade One in the middle of the briefing. He had known the pillar of calm and perception named Ise Koolen for a bit more than three years now, he reflected, and she still regularly surprised him with how she saw and did things.

Miz Holt lofted an eyebrow at Miz Koolen. There was a moment of silence where the two looked at each other with a quiet and steady professionalism. Hal reflected that he might have called the moment a prelude to a duel if this had been a Saturday evening stage play.

The Mission Services Mistress quirked a smile and nodded. "Request granted in principle. Get the paperwork in and I will sign off on it."

"Thank you, Miz," Ise answered with a polite nod.

"Any mission-specific requests that you would like pre-cleared as well, Captain?" Alodia asked Hal, sounding amused about something.

"Not at this time. I will need to meet with my Detail Leads and see if anything bubbles up. We did deliver some make-and-mend requests when we docked, but I presume those have all be seen to."

"Very well, Captain," Holt replied. She turned and picked up two brown leather portfolios. She then turned back to the pair and gave them each one. "That is a copy of the briefing, as well as the usual selection of in-depth information to accompany it. I expect your 'read-and-reviewed' sheets signed and returned within twenty-four hours. As stated, I expect the *Sheerah* to be clearing the docks in three days. If there is any reason that cannot happen, I expect to be notified immediately so that we can resolve the problem."

Hal nodded. "I am not aware of any reason that our departure would be delayed," he replied and then paused. "Counsellor Koolen, I have not seen any paperwork on Mister Martinsson. What is his status, officially?"

Ise tilted her head thoughtfully. "To the best of my knowledge, still part of our crew. I have heard nothing about his wife nor their child."

"Given the circumstances we discussed before we got home, I think we should get him home-posted for this cruise, at least," Hal stated.

"I will see to it, Captain. Fleet Staffing Services should be able to provide us a Hull-Tech on short notice."

"Make sure I am See-See'd on the paperwork, Counsellor, and I will ensure the process is expedited," Alodia offered. "Also, send me a memo with the details of the circumstances. The *Sheerah* is not known for switching crew around willy-nilly, so I presume this is non-minor in nature."

Ise nodded and borrowed Hal's notepad and pen to write herself a reminder.

"Very well," Alodia said. "That ends the briefing. I will see you off when you sail in three days. Make the Service proud."

# CHAPTER SIX
## *Ready, Aye, Ready*

### Jonas
### 08h12 SST
### Tuesday, April 19th

The music filtering through the air of his apartment was as moody and melancholy as Jonas Zupan was. He could not believe the state of his life right now. Beyond the physical pains he was suffering from a combination of the curt beating by the Chief Armsman and a substantially longer drubbing by a trio of rye-whiskey bottles, his heart and soul ached.

After that ridiculous disaster at the Parlour, how could he go back to the ship? Would they even *want* him there? He had been waiting for Public Security and Safety to stop by most of Sunday and Monday; apparently Christopher had decided, for whatever unfathomable reason, not to turn this into a Service issue.

That was a barely a mercy, Jonas reflected. Being tossed in the stockade for a week and pulled off the *Sheerah* would have been easier on him. Instead, he had to go back and face them.

Them. Hal. Cordelia. Marlon. *Them.*

How could he? He would look like the childish, foolish ass that he was. He was mortified at the aspect. But he could not stay away, either. His ship and his crew *needed* him.

He wiped a fresh trickle of tears from his eyes and shook his head. What could he do?

*Koolen.*

The Spirit and Morale Counsellor would know what to do. She might know how to fix this mess he was in. He reached for the phone nearby and hesitated. He sat back in his chair, feeling overwhelmingly guilty.

It was early. Very early. *Stupidly* early. The sun and lights would not be up for another two hours or so. Maybe he should not call. He did not want to be an inconvenience; more of a problem. He was enough of a problem already. He should wait until later. That would be better. He could wait.

He could all but hear her cool yet scolding tone lecturing him about failing to give her the opportunity to help someone in need. He sighed. He reached for the phone. He lowered his hand.

Maybe she did not know what happened? Then he would have to tell her. She would be disappointed in him. She was always so nice to him; so kind, so understanding. He desperately did not want her to dislike him, to be *disappointed* in him. He was tired of disappointing people. He could not call her. That would just be a disaster.

*Cordelia.*

He drove the heels of his hands into his eyes in sorrow. What a *fool* he was. She did not even know he was alive. She was all about the Captain; who could blame her? Hal was everything Jonas would never be; confident, handsome, athletic, charming, a leader, a good build, a good smile, good hair. Jonas never had a chance. He had been a fool to think he even would have been on her SONAR. What would a woman like that want with a wreckage like him?

The bottle was just below half. Maybe he would just finish it off in a few gulps, and then the noise in his head would go away, and he could get some sleep. At least when he was asleep, he was not a problem to anyone.

A choked noise escaped him, and he dabbed at his eyes. He sat in the gloom of his barely lit apartment. It would be just safer if he had a few more mouthfuls of 'Crown-Diamond', and went to bed. He could not deal with this. He just could not.

He nearly lunged at the telephone. It took three tries to get the number right, each prior aborted attempt demarcated by a fevered stab at the hang-up.

It rang. Once. A minor eternity passed. It rang again. Some longer interval of time went by. It rang a third time. She was asleep. He was being a bother. He should just hang up and leave her be. He should ...

"Ise Koolen," came the sleepy voice.

"Uh ... um ... I am sorry, Counsellor ... I ... I can call back later ... I ..."

"Nonsense," his Spirit and Morale Counsellor interrupted. "Is this Jonas?"

"Uh ... I mean ... um ... yes, Miz Koolen," he replied meekly.

"You are clearly not all right, so I will spare you the question. Meet me in Forest Room Number Nine in ...," there was a rustle of fabric, and what sounded like a mechanical 'click' that reached Jonas' ears.

"... Meet me there in twenty minutes. If you do not arrive in twenty minutes, I will have a Pee-Ess-Ess Detail knock your apartment door off its hinges and drag you there. I would expect that process would likely be exceptionally awkward for everyone involved. Do you understand, Pilot

Zupan?" she asked sternly.

"Yes, Counsellor Koolen," Jonas replied, involuntarily ducking his head as he answered her.

"In twenty minutes, then," she said amiably, and hung up.

*****

It had been one of the most miserably hopeful walks he had embarked upon in his life, Jonas reflected as he reached his destination. He had taken a handful of minutes to clean himself up so that he looked at least a notch less slovenly, regardless of the hour. He had hurried towards Forest Room Number Nine, suspecting that the remarkably wilful Spirit and Morale Counsellor had not been entirely speaking in hyperbole of the consequences should he be tardy.

Jonas had never been to this particular Forest Room before. There were twelve in Soumerville, spaced at equal intervals around the outer edge of the top of the structure. This one was essentially on the opposite side of the undersea colony from his apartment. Thus a certain level of extra haste had been required on his part.

"I hope she is there; I hope she is not. Save my soul; Let me rot" he sang under his shortened breath. Hmm. There might be a song in this. Albeit *not* a dance song, he thought ruefully. At its most cheerful, it would be a jazzy-blues. At most.

He slowed as he crossed the threshold for the Forest Space. The massive Flood Control Doors were closed by half of the generous width of the entry way to the Space. He knew that was normal for the hour, of course. Essentially, once most of the populace of Soumerville went to bed, the seafloor town rigged itself for disaster. Thus, if a fire or flood were to occur, any delay in response caused by a lack of available personnel would be somewhat offset by the restrictions already partially deployed.

Given it was still well before dawn, there was precious little light here; natural sunlight was entirely absent. A soft and muted "moonlight blue" filtered down from the artificial lighting mounted along the struts that supported the cerami-glass roof. Additional knee-level muted-white lights illuminated the walking paths for reasons of both comfort and safety.

He quietly and slowly made his way along the walk to where the cluster of picnic tables could expected to be found. Regardless of what was planted in them, each of the twelve Forest Rooms were all roughly the same path layout. To his mutual relief and anxiety, Ise Koolen was already sitting at one of them.

She had a trio of candles lit, a bottle of what looked like water, a couple of fancy-looking tall glass tumblers, and an enamel plate of what resembled baked sweets. She smiled when she saw him, and gestured to the spot opposite to where she sat.

He nodded, and took the indicated place at the table. "Look, Counsellor, I am really sorry about waking you at this hour," he began.

She raised a finger, which had the same effect as a spat of tape over his mouth. "First, for the duration of this meeting, call me Ise. Secondly, this is my job, Jonas. I am always available to help someone in need when they call," she said in a tone that managed to be both firm and friendly. She poured him a glass of what turned out to be a sparkling water, and passed him a couple of what looked like date squares. "Third, I can smell the 'Crown-Diamond' rye-whiskey on your breath from here. Have a bit to eat and some water. Then we can talk."

Jonas nodded at her and had a mouthful of water. He really did not deserve her tolerance and kindness, he thought guiltily.

"Stop that," she ordered, and his head snapped up to look at her in confusion.

"What? Stop what?"

"You were just feeling guilty about this. Stop that. It is okay, Jonas. I do not mind. I feel very complimented that you called me out of everyone you know. It is a wonderful display of trust, and I very much appreciate that. Now, enjoy the snack, and leave the guilt behind."

"Yes, Ise." He had no idea how she did that. It was like she could read minds. There was a persistent rumour that all of Counsellor Koolen's ilk actually *could* read minds, but that seemed far-fetched to him. Still, it was uncanny how she did that.

She poured herself some of the fizzy water and took one of the squares. She waited patiently, not pressing him.

"I, well, I think I am in trouble," he began uncertainly.

"Oh? Why do you say that?" Ise asked encouragingly.

"Well, ah, for one, I, um, got into a fight with the Chief Armsman."

"That does not sound very wise of you, Jonas. Christopher is very proud of his skills, and justifiably so. Besides, why would you do something like that? It does not seem much like you at all," she observed. Her voice was entirely conversational, without a hint of condemnation or recrimination.

"I was mad. I was so angry, Ise. So angry it felt like it burned. I had to let it out, and it was the only thing I could think of," he whispered, shame in his voice.

"Sssssh. It is ok. Rage can surprise a person with its intensity. Everyone deals with a moment of it, eventually. If someone tells you they have not, then they are either lying to you or they have not been passionate about something in their lives," Ise stated. "So, tell me, just you and me, who or what is your passion that gave reason for your rage?"

"You mean you do not know? I thought it would be obvious to

someone like you, Counsellor."

"'Ise'," she corrected. "And it does not matter what *I* see, Jonas. The question is 'what do you feel?' When we talk about what we feel, it becomes real. Then we can learn from those feelings, heal from the hurt they may have caused, and make a plan about how those feelings fit in our lives. You cannot run from a ghost, Jonas. You cannot heal from a ghost, Jonas. You cannot learn from a ghost, Jonas. Those are all things you can only do with what is real."

Jonas felt like he was at the edge of a cliff. If he said anything in the next moment, he would be dashing himself on rocks unseen on a beach beyond his vision. Safety was to turn away, to be silent, to avoid, to joke, to hide. *Anything* but forward was safety.

He opened his mouth, but no sound emerged. He closed his eyes, and suddenly Ise was sitting beside him. Her arm was around his shoulder, giving him a reassuring squeeze.

"Cordelia," he blurted. "Cordelia Baasch. I … I think I love her, Ise. And she is in love with Hal. And I feel like I am lost and alone … and … like … I am *always* going to be lost and alone."

Ise gave him a surprisingly strong hug and suddenly he found himself literally crying on her shoulder. She said nothing, instead letting him bawl without comment or action, beyond suddenly producing a damp facecloth and a dry handkerchief, apparently from thin air.

He hiccupped, then sat up and wiped at his face. Ise smiled encouragingly at him. "I am fairly sure you are mistaken about Miz Baasch's feelings for Hal Lum," she said quietly. "I know Cordelia fairly well, and both she and the Captain are married to their jobs."

"But, she *sang* to him! And what a song! And sat in his lap! And …"

Ise gently laid a slender finger over his lips and he stopped obediently. "You, of all people, 'Zee' should know that who someone is as a performer, can be very different from who they really are," she said pointedly.

He blinked at her. "Wait. You know?"

Ise giggled at him and flashed a pretty smile that entirely caught him off guard. "I am a *fan*, dear Jonas. A noticeable portion of my personal music library is the 'Jay Zee Clark Project'. Yes, I know. As part of my job, I know very well what the entire crew's 'Second' is. And, when Miz Baasch has her high-heel shoes and low-cut dresses on, she is very *much* a performer. I entirely expect she was trying to ruffle the feathers of our notoriously calm and smooth Captain," Ise said with a laugh.

Jonas hid his face in his hands. "And then I acted like a complete fool. Oh, Ise, what am I ever going to do? We sail in two days, and I feel so humiliated, so stupid. I cannot go back to the *Sheerah*! What will everyone think? What will *she* think?"

Ise "tsk'd" at him for a moment, but somehow still managed to look sympathetic. "Yes, you can go back; yes, you must go back; and yes, Jonas, you will go back. Firstly, you have to be honest with everyone."

He looked at her in horror. "I cannot just tell Cordelia how I feel!"

"Why not? You are afraid that she might not be interested? If you never tell her, she might never be interested. On the other hand if you do, then perhaps she might. Regardless of that, silence does not ever improve any aspect about a relationship between two people, Jonas. Besides, I did not say you had to run around posting bulletins about the ship, either. I said you have to be honest."

He took a mouthful of water and looked at the slender, dark-skinned woman seated beside him in a cheery palette of athletic attire. "I am sorry, Ise, I do not get what you are trying to explain here. I should be honest but not say anything?"

"Yes," she said. "See? You do understand, even if you are afraid of it. If someone asks you a question about what happened, then tell the truth as it pertains to them. If the truth does not pertain to them, then tell them *that* truth. And by truth, I mean 'big T' Truth, not 'little-t' truth. The Truth. The Truth that says who you are and what you believe in and what makes you Jonas the Pilot-Navigator of the *RSAV Sheerah*. If Cordelia asks you what happened or why, then tell her The Truth. If Hal asks, if Christopher asks, if Marlon asks, if *anyone* asks, you tell them The Truth as it pertains to them."

He thought about that for a while. "I ... I am not sure I can do that."

"You can. You do it every time 'Zee' writes a marvellous song for the dance halls that gets the girls out on the floor and the boys following behind. All of Zee's songs, *your* songs, are about Truths, Jonas. Truths about who we are as a people, as a place, and a time. You mask some of those Truths behind catchy foot-movers and bottom-shakers, just as you mask your anxieties in person behind laughter and jokes. But they are still Truths."

He simply stared at her. A suspicion bubbled to the surface unbidden; she had never mentioned his music before, let alone being a fan. She was likely just saying that to make him feel better, he thought sourly.

"And since you are wondering, my favourite is '*Dolphin Ranch Promenade*'. I would love if you would sign the vinyl copy I have as 'Zee'. I *adore* that song."

"How do you do that?" he asked, abruptly mentally face-down in a puddle of confusion.

"Practice," she replied. "Hours upon hours of practice. Plus, well, I am a product of the STADEs, just as much as you are. Every one of us are highly specialised freak-shows, ruthlessly optimised to be the best we can be at the jobs our society needs of us. Just as you can make the

*Sheerah* all but do a four-four time foxtrot, I can read people."

They sat together in silence for a while before he spoke again; long enough for another glass of water and an accompanying date square to disappear. "So, that is it?  Easy-peasy, just tell The Truth, all the time, every time?" he asked, sounding dubious.

She laughed gaily, a surprisingly pleasant sound given the circumstances. "Oh, Spirits bright, no, no, no, I did not say it was going to be *easy*, Jonas.  It is going to be a remarkably *difficult* thing to do, until you make it a habit.  But yes, all the time, every time.  Why would you not tell the truth?  Not telling the truth is lying, after all," she pointed out to him.

"I am still not sure I can face everyone after all of this," he said sourly.

"Yes, you can, Jonas.  Listen to me, now.  I promise you that if anyone, and I mean anyone from Captain Hal Lum down to Able Deckhand Danielle Hendry, *anyone* gives you a moment of trouble over the incident at the Parlour or with Christopher, I will be your advocate. You call me, and the three of us will sit down in my cabin and sort it all out.  That is my job, Jonas, and I am proud to be able to do it.  'It is my pleasure to Serve and Guide', as we say formally."

Jonas nodded at her.  "Really?  You would do that for me?"

"I would do that for *any* of the crew of the *Sheerah*, Jonas.  But yes, really.  I would do that for you, too.  You deserve that much," she said firmly.

He nodded at her slowly.

"Do you feel much better?" she asked.

He opened his mouth to answer and then closed it.  Big-T Truth, she had told him.  "Not much better, no.  A bit better, though.  At least I no longer feel like drowning myself in a rye bottle."

She smiled encouragingly at him. "That is wonderful news to my ears, Jonas. I will see you in a day or so, as we prepare the *Sheerah* for sea again. Your crew and your friends need their Chief Navigational Miracle Worker at the helm and in the light of good Spirits. Promise me you will do everything you can to be there for us."

He paused for a moment. Big-T Truth. Do not just blow off the question with a "yeah sure". Think about it. It was hard. He still wanted so very much to hide. But she said he could do it. So, he could. He took a deep breath and nodded. "I promise, Ise. Thank-you so much for all of this. I really needed someone to talk to. You have been wonderful."

She smiled at him and gave him another hug, which caught him a bit off guard. "It is my pleasure to Serve and Guide," she said warmly. Then, she added, "You are worth my time, Jonas. Never think you are not."

# Hal
## 18h51 SST
## Tuesday, April 19th

Captain Hal Lum made his way across the gangplank, with a duffle bag over each shoulder and a briefcase in one hand. Jokes about "officer privilege" concerning the amount of stuff he was lugging aboard were common, but in Hal's case, this was about the minimum he could sail with. The briefcase was full of the paperwork and documents that an RSAV officially required to let go the lines and drive down the Ramp. One duffle bag was full of uniforms, clothes, books, and the like; his personal things. The other duffle bag was loaded with books and AMTACs for the ship's Library for the cruise.

For some reason he never quite understood, while it was Ise Koolen's job to make up the list of what would be in the Library, it was

Hal Lum's job to actually stop by the Fleet Operational Support office to pick it up and bring it to the ship. His situation was not unique, of course; this was how every ship in the fleet did it. There was likely a terribly clever reason for it; with the Service, there usually was.

The *Sheerah* and her crew sailed tomorrow, two hours after sunrise, and so activity in and around the amphibious vessel was approaching its zenith. As Hal stepped onto the deck of the RSAV, the Day Watchman blew a series of shrill tones on his whistle that everyone within earshot easily recognised as "Captain coming aboard". Three years on, it still felt somewhat surreal to Hal that the sound meant *him*.

A chorus of respectful greetings began, and continued on with everyone he passed for the first time this cruise, until he reached his cabin. He snagged the two envelopes out of the "Day's Dispatch" bin outside his door, unlocked it and went in. The bags and briefcase landed on the bunk. The envelopes landed on the desk. Then he immediately left, heading for the Emm-and-Que shack. Might as well get that part of the boarding process out of the way, he thought.

# Damiano

The *Sheerah's* Medical and Quarantine facility was just as abuzz with activity as the rest of the vessel. A short line-up outside the "Emm-and-Que Shack" of crew members all yielded the head of the line to their Captain when he arrived.

"Well, hello, Skipper. Good to see you again," Damiano Émile offered charitably. The Ship's Doctor was not just making polite noises; that was something Damiano personally found infuriating, so he refused to do it. He genuinely liked Captain Lum.

Generally speaking, Damiano was the most consistently bored Doctor in the fleet and that was pretty much as he liked it. That boredom directly stemmed from Captain Lum's careful style of leadership.

"Hello, Doctor. It is good to see you as well. I hope your Seconds shift was relaxing. As you likely guessed, I am here for the pre-sail checkup," Hal said cheerfully.

"I thought as much, yes. Well, let us get this done. I know you are busy. So, shirt off, please, and up on the bench, as usual. Ok, so, questions first. Any sickness while alongside since last sail?"

"No," Hal replied.

"Any drinking or recreational drugs in excess of the equivalent of three pints of cider on any given day?"

"Once, alcohol only; somewhere around five pints in one night."

"Well, once like that in a ten-day is hardly a crime. Try not to make a habit of it, though," the Doctor admonished. Crew gossip being what it was, he had already heard that the Captain, Pilot and Engineer had gotten well into their cups at a particularly famous gentleman's club a few days ago. He was glad that Hal was honest about this sort of thing to him; it made Damiano Émile's job that much easier.

"No, of course not," Hal responded affably.

"Right. Aches, pains, diarrhea, difficulty breathing or fever in the past seven days?"

"No."

"Any contact with anyone exhibiting those symptoms within the past four days?"

"No."

"Good," Damiano nodded as he checked off another pair of boxes on the clip-boarded questionnaire. "Any problems with sleep, or other issues of fatigue?"

"Minor insomnia. Took a sleep-aide a couple of nights," Hal replied.

"Mmm. The usual anxiety issue, Captain?"

"Yes," Hal answered, doing his best to mask his discomfort at the question. From Damiano's perspective, it was as effective as using a tea-cozy to conceal a coal pile in a dance hall.

"Well then, as usual, please allow me to remind you that our Spirit and Morale Counsellor is top-notch, and has an excellent support organisation behind her. I would also remind you that intervention and reconciliation services are part of what she does for a living," Damiano intoned, waving his pen at his Captain.

"As usual, noted for the future," Hal replied gruffly.

There were days, the doctor noted to himself amusedly, that the good Captain was as stubborn as a post. "Very well then, lets get your two vials drawn, and your vital signs recorded," he said.

"Vampire tax," Lum sighed in distaste.

"You are hardly unique in your opinion, Captain," the Doctor said with a hint of amusement in his voice. "I am not aware of anyone, myself or Nurse Ji-Hye included, for whom the prospect of being stuck with a needle of any kind results in a resounding cheer of 'oh, goody'," he remarked in humorous tone.

All joking aside, Ship's Doctor Émile considered himself an empathetic sort, and hardly enjoyed hurting anyone. Needles and their ilk were part of the necessary evils of healthcare, however, and like the tools of any other trade, they had their time and place in the process.

Damiano quickly and expertly drew the two vials of blood; for Hal's minor theatrics a moment ago, there was barely a twitch or intake of breath when the needle initially went into his dark skin. Next was a blood-pressure check, politely done with the arm opposite where the spat of swab and tape now sat.

"Blood-pressure is a smidgen high, Captain. I will ask you to stop by in a couple of days for a re-check, okay? I expect it is likely a bit of pre-sail excitement."

Hal nodded. "Yes, that is likely. It is an interestingly curious mission profile, and it was a bit of an odd ten-day ashore. I will be much happier to be at sea again where everything is sane."

Damiano cocked an eyebrow in curiosity. He was going to ask exactly what Hal meant by that somewhat cryptic comment, but opted against it. He would, however, suggest to Counsellor Koolen she perhaps have a "chat" with the Captain in a couple of days, to see what was on his mind.

From his perspective as Ship's Doctor, he and Counsellor Koolen were very much two members of a precision team, he thought as he continued his exam of the Captain. They discussed each other's patients often, ensuring that matters physical and mental across the entire crew were clear and understood between them. Each had their particular health specialty, but certainly, they each leveraged the other's skills to make better diagnosis of their respective current patients.

"Very well, Captain. Your heart-rate is nice and regular, eye-dilation by light is perfectly normal, and your breathing sounds perfectly clear. I am happy to sign off on your 'healthy-for-sea'," Damiano announced.

"Glad to hear it, Doc. I would hate to be told I was staying ashore due to a health issue," Hal chuckled as he pulled his shirt back on.

"No risk of that right now, but I will see you in a couple of days about your blood pressure," the Doctor reminded.

Hal nodded and left.

Damiano did a quick bit of tidy up around the space, humming a happy-sounding tune under his breath. He filed the signed paperwork into the appropriate slot on the wall, added the two vials of blood to the set that would be sent ashore just before sailing tomorrow, and got ready for the next sailor in the line outside the door.

## Cordelia
## 19h21 SST
## Tuesday, April 19th

Cordelia was supervising boxes being chain-ganged down Salt Flats and into Stores Locker Five when Counsellor Koolen arrived behind her. In spite of her usual easy nature, Cordelia stiffened slightly, and found herself hoping this was purely a ship's-business issue.

"Hello, Counsellor, what can I do for you?" she asked politely.

Ise Koolen gave the Salvage Detail Leader the barest of arched eyebrows. "I wanted to ensure that the stores we are embarking are Gee-One-Ewe. I requested the upgrade due to our mission profile. While Mission Services Mistress Holt assured me she would see to the upgrade request personally, I wanted to be sure that there was no mix-up or late-hour change," the lithe, dark-skinned woman answered with a warm enthusiasm.

"Oh! *You* are the Goddess the crew has to thank!" Cordelia grinned. "Yes, oh yes, we did get the upgrade. You should *see* some of the stuff on the Ess-And-Ess list; fresh eggs, top-cut mutton chops, extra dairy butter, enough extra flour that the cooks are talking about English muffins and *croissants* being on the table for most breakfasts. There is a heap of fruits and juices, too!" The blonde-haired woman was looking forward to some very hearty breakfasts on this trip.

Ise openly looked relieved. "Oh, good! Do you know if we got venison and duck in the fridges, too?" she asked hopefully.

Cordelia's grin widened and she nodded. "Yes, Miz! Our fish allotment is about half what I would expect, and that portion of the protein count has been made up with venison, mutton and duck. I heard one of the Armsmen at the head of the chain here joking that it looked like we had robbed a restaurant."

Ise giggled in delight and Cordelia could not help herself but join in. She knew that part of the Spirit and Morale Counsellor's job was to keep an eye on the quality of food and accommodations aboard the RSAV, of course. She knew that a happy stomach and a comfortable cabin space made the difficult life of being an RSAV crew-member considerably more bearable. However, this was the first time she had ever heard of, let alone seen in person, a G1 stores upgrade done at the behest of a ship's Counsellor.

"Oh, before I forget, Cordelia" Ise said conspiratorially while leaning forward towards the woman she was speaking with. "They were going to leave your protege, Salvage and Dive Tech Third Class Klára Reed, ashore for this trip for 'additional rest'. I knew that would likely not sit well with you, so I pulled some strings and got her back on the roster," she finished in a low voice.

The chocolate-skinned woman winked impishly at the cream-skinned one she was speaking to. That just added to the surprise Cordelia felt at the Counsellor's sudden and uncharacteristic lack of formality.

"Oh, Ise! That is so good of you. She is so keen, and I know how much she wants to be out here. Leaving her home-posted for this trip would just make her miserable."

The other, unsaid, truth of the matter was that Cordelia was still feeling guilty about the incident that had gotten the younger woman injured to start with. At least Klára was not going to miss out on what was shaping up to be an interesting mission.

"No problem. That is sort of thing is what I am here for ... making sure everyone is as happy as they can be, and getting what it is they need," Koolen said with a smile and wave as she turned to make her way towards her cabin.

# Kimberly
## 01h51 SST
## Wednesday, April 20th

It had been a busy day at the Soumerville Music Conservatorium, Kim Cannes reflected as she sipped at a mixture of bourbon and water. On any given day, half to all of the seven of the recording studios were in use, and at least that many of the practice halls. From soloists to twelve-piece groups, there was space at the Conservatorium to learn, improve, create, collaborate and record.

Kim was very pleased that there was some promising stuff bubbling up out of all that creative industry. Whether they were on their First or their Second, there was a Generation of excellent musicians getting ready for the dance halls, parlours and music houses. The target was one new published piece every six months. That was the Conservatorium's contribution to the cultural zeitgeist of Soumerville and her undersea sister-towns. There was always something new to listen or dance to.

She considered herself remarkably fortunate to be a part of it all. Her "working retirement" was as good as anything she could have hoped for at this stage of her life.

In another ten minutes or so, she would go lock the doors and head home. She was a divorcee, or, as she preferred to put it, "experienced and available", so how late she was out was singularly her own business. On this particular night, that meant that she was considering a late-night picnic in one of the Forest Rooms with a portable AMTAC player and some of the new music that would be reaching public ears soon.

She had just about made up her mind to "cheat" and close up five minutes early when Zee came flying in the office doors, looking positively frantic.

"Kim! Kim! I am so sorry, I hate to do this, I know it is late, I need your help, please, please, please can you help? I need to get a song done before tomorrow morning! It is really important! Please, please, please?" he blurted as he bolted into her office.

So much for the picnic, she thought ruefully.

"Zee, slow down, breathe, and start over. Preferably in coherent sentences that use punctuation," she said with a patient sigh. The problem, she reflected, was that genius was rarely ever tidy, functional, or owned a pocket watch.

There was a long pause where the two of them just looked at each other with the only real sound being Jonas' breathing. She guessed he had run here from where ever he had received his current epiphany.

If you were not a serious artist at heart or at least knew one well, the concept of an "art crisis" or "art emergency" likely sounded like drama or hyperbole. In Kimberly's experience of thirty years of dealing with artists of all stripes and medium, it was not. Even she, at the height of her career as a recording artist, had experienced that moment where an idea or feeling or creative vibe was so intense that the only thing that mattered in the world was capturing it so it could be shared and exorcised.

Friends, food, sleep; all had to wait at such a moment. Poets, story-tellers, song-smiths, painters, sculptors, whatever; no one was exempt from the cost of having a genius-level muse pay a visit at an inopportune time.

"Um ... look, Kim ... this is going to sound ridiculous ... but ..."

"Just say it, Zee. Everyone deals with this sort of thing eventually," she offered, trying to sound reassuring to the pile of emotions and nerves currently trying to not explode in her office.

"I need you to record a song for me. I will be your doo-wop. It is a winner, Kim, but it is *nothing* like I usually do. It is all blues and jazz and pain, all in a burning bundle. I *need* your voice for this," he pleaded.

Kim blinked at the younger man across the desk from her. She anonymously did background work from time to time on recordings, of course, but it had been well past a decade since she had released her last feature recording. It was considered a bit *gauche* for the prior Generation to be seen to be "competing" with the current one. Guiding, helping, teaching, that was all good. Competing, on the other hand; not so much. Kim pursed her lips; if she headlined a recording for the 'Jay Zee Clark Project', she was certainly going to get some snarky commentary about it.

"*Please*, Kim! It is *important*," Jonas pleaded.

"Zee, sit," she ordered and pointed to the chair opposite her. She watched him comply before a sigh escaped her. "Look, I can hook you up tomorrow with a couple of really hot voices that are doing the kind of stuff now that I used to do back in the day. One of them is really cute, too; I think you will like her."

The young songwriter opposite her shook his head fiercely. "No. I sail tomorrow. In the morning," he stated. "It has to be tonight. Right now, kind of tonight," he said with the resolve of a battering ram.

Kimberly was a bit surprised. Officially, you did not *ever* talk about your "other life"; it was so that you actually could get away from your Main. So, even the mention that he was "sailing" tomorrow was ostensibly more than he should have said. She had already half-concluded he was Crew of some kind, just based on things that he had let slip over the time she had known him. That was not the point, though.

"Sell me on this, Zee. Why is it this cannot wait until you get back?" she asked, trying to be as reasonable as she could. She wanted to help him; she had always had a soft spot for Zee. Still, she knew that he had to own this. He had to earn it. Otherwise it would not be worth what it cost either of them.

There was a long pause where she could visibly see the struggle on the face of the young man pleading with her. He clearly made a decision and set his jaw before he spoke.

"I was awfully close to drinking myself to death in a depression recently, and someone was there for me when I needed it most. I want to record this as a thank-you note and that person is a crew-mate. My ribs are so bruised it hurts to breathe right now, and I am going to sing doo-wop on this. I want to be able to give them the recording to listen to on the cruise. I want them to hear it first in *private*, before they hear it at a parlour or club. I want them to know this is for *them*," Jonas said fiercely.

"Yeah, all right, that is one hell of a sales pitch, Zee," she said with a sigh, rubbing her forehead. "Fine, I cannot say 'no' to that. I will go turn on Studio Three and try and remember how to sing a scale," she said, shaking her head as she got up from her chair.

"Can we do vinyl before six in the morning, local?" he asked hopefully.

"Do not push your luck, kiddo," she admonished.

# CHAPTER SEVEN
## *Dearly Departing*

### Hal
### 09h04 SST
### Wednesday, April 20th

Captain Hal Lum looked at his somewhat dishevelled Pilot-Navigator standing in the office area of his cabin.

"You realise you are late for pre-sail check-in by almost twelve hours, Mister Zupan?" Hal asked sternly.

"Yessir," came the formal answer. Hal was a bit taken aback by the lack of Jonas' usual flippancy in the reply.

"You realise that we sail in less than four hours, Mister Zupan?"

"Yessir," the Pilot-Navigator replied in the same tone he had just used.

"You realise that you are already a tad low on good graces aboard this vessel for this cruise, Mister Zupan?"

"Yessir," Jonas replied, eyes fixed forward on the bulkhead opposite him, attempting something like a proper position of attention.

Hal got up from his chair and walked around to stand directly in front of Jonas. "All right, Mister. Who the hell are you and what have you done with my irreverent Pilot-Navigator?" he asked suspiciously.

"Um. Pardon, Captain?"

"You heard me. What is with this sudden Summer Serviceman routine?" Lum growled. He suspected this was an attempt at humour on Zupan's part, and Hal was finding it more and more annoying with each passing minute.

"Look, Skipper," Jonas started with a sigh, "I screwed up. I cannot say that I did not. I made a bunch of bad decisions in the past few days. I cannot change any of them. I can apologise for them and try and do better. I ... I am sorry, Skipper."

Hal tilted his head, looking at Jonas. "Does this have anything to do with that fiasco at the Crystal Parlour Lounge?" he asked his Pilot quietly. From the flash in Jonas' eyes, to the pursed lips, it seemed to Hal that it likely was.

There was a moment of stubborn silence before Jonas answered. "Yes. I am sorry for how I behaved."

Hal nodded. "Ah. So you would be 'the Door' then?"

"Pardon, Skipper?"

"My Chief Armsman apparently ran into 'a door', one which he refuses to answer questions about. Now, Mister Olivier is pretty terse at the best of days, but this is a new standard of tight-lipped for him," Hal suggested dryly.

Jonas turned bright red. "Um. I would not be willing to contradict the Chief Armsman, Skipper. I am sure he knows best what happened to him."

"You say so, hmm?" Hal questioned. He personally found the entire situation absurd. Marlon Pryce had been avoiding him except at the most strictly required level, Cordelia of all people had turned pink and changed course the first time she had seen him, and now Jonas and the Chief Armsman were covering for each other when Hal was aware neither particularly liked the other.

There were a few moments of pointed silence before Hal spoke again. "Just so it has been said Mister Zupan, I am not angry or upset at anyone, including my Salvage Leader, for a bit of public amusement 'inflicted' upon me by a torch singer at a gentleman's lounge. As an RSAV captain, I am required to be made of somewhat sterner stuff than that. I know it has likely never crossed any of your collective minds, but that is not the first place like that I have been to, nor is 'Samantha Shameless' the first attractive woman to sit in my lap in public.

"Now, whatever your issues are with whatever it is that you think that happened, sort them out with Counsellor Koolen and the rest of those involved. I need you back in the Pilot's chair and in top form. We are going into a bay and harbour that Mother Nature has recently remodelled with three successive monster hurricanes, and I cannot have any doubt your head is on the job at hand. You are my number-one weapon for keeping this ship and her crew safe when we get there. Am I clear?"

Jonas blinked and then stood straight and nodded. "Yes, Skipper. I will not let you down. I promise."

"Very good. Go get a shower, then get your backside down to Emm-And-Que right away so that we can get you signed off on. I am aware you might have walked into a 'door' as well."

## Marlon
### 10h10 SST

"All right Miz Lagounov, that is the last of the pre-sail checklists. Do you have any questions about the process?"

"No, Chief. How did I do?" the petit and auburn-haired engineer replied.

"Well. You missed a couple of the pickier items, but you had the important stuff covered. Keep at the manuals and you will get it. Once you get this down, I will be happy to sign off on your training ticket," Marlon answered in an encouraging tone.

"Thanks, Chief. There is so much to keep track of that it is dizzying. I will keep at it. I appreciate all your help."

"It is part of my job, Miz. Now, go check with Mister Darzi and find out if he needs help on getting those battery covers closed up. That is the last major item on the checklist for the electrical."

"Yes Chief!" Dasia chirped, and headed towards the battery banks.

Marlon Pryce climbed into the Watch Keeper's Chair adjacent to where they had been conversing. He sighed, feeling a bit stiff and a bit old. He remembered a time when doing a pre-sail checklist would not have been nearly so tiring. As he had recently told his beloved wife Annabelle, he was getting too old for this. However, it was still emotionally satisfying work. He was proud of his Detail; all of them worked hard and eagerly learned everything he had to teach.

He had little doubt that Davis and Lagounov would each have their own Details someday. The other two would go far, as well, though perhaps not to the top of the ladder. Regardless of how far they did or did not go, he knew that he had done what he could to give them the best training they could get in the Fleet. He was confident of that.

The light went yellow under the intercom box, and Hal's voice emerged. "Engine Room, this is the Comm. How do we stand?"

Marlon leaned over and pressed the "Talk" button and the associated status lamp glowed red. "Good morning, Captain. Chief Pryce here. We are on final checks prior to flash-up, and have no anticipated roadblocks.

No restrictions or warnings are expected to be in effect for a thirteen-hundred departure."

"Great news, Chief. At this time, all other Details are reporting 'go' for thirteen-hundred as well, so Command is one-hundred percent confident on that departure time," Hal answered, sounding a bit metallic over the intercom.

Marlon quirked a grin and shook a fist in delight. That meant that Jonas had gotten his backside aboard in time. Good; he knew that both Counsellor Koolen and Captain Lum had been looking for him last evening. In a pinch, of course, Fleet Staffing Services could get them a Pilot-Navigator on short notice, but no one really wanted that. Marlon, in particular, would have been worried about the young Pilot uncharacteristically missing a sailing.

"Glad to hear it, Skipper. I will let you know when the Pilotage requests power past the gearbox, as usual."

"Very good, Chief. Comm out." The yellow light went out, and Marlon flipped the "Talk" switch off.

## Ise
## 11h24 SST

Ise Koolen arrived back at her cabin after a very productive meeting and chat with the Ship's Doctor, Damiano Émile. Doctor Émile was very sensible and wonderfully easy to get along with, from her perspective. Amongst other things, he genuinely cared about the crew he was with. She had met doctors in the past who coped with their responsibilities by remaining detached and distant. Happily, Damiano was not one of those physicians.

As she reached her cabin, she noted a small bundle, wrapped in craft-paper, sitting in the mail slot for her cabin. She fished it out, and gave it a glance. The size, shape and weight suggested an AMTAC, as did the sound that an experimental shake made. She turned it over, curiously. On the opposite side was handwritten:

*To Ise, From Zee*

Her free hand flew to her mouth in surprise and she consciously suppressed the squeal of delight threatening to escape her mouth. She hastily unlocked her cabin, and darted in, barely remembering to close the door behind her. Wrapping paper flew in all directions until she was blinking at a standard "art grade" AMTAC with a new label adhered to it. Stencilled on the label was:

```
Track 1, Dolphin Ranch Promenade,
feat. Hugo Sanna. (Archive
Recording)

Track 2, Save My Soul, feat. Kim
Cannes.
```

Scrawled under it was:

*To my #1 Fan Ise Koolen, with thanks — Zee / JZCP*

Her eyes went wide and she did not even bother trying to contain the sound of glee she made. She was rarely wrong about what was going on in someone's head. However, this time she was delighted to have apparently missed the mark. She had been fairly certain that, given his emotional condition, as well as physical condition, Jonas had completely missed her request for a signed copy of her favourite song. Instead, he had gotten her a brand new copy and signed it with his *nom-de-chanson*. She was absolutely delighted at the gesture.

She paused and re-read the label. She was relatively convinced she either owned, or had danced to, or, in a few instances, had made-out to, everything that the "Jay Zee Clark Project" had ever released. She was just as certain that she had never seen the song title for Track Two before. To further stoke her curiosity was the detail that Ise was somewhat certain that "Kim Cannes" was a Gen-Six blues singer that had not done anything in around fifteen years. She dropped the cartridge in the AMTAC music player and hit 'play'.

# Cordelia
## 12h19 SST

Salvage and Dive Leader Cordelia Baasch slipped into the comfort of her curved and sloped oak crew chair in the Command Compartment. She happily wiggled into the down-filled leather padding of the chair back. Around her, the Comm was starting to buzz with the various positions checking in with their respective Details and areas of responsibility.

She glanced over at the Pilot-Navigator, who was sporting a fresh haircut and a fresh shave, she noted. He was also currently looking in her direction. Her eyes met his, and he blinked and immediately looked away, apparently suddenly needing to study a set of dials and gauges facing the other direction. She could not help the slight smile that played at her lips.

She was going to have to beat Marlon, she concluded, suddenly feeling sour. Hal Lum, Master of Impeccable Timing, interrupted her self-righteous annoyance.

"Miz Baasch, I did not see the RATT-net code books in the security satchel that came aboard. Is everything in order on that front?"

"What? Oh! Oh, yes, Captain. Everything is fine. I stopped by the Message Centre and picked them up myself. I decided to get all that taken care of earlier, so there would be less paperwork to handle at the last minute," she responded, feeling ruffled for some reason.

Hal tilted his head, looking at her for a moment. She had the impression he was going to remark about something and then changed his mind. He nodded and then merely answered with "Good thinking, and good work. Thank you, Miz Baasch."

"You are welcome, Captain," she responded, feeling uncharacteristically awkward for some reason. She rubbed at the nape of her neck, rather wishing the sensation would return to where ever it had come from.

She picked up her Detail communications phone and checked in with her team. A brief chat reassured her that everything was ready to go on the Supply and Salvage side of things. This was hardly a surprise; for the Salvage and Dive Detail, the work began once they arrived at their destination.

She glanced over at the Chief Armsman, currently looking at the contents of a clipboard. He clearly sported bruised chin and, to what Cordelia could see from her location, looked like a black eye. She involuntarily glanced at Jonas before looking back at Christopher. Jonas did not have a mark on him that she could see. The entire notion that the noticeably less muscled Pilot had done that much unanswered damage to the Chief Armsman seemed somewhat incredible to the Salvage Leader.

Jonas turned towards where Hal sat in the "big chair". Cordelia looked over reflexively. "Skipper, we are now thirty-five minutes to let-go," Jonas began, sounding a bit wheezy. "Engineering has signalled the Pilotage that they are ready to supply power past the gearbox, as well as control systems, at the Pilot's request. Gyroscopes are up, stable, calibrated and corrected. The autopilot is prepared, and our Arr-Vee point is set in. Pilotage is ready to go, Skipper."

"Thank-you, Pilot," the Captain answered. Hal then looked over at the Chief Armsman. "Update?"

Christopher turned towards Hal before answering, irritation mostly concealed in his voice. "Captain, we still have no contact with Traffic

Control via underwater telephone. We are pretty confident our side is working as expected, and we are waiting on checkouts from their side. I will let you know when the issue is resolved," the Armsman stated.

"Thank-you, Mister Olivier. Please do," Lum answered, frowning.

Cordelia could understand the expression on Hal's face and the tone of Christopher's voice. Without the underwater telephone connection to Traffic Control, the *Sheerah* was going no where. The risk of injury to someone working around the structure of Soumerville, or to the RSAV itself, was just too high. They would be sitting here until the communications problem was resolved.

The cream-skinned woman was hoping that would be sooner, rather than later. There were times she felt like the familiar routine of an RSAV at sea was about the only thing that made sense.

## Jonas
### 13h07 SST

Jonas rubbed at his chin, and glanced out the Command Compartment windows at the activity on the bow of the *Sheerah* and the dock beside her. They were uncharacteristically late to depart. First a problem with the underwater telephone, then a problem with a compressor in engineering, and then back to issues with the communications to Traffic Control.

He glanced over at the Chief Armsman, Christopher, who had the handset for the underwater telephone pressed to his left ear. If Mister Olivier had any particular ill-will towards Jonas for the completely uncalled for fracas between them, he gave no sign. Given that Jonas had instigated the incident without warning, this was somewhat surprising to him. In fact, the Chief Armsman had seemed vaguely amused about something when they greeted each other when they first came into the Comm.

Christopher wagged a free finger of his right hand, catching Jonas' eye, even as he was now speaking into the underwater telephone. The well-muscled Armsman tapped the phone at his ear with a finger and then gave a thumbs-up gesture. He then tapped both of his shoulders, gave a slight sideways back-and-forth of his hand, then made an equally slight chopping gesture. He twirled a finger in the air, jerked his thumb over his shoulder, and then gave two quick thumbs-up gestures.

Jonas nodded and smiled. The signal sequence was well known to both of them, and good news.

"Captain, Sir, Armsman reports good communication with Traffic and we have immediate clearance to let go, turn and depart. I am guessing this is '*go now while we can still tell you to do so*'," the Pilot-Navigator announced.

Hal Lum, from his position in the centre seat, glanced between the two men and then nodded at Jonas. "Thank-you, Pilot. Security; gangways off, lines in. Engines; standby for power past the gearbox. Salvage and Dive; standby lights and signals. Navigation; when we are free, make way," the Captain rattled off with practiced ease. He picked up the broadcast microphone and keyed it.

Chimes sounded from all the intercom boxes throughout the ship. "Attention all hands, stand by for Power, Drop and Ramp. Ensure all loose items are secured," Hal ordered.

"Pilot, Gangways are off and lines are in. Security confirms deck is cleared of items and personnel, and hatches are closed. Ready for sea," Christopher announced.

"Thank-you, Security," Jonas replied. He reached forward towards a brass plate on the console ahead of him. On it was an engraved schematic of a Mk.III Reclaimer, showing the power systems, caterpillar treads, and thrusters. Each one of these systems had a lighted push-switch set into the brass plate. Everything ahead of the gearbox on the schema of the ship was lit up green. Everything behind it was still dark.

The panel was one of the primary mechanisms for the Pilot and the Engineering team to let each other know where power was, and was not yet, currently available. Jonas quickly pressed down each of the buttons for the treads, thrusters and steering systems. Those switches now glowed yellow.

At Hal's spot, the intercom buzzed. Chief Engineering Artificer Marlon Pryce's voice emerged. "Comm, this is Eng. We have received a request for power past the gearbox to treads, thrusters and steering from Helm, and we are preparing to do so. Please confirm."

Hal looked towards the box and replied. "Order is confirmed. We finally have clearance to depart."

"Roger, thank-you, Wilco, Eng Out," came the reply and the lights changed under the intercom. Within a few moments, the yellow lights on the engraved schematic started changing one by one to green.

"Salvage and Dive, sound one prolonged blast, make a ten-second pause, then sound three short blasts please," Jonas requested, glancing over towards Cordelia.

"Salvage confirms signals request; one long, ten seconds, three short," she answered.

## Alodia

From the dock, Mission Services Mistress Alodia Holt quietly breathed a sigh of relief at the sound of the *Sheerah*'s steam-horn blaring a single-tone, three-second duration wail. The sound echoed off the steel and concrete walls of the North Bay Dockyard, and the group of workers, families and sub-chasers on the jetty cheered in reply. There was a dull, rumbling roar that emerged from within the RSAV, and water around it churned as thirty-two hundred kilowatts of diesel engines made their will known.

The RSAV shuddered and then three more blaring wails emerged from the horn. The combination was well known to Alodia; *"vessel getting underway"* and then *"vessel going astern"*. She had been living to the sounds of an RSAV's steam horn for over thirty years now; she had been watching from the dock for a bit more than ten of that.

To those who might have glanced her way, she would have seemed as she always did; well-dressed in fashionable attire for a lady of an older generation, stately in comportment, and with a quiet, impassive expression. She was on the jetty for every RSAV that sailed under her orders, and she was on the jetty for each one that came home. Regrettably, those two numbers were not equal.

She watched as the *Sheerah* slowly moved backwards until its bow was clear of the corner of the jetty. The vessel slowly turned in place, rippling a wave across the moon-pool of the Dockyard; the neatness of the turn and the minimal crest of the wave was a testimony to the skill of the Pilot-Navigator. The RSAV began moving forward; even as the sound of the diesel engines died, a rattling clatter was heard as the set of armoured vents along her stern deck snapped closed.

Her nose pitched down beneath the water and her stern kicked upwards, exposing her treads and underbelly. The treads threw water into the air behind them and foamed the surface as the *Sheerah* began her drive down the Ramp. Within moments, the waters of the moon-pool completely closed over the last bit of the stern. Then the sea around the shadowed bulk of the vessel suddenly glowed as she turned on her array of lights.

Alodia exhaled, conscious that she had been holding her breath as she always did when the "Power, Drop, and Ramp" phase began. The *Sheerah* was on her way. There was nothing more that she could do for them on this new adventure. She had stacked the deck as heavily as she could in their favour against the bitter realities of the world above. From here on out, until the *Sheerah's* bow once again broke the surface of a Dockyard moon-pool, it was up to the officers and crew aboard how those cards were played.

She turned away from the still-churning waters of the moon-pool and began slowly walking along the jetty for the Dockyard doors. She was feeling anxious about this mission, she realised. The crew of the *Sheerah* were an experiment, ultimately. The youngest crew under the youngest command in the Fleet, with only one carefully chosen Gen-Six aboard. Normally, the command crew would all be Gen-Six, and the crew would be Gen-Seven. However, for reasons she was not privy to, the Council had gone this route.

The Mission Services Mistress had been watching the *Sheerah* and her crew with some interest since the day the bottle broke on her bow. There was something different about this crew, beyond their ages, that caught her attention. It was something that Alodia Holt had never quite been able to identify, but still, it was there. Clearly the Council held a similar interest; the decision to cut the *Sheerah's* alongside time short by a couple of days and assign them to this mission had not be hers. Unusually, it had been the Council's.

She stopped and turned, looking towards the far wall of the Dock, scribed with a large arrow pointing downwards to the water's surface. That was the exit point for the Dock.

She tucked an errant wisp of greying hair back behind her ear. "Come home safe. I will keep a light on for you until you do," she whispered.

# CHAPTER EIGHT
## *Hearing Ghosts*

### Jonas
### 03h28 SST
### Tuesday, April 26th
### 42.89N,65.72W

The notion of electric window-wipers on a submarine had always amused Jonas, ever since he had first seen them as a boy. He recalled, during a school visit to a Dockyard, asking some grizzled sailor-type what use they would be underwater. The answer had stayed with Jonas ever since then; *"They work just fine, young fella! They just have to wipe faster!"*

Even now, an involuntary chuckle escaped him as he watched out the brass-framed windows ahead of him. The window-wipers "tick-tacked" back and forth in a steady staccato beat, doing a mostly acceptable job of keeping the combination of rain water and salt-spray from rendering the glass translucent. They had been surface cruising for an hour or so after spending most of the previous five days bottom-rolling.

The only divergence from that had been a few hours spent on the surface waiting to *rendezvous* with the *RSAV Emilia Lanier*, who had been almost six hours late to the designated location. It had turned out that the "minor incident" which had required the *Sheerah* to bring emergency supplies to the meet-up had involved striking something that had blown a hole in the hull.

The *Lanier's* Pilot-Navigator had told Jonas that the incident had reminded her of what her trainer had told her striking a mine might be like. There had been a sudden loud bang, immediately followed by a roar that shook the whole RSAV. Almost immediately flooding alarms were ringing. Of course, neither she nor Jonas could recall anyone in three generations encountering any kind of floating anti-ship mine, anywhere.

What ever it was that had happened, it had rattled the *Lanier* so badly that it was going to take a stay in a graving dock to get everything working right again. They had been sailing on speed and depth restrictions the entire trip back, which was why they had been late to the *rendezvous* position. By the time the two vessels parted ways, which should have been done well before noon, instead the sun was noticeably dipping towards the western horizon.

After that, they had eschewed bottom rolling for a bit more than half a day as they reached and crossed the so-called "Influence Zone" of the Great River. The raw volume of the current, even over eight hundred kilometres from the mouth of the Great River, had carved a noticeable trench in the seafloor all the way out to the continental shelf. The amount of sediment in the current meant you could never trust the area around the Zone to look the same way twice, nor to be stable enough to bottom roll on. Instead, they ran like a conventional submarine about half-way down the water column until they were past the Zone by at least twenty minutes. Then, it was relatively safe to resume the much more economical bottom-rolling.

Jonas rubbed at his forehead and glanced at his gauges and telltales again. He had been jumpy ever since the *rendezvous*, of course. His anxiety was mostly because the description by *Lanier's* Pilot-Navigator of what had happened to them was essentially *exactly* what Jonas had also been told hitting an anti-ship mine might be like.

So now, every damn seal curiously sticking its head out of a wave to watch the passing ship caused a moment of panic to wash over him. In what could only be deemed as a perverse synchronicity, it was spring on the North-East Coast; there were seals everywhere at this time of year, it seemed. That the water here was so deep, and the tides so severe, that there was no way a mine would have stayed anchored, was irrelevant, of course. The very nature of an unreasonable fear, he supposed, was that there was no reasoning with it.

Thankfully, it was well past sunset now, with the thin glow of a waning moon and a curtain of stars completely obscured by the clouds and rain. So, if there were cavorting seals watching the *Sheerah's* passage, Jonas could not see them.

They never ran with lights of any kind when they were more than a hundred kilometres away from Soumerville or any of its seafloor sister-towns. The only light in the Command Compartment were a trio of floor-level red lights, and the dimmed glow of the instruments and indicators. Running dark on the surface was a hold-over from the times of Generations One and Two. It was purely a book-habit, as Jonas called it; it was in The Book, and so it was habit to do it, whether it made any sense at all in this day and age. Hal Lum, however, was a staunch devotee of The Book, and ultimately Jonas Zupan did not care enough to argue.

He sighed and glanced at the moving map. Another two days or so of surface cruising, and they would be arriving at the mission location. With any luck at all, everything would remain quiet and dull.

They were on the surface primarily because they could move much faster this way. Using the caterpillar treads like a bizarre paddle-boat system worked surprisingly well, and the thrusters sorted out the steering. How it all actually worked was completely beyond Jonas' level of understanding. That was Marlon Pryce's problem, and beyond a visit once a cruise by Jonas to the Engine Room for the purpose of courtesy, the Pilot had no interest in it. It worked, Marlon kept it working, Jonas could do his job, and he was happy.

It was actually rather unusual for an RSAV to run on the surface during daylight hours for anything other than meeting another RSAV, or a *bona-fide* emergency. The normal routine was to bottom-roll, or at least cruise submerged, during the day while running entirely on batteries and canned air. An RSAV had power in her batteries for eight hours of fully electric operation. So, in broad-daylight, that was what they did. At dusk and dawn, they would run shallow, but not on the surface, and raise the *schnorkel* to be able to use the air-hungry turbo-diesels in a restricted power-range. In the full dark of night, they could run on the surface with full power available from the Tee-Dees. Like "running dark", the idea was to hide from possibly prying and hostile eyes.

Another book-habit, ultimately. One that, in this particular case, had been waived in the name of expediency.

In addition to being quicker and cheaper, running on the surface gave the Arms and Security team a chance to run the on-board weather station, which was recording a bevy of statistics that helped the scientists back home understand what was going on around them. That data was automatically recorded to AMTAC, and would then be sent back to Soumerville with the usual message traffic exchange. Again, the exact significance of water salinity and oxygen content in the thirty to forty metre depth band, or why a certain level of ultra-violet light reaching the deck was remarkable, escaped him. The Armsmen needed the data, so Jonas made sure they spent time on the surface to get the data, and everyone was happy.

That reminded him; his eyes sought the Command Compartment's wall clock, set to Standard Signal Time. That was the ship's reference time-piece, ensuring the steady routine of life aboard was accurate to within a tenth of a second. By his reckoning, in a couple of minutes Cordelia would be arriving to do the day's message traffic exchange, before the start of her watch.

Salvage and Dive Leader Baasch had been rather chatty with him this trip, particularly in the O-Room. He was still getting used to that; it was far from that he minded, of course. He was not entirely sure where this bit of good favour came from, but he was not daring to question it.

He thought he might get everything set up for her so all she would have to do is come in and plug in the AMTACs. That would be a nice surprise for her, he hoped, and he could use the practice anyway.

As a benefit, it would give him something else to do other than stare out the Comm windows looking for black seals in the rainy dark, he thought wryly. He set the vessel on gyroscopic autopilot, and then waited a few moments to make sure that it was doing what he wanted. He knew that it was a pretty reliable piece of equipment, but the safety of the ship and the sureness of her course was his responsibility. He then eased the throttles back, watching the indicator lights change to match his requested power setting. After a few minutes, the substantial mass of the RSAV had slowed down to just about five kilometres per hour. That was the safe speed for the floating antenna.

He moved over to where Miz Baasch usually sat, and leaned over past her chair to operate the controls to unroll the antenna behind the *Sheerah*. At this time of night, and being able to have the entire antenna on the surface meant they should be able to contact Soumerville, even at this distance.

Next, he flipped a series of switches and then turned a trio of dials to tune the set until a familiar high-frequency squeal emerged from the monitor speaker in front of him. It was faint, but audible enough he could tell what it was; that meant a very good chance of being able to get a RATT-net connection.

He was about to press the "Connect" button when what he heard emerge from the monitor speaker caused him to freeze in mid-action.

*"Cullhang unneewn ztay shun ... preeze, hany hun art dar ... hap, hap .... Preeze rheaspoon"*

That was a human voice. Jonas did not understand the language, but that was unmistakably a human voice. Except that was *impossible*. There was no one *else up here*, and anyone who had this frequency would never transmit except for encrypted RATT-net. In addition, every citizen of Soumerville and her ocean floor sister towns all spoke the same, single language. What ever he just heard, was *not* that language.

Just as he was about to let sanity win out over senses, he heard it again.

*"Preeze rheaspoon ... Ah don harf maech taeme ... Hany hun"*

He was a trained musician and worked with human singers and human language ten hours a day on his Second. He knew what he was hearing. That was a human voice, pleading for help.

# Cordelia

Cordelia Baasch opened the bulkhead hatch into the Command Compartment to find Jonas Zupan leaning over her chair with his eyes wide and his jaw agape. His entire expression and stance was so uncharacteristic that she herself stopped midway across the threshold.

"Jonas! What is wrong? Is everything okay?" she asked suddenly feeling oddly worried.

He looked over at her, blinking as though struggling to comprehend her questions. "I ... I heard ... I heard a voice, Cordie! On the RATT-net speaker!" he blurted.

"Hang on, hang on. You heard what?"

"A human voice, Cordie. I am sure of it," he answered, clearly still in some level of shock.

She closed the bulkhead door behind her slowly, considering what the Pilot-Navigator had just told her. He was a joker, for sure, so was possible he was just trying to be funny. Another look at his face, however, threw that notion away entirely. Jonas was visibly pale and agitated.

"Jonas, are you sure?" she started out carefully. She did not want to mock him or belittle him. "Everything we know right now says that would be ..."

"Impossible, yeah, Cordie, I know. Trust me, I know," he said. He moved back to his crew chair and sat down heavily, and then ran a hand through his hair. He looked up at her as she made her way to her own crew position. "I am absolutely sure what I heard," he stated firmly. "I am also pretty sure it was a distress call."

"A distress call?" Cordelia blinked. "What did they say?"

"I ... I do not know, honestly. I did not understand the language. But the tone of voice was unmistakable. It was a male voice, pleading for help."

Cordelia tilted her head, openly studying the Pilot-Navigator sitting across from her. Everything that every piece of history she had learned in school, and everything she had seen with her own eyes in more than three years of RSAV visits to coastlines within a thousand kilometres of Soumerville, contradicted what she had just heard from Jonas.

Living on the surface world for any amount of time was impossible. You could visit for a few days on carefully planned and managed voyages, but you could not stay. The depredations of the Precursors had left lingering and lethal effects on the world above the waves. The recent monstrous Green Fog event at Soumerville itself was just more reinforcement of that notion.

Yet, right now, the usually light-hearted and goofy Pilot-Navigator was stone-cold serious about what he had heard. That much was obvious to her; she did not need Ise Koolen's uncanny gifts for that.

"Okay. Before we go get the Captain out of his rack, let us work this backwards together," she said. "Give me a minute to get the ship talking to Soumerville and trading message traffic. While the AMTACs are turning we can talk."

"Sure thing, Cordie. The antenna is already out, we are surface cruising at speed five, and I already have the radios tuned for you, as you can likely guess from the squeal from the monitor speaker," Jonas grinned at her, looking a bit more like his usual self.

In spite of herself, Cordelia found his smile infectious and grinned back. "Thanks, Jonas. I appreciate that. It saves me a bit of time. So, a couple of minutes, and we can talk and sort out what we are telling Hal when we wake him up."

A little while later, the AMTAC drives were whirring quietly, mixing in to the concert and cacophony of other noises that the combination of the RSAV, its crew, and the sea around them produced. Jonas had thoughtfully gone to get them both a cup of coffee from the O-Room, since the ship was already running on autopilot. By the time he had gotten back with a mug each and a ginger-spice cookie to go with it, Cordelia had gotten the RATT-net side of things taken care of.

They were both sitting in their usual chairs, brooding over their coffee cups. She did not really know what Jonas was thinking, but Cordelia had two items on her mind. She looked up to say something, to find him looking towards her. As soon as their eyes met, he blinked and looked away.

She added an item to the list of things to talk about, immediately promoted the new addition to the top of the list and sighed irritably. "Jonas, this is weird to say, but you are allowed to look at me. Stop avoiding eye-contact with me, okay? It drives me nuts and it feels rather creepy."

"Pardon?" he replied, looking back at her, mostly meeting her gaze. "Creepy? I am trying to not be creepy," he said, sounding pained.

"Yeah, well, at the point I see you looking my way, and then you are suddenly trying to look at something else, that is just, well, it just feels like you are trying to hide it. If you are going to do something, Jonas, particularly around me, do it and own it, and be brave enough to take responsibility for it," she said bluntly.

"Cordie, look," Jonas began.

"No, *you* 'look', Jonzie ..."

"Jonzie?" he said, looking vaguely alarmed about something.

"Yes, *Jonzie*! If you insist on calling me by 'Cordie', then that makes *you* 'Jonzie'. If you do not like it, then start using my real name," she fumed, drumming the fingers of one hand on the console at her crew station. She looked out one of the Comm windows into the ink-black of the rainy ocean night.

"Since I seem to be telling you things that are really none of your business," she continued, anger edging into her voice, "I might as well continue on that track. Your drinking pisses me off. If you want my attention, that is *not* the way to get it. I *hate* knowing that part of the reason you show up half-drunk at my performances and then proceed to finish the job while I am singing is because you are afraid of me or something. That is unfair, Jonzie," she scowled, setting her coffee cup down with a loud clunk on the console beside her. "It is unfair to me, and it is unfair to you. Either dry up, or stay away from the Parlour when I am singing. I do not want that hanging around my neck, ruining my night."

When the ensuing silence caused her to look away from the windows and towards the Pilot-Navigator, she found him with his head back, apparently staring at the deck-head. "Cordie, look. Sorry, Cordelia, rather, then, it is just that," he trailed off. He looked at her, and visibly fought the reflex to look away from her. He actually had nice eyes, she noted, when he bothered to hold her gaze. "Never mind," he sighed with a shake of his head. "I will just stay away from the Parlour and keep my eyes to myself. I am sorry to be a bother." He turned his crew chair forward, to face the windows.

She bit her lip to prevent the sharp rebuke that sprang to mind from going any further. She also balled a fist to prevent herself from throwing the coffee cup at the side of his head in frustration.

"So. Work, then. You are the resident RATT-net expert. What are we going to tell the Captain about me hearing voices?" he asked her in a flat tone.

# Hal
## 04h40 SST
## Tuesday, April 26th

Hal sat in the O-Room, sipping some honeyed-tea, and listening to the Pilot-Navigator's rather incredible story for the second time. Unfortunately, it made as little sense in its repetition as it did in the original account. When the Salvage and Dive Leader had chimed his cabin from the Command Compartment with a request to meet with the two of them, Hal had been somewhat puzzled.

He had been hoping this was not more foolishness associated with the 'incident' at the Crystal Parlour. He needed his crew worrying about more pressing matters. This was in fact a much more pressing matter; he reminded himself to be more careful in the future about what he wished for.

"And you are completely certain about what you heard, Mister Zupan?" Hal asked, with a bit of skepticism audible in his tone.

"Yessir," Jonas replied. "Completely certain, Captain. A male human voice, twice, about half a minute apart. I did not recognise the language, but the tone sounded like pleading."

Hal glanced over at Cordelia, who had just poured herself a glass of water and seemed to be focusing entirely on Jonas. Hal rubbed his jaw for a moment. He had a suspicion about this, but he was not going to raise the question with the Pilot in the room.

"All right, Mister Zupan. You did the right thing by bringing this to my attention. I will give this some thought, and discuss the technical side of it with Miz Baasch. Once I have a bit more information to go on, we can make a plan. Go get some sleep."

"Ok, Skipper. Thanks," Jonas offered, and then rose and left the O-Room. That left just Hal and Cordelia there. Hal leaned over and flipped the "privacy" switch on the intercom box.

Cordelia looked surprised by the action. "The next couple of minutes are entirely off the record, Miz Baasch. I need your complete honesty, since it potentially affects the safety and operation of this ship."

"Well, yes, of course, Captain," she replied carefully.

"Was he drunk when you arrived in the Comm? Any evidence at all he had been drinking?" Hal asked.

Cordelia looked shocked. "*Jonzie*? Er, I mean, Jonas Zupan? No, no, not at all, Captain! He was stone-cold sober when I came through the hatch. I would swear to that before the Council or the Spirits," she said forcefully. "He is better than that, Captain. Much better."

Hal lofted a brow at the nickname, but said nothing about it. Her tone and bearing were also rather surprising to him; she was clearly offended by the idea that Hal would even have to ask.

"Fair enough. Do you think he is telling the truth? Or is this some game to garner attention?"

Cordelia put her water glass down. "The look on his face was no act, Captain. I do not know what he actually heard, but I am completely convinced that he is convinced it was a person making a distress call. We are only just a couple hundred kilometres from four different Precursor areas," she pointed out. "That would be within the sensitivity of our towed antenna on the surface, even for a poor radio."

"Except for the part where there is no one alive at any of those locations to be using a radio," Hal countered.

"At the point our destination has been remodelled by three back-to-back Category Five hurricanes, Captain, it is possible that it might be an old Precursor recording that has been activated," Cordelia suggested. "Something got churned up and turned on."

"Would not that be something extraordinary? Finding a cache of working Precursor radio gear?" Lum said quietly, boggling at the very notion of what that could mean.

Cordelia grinned at him. "It would certainly be newsworthy, that is for sure. Either way, Captain, regardless of what it turns out to be or not to be, Jonas is being honest here. He thinks that is what he heard. I really believe that," she said quietly.

Hal nodded at her. "Thank-you, Miz Baasch. I appreciate your willingness to say that. Hit your bunk, I will see you in the morning. I am going to go up to the Comm and I will stand your watch for you."

"Oh, Captain, that is very kind, but you do not have to …"

"I insist," he interrupted, and gestured towards the hatch Jonas had taken a few minutes ago. "Go get some sleep. We make landfall in less than twenty-four hours, and I need you sharp and at the top of your game."

Cordelia nodded with a mildly sour expression on her face, but did not verbally argue. She got up and left, leaving Hal in the O-Room with his thoughts. The implications of the Pilot-Navigator's incident report were staggering.

Given the cryptic comment by the *Lanier* about a "radio anomaly", it was not completely beyond imagination that Jonas had heard something, Hal reasoned. He was far from sold on the notion that it was the voice of someone currently alive, of course. That just seemed ridiculously far fetched.

He finished his tea in two gulps, put the cups and plates on the table into the automatic dishwasher, and set it to run. Officially, that was not his job, but he always felt awkward leaving the O-Room a mess for the morning Steward to clean up.

He made his way along Salt Flats, then up the ladder and into the Command Compartment. He checked on the autopilot, and once he was content that it was doing what it should be, he took his place in the "big chair" as everyone called it. He rubbed at his jaw, wondering what landfall tomorrow might bring.

# Christopher
## 12h43 SST
## Tuesday, April 26th

The Chief Armsman gestured to a map behind him on the front wall of the Briefing Room. "Everyone, listen up. That includes you, Hudson," Christopher began. "According to Navigation, we will arrive about two-and-a-half hours after dark tonight at our destination of 42.40N,71.10W. Our ship's mission objectives in the Operations Area are two-fold; first, survey the area for available new resources after major environmental impacts have rendered the area barely recognisable. The second objective is to deploy a set of two pairs of radio environment recorders.

"The mission of the Security and Weapons Detail is, as always, to provide eyes on the ground and security on-scene for each of the groups of Salvage and Dive teams as well as any other-department expedition teams. Any questions so far?" the Chief Armsman asked as he glanced at the group. The eight other Armsmen in the room shook their heads.

"Good. It is the current opinion of Command that there might be a Precursor radio source in the area, based on recent SIGINT from both our own ship and the RSAV Emilia Lanier, who we Arr-Vee'd with recently. This of course raises the potential risk associated with Precursor autonomous roving defensive systems. We are treating the Op Area as a 'moderate' threat area with a potential for rapid escalation into 'dangerous'."

A few eye-brows raised among the eight Armsmen. It had been some time since they had last heard a "dangerous" threat assessment issued in a briefing. Or the mention of murder-drones, for that matter.

"The thirty-eight millimetre deck guns will be deployed as soon as we enter the Op Area. The two bow mounts will be manned at all times until we depart. Standard watch rotation; eight hours on, four hours off, four hours on and eight hours off. The two stern mounts will be manned at any call of 'security' or 'contact'. The clip in the thirty-eights will be smoke, with a clip of 'moose' and a clip of penetrators in the ready-use tray. Guns-crew, any questions?"

The four Armsmen shook their heads while taking notes. "Moose" rounds were so named because, while non-lethal, they hit hard enough to persuade an irritated bull-moose to go else where to shake off its sudden headache.

142

"Good. Expedition security team, full charges on the tanks for the variable rifles. Your default pressure setting will be 'non-lethal'. Your carried ammunition will be six baker-boxes instead of the usual four; two smoke, two bull-dog, two lethal. Your default loads will be one smoke, one rib-cracker. Four grenades each; Two smoke, two thunder-strike. Full armour, melee and survival gear at all times when you are on-task."

A round of groans emerged from the four members of the shore-team. That last sentence nearly tripled their carry weight. Christopher quirked an amused grin and continued speaking.

"I have spoken with both Command and the Salvage Leader, and there is no intention to do any after-dark Salvage and Dive operations at this time. We will go ashore one hour after dawn, and depart back to safe water one hour before sunset. So, it is hats and bats from the moment the sun comes up until it is down. I want two Armsmen with the ship as a reaction squad, and two of you out with the Salvage and Dive Detail teams. You will rotate in and out every three hours."

"I will be out there as a Command escort as required, and as part of the reaction force if I am not actively escorting. So, I will be as loaded up as you four. Expedition security team, any questions?"

Christopher noted the shakes of heads and the scribbles. "Last two items. First, given the couple of injuries that the Salvage and Dive detail took on the last cruise, I will remind everyone to keep a prudent eye around them at all times, and actively judge the minimum safety distance for stupid."

The eight Armsmen all chuckled in amusement. "Second, Command has concerns about the safety of this Op Area. We are the eyes, ears, arms and armour of our crew. We are the first in, and the last out. This is our job; our reason for being. I want everyone extra sharp on this one. Get as much extra rest as you can when the hull is wet, because once it is dry we will not be able to let our vigilance lapse for a moment. The measure of our expertise and success is the safety of our shipmates. Am I clear?"

A chorus of "Yes, Chief!" was the reply.

"Very good. Make the *Sheerah* proud with your commitment to excellence. Dismissed."

# CHAPTER NINE
## *Running Aground*

### Hal
**01h12 SST**
**Wednesday, April 27th**
**42.39N, 70.88W**

It was less than two hours after sunset when the *Sheerah* began picking her way through the disaster zone of the Precursor harbour. Even now, the wreckage of ruined buildings jutted out of the water; some of the old towers must have been hundreds of metres tall in their glory days, Hal reflected.

They had all fallen, of course. Never designed to have their foundations covered by ten or more metres of water, never-you-mind the unforgiving and unrelenting abrasion of the three-metre tide itself, they had all collapsed. Most of the ancient towers were naught more than rubble-piles now, their tumbled ruins all roughly pointing out to sea, as though to convey a generations-too-late warning to their creators.

The *Sheerah* and her crew had been here three times previously in their careers. However, this might as well have been unexplored territory based on what the bottom-profiling SONARs were reporting.

"Skipper, I think I can confidently say this is the most spectacular mess I have ever seen made by weather," Jonas commented, frowning as he glanced at four small screens laid out before him on one of the facets of his crew station. Each screen showed the bottom from a different perspective angle as viewed from bottom of the bow of the RSAV. The first two were aimed downwards at a forty-five degree angle, looking towards the port and starboard sides. The third and fourth were aimed ahead, angled downwards at twenty-two and sixty-eight degrees.

This gave a talented RSAV pilot the ability to "see" the bottom as it might affect the vessel. In the three years that Hal had known Jonas, the Pilot had proven that if the gap was a metre-stick wider and deeper than the *Sheerah*, he could get the ship through without touching anything but water.

"You say the description of 'remodelled' was entirely too kind, Mister Zupan?" Hal asked, trying to sound amused. He was actually feeling much more concerned. The last time he had sailed into "unknown waters" was four years ago in a simulator. Since he had first sat down in the centre seat, all the *Sheerah's* travels had taken them to bays and harbours that other crews had already explored and documented.

"Yeah, entirely too kind, Skipper. The main channel is essentially gone. It is completely silted in, and log jammed with washed-in debris up to the size of full trees. The outer rise and mounts have all moved somewhat. The good news is that it looks like Mother Nature opted to take an average; a few of what were shallows are a now bit deeper."

This was not the news Hal had wanted he thought sourly. "What is your confidence level? Can you get us onto dry land around here?"

"Oh, do not sweat that, Skipper," Jonas said with a grin, looking back at Hal. "Nothing I am seeing on SONAR will stop us from getting ashore. The first trip in might be a bit more complicated than it needs to be, but I am still seeing a good-sized area with ten metres of water in it.

Once we are into the rubble field, we ought to be fine. Once the sun is up, we will scout out the outer and inner harbours, pick our shore zone, and get our feet dry."

Hal relaxed. "Thank-you, Mister Zupan. I do appreciate your confidence in the circumstances. Mister Olivier, Security and Weapons status?" he asked as he shifted in his chair to face the Chief Armsman.

"As per briefing, Captain, fore and aft deck weapons are up and un-caged. Bow deck weapons are crewed, and stern deck weapons will be crewed on five minutes notice. Both sets of guns crews have been briefed and have their rotations. I also have one Armsman in full gear as an upper-deck roundsman to ensure nothing comes up out of the water at us. If Trouble comes looking for us, Captain, then Trouble will have a very bad night," Christopher stated.

If there was one thing that Hal knew he could count on about his Chief Armsman, it was that he took his job personally. If Christopher Olivier told him that the team of Armsmen were ready to have an unarmed wrestling match with a couple of brown bears, then Hal's immediate reaction would be to feel bad for the bears. Olivier and his Detail were like that; second place was first loser. Those that chose to be Armsmen aboard the *Sheerah* did so because they wanted to be here; they liked being part of Chief Olivier's unrelenting quest for excellence.

"Very good, Mister Olivier. Normally I would consider the upper-deck roundsman excessive vigilance, if there is such a thing, but given the 'radio anomalies'," Hal glanced at Jonas before continuing, "it is likely prudent. I appreciate your diligence."

"Thank-you, Captain," the Chief Armsman replied.

"Very well, everyone, we are here. Salvage and Dive operations start once the sun is up, so everyone make sure your Details get good sleep and good breakfasts. We have a lot to do," Hal declared, and everyone in the Command Compartment nodded at him.

*****

In spite of his last instructions to his command crew, a couple of hours later Hal found himself in front of the door to Counsellor Koolen's cabin. The entire ship was bathed in a low, red light and largely silent. Almost everyone, other than himself, the Arms and Security crew and Engineering crew who were on duty, was asleep.

He knocked twice, and waited. As with many of his unscheduled visits with Ise Koolen, Hal found himself mildly hoping she was currently not entertaining visitors.

Fortunately, or unfortunately, she opened the door with an amused look of surprise. "Good evening, Captain. You have managed to surprise me; I was expecting this to be someone else's arrival," she said warmly. "Come in, and no, I do not mind the lateness of the hour. As I said, I was expecting someone might show up at my door." She turned and went into her cabin, leaving the door open for him.

Hal followed her in and closed it. "I am hoping you are not already feeling like you need a revolving door on your cabin to deal with the number of visitors?"

She poured them each a glass of fruit juice from a decanter, and glanced over at him. She raised an eyebrow, smiled and shook her head as she passed him his glass. "No, not at all, Hal. However, based on that remark I sense that perhaps you are here as a result of a reoccurring problem you have." She gestured to the small table and trio of chairs in the "office" area of her cabin. "Anxiety issues, Hal?"

He really wanted for her, someday, at least once, to have to take longer than five sentences before manifesting the ability to read him like a bold-print children's book. He sighed and took a seat in one of the chairs, and watched her gracefully move to sit opposite him.

"Yes," he admitted finally. "It is the usual, Ise. I keep wondering what either the Spirits or the Council thought about putting me straight into the Big Chair. We are out here with the looming potential to be making history, or sailing into a world of hurt. I know this is important; Mission Services pulled us off our shore stay two days early, so we got picked for this."

Ise tapped a journal sticking out from the stack on the table they sat at. "I was reading this morning that the average is one 'major injury' every six months for an RSAV crew. The *Journal of Safety And Recovery* defines a 'major injury' as a crew member being unable to sail for six weeks or more, and requiring at least one week of time in the Infirmary. There is an outright fatality about once every two years of operations of a given crew," she commented, apparently at random.

"What?" Hal asked. He was as perplexed by the change of topic as he was the numbers the usually attentive and on-point Spirit and Morale Counsellor had just quoted. "Good Spirits bright, that seems high. We have not had anyone miss a trip due to injury of any kind in … what? Nine months?"

"Oh? Is that so?" Ise asked, sounding politely surprised. "Jog my memory, would you? What was the name of that Third Class that we had to bury at sea?"

Hal was horrified at her question. That horror almost immediately gave way to indignation. "*No one* has died under my command, Miz Koolen, ever. *Ever.* You very well know that," he snarled.

She had a mouthful from her juice glass, looking at him over the rim of the glass.

"That was your point, I take it?" he said with a sigh, suddenly feeling very deflated and somewhat foolish. She had artfully baited him with his own insecurity, and he had taken it hook, line, and sinker. Perhaps with a bit of the rod, as well.

She nodded and then sat the glass down. "Indeed it was, Hal. The *Sheerah* is well below Fleet average on injuries, even when compared to captains with three times your in-rank experience. That would be *nine* years in the Big Chair, Hal", she pointed out with an accompanying gesture of a hand. "Under your command, the crew of the *Sheerah* is setting records for success and safety. She is breaking records that have stood, in some cases, for more than a Generation."

She paused, watching him for a moment. "But it is not your *past* record that worries you, is it, Hal?" she asked gently. Her voice was barely audible above the mild noises of the ship.

He put an elbow on the table and leaned his forehead heavily against his hand. "No. I am," he paused, his voice lowering as he continued, "I am really afraid of getting someone killed, Ise. We have really been lucky so far but …"

She interrupted him with a finger laid gently across his lips. "You are making two serious mistakes in your establishing statement, Hal. First, short of taking a knife or variable rifle and directly attacking a crew member, it is almost impossible for you to get someone killed. Secondly, the track record of our ship and her crew 'so far' has nothing to do with luck."

"But, Ise," he began slowly.

"Listen to me, Hal, please. First," she said, ticking a finger as she spoke, "everyone aboard this vessel, yourself and myself included, are here because we are well above the average for our Main disciplines. When you put this much excellence into this small a space, what happens might as well be magic, for what it looks like. But it is not magic, Hal, nor is it luck. It is what happens when the finest people, with the greatest love of their job, are given the best technology available and are guided by the finest leadership any of them will meet."

Hal nodded, listening. He was not entirely sure how much of this was platitude, but he was willing to keep an open mind. On the other hand, he had never known Ise Koolen to be prone to useless platitude, either.

"Now, you, my dear Hal Lum, have been perpetually afraid of being responsible for the death of a crew member since I first met you. You need to accept two simple truths, Hal. They are unkind, and awkward truths, but you must listen to me, and you must accept them. If you do not, you will drive yourself out of the Big Chair with your anxiety issues.

"The first truth, unfortunately, is that you will have a crew member die under your command. RSAV crews have been dying in action since Generation One; technically even before. In the course of your expected twenty-five year career, you will see at least six crew die. That is if you can double their odds of survival. If you can reduce the carnage by a full three times, then it will be 'merely' four lives lost. There is nothing you can do about that. Nothing, Hal."

Hal closed his eyes, a lump in his gut. If this was supposed to be a warming and inspiring pep-talk, Ise Koolen was missing her mark by a couple of kilometres. The notion that he was going be the reason that four, or six, or more, good people did not get to go home to their families sickened him

"Hal? You are not listening to me," she said pointedly.

"Yes I AM," he exploded. "What do you want me to do? A jig? Perhaps a foxtrot? Shall I press 'Play' on the AMTAC, and you and I will polka around the cabin together? Should I be cheering at the idea of being the reason why good people die? Should I be glad my mistakes are going to snuff lives out? What do you want from me, Ise?" he shouted at her.

"Well," she offered patiently, "you could start by listening to what I *am* saying instead of what you *think* I am saying." She tilted her head as she gazed at him.

There was a long silence. "Okay, Ise, I have no idea what you are getting at. I am listening to you. You just finished telling me that I would be the reason 'at least six crew die'," he said sourly. He was sitting directly opposite her; the idea he had misheard her was absurd.

"No, Hal, that is *not* what I said. That is what you *heard*. You are filtering my words through your own insecurities, your issues with your lack of approval from your father, and what you have heard via the rumour mill, and as a result you are substituting entire phrases," she said firmly, tapping a long fingernail on the side of her glass.

Hal blinked at her. He was *sure* what she had told him. He had been sitting *right here* listening to her, after all. How could he possibly have misheard her?

He rubbed at his forehead, suddenly feeling very tired. "All right, Ise. Explain it to me," he said wearily. "I am pretty much lost at this point."

"Good. Perhaps you will listen this time," she said, managing to sound both encouraging and sympathetic, in spite of her words. "What I said was that you will likely *see* at least six crew die under your command. I did not say you would be *responsible*."

"Hang on, Ise, you are playing word games," he barked irritably. "Of course I am going to be responsible! I will be their Captain! That *makes* me responsible!"

"No, Hal," she stated firmly, "it does not. It makes *them* responsible. Take Miz Reed; you were no where near her at the moment she chose to short-string that fir tree, instead of setting up the safety ropes properly. *She* made the decision to cut corners on safety. *She* is responsible for her injury. You are *not*. At no time did you try and encourage an attitude that is lax in safety and regard for personal well-being. You often and regularly do just the opposite.

"If that tree had crushed her flat," Ise continued coldly, "that would have been her fault and her responsibility. Not. Yours. You cannot let yourself be to blame for every mistake everyone you have ever met, your Father included, has ever made." She paused, beyond the tap-tap of her nail against the juice glass. "Are you listening, Hal?" she asked quietly.

The dark-skinned man sat back in his chair, staring at the dark-skinned woman across from him. Hal desperately wanted to argue with her; point out some flaw in her logic, some place where his command training proved him right and her wrong.

Except, of course, he could not. That was the infuriating part of dealing with his Spirit and Morale Counsellor. She was almost exclusively right. He sighed, and rubbed at his eyes for a moment. He refused to cry in front of her, even in what felt right now like an awkward flavour of relief.

"It is okay, Hal, you are allowed. I understand why you feel like you should not, but do not ever think you are not allowed."

He sighed again, somewhere between irritation at her mind-reading and relief at her message and wiped an eye. "So, what is item number two that I have to come to grips with, Ise?"

She smiled at him. "Bravo, Hal," she said, sounding both sincere and pleased. "Most people need to be reminded when I leave something like that hanging. You need to break the silence between yourself and your Father. You either need to reconcile your differences with each other, or you need to accept that those differences are irreconcilable. If they are the latter, then you need to walk away from your sea-anchor reflex to try and do bigger and better and brighter every time we sail to try and impress him out of his silence. Otherwise, one day, you *will* encourage someone to skimp on safety or common sense, and then what happens *will* be your responsibility. Worse, you will no longer be the Hal Lum your crew are so loyal to."

Her words stung at his heart like an upset hornet. He wiped an eye. "I … I do not know what to say."

"Well, then I guess you can listen to me lecture a bit more," she said with a chuckle, rubbing her hands together in mock glee. Hal laughed lightly as well, despite his mood. She grinned at him and refilled his juice glass. He picked it up and tipped it to his lips, thinking. He had let three years of silence become a crippling habit. Ise was right. He needed to stow this sea-anchor and start moving ahead once again.

"Thank-you, Ise."

"It is my pleasure to Serve and Guide," she said warmly. "Go get some good sleep and good breakfast. We have a lot to do," she quoted to him with a wink.

He laughed aloud.

## Marlon
### 09h48 SST
### Wednesday, April 27th

Marlon climbed up out of the stern deck hatch to the world outside the *Sheerah*. The Sun had just broken the horizon, and Marlon was here with his morning coffee to greet Him. Much as he expected, the stern section of the amphibious vehicle's weather deck was largely deserted, beyond the one Armsman currently walking towards the bow. Then, he noticed Jonas was also here, also with a cup in hand, watching the sunrise.

As Marlon walked over to where the younger Pilot-Navigator was, he noted to his abject horror that there were two empty glass bottles beside where Jonas sat on the deck. When full, those bottles would have each held one-and-a-quarter litres of rye-whiskey each. The Engineering Chief desperately hoped there was some explanation beyond that Jonas had knocked the two of them off over a couple of hours. If he had, and alcohol poisoning did not kill the gifted Pilot, Marlon was sure the Skipper would.

"Well, Pilot, good morning. How … how are you feeling this morning?" Marlon began cautiously.

Jonas looked over his shoulder towards the greying-haired Engineer. The cup his hands were wrapped around issued little curls of steam into the chill spring morning air. "Oh, hey there, Chief. I am doing ok. Just doing some thinking and watching the sun rise. Kinda beautiful. One of those things about being Crew I consider a perk; I get to see an awful lot of absolutely unique sunrises," the Pilot-Navigator responded, sounding surprisingly philosophical.

Much to Marlon's relief, it was obvious the younger man was completely sober as well. Pryce smiled at Zupan. "If you can hang on to that sense of wonder, Mister Zupan, you will never grow old. Regardless of what any future spouse or shaving mirror might tell you," Marlon said with a laugh. Jonas chuckled as well. "So," Marlon asked, nudging one of the empties with a toe, "what is with this pair of dry tankers?"

Jonas sighed, and looked back out towards the distant horizon. Nothing was said for long enough that the Armsman on patrol had time to come and go again before the Pilot answered him. "I quit," Jonas announced with a firmness to his voice. "I dumped them both over the side with the first sliver of gold on the horizon and I am not touching the stuff again for a long time, if ever. I will toss the empties into the recycling when I go back down below."

Marlon blinked at him. "Well, that is quite a decision, Mister Zupan. Congratulations to you," the older engineer said, trying to sound as encouraging as possible without actually cheering. Marlon had been worried about the younger man's drinking for some time. This was remarkably good news as far he as was concerned.

"Thanks, Chief. It is something I should have been brave enough to

155

do before now," Jonas said quietly. He had a sip from the steaming mug he had; Marlon guessed it was hot chocolate.

Marlon sat down beside him, folding his arms and resting his elbows on his knees. "Do not be too hard on yourself, Jonas," the older engineer offered, lowering his voice. "We all do what we can to try and make the world make sense. You are not the first, nor will you be the last, to try and use a liquor bottle as a filter. Spirits, lad, even I did that at one point."

"You did?" Jonas asked, sounding surprised.

"Aye. My wife and I got into a bad patch after we had been together a few years. Some charming young buck had caught her eye, and when she tried to talk to me about how she felt I was an insecure, self-righteous arse. Predictably, when someone is wanting to talk to their best friend and instead gets beaten about the heart and self-confidence, it does not improve the relationship much. So, she packed her bags and went elsewhere for a little while. I took to the bottle out of self-pity," Pryce stated with a sigh. "Not one of my finer moments, I must say," he concluded ruefully.

Jonas stared in horror at the older man beside him. "But, what ... what happened?" he asked anxiously.

"Hmm? Oh, my sister got tired of my foolishness and came over and gave me an earful one weekend. She helped me write the most awkward apology letter in the history of romance and took it over to my wife. Annabelle and I got back together, sorted the whole mess out, and it has been happily ever-after since then. That was a few years ago."

Jonas relaxed visibly.

"Jonas, lad," Marlon said with an encouraging smile, "spats are just part of caring about someone. The more you care, the more likely someone is going to get bruised. The more you care, you see, the more you take off the armour and the padding. So even silly stuff can sting more than it ought to. You accept that, and you learn to talk to each other, even when it is no fun. Or you can learn to be single," Marlon concluded with a shrug of his shoulders.

There were a few moments of silence. It seemed to Pryce that the younger man beside him was thinking about that exchange rather in detail.

"So, what prompted you to quit drinking now, Mister Zupan?" Pryce asked casually.

Jonas shifted his gaze towards the horizon for a moment, watching a couple of gulls wheeling over the bay. He then looked back towards Marlon. "It might be 'free' to folks like me as Crew, but even then it turns out that it is damn expensive stuff," the Pilot said quietly.

# Cordelia
## 10h41 SST

It was a bit shy of an hour after sunrise as the *Sheerah* picked her way through the ruins and debris of the Flood Zone. Cordelia was at her crew station, watching via a combination of instruments and the Comm windows as they approached dry shore.

Jonas had been doing an outstanding job at moving the substantial mass of the RSAV through the maze-like area of rubble and wreckage. Once upon an eon ago, this area would have been homes, businesses, parks and factories. Then the sea moved inland, in some cases by a few dozen kilometres, and it was all inundated. What the sea did not take directly was drowned by proximity; storm surges that in some cases doubled the height of the tide pushed sea water over barriers and into the already beleaguered Precursor habitations.

Hundred-year storms now hammered the coastal zones every two or three years. What would have been dubbed millennial monsters instead now mauled the remnants of the Precursor world roughly once a decade. The devastation of these events could reach more than a hundred kilometres inland, from what Cordelia had read.

"Skipper," Jonas began, "We are about two hundred metres from where I want to take us ashore. From what I can see with side-scan SONAR and eyeballs, it looks like the best candidate. Then it is just about the same distance inland to where we are supposed to unload the first set of Arr-Eee-Arr's."

"Very good, Pilot," Hal replied. "Chief Armsman, please make sure your people on the weather deck know to tie down and hang on."

"All ready done, Captain. Weather deck team is ready for a Rubble Roll," Olivier answered.

"Very good, Security. Pilot, take us ashore," Hal ordered. Cordelia watched him cue his microphone for the RSAV's main broadcast. "Attention all hands, stand by for Rise, Beach and Rubble Roll. Ensure all loose items are secured. All Salvage and Dive, and all Arms and Security personnel make ready for deployment," he ordered.

Cordelia picked up her Detail communications telephone. Tech First-Class Anna Longo answered. "Miz Longo, as you just heard from the Captain, we are almost there. Make sure everyone is ready to be rigging that derrick and shifting those pallets as soon as the door gets open."

"Sure thing, Chief," the cheery voice answered. "We are already on it."

"I figured you would be. I will be down to help as soon as we are wrapped up here in the Comm," she said, and then hung the receiver up. As she did so, a dull rumble began to vibrate the hull. That, she knew, was the sound of thirty-two hundred kilowatts of turbo-diesels coming to full power in anticipation of the *Sheerah*'s caterpillar treads hitting bottom.

She looked forward, out the windows. Curls of water broke against the bow of the RSAV as it moved sharply forward.

"One hundred to shore, fifty to bottom," Jonas announced. "Here we go!" A few moments later an audible crunch and thud that Cordelia could feel as much as hear announced that the treads had touched bottom. The RSAV shuddered and surged forward as Jonas guided the massive machine onto the shore.

The guttural sound of the Tee-Dees deepened as the gears and linkages that sorted out where and how much power from the engines went to which treads did their magic. As more of the *Sheerah* moved out of the water, her pace increased, due to the decreased effect of the water on her hull.

Cordelia absolutely loved this feeling of the raw power of the RSAV as it drove up onto the shore. The *Sheerah* was free entirely of the sea now, and she watched Jonas skilfully manage the throttle-requesters and the steering controls.

She glanced back at Hal, who was leaning forward in his chair, a solid hold on the armrests, watching out the windows towards the two gun-turrets. Each of the Armsmen occupying those turrets would be watching around them for anything that might be a problem; a sudden turn of the turret would prompt Hal to action.

The *Sheerah* eased to a stop, and then turned in place so that her hull was parallel to the shoreline they had just exited.

"That is it," Jonas announced. "We are here."

"Another talented job done, Pilot. Miz Baasch, you are clear to start Salvage and Dive operations as soon as Security clears the area. Mister Olivier, get your people on the ground and looking around. I would like a go / no-go report from you on channel nine in fifteen minutes."

"Yes, Captain. Report channel is nine, and I will get the Armsmen moving right away," he confirmed, picking up his Detail telephone.

Cordelia immediately was up and out of her chair and giving Hal a polite nod. Then she was heading for the hatch and ladder leading down out of the Command Compartment. She moved down Salt Flats towards the bow of the RSAV. She could hear the whine and growl of substantial hydraulic systems spinning up, then a metallic grind and rumble.

She came through the hatch of the forward cargo bay, known as the Load Bay, as the first crack of light shone through the bow ramp-door as it began to lower. Her Detail were already in the process of moving the gear they would soon require. Four heavily armed and equipped Armsmen stood at the top of the ramp, watching as it lowered before them. As soon as it was about half-way to the ground, which was admittedly a slow-moving process, one by one the Armsmen moved up to the opening, dropped and rolled off the lip to land in a crouch on the ground below. They then moved away to clear the spot for the next to descend.

She appreciated the work they did, but did not envy them their calling. Armsmen were the most likely members of an RSAV crew to be buried on a beach or at sea. It had nothing to do with being "meatheads" or unintelligent, she knew. Armsmen were as technically proficient and well trained in their disciplines as any of her own Ess-And-Dee Techs. The world above the waves was just that damnably dangerous.

She was surprised to find herself suddenly glad that Jonas was not an Armsman. Equally surprising to her was the arrival of the notion that she also likely owed the charming Pilot an apology for her behaviour.

"Reed! Careful with that rigging kit, before you drop it on yourself," she barked irritably at the Third-Class tech. "I do not want to see injury paperwork with your name on it again any time soon, understood?"

# Christopher
## 18h01 SST

Christopher Olivier flipped the visor of his helmet up and looked towards the sun, high in the sky. It was past midday now, heading towards mid afternoon, and it was easily too warm to be comfortable in the full battle gear he wore. Still, it was staying on until the *Sheerah* and her crew were safely idling in the bay for the night.

Christopher was hardly superstitious, nor was he terribly pious. There were those he knew and worked with who Blessed and thanked the Spirits, Sun and Moon for everything that happened around him. He was not one of them.

That said, he was a firm believer in gut instinct; that feral left-over from a time long before either the Precursors or any other civilisation, when humankind had first been at the mercy of nature. When the heart and mind argued, Christopher let his gut make the decisions. It had worked out for him every time so far.

As he flipped the visor down and resumed his march back towards where the RSAV was currently parked, his gut was telling him that something "bad" was in the neighbourhood. So far, neither Armsmen nor Salvage Techs had reported anything of concern. He was not convinced that trend would hold.

The *Sheerah* had changed positions twice so far today. Captain Lum, in a rare spate of reasonable planning, had determined that the highest order of priority would be getting the two "Radio Environment Recorder" systems deployed on opposite sides of the bay. Given the report from the Pilot-Navigator of the possible nature of the "radio anomaly", that seemed to be the obvious course of action to the Chief Armsman.

Given that both the weather and the breathability of the air itself could be capricious, there was no guarantee how much of the week they were slated to be here would actually be usable. So, getting the bulky

Arr-Eee-Arr's deployed first ensured that a critical SIGINT opportunity would not be lost.

Each Arr-Eee-Arr was two full pallets of armoured equipment, and so took a significant amount of time and effort to unload, position, unpack and activate. It was all too easy to imagine Hal having stupidly decided to harvest first, and then suddenly find that a storm or a Green Fog forced them to head to sea before getting the equipment in place.

So, after they had gone ashore just after dawn, they had gotten the first Arr-Eee-Arr positioned and turned on. Then, everyone had returned to the RSAV, and she had rumbled back the way she had come, driven back out into the water, paddled across the bay to the South side of its crescent coast, and driven ashore again. They had repeated the process again, and then returned out into the bay.

After a bit of deliberation and path-finding by the mercurial Pilot-Navigator, they had worked their way east through the extensive Flood Zone. Then, for the third time that day, the *Sheerah* had rolled ashore. Jonas had cozied the RSAV up to a substantial pile of metallic wreckage, liberally surrounded by reinforced concrete slabs and debris. The ever-outrageous Miz Baasch had been visibly licking her lips in anticipation of the haul that a few days here would net them.

As always, when there were teams of Salvage Techs out, either on land or underwater, it was the job of the Armsmen to watch over them. The Ess-And-Dee Detail were working in two groups, so each one had an Armsman guarding them. Christopher was coming back from paying the two groups a surprise visit.

Ostensibly, he was bringing a couple canteens of fresh chilled water out to the Armsmen. In reality, he was making sure they were alert and paying careful attention to both anything alien in the surroundings, as well as Miz Baasch's "safety-unconscious" Techs themselves. So far, so good.

His radio crackled with Hal Lum's voice. "Mister Olivier, Counsellor Koolen wishes to stretch her legs and check up on the crew on the ground. Please check in when you get back to the ship; I would like you to escort her."

A smile curled Christopher's usually stoic visage. His day had just improved noticeably.

# CHAPTER TEN

## *A Voice in the Distance*

**Ise**
**00h01 SST**
**Thursday, April 28th**
**Vicinity 42.4N,71.1W**
**14C, Winds SE 7kph**

It was a little less than a half-hour after sunset when Ise Koolen hit 'play' on the AMTAC music player in her cabin. She was fresh out of the shower, wearing her favourite purple and blue babydoll styled nightgown. Kim Cannes' smokey, sexy voice filled the air and Ise gleefully shimmied and belly danced barefoot around her cabin to the sound of her new favourite song.

One of the reasons that she and many others appreciated the work of the "Jay Zee Clark Project" was that "Zee" was a composer and partway sound-engineer. All the instruments and voices were chosen as part of the composition; each one being a distinct texture or flavour in the finished song. Ise could guess that Zee had specifically chosen Miz Cannes for the lead singer exactly for the distinctive flavour of her sound.

The lyrics and the arrangement were the message, and everything else was an emotionally weaponised delivery mechanism. You could make the mistake of getting caught up in the beat and just dancing your heart out to any of Zee's songs, and many club-goers did. Any of the Project's serious fans, on the other hand, would tell you that you were missing out on sixty percent of the beauty of the music.

So while this smokey and melancholy blues anthem might seem uncharacteristic of Zee's work, most snobbish "true fans", which Ise Koolen would sheepishly confess to being one of, would find this right at home in the music collection. The fact that Miz Cannes' voice turned this into make-out music was just extra value.

She giggled to herself that poor "Zee" was going to have to be extra careful with keeping his true identity a proper secret for the next few weeks, or there was going to be a line up of fan girls at his bedroom door. She giggled again, this time at the idea of how the shy and awkward "real world" Jonas Zupan would deal with that kind of "attention" from even a couple of very, ahem, *enthusiastic* fans.

If she had been more of a boy's-girl and did not have to work with him after, Ise would have considered adding herself to the queue, she thought to herself with a bawdy chuckle as she listened and danced. It was so sweet of him to have written and recorded his thank-you note for her.

However, one of those things you did not ever do as a Counsellor was spend time even just making out with a crew-mate. Even if it did not skew your judgment, it would skew theirs, every time. Given that taking care of people's minds and souls was part of the job description, skewed judgement anywhere in the equation was a disaster waiting to happen.

So, while there were a couple of very attractive crew-mates that had caught Ise's eye, she saved any of that sort of thing for ashore and a dance club with people from a life outside the RSAVs.

"*Save My Soul*" wound out its final notes, and Ise came to a stop in her dancing over by her small fridge. She opened it and fished out a carafe of chilled juice and poured herself a glass. As the actually much more danceable "*Dolphin Ranch Promenade*" began, she gulped a couple of mouthfuls.

Sex and dating were one of those weird social spaces in the world of Soumerville, she mused as she sat on the edge of her little table, her bare feet dangling. Officially, morally, anyone could do what ever or who ever they wanted, so long as everyone involved was a clearly consenting adult, and no children resulted from it.

Even *that* awkward detail of the entire affair was handled by Official Protocols, she thought amusedly. The odds of unexpected pregnancies were essentially zero; as part of the every sixty-day medical check-ups that were just part of life in Soumerville and her sister towns, both men and women got a birth-control injection. The injection was good for ninety days, thus unplanned families were functionally unheard of. Both sides of the fun-fun dance were equally responsible for keeping their shots up to date, and that meant that everyone had the same amount of social pressure. The aggressive and progressive medical routine meant that social diseases were also functionally non-existent. Sex between consenting adults was clearly labeled "to be enjoyed by owner", and it could be, if that was what you wanted.

However, by way of paradox, everyone was aware of the entire process of officially sanctioned match-making. A full third of the women on board the RSAV would have gotten "The Letter" in the past year, Ise knew. She did not know exactly who, officially, but she knew roughly how many. Several of them had been in her cabin to talk with her. Few things were more heart-breaking than having to explain to a young woman why her love of the past couple of years was arbitrarily not ever going to be the father of her children. But that was how life was. Once again, the needs of the many outweighed those of the few.

Ise was expecting her own copy of "The Letter" to be arriving any day now. She had no interest in an official husband or raising children herself, so she had already decided she would be going the artificial route for getting started. Twice would be plenty, and then she would be back to both RSAVs and wounded souls, as well as dance halls and pretty girls.

She yawned, had another gulp of juice and bounced to her feet. She hit play again, and started dancing around her cabin with renewed delight. One of the benefits of being the Spirit and Morale Counsellor was that the walls of her cabin were sound-proofed for "patient privacy". This had the delightful side effect of letting her be as obnoxious with her music and antics here as at her apartment.

She loved few things more than the abandon of dancing. Her legs were already sore from walking on shore, but she flatly did not care. "*Dance like no one is watching*" was the ages-old maxim, and regardless of if anyone ever was, Ise Koolen always did.

Christopher Olivier's chiseled features and gold-brown skin crossed her mind, mid-lock-step. She felt sorry for him; it was as obvious to her as a printed note that he was completely infatuated with her. She was careful not to lead him on or give him any hints of encouragement that were beyond what she would do or say to her other crew mates. She was fairly sure he was politely taking the hint; certainly he had never done anything or said anything that made her uncomfortable.

She *was* somewhat perplexed, however, as to why he was still aboard. She had fully expected he would have been reassigned to another RSAV before the *Sheerah* had sailed again. Yet, that had not happened. That concerned her; it implied that either her immediate superiors had over-ruled her assessment, or the Council itself had.

She ground to a halt, chewing the corner of her lip and frowning. Had she read the situation wrong? Had her judgment been clouded by his obvious romantic and sexual interest in her?

She sighed and her shoulders sagged slightly. She went over and pressed "Stop" on the AMTAC player, then padded over to the brass-and-cherrywood intercom by her desk. She pressed the button for the "Emm-And-Que Shack". Damiano Émile's distinctive cigars-and-gravel voice emerged.

"Sickbay," he stated.

"Damiano, it is Ise. Do you have some time to play Counsellor with me?" she asked, still biting at her lip.

"With or without the tequila?" he asked, sounding entirely too reasonable.

She gave that question a hard moment of thought. "Leave it in the cabinet," she decided aloud. "I think that falls under the category of 'terrible mistake' this evening."

"Fair enough. Your cabin or mine?"

"Likely better for you to come here," she answered. She glanced down at her attire and then sighed. "Give me ten minutes before you show up, though, Dami?"

"No problem, Ise. Talk to you in ten." The light under the intercom box went out, and she flipped her side to "Privacy".

She went to her closet-locker and pulled out a ship-suit, and tossed it towards her bunk. She pulled the nightgown over her head and shoved it under her pillow. As her ship's doctor, Damiano had seen her in less than her babydoll nightgown a couple of times. However, that was entirely different circumstances and context, from Ise's perspective. She was completely confident that if she opted to stay in her nightgown, Damiano would have officially "failed to notice" what she was wearing and would have been both professional and a perfect gentleman. Still, even with as much of a spectacle as she could make of herself on a dancehall floor, her body was her space, and she tended towards a fairly conservative style of clothing for the combination of her emotional and physical comfort.

Once she was dressed, she went out to her "office" to make sure the juice container was at least half full.

\*\*\*\*\*

A bit more than ten minutes after Damiano had hung-up, there was a knock at her cabin door.

"Good evening, Ise," the ship's doctor said with a smile as she opened the door.

"Hello, Dami. Thank-you for stopping by. Come in; the fruit juice is fresh and cold. I poured us each a glass already."

"Oh, thank-you. The Emm-And-Que is always a bit dry," he responded, moving past her at the door, and then towards the table and chairs in the front half of her cabin. "So, what is on your mind, Ise?"

She closed the cabin door, sighed and then made her way to the chair opposite the short and stocky fellow sitting there. "I wiggled my fingers and nothing happened," she said with a pout, miming her words.

"Ah. Can you share some details for context?"

"It is a bit awkward, Dami," she said with a sigh. "It is Christopher Olivier." Her sandy-haired conversational partner merely arched an eyebrow. "He wants me, Dami. Or, at least his mythology of me, anyway. I am not entirely sure how well he actually knows who I am."

"Ah, yes, I can see how that would be awkward for you, Ise, as his Spirit and Morale Counsellor. Now, just to keep up with that theme of awkward, have you actually considered him as a pillow pal? While you primarily identify as lesbian, I know in practice you are bisexual."

Ise quietly sighed. This was the problem with Damiano; she adored him as a coworker and confidante, but he sometimes completely missed the point of a discussion. Charming, professional, empathetic, an excellent backgammon player, a talented bartender, a reasonable dancer, and sometimes incapable of reading street signs; that was the Damiano Émile she knew and was periodically frustrated by.

"No, Dami. I am sure that Christopher is easy on the eyes for a few of the girls and boys onboard, but he is absolutely not my thing," she replied firmly.

"So, what is the specific issue?"

"Well, there is significant friction between him and Hal Lum," she said. "I am sure you know that." When he nodded at her while having a mouthful of his juice, she continued, "It is a bad interpersonal fit. One of them will do something stupid eventually regarding the other, and someone's otherwise perfectly good career is going to get ruined. More importantly, it will cause chaos for the *Sheerah's* crew. So, I recommended Christopher be switched out."

Damiano blinked at her. "You can do that?"

She nodded at him. "Yes, but please do keep that as a professional confidence, Dami. I have a mechanism where I can have crew members moved off the ship for what look like innocent and obtuse administrative reasons. No one has their feelings hurt, no one has their careers marked, and there is nothing to be grumpy about, other than so-called 'bad luck'."

"Well, that is handy. I will endeavour to forget about it once we are done talking," he chuckled. "I will point out that your vile sorcery seems to have some limits, my friend. To wit, Ise, our current Chief Armsman looks and sounds suspiciously just like the last one."

"Yes, I noticed that as well," she said with a sigh. "Which is why you are sitting here drinking with me. That means that someone up the chain overruled me. That rarely happens, and what I have been taught is that when it does happen, I really need to stop and look at myself and ask why."

"Ah. And so, our intrepid readers find the heroic and attractive

Counsellor Koolen in her cabin on a spring evening having a crisis of faith," Damiano said with a dramatic wave.

"Correct. She therefore opted to call on her long-time confidante and sounding board, the charismatic and charming Ship's Doctor Émile."

"Smart character, she is. An excellent judge of others, too," Damiano asserted in a deadpan. There was a moment of silence and then they both dissolved into giggles and snickers. Once they had both regained their composures and sipped a bit more of the juice, he looked over the rim of his glass at her. "So, you are officially better at this 'Counsellor' thing than I am, Ise. What is the most obvious reason your recommendations would be countermanded?" he asked. "Also, and a near second in importance, are there any date squares?"

"Oooh! Yes, there are. One moment!" She quickly was up and out of her chair, and then darted over to the refrigerator. Date squares were a favourite treat of hers, which Damiano very well knew. A few moments later she was back, there was a plate of the flavourful sweets on the table, and each of them was enjoying one.

"And?" he prompted.

"Hmm? Oh! Yes, right! Ah, well, if I had to guess, it is because I do not know something relevant to the calculus. As with most things in the Service, there is a certain amount of 'need-to-know' applied as a filter to anything I am told from 'on high'."

"Okay. So, did you recommend anyone else be transferred off, and if so, did it go through?" Damiano inquired.

"Um. Yes, and yes. In fact, now that you mention it, there were six recommendations and four happened," she answered slowly. That in and of itself was puzzling to her, now that she thought about it.

"So we can conclude that the request was not lost in bureaucracy, nor was it given a blanket treatment. Your recommendations were considered individually," he suggested, gesturing with his unoccupied hand.

"It would seem that way, yes, Dami."

"Then you need to start over. As a doctor, when I am training a medical staffer of any level, it is all about the procedure. Often an otherwise competent Tech or Nurse gets caught up in the intensity of a moment and takes a shortcut or just discounts the need for a particular step. For example, one of the things you should always do as a First Responder is a pat-down and full-body injury exam. A lot of times, that step gets skipped, because things like a wound spitting blood makes it *seem* obvious what the extent of injury is."

"Right," Ise answered, "and yet, a bandage on the arm only solves part of the problem if you did not check to see if they have a broken leg to match."

"Exactly. Being outside the sort of magic that you Spirit and Morale types do, Ise, my first instinct is that someone up the chain thinks you skipped a step. So, go back to the beginning of whatever process you folks use for a 'diagnosis' and determining a 'course of treatment' and start there. If you do the whole thing over and get to the same place, then at least you can be sure that you are not part of the problem."

"That makes perfect sense, Dami. Thank-you so much."

# Marlon
## 10h06 SST

Chief Engineering Artificer Marlon Pryce, veteran of more than twenty-five years in the Reclamation Service, the technical wizard who ensured that a vast and complex mechanical and hydraulic world could be depended on to deliver thirty-two hundred-thousand watts of power where ever and whenever his crew-mates demanded had, yet again, been thwarted by the toaster. He hated burnt toast, he thought with a sigh. On the other hand, he always felt bad about throwing food away just because it was not exactly to his liking. He slathered the charred disaster in a liberal measure of honey, and set it on the edge of his plate.

Cordelia came into the O-Room, increasing its current population by one hundred percent. "Good morning, Marlon. Some personal traffic came in for you via RATT-net last night," she said, offering an envelope to him.

"Oh, thank-you, Cordelia," he said, suddenly feeling much better. He sat his plate down at his usual spot at the table, and wiped the excess sticky onto the pants of his ship-suit before he took the letter from her. "I appreciate the personal delivery first thing in the morning," he said with a smile.

"Entirely happy to oblige, Marlon. I know that it brightens your day a bit," she answered as she moved over to the steward window to request her breakfast.

Pryce sat down at his spot and neatly opened the left-hand edge of the envelope with his work knife. He unfolded the contained page and adjusted the position of his glasses.

*Dearest Marlon,*

*Your silly, excitable wife could not wait for you to come home to share some news with you, so she spent a few line-credits to have this sent to you out on your ship, where-ever you are right now. She hopes you do not mind.*

*Clarissa has already made her big decision!! Do you recall the chap she was all smitten over and totally beside herself about a couple of years back?*

*She had been in a tizzy back then about how to ask him out to the theatre. She had gotten tired of waiting for him to ask, as I recall. Anyway, his name is Mahomet Zaman; not a bad looking young man, with a square jaw and sharp eyes. Well, he was one of the ones on her List.*

*(Do not even \*dare\* to consider telegramming me in reply with "what List?". You have been warned!)*

*She managed to talk herself into calling him up for a dinner and dancing night. It went swimmingly well; I will spare you the 'girl talk' that she and I had. They had fun, she is completely over-the-moon all over again, and you do not need to adjust your blood-pressure medication.*

*Unless he turns out to be a cad of some species, he will likely be our son-in-law, and we will likely be grandparents within the year. I am so proud of her for having gotten past her shyness and screwed up the courage to do what was in her heart. You have done a smashing job as a father, Marlon. She even said so when we were talking.*

*Naturally, Simon, is acting like an over-protective older-brother. Never mind the part where she is a year older than he; a point she \*ahem\* firmly reminded him of at the dinner table last night. He is worried that Clarissa is 'rushing' things. I expect you will have to have some 'guy talk' and help him sort himself out over all this.*

*So, that is the big news. I hope that this telegram finds you in good spirits, beyond a bit of boredom. Come home safe, and know that I will be waiting for you on the dock.*

*All my love and loyalty,*

*Annabelle*

"Well," Pryce said gruffly, "that escalated quickly." He sighed and refolded the letter and slowly put it back in the envelope. He was going to be a grandfather within a year? Good grief the time was flying past him.

"Hmm? What is afoot, Marlon?" Cordelia asked as she sat down at her usual spot at the other table.

"Oh, my daughter got 'The Letter' about a month ago. It turns out her teenage sweetheart was on one of the pages. She has apparently put him at the head of the list and has been out to a social or two with him. So, unless he does something to upset the gilded applecart he was just handed, I expect I will have a son-in-law in the next few months."

Cordelia blinked at him. "That sounds like wonderful news to me, Marlon!" she grinned.

"Oh, it is, it is. I recall the chap. Smart spoken, good deportment, good tradesman, and seems to me to be a genuinely kind lad. I am sure he will treat Clarissa as she deserves. I am just perpetually surprised by how fast that young lady moves when she has a bee in her bonnet. Rather much like her mother," Marlon laughed.

# Christopher
## 00h17 SST
## Friday, April 29th

Chief Armsman Christopher Olivier was pleased that his gut had thus far been wrong. Other than a minor bit of target practice that the thirty-eight gunners had been obligated to perform against a curious bear, things had been quiet. The two bow deck guns had each fired a couple of "Moose" rounds into the trees adjacent where the animal had emerged from the nearby forest. The sounds of shattering saplings at close proximity had been more than sufficient to persuade it to take its ursine curiosity elsewhere.

Other than that one incident, the day's operations had been dull. No dramas, no problems, no dangers, no mistakes, no worries; either from the surrounding environment or Miz Baasch's Detail.

He was currently sitting in the Command Compartment as the on-Watch Officer. As with the previous night, about an hour before sunset, salvage operations had wrapped up, everyone returned to the *Sheerah*, and the vessel had returned to the relative safety of the open waters of the bay. They would stay here, with the autopilot using the submerged thrusters to keep them from drifting with the tide, until after sunrise tomorrow. Then they would drive ashore once again, and begin another full day of dry-land operations.

Of course, the autopilot was not infallible. As well, there were Armsmen on the weather deck for security. Ergo, an officer of some rank or description needed to be in the Comm in case something significant happened. Generally speaking, nothing did, but when the exception to the rule arrived, it always did so both swiftly and unexpectedly.

He had a sip of tea and shifted slightly in the chair at his crew station. He had brought a book up with him to read, but he had only been here a little while. Across the Compartment, the AMTAC signal monitor speaker hissed a soft waterfall of white noise. Both Jonas and Cordelia had taken to leaving the speaker on, and the Comm antenna extended, anytime they were on watch.

At this distance, which was apparently beyond the edge of maximum range for the *Sheerah* from Soumerville, the short Comm antenna would never hear anything on the RATT-net, of course. In fact, the only way they had gotten this far from home was by packing one of the cargo bays with collapsible bladders full of extra diesel fuel, and then transferring that to the main fuel tanks once they were here. That was the margin they would require to run the RSAV for the eight days they would be here, before setting sail for home.

A change in the sound of the white noise from the monitor speaker caused Christopher to glance over towards it. There it was again;

something definitely non-random in the noise. He immediately dashed over to the Salvage Leader's crew station and turned the volume up on the monitor.

"...*Nee brodee ... Preeze rheaspoon ...*"

The Chief Armsman's eyes widened at the sound of a clearly human voice; Jonas had been right. Christopher rapidly shoved a to-be-re-used AMTAC into the empty slot marked "Incoming Traffic", and his other hand slammed down on the "Record" Button.

Ever since he had heard Jonas' account of what had happened, he had mentally gone over the what-if-me scenario in his head. He had skimmed the emergency procedures manual for the RATT-net system. He had done what he usually did; he prepared.

Thus it was only another moment or two before he found the combination of switches that put the RATT-net keyboard into "emergency" mode. In other words, the keyboard did not try to send its signal to the AMTAC recorder. Instead, it went straight to the transmitters.

He hit the spacebar five times quickly, and then five times slowly. He waited a few moments and then repeated it.

"*Aeye keen haar hue ... unneewn ztay shun ... keen hue raensmeet varce?*"

Jonas had been very right; it was a male voice. This did not sound pleading, however; more measured, and intended. Christopher tapped out a simple pattern with the spacebar.

"Come on, keep talking, whoever you are, the Arr-Eee-Arr's are listening, give them a minute, we can pull a fix from the records in the morning, come on," he muttered under his breath.

"*... Unneewn ztay shun aeye dhoo naet ... stan ... warel bee in bleck* *stane heerbeer ... deez ... "*

Christopher listened for a few more moments, then tapped out another pattern. He pursed his lips and drummed fingers impatiently. Nothing. Another pattern was sent out over the airwaves; he was conscious that he was possibly giving away the location of the *Sheerah* to whoever else was out there. No reply.

He pressed "Stop" on the AMTAC recorder, took the system out of emergency mode, and then called Hal Lum's cabin on the intercom.

"Captain Lum, we have an incident."

## Hal
### 01h21 SST

"So, Chief Pryce, you are convinced this is a Precursor language transmission?" Hal asked, quietly. All of the officers were in the O-Room, the door was locked and the intercom was set to privacy mode. The recording that the Chief Armsman had made was stunning. There had been dead silence in the O-Room when Christopher had played it back with everyone assembled for the first time.

Marlon nodded at Hal. "Yep, Skipper. No doubt about it. I teach Precursor Studies and Precursor Archeology as my Second," he reminded everyone. "I have studied the language enough to be able to speak it and understand it. Now, whoever that is, they are speaking a very dialectal version of it; but it has been seven Generations, you could expect some linguistic drift in that time, I should think."

Everyone glanced around the two tables at each other in shock. What the greying Engineering Chief had just said was that they were collectively at the epicentre of a moment of history.

Marlon lifted a piece of paper, and adjusted his reading glasses.

"The first transmission in the recording is '*I can hear you, unknown station, can you transmit voice'*. Obviously, they could hear our resourceful Chief Armsman on the circuit. Then, the speaker says *'unknown station, I do not ... something ... will be in Black Stone Harbour ... something ... Days'* Now, that sounds to me like whoever they are was trying to arrange a *rendezvous* with us," Marlon concluded.

Hal tried to keep his combination of shock and excitement under control. The implications of this were staggering. Not only was someone living up on the surface world, but they had a working radio, they had been listening to RSAV operations enough to know what frequency to call out on, *and* they wanted to meet. Hal rubbed at the back of his neck.

"Pilot," Hal began, looking squarely at Jonas, "firstly, allow me to apologise in front of everyone for doubting you. You were right, you heard what you reported and I was wrong in considering anything else."

Jonas shrugged. "Do not sweat it, Skipper. I was not sure I believed myself, and I hardly started this cruise out in the most reassuring way." Jonas quirked a broad grin at Hal.

As Hal turned towards Christopher, from the corner of his eye, he noticed both Jonas and Cordelia look at each other with a grin and then both look away while reddening slightly. He opted not to comment.

"Mister Olivier, excellent work. This is exactly the kind of preparation, planning and presence of mind that I have learned to expect from you, and you delivered the goods, well in excess of expectations this evening. Your visible commitment to top-notch performance has done you well, yet again. You have likely just put this ship into the history books," Hal stated.

The usually stoic Chief Armsman lifted an eyebrow while looking back at Hal. "Ah, well, thank-you Captain," he began slowly, as though actually caught unprepared. "I am, ah, glad I could contribute," he said somewhat stiffly, punctuated with a polite nod.

Hal noted Ise Koolen eyeing the Chief Armsman with a similar expression than the one Christopher had just given Hal. He glanced around the room before continuing.

"As of an hour ago, our mission profile has changed. In the morning, we are going to be getting copies of the logs from the Arr-Eee-Arr's, and analysing them. With some luck Miz Baasch and Mister Zupan will be able to get a simple fix on the transmitter. From there, we will make an assessment about our next course of action."

Hal looked over at Damiano and then continued "Doctor, please start considering contamination and quarantine, if you have not already. Chief Pryce, please work with Counsellor Koolen to try and sort out where 'Black Stone Harbour' might be. Miz Baasch, all Ess-and-Dee Operations are suspended until further notice. Mister Olivier, please ensure the ship is ready for combat."

There was a pause and Hal ran his hand back through his hair. "That was an order I was hoping to never give. However, here we are. We have no reason yet to consider whoever they are hostile, but we have an awful lot of history to suggest they may not be friendly. Until further notice, this ship and crew should consider themselves in a full-fledged Contact Event. I have no interest in a repeat of Aquarius Reach. Any questions?" Hal asked.

# CHAPTER ELEVEN
## *History On The Wind*

### Damiano
**03h58 SST**
**Friday, April 29th**
**Vicinity 42.4N,71.1W**

Damiano Émile closed the medical book, leaned back in the chair at his desk, looked at the ceiling and gave a heavy sigh. This was an absolute nightmare scenario, whether or not the Captain and the other officers saw it as such. Supposing that there was a culture living on land, somehow, against everything that the world of Soumerville understood, they then represented a seven-generation separation of microbiology.

In other words, a potentially substantial list of diseases that the crew of the *Sheerah* had never been exposed to and thus had no resistances to. Likewise, the crew of the *Sheerah* represented an equally lethal probable threat to those on the surface. Even if everyone involved were completely friendly and only wanted to conduct peaceful trade and diplomacy, there was a significant risk of genocide.

He pulled out a clean sheet of paper and picked up his pen.

*To: Captain Hal Lum*

*From: Ship's Doctor Damiano Émile*

*Sir,*

*You have requested my advice on how best to minimise the risk to the Sheerah and her crew in what is almost certainly a Contact Event, per pp 227 - pp 230, "Official Reclamation Services Standards and Procedures Manual".*

*I unfortunately must advise you that, based on current medical theory and my own professional opinion, any contact at all comes part-and-parcel with a tremendous risk of genocide to both sides of the Contact Event. Essentially, we are in excess of 150 years apart, in terms of our immune systems. What to us might be the Common Cold, might be as fatal as Ashen Fever to them.*

*Thus, the only way to properly minimise the risk is to avoid it. In other words, we must determine the areas that this supposedly 'top-side' culture inhabit, and then we do not ever go there. With regard to the apparent desire for a pre-arranged meeting, I can only emphatically recommend against it.*

*Since I am aware that you are potentially going to ignore this recommendation, I will state that the minimum we can do after a Contact with these "Top Siders", would be to not return home immediately. Modern doctrine from both epidemiology and general health perspectives would suggest that we would inform 45N50W that we are potentially contaminated. We would then remain outside Dock, on seafloor, using work-shack tethers for power and air, for at least two weeks.*

*This is standard contamination quarantine procedures, of which I am sure you are aware, pp 321-322, "Official Reclamation Services Standards and Procedures Manual". After two weeks without any evidence of outbreaks of unknown disease, we would be able to then return to Dock.*

*I will be requesting that the ship's company be issued standard broad-scope immune-system boosters, in tablet form, each morning as part of breakfast rations until we depart the current operations area. In essence, since we do not know where 'Black Stone Harbour' is, we must presume we are currently in it, for medical risk purposes, until we are certain we are not. Therefore, it is possible this area, and therefore we, are already contaminated at some level.*

*Any crew reporting even a mild fever, runny nose, scratchy throat or any similar "flu-like" or "cold-like" symptoms must be brought to Medical and Quarantine for immediate assessment and treatment. I cannot stress enough this must be without hesitation or worry about "false alarms". I would rather treat the entire crew for "nothing", then have any of us die because someone ignored what they thought was "just a sniffle".*

*I must now issue you the grim reminder that, statistically, it is your medical team who will be the first to succumb to any such sickness. Since we will be the ones in contact with everyone exhibiting any symptoms, without yet understanding vectors of propagation, et al., it is almost unavoidable that either I or Nurse Ji-Hye will fall sick, as a minimum. While I do not relish our job as the proverbial canary, and we will do everything within the scope of diligence to avoid this outcome, preparations must be made.*

*I therefore am requesting, as per pp 376-377, "Official Reclamation Services Standards and Procedures Manual", "one crew member per detail, including Officers as required, for addition daily pre-battle medical training, such that they may be able and capable of undertaking those tasks normally associated with the Nurse position of a Reclamation Services Vessel". I would request this daily training begin effective today, Friday, April 29, forenoon watch.*

*Obviously, beyond concerns about Top-Sider disease, there is*

*the detail that our history is littered with the names of victims of*
*previous contacts between we ocean-dwellers and the remnants of*
*Precursor surface cultures. I will close this letter with the remark*
*that while I am very capable of sewing up holes in my crew-mates as*
*well as mending their broken bones, it is essentially the least*
*favourite part of my job. I would encourage you, my Captain, to*
*avoid situations that might lead to such work on my part, if possible.*

    *Sincerely*

    *Damiano Émile*

# Jonas
## 06h39 SST

Jonas pushed open the hatch leading up to the stern section of the weather deck. He blinked a couple of times, letting his eyes adjust to the darkness. It was not much of a delay, since the entire ship was only using night-light red at this hour. He climbed out and closed the hatch gingerly.

There was not much sound, he noted. Just the water lapping and flowing past the *Sheerah's* hull as she idled in the tidal current, a bit of a breeze, and the infrequent sound of a seabird. Jonas liked the sound of seabirds, no matter what they were. Firstly, it was Nature's own kind of music, and it had its own rhythm and cadence. Secondly, somewhere along the arc of seven Generations of RSAV crews, it had been figured out that sea birds could sense a Green Fog before it was fatal to them. If there were not any in an area, that was rarely good news for the humans noticing their absence.

He made his way towards the stern, where the weather deck sloped to disappear beneath the inky black water. He sat down, knees under his chin, facing the starboard side, and looked up at the stars. A new moon and mostly clear skies had laid out the jewellery store of the Universe before him in a dazzling vista. The RSAVs two vertical stabilisers jutted out of the water, like a pair of metallic orca fins, a dozen paces across the water at his shoulder. He felt a mild thrum through the steel of the deck, and the water churned slightly to either side of the stabilisers, briefly suffused with a soft blue light; the autopilot triggering the thrusters to adjust their heading and position.

A hefty metallic clunk signalled the deck hatch opening again, and a similar sound a few moments later was its closure. Jonas looked over curiously to see who else would be up here at this hour. The Armsmen all used the forward hatch to come and go, so it was unlikely to be one of them. He was surprised to see Cordelia's distinctive figure moving his way in the starlit darkness.

The blonde Salvage Leader stopped a couple of paces away from him. "Fancy meeting you here," she offered.

"Uh, yeah, how about that?" he answered, feeling awkward. "Come here often?" he joked.

"Only on nights featuring cultural upheavals. It is a pretty restricted billing," she answered with a chuckle.

"Lucky me. Front row seats," he answered, feeling like he was both giggling in delight and juggling butcher knives in terror at the same time. "You, uh, I mean, feel free to have a seat, Cordie … lia."

She snickered audibly; he could not tell if it was at him or with him. She eased herself down beside him, outside his personal space. Not that he would have minded if she had parked herself against him and put her head on his shoulder. He had dreamed of that more than once. It would never happen, he knew, but he still dreamed.

"So what brings you up here at this time of night? Or, morning, I suppose," the blonde Salvage Leader asked him.

"I, uh, could not sleep. Just kind of wound up about everything going on." In the back of his head, he could hear Ise reminding him about "Big-T Truths". That was not exactly what had just come out of his mouth.

"Yeah. I understand that. I finished my Watch in the Comm, got a shower and then realised I was wide awake. No point going to my bunk," she said with a sigh.

The mental image of Cordelia in the shower brought a heat to his cheeks. He was very glad they were both sitting in the darkness. "Um, well, I am glad you came up for some fresh air, then. Did you, er, I mean, have you given any thought to what might be on the Arr-Eee-Arr's?"

She looked over at him in the darkness, most of her features lost in starlit shadows. She shook her head. "Not really. I do not want to get my hopes up. The odds of getting meaningful signal fixes are pretty low," she said. As she spoke, she reached up and undid the work-kerchief she had her hair put up in and let it tumble down. She stuffed the kerchief in a breast pocket and then finger-combed her hair lightly as she kept speaking. "We would need two minutes of signal for the gear to get a solid fix. Unfortunately, or fortunately I suppose, depending on your perspective, two sentences is not two minutes."

"I still think we should try," Jonas stated. From his point of view there was too much at stake to not know where that transmitter was, even if the decision was to avoid it for safety's sake.

"Oh, so do I, Jonas. Besides, it does not matter what we think, anyway. The Captain said we are doing it, and so we are doing it. If we can wring a plausible fix out of those logs, I do not care if it takes all day to do it, we will. I do not do anything half-assed or planned to fail, regardless of what anyone thinks," she concluded with a growl.

"I never meant you did, Cordie … lia. I was just wondering what your opinion was, is all," he replied, wondering how he had managed to put his foot in his mouth this time. She was visibly upset about something, and he was the last one to speak after all.

She sighed and shook her head. "No, no, Jonas, not you. I am sorry. I found out today that the Chief Armsman has a pretty low opinion about my professionalism and safety standards."

"What? He said that to you?" Jonas asked, feeling a bit bewildered. That made no sense to him. Why would Christopher lie to protect Jonas, and then bad-mouth Cordelia? It seemed obvious to him it would have been the other way around.

"Hmm? Oh, no, our brave Chief Armsman did not have the brass fittings to do that. Oh, no, no. One of his Techs is kind of sweet on one of mine, and they were talking on a break and she let slip what had been said in a briefing. So naturally my guy told me, because he was pretty pissed off about it."

"Oh, that is awful, Cordie ... Er, I mean Cordelia ..."

"Jonas, hang on a moment, would you?" she interrupted him, raising a hand in signal.

Emotionally, Jonas "braced for impact". He was pretty sure she was about to get upset with him for something he had done. He just nodded to her, keeping his mouth shut. He would just nod yes, apologise and cry in the shower later, if he had to. That was the usual routine when dealing with people he cared about, but did not know why they were upset.

"Jonas? Could you, I mean, Spirits bright this is awkward, could you please keep calling me 'Cordie', would you?" she asked with a sigh.

"What?" he asked, boggling intelligently at her. To Jonas, this was almost as improbable an event as hearing someone speaking on the RATT-net monitor in the middle of the night.

"Look, about the other night. I was completely out of line. I am sorry for how I acted. You are welcome to come to my shows, and you can call me 'Cordie', and what you do in your off-time is your business, not mine, and I need to learn to be less of a self-righteous, self-important bitch," she said quietly, intently looking off at the starlit shoreline in the distance.

"Um ..." Jonas began and then absolutely stalled. Had Cordelia Baasch actually just apologised to him? He was pretty sure that was what he had just heard. Maybe.

There were a few moments of quiet as the Armsman on upper deck rounds made his way to the stern of the ship where they were, a red-lensed electric torch in hand, checking around the water line and back towards the stabilisers. He then went back forward after a quick exchange of "hello's".

"I made a stupid mistake, Jonzie, and yes, I am calling you Jonzie, because its fun and it sounds fun, just like you can call me Cordie. I made a stupid mistake, Jonzie. I just sort of lumped you in with a bunch of other guys I have met singing at the Crystal Parlour. All they know about me is my bra size, my hip measurement and my inseam, and the only thing they care about my vocal range is what it would sound like muffled in their bedroom pillow," she said bitterly. "But that is not who *I* am;  there is an awful lot more to me than the show at the Parlour. I was so busy being indignant about that, though, that I did not stop to find out who *you* are."

She paused for a moment, before continuing on in a quiet voice laden with contrition. "In other words, I sort of did to you what I was mad about other guys doing to me. I ... I am sorry, Jonzie."

There was very long moment before Jonas could unlock his brain. Part of him was trying not to jump for joy, and part of him was telling him this was likely just a cruel prank. There was no way that Cordelia Baasch had just told him that she had misjudged him. Or that his having a pet-name for her was fun.

While he sat there, trying to sort out what was or was not a landmine or pit trap, she quietly got up. "Of all people, *I* should have known better, Jonzie," she said. "I bought into the whole RSAV Pilot mythology, because it was easy. You know; the flippancy, the drinking, the disposable relationships. I guess it is like Ise Koolen says; you can usually see what you look for. I only realised just a little while ago that you are nothing like any of that, if anyone gives you a chance."

As she turned to head back to the hatch, he found himself blurting out "I love your singing voice, Cordie. That is why I go to your shows; it is your music. Honest!"

She paused and turned slightly, looking back at him over her shoulder. The starlight showed enough of her features that he could see a smile on her lips, and maybe surprise in her eyes. "Thanks, Jonzie. That actually means a lot to me. I will see you at breakfast and then we can get those AMTACs pulled and reviewed."

"Sure thing, Cordie. Sleep well. I, uh, I will see you then," he offered, trying to sound pleasant and sincere. As opposed to emotionally unhinged and about to fly in all directions at once, which was how he actually felt. He watched her silhouetted by the starlight above and then the red night-light from below as she opened the hatch and went down the ladder. He watched the hatch swing closed and heard it audibly latch shut before he dared breathe.

"Big-T Truth. Yeah, right. How about I *not* do that?" he said aloud. Once upon a time, he too had been one of those dumb guys that had memorised the measurements of "Samantha Shameless", torch singer of the Crystal Palace. She was one-eighty-five tall, ninety kilos, and a damn near perfect, to his eyes at least, ninety-seventy-eighty-five hourglass figure. She was further graced with a solid "D" cup, and a remarkably leggy eighty centimetre inseam. She had exactly the kind of figure that, in the exact kind of gowns she wore, had a tendency to provoke open stares and wolf-whistles from the exact kind of patrons who went to a place like the Crystal Palace.

Jonas tilted his head back and looked skyward at the stars above, slowly being occluded by a creeping cloud front from the South. He had even had a couple of pin-up pictures of her at his place for a while; that sort of made his moral position a bit less defensible, he supposed. He had taken them down after a while, but they had been there.

He had to admit that when he first saw Cordelia as her "alter-ego" of "Samantha Shameless", music was pretty much the *last* thing on his mind. Truthfully, it was pretty much the same experience every time he saw her in her latest singing gown.

But, every time, all that mattered to Jonas when she sang was the music. He was pretty much convinced that if all she ever wanted to do in private was sing jazz, blues and torch songs to him all night, he would be a very happy fella.

Suddenly he could clearly recall Counsellor Koolen's advice to him. *"If you never tell her, she might never be interested. On the other hand if you do, then perhaps she might. Regardless of that, silence does not ever improve any aspect about a relationship between two people, Jonas. Besides, I did not say you had to run around posting bulletins around the ship, either. I said you have to be honest."*

He nodded to himself, and then rubbed at his forehead. Ise had told him that he had to be honest, but he did not have to volunteer to tell Cordelia things that were not immediately relevant. If she ever asked what he thought about her looks, he would tell her. But otherwise, it was all about everything else about her.

He blew a long exhale into the air. He had, apparently, just made a decision. He did not know where it came from, but it was a decision. He would no doubt live to regret it, but it was a decision. When they got home after this cruise, Jonas was going to ask Cordelia out to dinner and maybe to a music hall.

Maybe he would even tell her what his other name was. It seemed fair, since he knew hers.

# Hal
## 17h31 SST

Hal leaned back in his cabin's office chair, and set his pen down on his desk. He ran both hands back through his hair. The day so far had gone as close to perfectly as could be imagined, and yet he was still unsettled.

They had used one of the pair of inflatable dispatch boats the RSAV carried, instead of driving the RSAV ashore to visit the South shore Arr-Eee-Arr. Once the sun was up, they had sent the small boat in from their holding position, out in the approximate middle of the deep-water area of the bay. The boat crew was composed of two Armsmen and two Salvage techs. That ensured the best balance of skill and safety for the expedition.

They had switched AMTAC tapes in the Arr-Eee-Arr without incident, then stopped at the *Sheerah* to deliver the precious cargo. Then they had repeated the process with the North shore Arr-Eee-Arr.

Once the boat was recovered and the second tape in the hands of Cordelia and Jonas, that pair had spent a couple of hours simply fast-forwarding through the twenty or so hours of recording already on the tape, looking for signals. Then, they spent almost as much time in the O-Room doing a dizzying amount of algebra and trigonometry while looking at a two-metre wide chart of the area around 42.4N,71.1W. By the time the duo was done, they were convinced that there were in fact two transmitters, not one. The second transmitter had been picked up by the Arr-Eee-Arr's about ten hours after Christopher's transmitter was heard.

The closest was about thirty kilometres away to the Southeast, and the furthest was fifty in about the same direction. However, due to the brevity of both sets of transmissions, the margin of error was about twenty-five percent.

Working together in parallel to Cordelia and Jonas, Ise and Marlon had gone through everything in the *Sheerah*'s library, as well as Marlon's own books. The conclusion they had reached was that the current location of 42.4N,71.1W was likely to be Black Stone Harbour. Firstly, Precursor artefacts recovered in prior explorations of this area had a similar-sounding name. Secondly, there was really no other bay or inlet nearby to ascribe such an auspicious-sounding name to.

When combined with the proximity of the transmitters, it was hard not consider this a convincing argument. That brought him to the letter from Damiano. The Doctor was concise and absolutely unambiguous about the complexity of the risks facing even an entirely peaceful contact. How do you not offend a culture you know nothing about when one of the first things you have to say is *"please stay six metres away from me so I do not accidentally murder your entire home town"*?

The only thing that remained was to decide what to do. That was entirely up to him. He reached forward to his desk, and picked up the travel and fuel calculations that Marlon and Jonas had cooked up. They could follow the river for a sizeable portion of the distance, and then just simply drive the remainder of the way. It would be less than three hours to the probable location of the first transmitter.

The expenditure of resources for that trip was not extravagant, Hal mused. They would need to resupply on the way home, specifically fuel, but that was hardly unheard of. A spate of bad weather or a mechanical issue would cause that, even for RSAVs operating closer to home.

On the other hand, if things went badly on the drive or at the transmitter location, they would be between twenty and forty kilometres from the safety of deep water. The refuge of deep water had always been the greatest defence of the RSAV; the ability to just submerge, go deep, and ignore a threat. That option would be off the table. If something went wrong, they would be stuck inland with unknown circumstances to plan against, and with limited, dwindling resources to mitigate that.

Hal sighed and sat back in his chair. He rubbed at his eyes and then picked up the travel plan again, and looked it over one more time.

He *wanted* to do it. The name of the *Sheerah* would be engraved in the history books; an over land distance record, the first Contact Event in three Generations, plus whatever knowledge, diplomacy and trade might come out of that meeting. His family name would be toasted in Soumerville and beyond. His father might even realise that Hal had been right, after all.

Suddenly, Ise Koolen's voice was full in his memory from their talk the other night. "... *you need to walk away from your sea-anchor reflex to try and impress him out of his silence. Otherwise, one day, you will encourage someone to skimp on safety or common sense, and then what happens **will** be your responsibility ...*"

Hal closed his eyes. He took a deep breath, looked at the sheet of paper still in his hands, and then crumpled it.

He leaned forward, and flipped the switch on the Intercom and called the Command Compartment.

"Mister Zupan?" he inquired.

"Yep, Skipper," came Jonas' voice.

"Coordinate with Miz Baasch and Mister Olivier. Find us a quiet spot on the North coast of the bay that we can pull in a mixed profile of resources. We will work that area over, and then when the sun goes down, we are departing the Op Area. For home. Understood?"

There was a pause before the Pilot answered. "Yep, Skipper. Understood. That makes sense to me. Like you have said before, there is nothing out here worth getting killed over."

Hal flipped the intercom back to stand-by and sat back in his chair. He decided his father was going to hear about this, in person, when Hal got home.

# Cordelia
## 19h09 SST
## Temp 32C, Winds ESE 22 kph

She pushed her brass-and-leather safety goggles up from her eyes, and wiped a sheen of sweat from her brow. Cordelia exhaled through her nose and then took a deep breath. The mild, almost chilly breeze carried with it the smell of the salt, of sun-warmed mud flats, of fish and of the deep ocean. The sun was high in the sky, making the full gear that she and her Detail were wearing uncomfortably warm.

She licked her slightly dry lips and sighed as she realised that she was going to have to talk to Ise. Specifically, she was going to have to request that the Spirit and Morale Counsellor arrange a discussion and mediation session between she and Mister Olivier. She was still angry about what she had been told had been said in the briefing to the Armsmen. In addition, the general attitude that the Chief Armsman apparently held toward herself as Salvage Leader, as well as the members of her team, was unacceptable.

She turned a critical eye towards the two techs that were running a concrete cutting saw. They were carving up slabs of a ruins into manageable pieces that an electric "mule" then dragged over to a trailer-mounted crusher, operated by another Ess-and-Dee tech. From there the thumb-sized pieces were bagged to about one-hundred and sixty kilos each, then loaded onto an electric cart with a swing-derrick, and driven back to the load bay of the *Sheerah,* by yet another tech. There were two such teams working this site, totalling her full Detail of eight crew, besides herself. Not far from each of the crusher units was an Armsman, keeping a watchful eye on the surroundings.

Cordelia pulled her "safety-watch" out of her pocket and flipped the scratch-cover open. The safety-watch did not show time, *per se*. It showed how much time was left before the "safe window" for working would close, and they would need to start packing up to leave. There were just two hours left to pack-up time, which would leave them a thirty-minute margin to get back to the RSAV and onboard before the "yellow line" of one hour before sunset was crossed. Another hand sweeping around the clock face suggested it was about an hour that they had been working out here. She snapped the scratch-cover closed and fumed mildly. She pulled a brass and silver whistle from a breast pocket and blew a shrill noted on it. All of her techs looked in her direction, and she hand-signalled for a ten-minute break. Gear was powered off, goggles were raised, and filter masks pulled down.

Salvage Tech First-Class Anna Longo, Cordelia's second-in-command and infrequent nightclub wing-guard, came over to where the Salvage Leader was as she took a seat on a relatively flat piece of rubble. Anna was significantly shorter than Cordelia, but she was nearly the same weight; unlike Cordelia, that was almost entirely muscle. Anna sat down beside her, and took a swig from her water bottle.

"So," Anna began in a quiet but conversational tone, "what has got your knickers in a bunch today? You have been a right regulated bitch since breakfast."

"Watch your mouth, Tech, or the next time you have a club corset on, I will hook your sparkly nose chain to a tram car and let you go for a jog around the Ring," Cordelia replied in an attempt at a cheerful rejoinder.

"We really do need to get you some 'hysteria treatment' next time we are in port," Anna sighed and gave Cordelia a wink. "You have stress issues."

"I probably do, but those stress issues are related to lippy First-Class Techs and snotty Chief Armsmen, not whether I can get a handful when I want it," Cordelia muttered caustically in reply.

Historically, 'hysteria treatment' in the early Precursor period had essentially been a doctor-administered pelvic massage which was said to improve a woman's 'humours', reduce stress and anxiety and a few other benefits. Most of those benefits had more to do with orgasm than anything else, but for whatever reason the idea that women might derive some pleasure from intercourse seemed to escape early Precursor culture.

Then the phrase had been appropriated in late Precursor culture as a coy and somewhat derogatory joke about a woman openly being desirous of a purely sexual liaison, which for some reason was considered inappropriate. Again, the somewhat bizarre way that Precursor culture viewed women seemed to preclude the idea that women and men were sexual equals.

Now, in the modern world of Soumerville and its sister towns, the phrase was a silly, counter-culture saying, that was a way of expressing a woman's desire, or perceived 'need', for sex. It was commonly a slang between women, usually good friends, and usually light-hearted.

"Ah. You are still lit up about that, huh? Look, Officer Goon Gaggle is a gung-ho jerk, and we all get that, but you are kind of beating up on your Detail about it. It does not matter what he thinks, Boss. We all know who you are, we all do our best, we all play safe, we all try not to talk at the theatre, and we all get stuff done. Relax, okay?"

"Yeah, you are right, I suppose. I have just had it eating at me all day that maybe he was right, that I do play too fast and loose with the rules."

"Babe," Anna said with a smile, "I think you do not play fast and loose enough, and with a lot of things, not just rules. Do you really think that Captain Tight-Shirt would *not* say something if you were cutting too many corners?"

"That is Captain *Lum* to you, Tech. But yes, of course he would. He is doing everything he can to make sure we all stay safe."

"Right, like I said, Captain Nice-Ass will make sure the important rules get followed. You focus on getting holds filled," Anna chuckled.

"Captain *Lum* said that nothing we pull in is worth getting people hurt over," Cordelia said pointedly. It was pretty much common knowledge amongst the Detail that Anna was desperate to figure out a way to have a shower scene with Hal Lum. It was also common knowledge among the Detail that for all her cavalier and earthy talk, she always had an excuse why she had not just opted to approach him.

Hal, of course, was persistently oblivious. It occurred to Cordelia that in her off-time maybe she needed to get Anna into a dance gown at the Parlour and teach her a bit about lap-sitting.

Anna looked around and gave a two-fingered whistle that had the two women suddenly the centre of attention. "All right, Salvage, who was the last person to seriously screw up here?" Anna called out.

Reed's hand went up, she hung her head, and everyone else pointed at her.

"All right, Salvage, who was the person before that to seriously screw up in the shop?" Anna called out the second time.

Hernando Wiecenski's hand went up with a belaboured sigh, and everyone pointed at him.

"One more time, Salvage, who was the person before that to seriously screw up concerning job safety?" Anna called out the third time.

Everyone pointed at her.  Anna looked around, blinking.  "Hey now! No need to be like that," she laughed.  A ripple of laughter went through the Detail, and most of them gravitated towards where Anna and Cordelia sat.

"Ok, last question, Salvage!  Whose fault is that?"

"Yours!" Wiecenski laughed, "You are the goon that did not check the setting on the air pressure value."

"Hey now!  No need to be like that," Anna repeated, this time hamming being deeply chagrined.  Everyone laughed, including Cordelia.

Anna jerked a thumb at Cordelia.  "The Boss here thinks she has been letting us down.  Any comments?"  Cordelia's eyes went wide and her jaw dropped at the audacity of the question.

"Moose Jacking," Rainer Estalell suggested, and everyone sniggered at the bawdy-house slang.

"Pretty much, yeah, only maybe a bit more adult-like," Klára Reed said with a shake of her head.

Cordelia looked around at the eight Salvage Techs all sitting around her, and realised that everyone here was happy.  Including her.  She nearly did not know what to do with that realisation.

"Okay, everyone, no scrap; honest Detail business on the table. Anyone got issues that need to be brought up?"  Cordelia asked, feeling much better all of a sudden.  She wanted to make sure that things were as good with everyone as the jovial mood suggested to her.  She looked around at everyone, who were all looking around at everyone, and all shaking their heads.

"Yeah," Frazer Kingsley said after another moment.  "Now that you mention it, I think I am not entirely comfortable doing another mission with this kind of profile." A lot of puzzled looks went towards the Second Class Tech.

"What do you mean? What is the issue?" Cordelia asked, concerned.

"Well, apparently when stuff gets real around here, they seriously increase the calories on the menu," he stated flatly. "We do another one like this, I am going to gain five kilos!"

# André
## 22h52 SST

Armsman Third-Class André Lindo paced the deck of the *Sheerah* in the golden-red pre-sunset light. It was a beautiful evening and life was pretty good, from his perspective. They were on their way out of the bay, running on the surface, and heading home. This was going to be the last upper-deck rounds of the cruise. They had already pulled in the deck guns and caged them up. He walked past the bulk of the Command Compartment, heading forward towards the bow as part of his circuit. He took a deep breath of the warm sea air, savouring the smell.

So far, in spite of everything that everyone had been worried about, this trip had been quiet. He had been hoping for a little bit of excitement, admittedly. Being the newest of the Security and Weapons Detail, and working for someone like Chief Olivier, André vaguely felt like he had something to prove. He had hoped he would have gotten the chance to do something or be part of something that would have let him show to everyone else that he could pull his weight. On the other hand, no one had gotten hurt this trip, and the Chief said that was the best metric of the success of the Detail's mission.

As he reached the bow of the RSAV, he took a moment and looked around. It was a beautiful vista here; the open ocean spreading before them, and the ruins of the Precursor city laid out in a crescent behind. Ahead, at a narrow angle off the bow, he spotted the black bobbing head of a seal.

André Lindo had always loved seals. Most folk from Soumerville adored dolphins, but for him it was the seals that captured his imagination. On his Second, he was working towards becoming a Marine Biologist, and focusing on how seals could play a part in undersea life in some way.

He lifted his binoculars up and focused in on the seal in the water, interested to see what distinct markings it might have. What he saw was not a seal.

The black blot in the water was further away than he had thought. So, his brain had adjusted what it saw for the distance, telling him it was about the size of a seal. Looking at it via the binoculars, the detail revealed told a much different story. Firstly, based on the wave height for comparison, it would have likely been two-thirds his height if it had been on the deck beside him. He could see the object was sort of oval-shaped, dark in colour, and was drifting with the motion of the waves. It had spikes covering most of it; he guessed those would be the length of his forearm.

A wash of cold, primal fear flooded over him. It was an anti-ship mine. He had never seen one outside of a book or training video, but he was certain that was what it was. It was drifting right into the *Sheerah's* path; she would certainly strike it.

He could hear his training instructor's voice echo in his memory. *"Panic is the enemy of success. In the face of any danger, your priorities are always to 'Assess' the situation, 'Inform' command, and then and only then take any 'Action' appropriate. Assess, Inform, Act. That is your job as an Armsman on scene."*

He keyed his communicator and spoke quickly. "Command, this is Arms..." he stopped mid-start. There was no "bleep" to signify the transmission had started. There was no comforting hiss of an open circuit. His radio was dead.

He turned and waved both arms back towards the Comm, and then pointed towards the object. There was no change in the rumbling sound of the *Sheerah*'s turbo-diesel engines. He ran to the windows and shielded them against the glare of the setting sun, trying to look inside. He thumped the armoured glass with a gauntleted fist, and pointed at the looming danger. Nothing about the course or speed or sound of the RSAV changed.

In just a few moments, the *Sheerah* was going to die. He knew it. It was time for him to Act. "Be careful what you wish for," he said aloud with a suddenly dry mouth.

He ran forward to the very bow, unslinging his rifle as he went. He snapped open the breach, fumbled with his munitions carrier and dropped two armour-penetrating darts into the open barrels. He then closed the weapon to firing position with a jerked action. He pushed the pressure slider all the way forward, past "Lethal" and into "Anti-Armour", took careful aim against his shaking hands and hammering heart, and fired both barrels.

A wall of sound filled his ears, what felt like a tram-car hit him in the chest, his helmeted head hit the steel foredeck of the RSAV and he plunged into darkness.

# CHAPTER TWELVE
## *Connections*

### Alodia
**23h18 SST**
**Friday, April 29th**
**Soumerville**

Mission Services Mistress Alodia Holt stood at the picture window of her office, overlooking the Reclamation Services Graving Yard, where the *RSAV Emilia Lanier* was currently having two of her six turbo-diesel engines removed by cranes. What ever had happened to the vessel had not directly punched a hole in her hull, but the shockwave had battered and broken a whole laundry list of fittings, assemblies and systems. The water she had taken on was from a broken weld in one of the cargo modules' outer skin. The current repair estimate for a return to sea by the *Lanier* was past ninety days.

Miz Holt was, to most people's eyes, the stately image of a modern woman of power. Her current attire was composed of a sleek Prussian blue skirt topped by a complementary blouse in a slightly paler shade, which wrapped around her hips in a silver blue sash; the entire ensemble unified by silver and sapphire trim. Her greying hair was pinned up high and created with a jaunty cap. Silver and sapphire jewelry adorned her ears, throat, and left nostril. Her hands were folded behind her back, and she was motionless in the soft light of her oak and teak office. For all that picture might have been worth to someone else, she currently felt none of it.

A knock sounded at the door. "Come in," she ordered, still unmoving.

An aide entered the room, looking unhappy.

Alodia looked over her shoulder at the young man, a full generation apart from her in age and responsibility. "Still no word?" she asked, trying to sound as neutral as possible.

"I am sorry, but no, Miz. I checked with the Message Centre myself personally. All RSAVs currently on deployment have had RATT-net contacts within the past twelve hours, except the *Sheerah*. She has now missed both her sunrise and sunset radio check-ins," he said. Alodia must have frowned, or something similar, despite her best efforts because the Aide blinked and hastily added "The Signals Chief on duty at the Emm-See did say that, with the *Sheerah* right at the edge of her operational radius, it could just be poor weather preventing a connection." The young man was clearly trying to sound reassuring to her.

She turned away from the window, towards him, and offered a light smile. "Thank-you, Jamie. You might as well call it a night. You put in more than enough hours as it is," she lightly admonished him. "I do not wish your sweetheart thinking himself a work widower."

The young man bowed formally. "Thank-you, Miz Holt. He is very understanding of things like this cropping up. I will close up the front office as I go. I made you a pot of tea and some sandwiches; I can bring them in for you before I go, if you like."

Alodia broke in to a relieved smile, in spite of herself. "You are a darling, Jamie. I have no idea how I would run this office without you propping me up at times like this. Just put the tray on the table and then go home."

"Thank-you, Miz. I will see you in the morning. Try to take care of yourself, too," he reminded politely. She smiled at him and watched as he departed and then returned carrying a silvered tray of tea, sandwiches and treats. He insisted on pouring her a cup of tea and bringing it and a plate with a couple of sandwiches and cookies to her polished mahogany desk.

Once he had left, she returned to the window with a cup in hand, to once again watch the work on the *Lanier*. The evening shift at the Yard was just beginning; they would work until midnight local time, then everything would fall quiet until morning. Bright flashes of welders periodically lanced out, as an overhead crane slowly rolled along its tracks with one of the twelve-cylinder engines in its grasp.

The *Lanier* had made it home.

The *Sheerah* would, too.

# Hal
## 00h37 SST
## Saturday, April 30th
## Vicinity 42.4N,71.1W

"So, let us start with the damage report," Hal said, quietly. All of the officers were in the O-Room, the door was locked and the intercom was set to privacy mode. He was tired; he expected everyone else was as well. The past hour or more had been the chaos of damage control, casualty recoveries, and flood management. Things that everyone, other than Marlon, had practiced many times, but had never had to do for real. Then, in one violent moment, hours of theory and study became urgent application.

They were back in the middle of the deep-water zone of the Op Area, which everyone now referred to as "Black Stone Harbour". They had immediately turned back after the incident, if only so that Hal had the option of driving the *Sheerah* onto a sandbar to stop her from sinking. Even now, repairs were still being made, while repairs that had been made were being reviewed. The RSAV was buzzing with activity as the crew worked steadily to secure their home.

Marlon took a mouthful of water from his bottle before he spoke. His right eye had a bandage over it, and the bottom of his water bottle did too. The shockwave had introduced one to the other with significant force in the Engine Room. Hal had found out that Marlon had been carrying that bottle with him since the day he joined the Service in Gen-Six, hence the whimsical application of first-aid to it.

"Right, so, we are not dying," the Engineer began in earnest. "That is the good news. We are injured, but we are not dying. We had some sea-water get into the batteries, so we had to run emergency ventilation for a while. Latest assessment, still progressing as we speak, is that we are still good on fifty percent of cells. One Tee-Dee is past-tense; it is an ex-engine. It is an absolute miracle no one got hurt when the piston came out the top of the block and ricocheted around a couple times before deforming the aft emergency hatch. The aft emergency hatch, of course, is leaking; damage control solutions have restricted that to less than a tonne of sea water per hour, well within the capacity of automatic pumps.

"Two more of the Tee-Dees went into auto-shutdown, but we do not yet know why. Entirely possible just over-pressure from the blast, but since we do not know, those are tagged out 'Yellow' until they can be gone over in greater detail," Marlon continued. Hal winced; that was half the main power for the RSAV out of commission.

"Eleven other leaks, between hull and pipes, have been identified," the greying Engineer said with a gesture. "Dee-See-Ess has reduced those to around seventeen tonnes an hour at surface pressure. Again, that is within what standard hull pumps can manage. If we dive deeper than thirty metres, then water pressure will increase the rate of flow past our ability to pump out without special Dee-See-Ess.

"Of six thrusters, one is a write-off. The only thing we can do for it is pull into a graving dock and light a cutting torch. One more has a red card on it; estimated time to being serviceable is eight hours. One is a yellow card; emergency use only, repair estimate is three hours.

"Lastly is a laundry list of electrical systems issues; twenty hours worth of a variety of warning lights and failed systems. Everything from steering to climate control.

Hal wiped his face with a hand. "Ouch. Very ouch."

Marlon nodded. "Now, good news; about two-thirds of the flooding is because the cargo ramp-door is leaking around the seals. I strongly suspect if we get the Old Girl onto a beach and get the door open, then we can beat-bang-bend the issues out, pack the gasket with some expansion foam, close it up and get good enough closure to get us home.

"That is a 'one Engineer, and six other bodies' job that will probably take four hours. So, while that is being done, we can clear cards off the two thrusters, and maybe one Tee-Dee. At that point, we can stay shallow or surface-cruise with confidence while the other cards around the ship get cleared off. Then we can head for the bottom without worry once we are across the Great River Influence Zone."

Hal nodded. "That sounds like a reasonable plan for now. Doctor, casualty report, please?"

Damiano Émile picked up a clipboard, and flipped back and forth a couple of times between the top two pages before speaking. "First, Pilot-Navigator Jonas Zupan; concussion, cracked ribs, sprained ankle, black eye and scalding on his left hand and wrist. Officially, no door was involved," the Doctor said dryly with a side-eyed glance towards the Chief Armsman. "He was knocked off the ladder leading up to the

Command Compartment by the blast and was injured by the sudden arrival of the deck plating on Salt Flats. He was then further injured by the arrival of the coffee cup and its contents which he had left behind when he began his unplanned descent. I anticipate at least three days recovery time in Emm-and-Que." Hal did his very best to keep a straight face at the combination of the needling of the ever-stoic Armsman and the cartoonish description of the poor Pilot's misfortunes.

"Second injury, Spirit and Morale Counsellor Ise Koolen; broken arm, bruised ribs, sprained shoulder, twisted ankle. She broke Jonas' fall involuntarily. Currently in good enough mental health to be pursuing her duties from her bed in Sickbay by teasing the Pilot for being unexpectedly rough with women, and throwing himself into her arms," Damiano said, tapping his pen at an entry on the clipboard.

Cordelia burst out laughing at the description, and when everyone looked at her, she turned beet red and fell silent. "Sorry," she said from behind a hand, clearly still trying not to laugh. Hal sighed, and allowed a chuckle to escape him. "It is quite all right, Miz Baasch. Mister Émile is making the most of his floor time at this evening's unscheduled show," he said with a shake of his head combined with an amused roll of his eyes. Hal found the idea of the shy and mild Pilot-Navigator "throwing himself", in the usual connotation, at the rather conservative yet worldly Counsellor remarkably amusing as well.

Damiano merely gave a gracious dip of his head and continued speaking. "Salvage Tech Third Class Hernando Wiecenski, functionally suffering from a gunshot wound to the chest. The shockwave broke something that Chief Pryce will be responsible for later fixing. One of the currently missing parts to that item, a bolt of some description, was found lodged between the seventh and eighth ribs on Mister Wiecenski's left side. I am given to understand that the See-Eee-Arr-Aye does not want said bolt back, now that it has been surgically extracted. Mister Wiecenski will be in Emm-and-Que for at least a week; he will likely require time in Infirmary when we get home. He is currently sedated for comfort."

"Lastly, our hero of the day, Armsman Third-Class André Lindo. Allow me to preface my remarks by saying he is a very lucky man. Simple math says he was well inside one-half the atmospheric over-pressure danger-radius for an explosion of that type. He likely should be crippled, or worse. His actual injuries are a burst ear drum on his left side, multiple blood vessels burst around his left eye, mild concussion, bruised jaw, cracked ribs on his left side and a sprained wrist. He is expected to make a full recovery, but most certainly will need time at the Infirmary once we return home. Also, he is suffering from seriously injured self-confidence; he is extremely concerned about his career as an Armsman at this point," Damiano said, looking squarely at the Chief Armsman while tapping his pen on his clipboard.

"Care to explain?" Hal prompted.

Christopher Olivier looked back at Hal with a surprisingly icy expression. "He made an amateur mistake and nearly got everyone on this vessel killed, Sir. He failed to check the battery on his radio before he went on rounds. That is a breach of the most basic of Standard Operating Procedures. I will not toler..."

"That is enough, Chief," Hal said, interrupting sharply. "More than enough. Allow me to spell this out to you in detail, Mister; when everything went wrong, he made a snap of the cuff decision that *saved* the lives of this vessel and her crew.

Hal stood up from his seat and leaned forward, each hand resting on the table in front of him. "You are an excellent Chief Armsman, Mister Olivier, but if you are going to stay on this ship, you might as well learn to look with your eyes open. If the only thing you see in that young sailor's action this evening is a career-scuttling mistake, then you had better look again. If I so much as hear a *hint* of you taking administrative or 'unofficial' action against him, you had better have some damn air-tight explanation for it. Am I clear, Mister?"

There was a long pause before the Chief Armsman nodded and replied "Yes sir. Perfectly clear."

"Good," Hal said, folding his arms and drumming the fingers of one hand on his other sleeve. He looked around the O-Room to the surprised faces of his command crew. "Listen up. And I mean everyone present. At this point, all we know is that somehow a Precursor-era anti-ship mine got into our sail path. I personally find it very suspicious that the damage we suffered is similar to what happened to the *Lanier*. I can only conclude that it was, in fact, a mine that damaged her as well.

"That would be two RSAVs damaged by mines while leaving 'Black Stone Harbour' after detecting 'radio anomalies'. Until proven otherwise, I am presuming this was an intentional hostile action on the part of unknown parties. Perhaps I was not clear when I stated earlier that I wished this vessel to be made ready for battle.

"If Mister Zupan was falling down a ladder into Miz Koolen's arms, that means that this vessel was operating on autopilot at the time of the incident. In other words, dead radio or not, there was *no one* in the Comm at the time of the incident to take action based on the Armsman's warnings. I will speak to Mister Zupan myself later, but I want everyone here and now to listen to me.

Hal looked around the room, ensuring he held everyone's attention before continuing. *"Someone or something just tried to kill us,"* he growled sharply. "We know that there are members of what is apparently a 'Top Sider' culture in the area. This is no longer 'the usual' circumstances in which we operate. As a reminder, part of the battle footing for an RSAV is that Comm watches are doubled; two people per watch, and only one is allowed to leave the Comm at any time. It *must* be manned *at all times*. Go look at the Watch Chart and start bloody doing what you are supposed to. Am I clear?" he growled sternly.

A round of meek "yessir"'s came from about the room. He looked about at each of them. "Now, come sunrise, I will demonstrate why you would much rather have Mister Zupan at the controls," he said wryly. The last time he had steered an RSAV was in a simulator during his annual safety requalification. He frankly had no illusions that he was even close to Jonas' skill level. It was going to be a rough ride ashore, and he was already hoping he did not break anything else in the process.

"We will get the RSAV up onto the South beach, above the high-tide line, and get some repairs done," he continued. "Once that is done, we will try to get out of the harbour again. This time I want all stations closed up and ready for action. I want to be ready for another mine so that we can set it off at a much further distance this time."

"Miz Baasch, no Salvage Ops. Your Detail will be supplying assistance to the Engineers with repair work until further notice. That will probably be every day until we get home. Understood?"

Cordelia nodded at him. "Makes sense to me, Captain," she replied.

"Security, I want the full Detail up and ready for action from sun up until we get out into deep water. All guns, all walks. Presume that the mine was intentional and someone is going to try and finish the job while we are on shore tomorrow. Understood?"

The Chief Armsman gave a curt nod. "Yessir."

"Good. Chief Pryce, have the work plan prioritised from the moment we get parked. I want to get as much done as we can to maximise our sea-worthiness and minimise our stay on land. We are exceptionally vulnerable on land. At the point that someone knows what frequencies we use for RATT-net, it is entirely possible they have at least an idea of our strengths and weaknesses. I want to keep our risk exposure as low as we can while making sure that we are not going to get half-way home and have something break badly. Am I clear?"

"Absolutely, Skipper. I agree with you a hundred percent. I will have that work plan sorted out before I go to my rack," Marlon replied.

"Good. That is all for now, everyone. Please pass on my appreciation to your Details for a job well done in keeping the aftermath of that blast contained. Everyone pulled hard and that is part of why we are all still here. Tomorrow morning is going to be another hard pull, and then we are getting out of here and making best speed for home. We need to make sure that what we have learned does not die with us out here. Dismissed."

# Cordelia
## 01h18 SST

Cordelia stretched her shoulder and spine and then eased back against her chair in the O-Room. She exhaled audibly, and sighed. She fiddled with the book she had been trying to read, then closed it and set it on the table in front of her. She really should have been in her bunk trying to get some sleep, she knew. She looked up at the brass, glass, and teak wall clock; a bit less than three hours before she was supposed to go on watch in the Comm with Marlon. He was her partner for Comm Watches under combat conditions.

She picked up a piece of toast from her plate, and gave it a speculative nibble for the fifth time in twice as many minutes. She sat it down on her plate, yet again frowning at the fact it tasted like buttered toast instead of an almond mousse.

She was being ridiculous, of course. She knew that, which in turn only served to annoy her. She was stiff and sore from head to toe; like everyone else onboard, she had taken a bit of a bounce when the several hundred-tonne *Sheerah* went from eight kilometres an hour to dead in the water in her own length. Cordelia had taken some pain-killers and muscle relaxers as prescribed by Damiano, which thankfully had taken the worst of the edge off.

She looked around the otherwise empty O-Room. If she was honest, she was just a little bit scared. She did not know how anyone else felt, but she was scared. The grand adventure she had been on thus far in her career had just gotten deadly serious. This was the first time, outside of a single training exercise in a simulator, she had ever heard the phrase "ready for battle" on an RSAV. That was something you read about in books or in saw theatre dramas, from Gen-Two, or something.

It was hardly news to her, or anyone else, that being RSAV crew was a dangerous profession. Like every other Officer or Tech in the Service, she had taken the courses that taught her what to do and when to do it when things went to scrap in an RSAV. Fires, floods, broken bones, deep water dives, poisonous atmospheres, underwater emergency escapes, whatever; ostensibly, at twenty-five years of age, Cordelia Baasch was a highly trained professional.

For some reason, right now however, she really did not feel that way. There was an awful lot of ocean between Black Stone Harbour and Soumerville, and an awful lot of opportunities for things to go from bad to worse. Of course, she could not say that. Her Detail was looking to her for leadership and confidence. They needed to know that she fully believed everything would be okay, regardless of what she felt.

She really wanted to be back home, sewing sequins onto her new gown, or maybe rehearsing for the next show. She wanted to be doing something happy, she thought.

"Spirits," she said aloud with a shake of her head, "that sounds whiny, even for me."

She got up, and dumped the toast into the composter, and set the plate in the rack. She picked up her book and headed for the O-Room door. She decided that sitting here alone and moping was not going to improve anything. Instead, she was going to head down to Emm-and-Que to visit and chat with Jonas and Ise. That would cheer her up.

# Jonas
## 10h03 SST

"Care to explain to me what you think you are doing, Mister Zupan?" Hal asked from the hatch door leading into the Comm. He sounded fairly irritated to Jonas' ears, which was pretty much what the Pilot had expected.

"Getting ready to drive the *Sheerah* up onto the beach for you, Skipper," he answered, trying to sound chipper. He felt nothing close to chipper; between the pain from his ribs and his ankle, getting up the ladder damn near killed him. Just sitting in the crew chair at this angle required an effort to not grit his teeth. However, Jonas was pretty sure that if Hal suspected he was in any kind of real pain, he would find himself being carried back to Sickbay by a couple of Armsmen.

Hal had just come into the Command Compartment; Jonas had been in the Pilot chair for about fifteen minutes already. Mostly because he had not been convinced that he would not need most of that to get from his bed in Sickbay to his chair in the Comm. As well, if he was here already, he figured it made Hal's path of least resistance to let him stay in the chair.

When Cordelia had arrived for a surprise visit last night, Jonas had managed, along with Ise Koolen's unexpected help, to persuade her to meet him at the Sickbay door before sunrise and help him get here. Doctor Émile was completely against the idea, but at the same time was not willing to force the issue with a call for an Armsman. When Jonas had departed Medical and Quarantine, limping and leaning heavily on the Salvage Leader's taller frame, Damiano had made a glib comment about preparing the casualty clearing area again for the end of the Watch.

For her part, Cordelia was a lot stronger than Jonas had guessed. If she had any problem helping him down Salt Flats and then up the ladder, Jonas had not been able to tell. He had been leaning against her fairly heavily for the last third of the trip. He supposed it should not really have been a surprise to him about her strength and endurance; she was hardly a small woman, and he had seen her one-handing twenty-kilogram supply boxes in the past.

He glanced at her reflection in the bridge windows; turning to look at her hurt his neck. She was intently occupied with stack of paper at her crew station. He glanced at Hal's reflection to see the Captain heading his way.

Hal moved to stand just ahead of his left shoulder and then turned to face the Pilot, which was a bit of a blessing for Jonas; that angle did not hurt too much. The Captain folded his arms across his chest and gave him what could only be described as a remarkably disapproving look.

"Mister Zupan, I am fully aware of the extent of your injuries. You should be in Emm-and-Que right now getting some rest," Hal scolded him. "You must be in a significant amount of pain."

"Nah, Skipper, I had three or four shots of whiskey before I came up, so I am fine," Jonas said offhandedly, and gave a dismissive wave.

Cordelia audibly emitted a mortified "eeep" from her crew station. "Jonas!" Hal bellowed at him after a moment of shock.

"Joking! Joking!" the Pilot replied hastily. "Totally dry, Skipper!"

Hal glowered at him for a moment. "Explain to me why I should not have the Chief Armsman drag your injured backside down to Emm-and-Que, Mister Zupan? Allowing you to further injure yourself up here is of no help to anyone."

Jonas sighed and tilted his head up to look Hal squarely in the eye. "With all due respect, Skipper, you drive the Old Girl like she is an armoured car. Even with me all bent up, I am still a better driver than you are. Right now we have a whole lot of stuff busted, and more than just a few other things on the 'nearly busted' list. I am pretty sure that if you take the *Sheerah* ashore, you will wind up moving stuff from the second column into the first.

"This needs to be a finesse process," Jonas continued carefully, "and you are just not that good an RSAV pilot. Besides, I am going to wind up getting kicked around in pain either up here with my driving, or in a Sickbay bed with your driving. At least up here, it is my own damn fault," Jonas concluded forcefully.

Hal looked at him, expressionless and motionless beyond the drumming of one set of fingers on the other crossed arm.

"Captain," Cordelia began.

"Keep it to yourself, Miz Baasch," Hal interrupted without breaking eye contact with the Pilot-Navigator. "The expression on Mister Zupan's face suggests that with the amount of pain he is in just sitting there, there is no way he was climbing that ladder unassisted. Since you are the only other person here, you are teetering on the edge of falling on to my scrap list," Hal replied coolly. Cordelia fell silent; a glance at her scowling reflection in the windows suggested to Jonas it was mostly by willpower.

"So am I calling Engineering for power, Skipper, or are we just going to sit here in the middle of bay until sunset?" Jonas asked. He realised he sounded a bit more confrontational in that question than he had intended.

Hal pursed his lips for a moment before speaking. "Get us ashore, Mister Zupan," Hal answered sternly, and then turned to head to his command chair. "While I do appreciate your dedication to your job, once we are parked, I want you back in Emm-And-Que. I need you recovered as soon as possible, Pilot. We have an awful lot of ocean between us and home. Miz Baasch?"

"Yes, Captain?" Cordelia asked in a flat tone.

"Since I presume you got him up here, it is your job to get him back to Emm-and-Que. Understood?"

"Yessir."

Jonas ignored the jab of pain, and looked over towards Cordelia. To his surprise, she glanced over and flashed him a grin and a wink. Jonas blinked, trying to contain his surprise, and offered her a smile. He looked towards his controls, took a deep breath, and immediately regretted it.

# Christopher
## 11h08 SST
## 20C, Fog, Winds 11kph SSW

The sun had barely been up two hours and the warmth of the late April morning was already getting uncomfortable. Right now, that discomfort was being mitigated by a cool fog that engulfed the Op Area, as well as an onshore breeze. The *Sheerah* had rolled ashore about a half-hour ago, and the Armsmen, Christopher included, had been on full alert. The three operational thirty-eight millimetre gun turrets were deployed and manned; the fourth, it turned out, was jammed in the "stored for sea" position. They had angled the RSAV so that the dud turret faced the sea, and the other three covered the inland sectors as best they could.

Captain Lum was staying out of his business this morning, which suited Christopher Olivier just fine. He was still a bit stung over the dressing down he had gotten in front of the other command crew in the O-Room. Right now, however, other things were more pressing. He was down one Armsman, and one deck gun, and they were a hundred metres distant from the water in what he considered hostile territory.

The terrain here was broken ruins. Heaps of collapsed Precursor structures, mangled beyond recognition by time and tide kept lines of sight uncomfortably short from ground level. Trees and bushes also dotted the mess, growing out of any crack or crevice that might be vaguely construed to have topsoil in it. Many would have viewed this as the poetic expression of the tenacity of life in the face of adversity; Christopher viewed it as another complication to ensuring the safety of the *Sheerah* and her crew. The fog just made matters even more difficult, as it restricted visibility to around one hundred metres in any direction.

That left the job of spotting incoming threats to the trio of Armsmen on the deck guns, to take advantage of their roughly seven metre higher vantage point. One Salvage Tech was atop the Command Compartment, in the "crows nest" for more height, as well as just having another set of eyes on lookout duty. The remaining Armsmen, five plus himself, were working in pairs to patrol an arc about fifty metres from the parked RSAV. It was about as far as made sense, given the conditions.

"Scrap morning, huh, Chief?" Armsman Third-Class Valerie Bernet commented, from where she trailed along behind him. She was a gunner, but since her turret was the one that was unusable, Christopher had opted to pair her with himself to get a third patrol on the ground. Each patrol was a senior, experienced Armsman paired with a more junior, less experienced one. That maximised the learning opportunities while minimising the risks posed by inexperience. The Service Manual was full of great ideas, if you bothered to read it regularly, Christopher thought to himself wryly.

"Pretty much, Bernet," the Chief Armsman replied. "Just view the circumstances as an excellent personal training oppor..."

"Contact, Contact, Contact!" Armsman Gerstenheim's voice cried excitedly on the radio. "Patrol One, one individual, unknown gear, approaching from the West! He is walking right down the middle of a lane, no attempt to cover his approach."

Christopher whirled in place, pointed at Armsman Bernet and ordered "Assume cover-and-watch position, ignore my next converge order on the radio."

He then hit his transmit button while immediately breaking into a run towards the area west of the RSAV. "All Patrols, All Patrols," he barked into his microphone, "hold position, assume cover-and-watch positions. All Third-Class, converge on West sector, mission is to support Patrol One. Do not fire unless fired upon. Weapons check; on the ground, non-lethal with double bull-dog. Thirty-eights, tray of smoke in the mount, tray of Moose on ready, set non-lethal. Patrol One, start Contact hold-back procedures. Break, Break, Break. Comm, this is Security, we have Contact. Contact security perimeter procedures are in effect. Request the Contact Team in West Sector."

"Patrol One, starting Contact hold-back, will call if deviation from the script," Armsman Gerstenheim answered.

"Security, this is Comm," came Hal Lum's voice, sounding on edge. "We are mustering the Contact Team and we will meet you in the West Sector."

It was the longest hundred-metre dash in full gear that Christopher Olivier had ever done. He was brutally aware that this was very likely to be a set-up; put one attacker in the open and visible to draw attention, and then hit from another angle. Which meant that right now, he was probably leaving one of his other two senior Armsmen to get slaughtered by that off-angle attack.

"You cannot play chess with an enemy you do not know," he reminded himself as he came to a halt near the two Armsmen of Patrol One. He glanced around, visually confirming the situation.

Gerstenheim gestured to the subject of the excitement, now sitting cross-legged in the middle of the ruined road. The other "Armsman" was in fact an on-loan Ess-and-Dee Tech; officially, in the Service, "*everyone is a Sailor, everyone is an Armsman*," before whatever Detail you actually made your career in. However, it was fairly obvious to

Christopher Olivier that the Third-Class Salvage Tech was struggling with the weight of the gear.

"Tech Niemcewicz, I want you to take up position over on that rubble pile over there, prone position. I want you to keep overwatch on our guest, and the direction he approached from," the Chief Armsman ordered her. "Armsman Gerstenheim, status?"

Everything about this scene had been carefully scripted and tested dozens of times over the years. Every Armsman could recite it rote from memory.

First, one Armsman steps into view and into path; weapon muzzles down, body-language loose. Call to the Contact, friendly tone. Observe reaction of the Contact. Now wave, then hold up hand in a "stop" motion. Say "Stop". Repeat. Observe. Point at a spot a metre or two ahead of the Contact, point and then make a back-and-forth gesture, hands low about waist level, to describe a line. Say "No closer, please." Now signal stop. Say "Stop". Repeat both steps again. Observe. If the contact complies, give a thumbs-up and then pat over your heart with the opposite hand. Say "Thank-you." Repeat.

If at any step the Contact does not comply, raise the weapon and start from the beginning, with the weapon aimed at them. If the Contact again fails to comply, the second Armsman reveals themselves, with their weapon aimed at the Contact, and then start over from the beginning. If the Contact covers more than one-third of the distance, fire one shot into the ground. If the Contact covers more than two-thirds of the distance, fire one shot into them.

Gerstenheim currently had his weapon in his off hand, pointed at the ground. "It took two tries, but he did what I signalled. When I drew the line, he just sat down where he is. He does not speak our language, Chief, but the hand-signals seem to work."

The Chief Armsman turned his head to look towards the raggedy looking character sitting in the ruined lane. Whoever he was, he was solidly built; even at this distance and under the heavy gear he was wearing, there was no question of it. He had what looked like a spear and a linear-bow laying on the ground in front of him; neat, evenly spaced, perpendicular to the line between himself and where Christopher stood. A man proud of his weapons, and openly declaring that he had them.

The rest of the man's attire was a mixture of animal furs, worked leathers and either plastic or metal plates. The plates were easily identifiable as armour; anywhere there was a pressure point or a vital organ, there was a plate. The rest of the softer stuff was comfort and cover. This was a warrior. Christopher did not even need to guess. Was this their mystery voice?

Marlon Pryce and Hal Lum arrived, panting slightly at the speed they had moved to get here in a reasonable amount of time. Bringing up the rear was Nurse Ji-Hye, with a field medical kit on her back. Each of the trio were carrying a thirty-centimetre diameter impact blocker on one arm made of a translucent material, and riot-stick with an enclosed hand guard, the same as the Armsmen all were. If they were attacked in hand-to-hand while ashore, they could defend themselves.

"Damn, Skipper! Keep in mind you are half my age," the greying Engineer grumbled.

"You should have twice the experience I do in sprinting then," Hal countered. "Mister Olivier, situation report, please."

"Situation is passive and on-script, Captain. Contact is one individual thus far," the Chief Armsman replied, gesturing towards the figure in the street, "who does not speak our language, but has complied with signalled instructions. He is armed, armoured, and carrying enough gear that I would say he is on some kind of a long-distance trip. One moment, Captain." He keyed his microphone. "Armsmen, this is Chief. Guns, call your sectors."

"East clear."

"South clear."

"West, one Contact, under procedures."

"Patrols, check in," Olivier ordered.

"One, one Contact, under procedures," Gerstenheim answered over the radio, even though he was just a couple metres away.

"Two, clear."

"Three, clear!" came Bernet's voice.

Christopher looked at Hal. "This is it. The rest of the area is clear at this time."

Hal looked at Marlon, his expression serious and his tone grave. "You are on, Chief. Please say hello to the man."

Marlon nodded, had a quick sip of water, and shouted something short and incomprehensible, beyond Marlon's name, in what Christopher presumed was Precursor.

Much to the Chief Armsman's surprise, their visitor clearly perked up. He cupped his hands over his mouth and called back. Marlon looked somewhat puzzled.

"He says his name is 'Exile'," the Chief Engineer said slowly, "and there are a group of hunters chasing him."

Echoing out of the fog ahead of them was the unmistakable whinny of a horse, and the sound of metal clanking. The man calling himself "Exile" slowly picked up his spear and linear bow, stood to his full height, and turned to face that direction. Christopher had seen that body language before, in people sentenced for crimes; that complete defeat, that acceptance of fate, whether it was deserved or undeserved.

The Chief Armsman's military mind raced through what he knew. Why was "Exile" here? If he was being chased, why run right into the face of another culture? Why radio ahead? Why just sit down at first meeting?

"'*The enemy of my enemy is my friend*'", he breathed in sudden realisation. "Captain, Sir," Christopher said forcefully, "I am pretty sure he thinks they are going to kill him. I am also pretty sure that he thinks that if we do not interfere, those 'hunters' will do it right in front of us."

# CHAPTER THIRTEEN
## *The Ironclad Kingdom*

### Hal
**11h11 SST**
**Saturday, April 30th**
**Black Stone Harbour**

"That is simply not going to happen while we are here," Hal stated flatly. "Mister Pryce, please ask 'Exile' to reduce the distance between us by half. Mister Olivier, prepare to take action on my order."

Saving lives, no matter whose they were, was part of the credo of being an RSAV crew. Since Generation One, Captains and Crews alike had been stepping into harms way instead of walking away. Hal Lum was not going to change that now.

Emerging from the veil of fog came more than a dozen figures. Each was dressed similarly to Exile. A couple carried banners on poles; the iconography was a red and blue background with a white star occupying the middle third, and a black cross on the star. Hal had never seen it before. One of the figures rode a horse, and completely dominated the unfolding scene.

Hal had never seen a horse before, in person. They did not have them in Soumerville, of course; too resource intensive for not enough return. He had seen pictures in books, however. The pictures failed to approach the magnificence of the creature he now beheld. It was a remarkable beast of dark hair, lean muscle, and liquid grace.

The rider and steed were dressed in a more elaborate version of the armoured leathers that Exile and the others wore. It was adorned by hints of silver and gold hues, as well as gem tones, and flickered in the foggy sunlight.

The rider and the others with him were all armed; spears and what Hal guessed were the above-water version of a speargun, called a 'linear bow'. As the approaching group collectively saw Exile, several of them raised weapons and shouted at him. Exile, for his part, kept slowly backing up, towards Hal and the rest of the *Sheerah's* crew.

"Mister Pryce, please introduce us, and inform them that we would like them to lower weapons before any misunderstandings happen. Mister Olivier, if any of them fire on Exile, drop them with bulldog rounds, please."

Both men acknowledged and acted on their orders. Marlon shouted out in their language via cupped hands. Christopher and the Armsmen all made a point of cracking open their weapons, checking the loads, and snapping the breaches closed. Visors got lowered, as well.

Hal took two steps forward, ahead of the rest of his crew. He wanted it obvious who Marlon was speaking for. He offered the man he considered his opposite number in this emerging standoff a polite salute.

Unexpectedly, laughter and what could only be described as a chorus of unfriendly replies greeted his action. The Horse Rider barked back a harsh-sounding answer coupled with a sharp gesture. Hal was puzzled. A certain amount of grandstanding was expected; both leaders needed to establish their authority over their part in this encounter. Hal knew that. But something akin to hostility already? Hal glanced towards Exile, wondering exactly who he was and what he had done.

Marlon cleared his throat uncomfortably. "Uh, well, Captain," the Engineer-now-translator began slowly. "I will spare you the direct translation; it was rather coarse."

Hal raised an eyebrow. That was not an encouraging start to the encounter.

"In short, their leader says that 'Exile' is a criminal of the 'Ironclad Kingdom' and if we protect him, so are we. In addition, because you are dark-skinned, he refuses to deal with you; he said something about inferior genetics and only being fit for draft labour. On the other hand since I am light-skinned, but old, he will listen to me, but I need to be careful in my 'respect' or he will have me killed."

Hal looked at Marlon, feeling completely flummoxed. "What? What does my skin colour and your age have to do with anything?"

"So-called 'Racial Profiling' is part of the Precursor mythos," Marlon explained, while watching and listening to the Horse Rider. "The Precursors believed that lighter skin, lighter eyes and lighter hair was a sign of 'genetic purity', and thus points of both social and economic privilege and entitlement. Their entire society was founded on it; economics, the design of their cities, the kinds of work an individual was permitted to do. Additionally, youthfulness was worshiped, while age was associated with a decay of social relevance and economic standing."

"That is absolute rubbish," Christopher growled, watching the group across the no-man's land between them.

"Of course it is," Marlon replied with a shrug. "But it is part of what they believed. Apparently, this group adhere to those ideals."

The Horse Rider was bellowing something and shaking a fist in the air, while prancing his steed back and forth in front of his allies. Marlon frowned. "He seems to be reciting a family linage," the Engineering

Chief said. "These clowns are right out of a Precursor Studies text; blood-lines determined wealth, political power and even if the public laws of the land applied to you or not. He seems to be expecting us to be awe-struck by his being part of the 'Barusch' family tree of the 'Ironclad Kingdom'."

Hal rubbed at his forehead. This entire situation was going to go badly, and he could already see it from here. The Horse Rider was some kind of irrational zealot, parroting the beliefs of a bygone era, whether or not they made any sense at all. "Mister Pryce," the Captain began patiently, "please tell 'Mister Barusch' over there that since 'Exile' is a criminal to the 'Ironclad Kingdom', we will be happy to take the problem off his hands. We are happy to pack our bags and get out of his territory in the next hour or so. Also please let him know that while we have no interest in conflict, we do have the means to defend ourselves."

Hal watched the group opposite them while Marlon shouted by cupped hands. He noted that Christopher Olivier immediately stepped in front of the Engineer as he finished speaking.

A chorus of derisive shouts and howls was the reply, followed by the Horse Leader pointing across the no-man's land towards the *Sheerah's* crew. Hal could clearly see the scathing demeanour in the gestures.

Marlon sighed. "Mostly invective and mockery, Skipper," he said, sounding apologetic. "None of it particularly creative or worth repeating. The short version is he refuses to acknowledge your authority in anything here because of your skin colour and if we do not turn tail, abandon 'Exile' to 'justice', and leave Miz Ji-Hye as 'tribute', they will slaughter us."

Hal's eyes narrowed. "Mister Olivier, get that ass off his figurative and literal high-horse, would you?" he requested in a growl that resulted in Marlon giving him a side-eyed glance. Hal was aware he was verging on losing his temper; the entire notion of leaving any of his crew behind to satisfy some bunch of Top-Sider barbarians' threats infuriated him. However, he needed to do his best to stay cold, calm and calculating to minimise injury and insult to both groups. He took a deep breath.

"With pleasure, Sir," was Christopher's snarled reply.

"Mister Pryce, as soon as the kinetic message is delivered, please tell them that anyone advancing, aiming weapons, or anything else I do not like the look of will get similar treatment," Hal ordered. Marlon nodded.

The Chief Armsman raised his Variable Rifle in one fluid motion and fired both barrels simultaneously the instant the stock was against his shoulder. The two projectiles, hollow-cored and made of a rubber-like bio-plastic, slammed into the Horse Rider. The Armsman's target tumbled backwards out of the saddle, landing flat on his back. The Chief Armsman was already reloading by the time his victim had hit the ground. Christopher keyed his microphone and said "All Patrols not in West sector, converge now. Weapons check; load one smoke, one whistle. Follow-up will be bulldog. All patrols, fire policy is aggressive self-defence. Relay fire, by number."

Stunned shock fell over the group opposite them as they watched their leader convulsing on the ground, clutching his chest in the area of his solar plexus. Two of Horse Rider's followers moved to assist him. A trio of others made an attempt at running with brandished weapons towards Exile and the RSAV crew beyond, only to be similarly picked off.

"Thirty-Eights, smoke wall, three-quarter range, fire now!" Christopher ordered into the radio. Behind them by half a football pitch, the three hull-mounted guns opened fire, each unloading their five-shot tray of shells in half as many seconds. Each round was subsonic, and made a shrieking hiss as it passed over them. The guns each spread their shots in a left to right pattern; each shot began belching clouds of thick orange smoke into the air from the point of impact. Within a few moments, the breeze carried the streaming clouds into the midst of the Top Siders obscuring them completely. Sounds of chaos and anger reached the ears of Hal and his crew.

"Mister Pryce, please tell them anyone stepping out of that cloud is going to get badly hurt," the Chief Armsman requested.

Marlon glanced at his Captain. Hal nodded, and the Engineer-now-Diplomatic Translator complied.

"I suggest we get out of here, Captain," Christopher Olivier stated. "The thirty-eights are reloading with moose rounds; but that will likely kill any of them they hit, so I would rather not use them for direct-fire. Our bulldog rounds deliver a good punch, but the worst it will do is crack a rib. They will get back up in a moment once they can get air back in their lungs. Unless we want to go lethal, they outnumber and out-stupid us, and that means we are more and more likely to come out poorly, the longer this goes on."

"I would tend to agree. Mister Pryce, please tell Exile to get himself over here double time, and let us get ready to retreat back to the *Sheerah*. We will get off the beach as we are, and find somewhere else to put up for repairs."

As soon as Marlon had shouted Exile's name, a group of figures charged out of the smoke screaming in fury. A couple had axes, the others had linear-bows. Shots from both sides of the battlefield flew through the air; Exile fell with a projectile jutting from his leg. Marlon clutched at his guts and tumbled to the ground with a choked cry of surprise and pain. Every one of the visible Top Siders were struck down, one rag-dolling backwards like he had been hit by a tram-car; one of the thirty-eight gunners had fired.

"Nurse Ji-Hye, take care of the Chief! Mister Olivier, the Security Detail are authorised for lethal pressure setting. Everyone hold position. Mister Olivier, you are with me!"

Hal unhooked the riot-stick from his belt, raised his impact blocker, and charged into no-man's land heading towards the injured mystery known only as 'Exile'.

# Christopher

Chief Armsman Christopher Olivier had barely repeated the order to dial up the pressure settings on the Variable Rifles when Captain Hal Lum bolted towards the wounded non-crewman about twenty metres ahead of them. It took him an eternal split second to fully comprehend that his captain had just volunteered to die in the name of saving the life of a stranger. It was barely another eternal moment longer before the Chief Armsman sprinted after him.

"Cover me!" the Captain bellowed at him.

"Yessir! A bit more warning next time would be good!"

"If I have some next time, you will get it, Mister!" Hal shouted back.

The pair reached Exile, who had dragged himself behind enough rubble to provide minor cover. Linear-bow shots periodically flew out of the smoke and figures could be seen moving around in apparent confusion.

"That smoke only lasts a little while longer, Captain. We only have so many rounds of it with the thirty-eights. When it blows out, we are dead men," Christopher stated.

Hal nodded. "You had better hope I work quickly then," Hal replied grimly as he pulled a bandage pack out of the first-aid pocket of his ship-suit. He began working to bandage Exile's wound, immobilising the forearm-length projectile shaft jutting out of the meat of his thigh, even as the other man eyed the other pair fearfully.

Christopher ground his teeth and queued his microphone. "All Patrols, all Guns, crowd control volley; split mixture of smoke and whistles. The Captain and I are in the middle of this. Keep them off us. After the crowd control volley, set lethal pressure and bulldog ammo."

A fusillade of shots flew over them; the whistle rounds were a less dangerous bulldog variant that screamed like a bird of prey as it went past. The primary use for the round was to scare animals. Based on the ruckus from the Top-Sider group, they worked against this particular group of animals as well, Christopher thought caustically.

The Horse Rider charged out of the smoke, astride his horse at a full gallop. In his grip he had a long-handled, spiked club of some kind. His destination was unmistakable; he was heading straight for the trio trapped in no-man's land.

"I will feel bad about this later," Christopher muttered, cranked the pressure setting to 'anti-armour' and coolly shot the mounted man in the face, with both bulldog rounds.

The Horse Rider's head snapped back and his helmet flew off at an awkward angle with a splatter of blood marking its arcing flight. The rider hit the ground solidly in a tumbling heap, and was still.

With the right ammunition loaded, the "anti-armour" setting on a Variable Rifle would drive a nineteen millimetre diameter dart through a sheet of steel. With the soft, squash-head bulldog round, it would be like getting hit full-force in the face with a cricket bat a couple of times.

If the pair of projectiles had somehow not killed the Horse Rider outright, and the fall had not broken his neck, then Christopher still knew that internal injuries would likely finish the job within a day or two, short of expert medical care. For his part, Christopher would try to feel regret about that choice once there were fewer howling barbarians trying to kill him and his Captain.

The horse whinnied in fear, and careened past the pile of rubble that Christopher was kneeling behind, adjacent to the Captain and the injured man. It passed by him so closely he could have reached out and touched the rippling flank of black hair, muscle, armour and flowing tail if he had wanted to. He could not help but watch in awe as the beast veered off at a full gallop and vanished into the mists away from both the battle and the bulk of the RSAV.

Projectiles from linear bows were regularly bouncing off the front of the rock pile they were hiding behind. He glanced over at Hal and Exile, to see that Hal had trimmed the thick, arrow-like projectile off about ten millimetres above the skin and clothes, and had it solidly bandaged. Hal was putting away a now-empty needle of painkillers, and Exile's eyes were already glassy.

The wall of smoke was a double-edged sword. It meant that the enemy had no clear targets to fire on. It also meant that anyone darting forward to press the attack were clearly exposed to the group of highly trained Armsmen. On the other hand, it meant that Christopher had no idea how many enemy were still standing, what they were aiming at or how they were moving. They would be idiots to not be trying a flanking manoeuvre right now, given their superior numbers.

Almost immediately after that thought had crossed his mind, one of the deck guns fired three shots at something off to his left; two bulldogs and one whistle from the sounds the ammunition made. He glanced over to see concrete dust pluming into the air, but no enemy were visible.

"Captain, if we do not move soon, we are going to get flanked and murdered here. We do not have the man power to cover all the angles against this."

"I know, Chief. I will have to rescue-carry Exile back. You will have to bring up the rear and keep them off us," Hal replied grimly. It was clear from Hal's tone that he understood the peril they were in. There was no regret or remorse, just a clear understanding of the situation. Christopher was surprised at just how calm and straightforward

Hal was under the circumstances.

Suddenly a tremendous roar filled the air as the *Sheerah's* several hundred-thousand watts of working turbo-diesels wound to life. Christopher glanced back over his shoulder at the RSAV; uncharacteristic plumes of black smoke belched into the sky from the vents on the aft deck, probably ten metres into the air. The RSAV lurched, turned in place towards the battlefield, and surged forward.

Jonas *had* to be at the helm, Christopher thought. No one else would even think to use an RSAV that way. The massive caterpillar belts, combined with the several hundred-tonne mass of the machine, simply ground everything it drove over into scrap.

Shouts of terror emerged from the smoke; two figures ran out. They halted, jaws agape at the sight of the massive machine rolling forward, flattening a rubble pile without pause, snorting smoke into the sky, and with the echoing sound of the howling engines filling the air. Before anyone had a chance to shoot them, they both turned and ran back into the smoke shouting and waving their arms.

The *Sheerah* somehow spun around and kept moving, now in reverse, towards the trio in no-man's land. The one functioning, stern-facing, deck gun was now firing an alternating pattern of whistle and smoke shells constantly, into the confusion of the smoke itself. Jogging along at the sides of the bulk of the lumbering machine was the entire Security Detail, injured or not. They advanced in a hunched-over jog with their weapons shouldered, scanning for targets and firing at anything that was unfortunate enough to be vaguely glimpsed.

In short order, the RSAV was parked behind them and the Security Detail was hustling the now-rescued trio around to the cargo ramp. At the top of the lowered ramp, with a Variable Rifle in hand, was the Salvage Detail Leader, Cordelia Baasch.

She gave Christopher an apologetic look. "Sorry to steal your thunder, Chief. I know you probably had that whole thing under control, but it looked to me like you could use the help, and Mister Zupan agreed."

# Cordelia
## 11h59 SST

"That was some amazing rubble-rolling, Jonzie," Cordelia said quietly. "I do not think I have ever seen an RSAV move like that before."

Jonas grinned at her from where he sat up in his Emm-and-Que bed. "I was highly motivated, Cordie. There was no way I was letting those goons hurt the Skipper and the Chief Armsman," he said in a fierce tone.

It was a bit less than three-quarters of an hour since the battle with the members of the "Ironclad Kingdom", as Cordelia had found out they referred to themselves. Once everyone was onboard the *Sheerah*, Jonas had aggressively driven the RSAV down to the waters edge and then parallel to it until the furiously working engineers had been able to get the ramp closed up and sealed "tight enough".

Hal had ordered the RSAV straight out to sea, and had every able-bodied Armsman and Salvage Tech on the upper deck with Variable Rifles as anti-mine lookouts. The Captain made it clear he wanted as much distance as they could manage between Black Stone Harbour and the *Sheerah* as fast as they could manage it.

Once they were safely out of the bay, without a mine seen anywhere, Hal had ordered Cordelia to get Jonas back to sickbay. The Pilot was starting to look pale from the pain he was in. Hal took over the Pilot chair himself and, thus far, had managed to not sink the RSAV.

Cordelia had no problem with her assigned task; Jonas was a bit shorter than she was, and only about three-quarters her weight, at most. She was fairly certain that she could have just rescue-carried him if she had wanted to, but that would have been a bit hard on his dignity. So, she had let him lean on her as hard as he needed, and set the pace, one hand on her shoulder and one arm around her waist.

Damiano was treating the injured when they arrived; once Jonas was back in his bed, Cordelia had been pressed into the role of medical assistant. She got a glimpse of the refugee that had caused such a stir; one of the only things she noted was that he was as tall as she was, which was unusual to her. He was mostly heavy muscle as well, with a chiselled jaw; it crossed her mind that he would have little problem attracting companionship in Soumerville, regardless of his preference.

Both the refugee and the Chief Engineer were unconscious in their beds, under medical sedation for now. Both were expected to survive, albeit with fresh scars and stories. Three other Armsmen had suffered injuries in the battle, and were also occupying beds.

The chaos in the Emm-and-Que Shack had abated, and it was now quiet, cool and dim, in spite of the hour. Damiano had said it was to assist in ensuring everyone got rest, and antibiotics had time to work on infections.

Ise Koolen, also in her patient bed, looked over towards Cordelia and Jonas, with an amused expression about her. "You are our very own hero, Jonas," Ise said. "I am given to understand that things were starting to look grim out there, from the Chief Armsman's perspective."

Jonas blushed slightly at the praise, and looked back and forth between Ise and Cordelia. "Well, it is not anything *that* special," he said modestly. "I mean, the tactic of using a Reclaimer for close ground support is in the Service Manual. It works better if you can drop the cargo ramp by only about two-thirds, and have a bunch of Armsmen with guns there, but, you do what you can with what you have got, right?"

"Jonzie, I think you are the only person I have ever met to have actually read that part of the Manual," Cordelia said with a laugh. "I had no idea that it was a sanctioned tactic. Even if it is, you are the one that pulled it off. That mid-course reverse was a bit of a wild ride; the engineers were cursing at you about that."

Jonas smiled and laughed. "I told you to make a warning call about 'heavy rolling'!"

"That is usually given at sea and in large waves," Ise giggled. "I expect no one quite anticipated your interpretation of it when you swapped ends on the Old Girl."

"*Phrasing*, dear Counsellor," Cordelia said dryly.

There was a blink as the Pilot and the Spirit and Morale Guide looked at each other and then back at the Salvage Leader. Jonas went wide-eyed and beet-red at the *double-entendre*, and Ise convulsed in giggles, with her good hand at her mouth trying to contain her mirth and her injured and casted arm pressing at her waist.

"Ow, ow! Ribs! Giggles and ribs! Ow! Miz Baasch, I may not like you right now! Ow!" Ise said, still snickering.

"It came out of your mouth, Miz Koolen. I just pointed it out," Cordelia replied, grinning.

"I do not believe you heard it that way," Jonas said, still red.

"Oh, please," she retorted with a roll of her eyes. "Between being a woman in the Salvage and Dive Detail, and a torch singer at a 'Gentleman's Club', I am pretty sure I have heard every dirty joke and innuendo in the whole damn town," Cordelia said with a laugh. "Innocence is not something I even *pretend* at, Jonzie. Get used to it, if you want to keep company with me," she said, giving him a saucy wink.

To her delighted amusement, the gesture just resulted in a rapid return of the Pilot's blush and stammer. She had to admit to herself she found him charmingly "adorkable" when he was like that.

Ise clearly enjoyed the spectacle as well, given a fresh round of giggles and subsequently pained complaints.

"So where is the Skipper taking us?" Jonas asked, after everyone had regained their composure.

"We are running up the coast on the surface at half speed; I think the idea is to go for about eight hours and then pull into a cove or inlet somewhere to finish repairs."

Jonas twisted his face for a moment while doing the math in his head. "So about a hundred kilometres, then. We really do not have fuel for that, but I understand what the Skipper is thinking. We cannot get down under without more repairs done, and we barely got started before the shooting began."

Cordelia nodded. "We have a lot of folks hurt, now, too. We need to get back home. This has been a terrible cruise," she said quietly.

"Once we get back to radio range, we can call for a *rendezvous* for supplies and a crew change, if we need," Ise pointed out.

"Like the *Lanier* did," Cordelia nodded. That made her feel better, now that she had been reminded that they were not alone to solve these problems.

"Exactly," Ise said. "We have the resources of the entire Service at our call, if we need it. The Top-Siders may be some self-styled 'Kingdom', but we are the Reclamation Service, with the assets of Soumerville and all of her undersea sisters to tap."

# CHAPTER FOURTEEN
## *Weathered Storms*

### Marlon
### 17h20 SST
### Sunday, May 1st
### 21C, Light Rain, Winds 21 kph ESE

Marlon opened his eyes, feeling a combination of groggy, disjointed and in pain. It was dark and cool, and his eyes did not really want to stay open or focus. He looked around slowly, realising he was in a bed in Sickbay.

This was good news; he was waking up and Damiano was a good doctor. From Marlon's perspective, this meant the odds of his continuing to wake up were very good indeed.

How did he wind up here?

He could recall being out with the Skipper and the Chief Armsmen, trying to save lives and avoid a wasteful fight … and then it all went fuzzy on him.

"Awake, Marlon?", Ise Koolen's warm, smoky voice greeted him. He turned his head towards the sound, to find her in a nearby bed, with a book in one hand and a cast around the other arm.

"Apparently so, Counsellor," he replied in a low tone. As his wits gathered around him, it looked to him like all twelve beds down here had someone in them. That was not good news.

"You took a dart from a linear bow to the abdomen, if I recall the good Doctor's commentary correctly," she said, sounding entirely cheerier than instinct suggested was appropriate for the subject matter. "Very lucky; all it cost you was your appendix, I believe. Your darling wife Annabelle will have a couple of new scars to marvel over when you get home; it was a sixty centimetre by eight millimetre projectile, with an end sticking out both sides of you."

"That would explain the bandages and pain in my gut, for sure," Marlon replied with a wince. "And how are you feeling, Counsellor?"

"Just call me, Ise, Marlon. Everyone is equal under the Doctor's care," the dark-skinned Spirit and Morale Guide said with a bright smile. "I am doing well. Another two or three days and I should be able to start getting around with a cane. I am stiff and sore, of course; I will need to spend time in the ship's gym to regain full mobility. Generally speaking, my most significant affliction is boredom," she concluded with a chuckle.

Marlon nodded and looked around again; Jonas was here, too, in the bed adjacent to Ise. Several Armsmen, a few Salvage Techs, and 'Exile' occupied the remaining beds. Other than Ise, everyone else seemed to be napping.

"He has been quite fascinated by me," Ise said, indicating where Exile was asleep. "And Nurse Ji-Hye, as well. And I mean more than just because we are a couple of pretty girls," she said with a quiet giggle.

"Oh, I am sure he has been, Counsellor. Based on what we learned of the Top-Sider culture we encountered, he has likely never seen anyone with skin the colour of either of you. If he has, it certainly has not been in positions of equality or authority," Marlon answered quietly.

"Oh! So those horrid stories about slavery, segregation, disenfranchisement and such in Precursor culture are true?" Ise answered, sounding aghast.

Marlon nodded. "Yes, apparently so; as hard as that might be to believe or swallow. I hope he is willing to learn a better way."

Exile stirred, apparently at the sound of the quiet conversation. He raised himself on an elbow and looked towards Marlon.

"<<*Thank-you*>>," Exile said quietly in the Precursor tongue, after a long moment. "<<*You saved my life.*>>"

"<<*Do not thank me yet*>>," Marlon replied. "<<*Our Doctor is worried we might make each other deadly sick.*>>"

"<<*Better here with you and your kind for while longer, than already dead with mine,*>>" Exile replied.

Ise was watching back and forth between the two men speaking. "His body language is ... odd. It is a mixture of fear, pride and remorse," she said thoughtfully, keeping her tone low to avoid waking the whole sickbay. "Could you introduce us, Marlon? Please offer him my welcome?"

Marlon nodded at her and then looked towards Exile. "<<*The lady is Ise Koolen. She is a counsellor, helping those with worries or anxiety find peace within themselves. She asked me to offer you her welcome to our ship.*>>"

Exile looked at Ise curiously for a moment. She smiled at him and offered a small wave to him. He returned the gesture and then looked to Marlon. "<<*Thank her for her kindness. How was she injured?*>>"

"<<*She was trying to save another member of the crew who was in danger.*>>" Marlon answered, opting to give a more heroic version of the truth.

Exile nodded, and looked back at Ise for a moment.

"What is his name, Marlon?"

"The translated version is 'Exile', Ise."

The Spirt and Morale Counsellor grimaced in obvious distaste. "That is very much *not* his real name. That is a name *forced* on him. What is his real name? Please ask him for me. I want to know," she said firmly.

"*<<She is wilful>>*," Exile suggested with a delighted tone.

"*<<You understood her?>>*" Marlon asked, surprised.

"*<<Her words, no. Her tone and demeanour, yes. She is used to having her demands met, I think.>>*", Exile answered, visibly amused.

"*<<That is our Counsellor Koolen, yes>>*," Marlon answered with a chuckle.

Ise raised an eyebrow, clearly aware that she was the subject of the amused conversation between the two men. Marlon had no doubt she would have folded her arms across her chest and glowered, save for the cast on one arm.

"*<<She would like your name, if you would?>>*" Marlon asked carefully.

"*<<I am Exile>>*"

"*<<She does not believe you. She says that might be your title, or your judicial sentence, but it is not your name. She requests your real name. I anticipate she will be quite stubborn about the request.>>*"

There was a stony silence as Exile and Marlon simply looked at each other. Marlon had the feeling he had possibly made a grave error in translation, or in cultural mores.

"Marlon, please tell him that he is safe here," Ise said fiercely. "His freedom might be restricted with us for a little while, but he is safe. I promise him that. What ever it is he is escaping from, where ever he is from, he is safe here with us. The Captain risked his life, and the entire Security Detail *fought* to make sure he is safe. He is allowed to have his name here."

Marlon repeated the message, watching the younger man in the bed adjacent to him. Exile, as he was known for now, was almost a full head taller than Marlon and easily out-massed him by a third.

Another long silence passed before Exile finally spoke. "*<<I am Veerhulm Klientan. Or I was. I am unsure that your Counsellor understands the potential cost to your people for offering me shelter and protection. The Kingdom does not like to be thwarted.>>*"

"'Veerhulm'? Oh, that sounds nice; very masculine. It suits him," Ise said thoughtfully after Marlon translated. "And I could not care less about that 'Kingdom'," she said with a wave. "If the Captain was willing to get into this fight, then we are *all* in this fight. We have been saving people left behind for seven generations; we are not going to stop now because yet another group of overbearing, self-important warlords might throw a temper tantrum," she concluded with a roll of her eyes.

Veerhulm laughed aloud, trying to keep his mirth to a manageable volume, at Marlon's translation. "*<<She clearly does not understand, does she?>>*"

Marlon tilted his head and raised an eyebrow at Veerhulm. "*<<I think, perhaps Veerhulm, it is you that do not understand.>>*" the Chief Engineer replied slowly. "*<<There is a fleet of nine ships like this one, in the city where we come from. Three more, even larger, are dedicated to travel and trade. There are more than a dozen-dozen such cities, dotted around the world at the edge of deep waters. If you wish to join us, then you are welcome to do so. We have more than enough space and*

*resources for you to be welcome. If not, then once you are in good health, we can drop you off somewhere on land that we know you will be safe from your old people. There is quite literally nothing they can do about any choice you make.>>"*

Veerhulm blinked at Marlon, visibly gobsmacked. "*<<And the woman Koolen has the authority to make such an offer to me? To assure my safety? Even at the risk of war?>>*" he asked, apparently not entirely believing what he had heard.

"*<<That is something you will have to get used to, Veerhulm. Our culture makes no distinction about gender or skin colour. Your merits and mistakes are entirely yours to make. They are never the 'sins of the father', as it were. Counsellor Koolen is functionally almost equal in rank to the Captain. In some situations, he will defer to her judgment. If she says you are welcome here, and the 'Kingdom' be damned, well, they are going to have to get used to disappointment, as concerns you.>>*" Marlon replied affably.

"What about me?" Ise enquired. "I heard my name a couple of times in all of that."

"He was having some difficulty believing that you might have the authority or wherewithal to be able to actually make your offer stick. I made sure he understood that you were easily more than obstinate and contrary enough to make the mighty Ironclad Kingdom regret irritating you," the greying Engineer explained blandly.

"Marlon Pryce!"

# Cordelia
## 18h17 SST
## Vicinity 44.2N,68.1W

The sun would have been about two-thirds of its track towards sunset, Cordelia thought, if the weather had allowed it to be visible.

Instead, a wind-blown mixture of rain squalls and fog obscured it. They were parked in the ruins of another, albeit smaller, Precursor town along the coast, making repairs. She was currently working with a couple other Salvage Techs and a Steward to repack cargo and stores in the Loading Bay. Each ostensibly water-tight box, containing food, replacement parts, clothes, or the myriad of other items that kept a thirty-two person ship at sea for ten days at a time, had to be opened and checked for signs of water damage.

More than a few had failed inspection so far; leakage caused by the blast from the mine in Black Stone Harbour. The "good goods", as Rainer Estalell referred to them, were being moved to other cargo holds. Conversely, the "not good goods" were being repacked well away from the cargo ramp. Shortly, the ramp-door would be sealed shut; unable to be opened again until they got back to a graving dock at Soumerville.

Captain Hal Lum had changed his mind early on in their flight from Black Stone Harbour. Instead of stopping about a third of a day's sail away, they had pressed on for almost a day and a third. To Cordelia, the reasoning was sensible. Just because they had only seen horses and foot travel did not mean the Top-Siders did not have something faster. They had radios, so initial behaviour aside, they were not barbarians. Fifty-percent restrictions on speed slowed the *Sheerah* significantly, even while surfaced, but just the same the distance they had covered was formidable.

The *Sheerah* had landed a team of Armsmen via the two inflatable dispatch boats, and they had scouted the area in the drizzle and rain for an hour before declaring the place devoid of evidence of recent visitors. The RSAV gingerly made its way ashore, up onto a level patch of dry land and then repair work resumed immediately.

Cordelia paused, and had a swig of water from her carried bottle. Beside her, Third-Class Salvage and Dive Tech Lizabetta Niemcewicz wiped her nose and then violently sneezed. "Bless you," Cordelia offered absently.

As she grabbed at another thirty-kilogram crate, the blonde Salvage Leader reflected that it had been a very long two days. The usually semi-relaxed atmosphere of life on the *Sheerah* had been entirely replaced by around-the-clock anxiety and urgency. Few things worried an RSAV crew person more than leaks, and the damage control pumps had been running constantly since the mine had detonated, trying to stay ahead of the persistent invasion of the sea. Now, the only remaining front on that battle was the cargo ramp-door into the loading bay.

She, and everyone else in her Detail, were tired. It was written on their faces, showed in voices, and was visible in their pace of work. A third of the crew were in Emm-and-Que right now; all twelve standard and emergency beds were full. That made watches and shifts longer, and life harder, for everyone else.

Niemcewicz sneezed again, wiping at her nose with a handkerchief out of her pocket. Something nagged at the back of Cordelia's mind. The Detail Leader set the waterproof crate she had just checked onto the "inspected, contents dry" pile and looked at the Third-Class Tech critically. "Are you feeling all right?" Cordelia asked Lizabetta.

"Huh? Oh, yeah, Chief. Just started with a cold today. Nothing serious," Lizabetta replied.

"Hold up, there. You were out on foot patrol with the Chief Armsman when the shooting started, right? In Black Stone Harbour?" Cordelia questioned, suddenly feeling uneasy.

"Well, yeah. Scared the scrap out of me, Boss. I have never ..."

"Stop. Go directly to Emm-and-Que. Report directly to Doctor Émile and tell him you started with cold symptoms this morning. Do not talk to anyone else. Get your backside in motion, Tech," Cordelia ordered.

"Aw, Chief, it is just a few sniffles! We have too much work to do for me to be down in Emm-and-Que for a runny nose!" Lizabetta protested.

"For all we know, you now have the local version of Ashen Fever. Haul ass, Tech. Go!" Cordelia barked and gestured towards the hatch door. She watched the Third-Class Tech head dejectedly back towards Salt Flats, destined for Sickbay. Disease aboard the *Sheerah* was the last thing they all needed right now, Cordelia knew. Even a relatively "benign" influenza outbreak could be fatal at this point, robbing the *Sheerah* of the manpower she needed to heal and make for home.

"Scrap, Fog and Jetsam," Cordelia muttered under her breath.

# Ise
## 18h42 SST

Ise Koolen gingerly lowered herself down onto her bunk, in the quiet of her own cabin, with a sigh of relief. She leaned the cane she was walking with against the head of the bunk, and then paused. She had a momentary mental vision of it flying like a javelin across the cabin the next time the *Sheerah* rolled down the beach or got into some waves. She therefore took a moment to fashion a couple loops with some finger-braided leather thong to "holster" it into. She could still use it when she wanted to move, but it was far less likely to become a problematic projectile like this.

The arrival of Third-Class Salvage Tech Lizabetta Niemcewicz as a possible plague rat had resulted in Doctor Émile sending the Spirit and Morale Counsellor back to her cabin a day earlier than he had intended. On the other hand, there was no specific need for Ise to still be in a bed in Sickbay, either. Her arm was in a cast, her shoulder was tightly wrapped, as was her ankle. She could get around with careful use of a cane, and only had to stop into Emm-and-Que once a day to have the isolation wrappings redone.

Spirits knew that she was relieved to be out of Sickbay. She was, by nature, perpetually in some kind of motion. Being confined to a bed beyond trips to the small bathroom in Emm-and-Que was aggravatingly restrictive.

The brass and stained wood intercom box above her desk chimed softly, and a blue light illuminated beneath it. For the first time in a while, she was left guessing as to who might be calling her. She unhooked her cane, pulled herself up with it, and hobble-stepped over to her desk. She flipped the 'Talk' switch.

"Counsellor Koolen here," she offered.

"Hello, Counsellor," came Hal Lum's voice. "How are you feeling?"

"Like a songbird sprung from its cage," she said with a laugh. "How are you holding up, Captain?"

"Like I have been in a two-day boxing match with a brown bear," Hal offered, some humour in his voice. Ise chuckled, glad to hear his light tone. She knew that Hal struggled with the weight of command on his shoulders.

"I am glad to hear that you are thus far the victor," she answered with mirth in her voice. "What is the occasion for the call today?"

"I just wanted to check in with you. The good Doctor let me know you were out of Emm-and-Que early, so I wanted to see how you were doing, and give you a quick courtesy update."

"Oh, why, Captain, that is very kind of you. Thank-you."

"You are very welcome. So, we are currently on the ground, in the cove near 44.2N,68.1W. We expect to be keeping the hull dry for another four hours or so, and then will be putting back to sea. The intention is to make best speed on surface for the waters at the southern tip of the Grand Peninsula. That will be close enough that we can hopefully get a RATT-net connection to work and get a situation report sent in," Hal said.

"Do you plan to request support services for the trip home?" Ise enquired. She had no doubt he would; Hal rarely left anything to chance, even in the name of love or pride.

"Oh yes, I do. I want us under escort before we make the Great River Influence Zone, particularly if the weather is bad and we cannot make the trip home on the bottom. I will need Mister Zupan to check my math, but I also think that we are about two days short of fuel, so we will need an at-sea replenishment."

"What are your thoughts on our new immigrant, Veerhulm Klientan?" Ise asked. She was of mixed feelings herself, and was keenly interested in Hal's perspective on the matter.

"Well, generally speaking, I am rather excited to have him with us. His mere existence changes everything we thought we knew about habitability above the waves. Once we get off the beach, I want Marlon to spend the trip home learning everything Mister Klientan can tell us about this Ironclad Kingdom. On a different front, we need to get that information relayed ahead so that the Fleet can be warned about operations anywhere near 42.4N,71.1W. We also need to ensure that Dockyard Ops and the Council know we will need to be under quarantine restrictions when we get home," he concluded with a sigh of resignation.

"That will be difficult on crew morale," Ise said quietly. "To be so close to home, yet forbidden entrance while waiting for a possible biological bomb to go off amongst us. We will have to do everything we can to keep reassurances high."

"I know, Counsellor, I know. I will be leaning on you heavily for your insights for the next fortnight or more."

"As always, Captain, it is my pleasure to Serve and Guide, and my honour," she said in an easy tone.

"Thank-you, Counsellor. I will let you get some rest. If you need me, I will most likely be in the Comm. We have so many people in Emm-and-Que right now that our Watch rotation is a mess."

"Be sure to take care of yourself, Captain. You cannot be much of a fearless leader from the position of medical sedation in Sickbay," she observed pointedly.

Hal laughed. "I will keep that in mind, Counsellor."

The light went out under the intercom, and she flipped the 'Talk' switch back to its original position.

Ise sighed. She took her cane back in hand and made her way to her mini-fridge. Thankfully the fruit juice was still fresh enough for her to have a tall, chilled glass of the stuff. She then slow-stepped her way to the easy-chair in her "office", and sat down.

She covered her mouth to stifle a yawn. She wondered how "Jonzie" and "Cordie" were doing; the pet-names and daily visits had not gone unnoticed by Ise. It was clear to her that a strong friendship and possible courtship was starting to gel between the two, but she was equally sure that neither of them could see that. Both were so crippled by their insecurities and scars that they could barely move, emotionally.

It was Ise's fond hope that they might be able to provide the healing for each other that they needed. Even if "nothing more" than friendship came of it, they would both still benefit substantially; as though a solid friendship was the lesser of *anything* by comparison. Still, both of them were loners by nature; surrounded by people who cared for them and about them, but never grasping that feeling.

Of course, Cordelia Baasch was at "that age" when "the Letter" would be showing up in her mail slot any day now. That sort of knowledge tended to put a chill over even remote prospects of romance until the practical details of the matter were sorted out by the woman in question.

Ise yawned again. It was, apparently, time for a nap. She tired so easily right now; it frustrated her. She would be much happier once she had fully healed and was back in top shape.

# Christopher
## 00h15 SST
## Monday, May 2nd
## Vicinity of 44.1N, 67.9W
## 13C, Heavy Fog, Winds 11 kph SSE

The Chief Armsman was leaning over the Pilot's station, checking the autopilot status when Captain Hal Lum came through the hatch leading into the Comm. Christopher suppressed a sigh. He had hoped that his usual on-Watch companion, Damiano Émile would be with him. Instead, the Ship's Doctor had not arrived for the start of Watch, and the Captain had now just arrived.

"Good evening, Captain. I take it Doctor Émile is occupied in Sickbay right now?" Christopher asked, trying to remain neutral sounding.

"That is correct, Chief. I do not know if you heard, but we have two new occupants back there, both with sniffles, a fever and a rash along the spinal column. One Salvage Tech, and one Engineer. So, Doctor Émile has locked the door and no one leaves until further notice. The only people going in will be anyone else with symptoms."

"That is entirely unwelcome news, Captain," the Chief Armsman replied grimly.

Hal walked over to Christopher and passed him a flask of coffee and a sandwich. "Here, I grabbed us a bite before I came up. And no, no, that is not welcome news."

Christopher took the offered snack with a mild feeling of surprise. Of course, one of those lessons you learn as an Armsman is that there are three things you never pass up;  a chance for sleep, food or to reload. "Thank-you, Captain," he offered as he took the flask and food.

Hal took his usual chair and had a sip from his own flask. "Think nothing of it, Chief.  How does our track look?  I noticed you were checking the autopilot when I came in."

"Oh, yes.  Slight drift in track to the South, but that is to be expected with the speed of the tide coming down Force Bay.  The wind and the waves are pushing us around some as well, but we are essentially following the intended track within 'acceptable' tolerances," the gold-brown-skinned Armsman replied.

Hal nodded. "We need to be able to dive," he said with a sigh. "We have a lot more control and stability that way."

"Agreed, Captain, but we both know that is not an option."

Hal gave his Chief Armsman an amused look over the top of his flask. "Hopefully the Engineers will get another Tee-Dee off the 'tagged' list in the next eight hours.  Our Pilot should be moving under his own steam within a day; he was sent to his cabin before the Doctor locked the Sickbay.  I am sure Mister Zupan can do a better job of this autopilot set up than I did.  Speaking of Mister Zupan, Chief, do you mind a question?"

"I prefer not to gossip about my crew-mates, Sir," Christopher replied stiffly.

"That is an interesting presumption on your part," Hal observed. "But no; no gossip. I am curious about that 'door' problem you two had."

Christopher frowned.  He had rather hoped that foolishness was behind him. "What about it, Sir?"

Hal sat his flask down in the holder on the side of his chair and rubbed at his forehead for a moment before speaking. "Mister Olivier, allow me to be direct, since it is just you and I here, and the ship we are mutual crew on seems to be at war all of a sudden. I am perpetually left with the feeling that you do not trust me as your Captain. I am not sure I understand why, and I am not sure I understand much else about you, either. Your quest for excellence is as visible as a lighthouse; beyond that, very little you do or say makes sense to me."

Christopher Olivier blinked. When the Captain had prefaced about being "direct" he had not been kidding. Of course, this left him in a quandary, implicit in the Captains own commentary. Under normal conditions, he would just use stonewalls and silence. Right now, however, after the events of the past seventy-two hours, his personal reserves of "polite" and "discretion" were running on vapours.

"Permission to speak candidly, Sir?" the Chief Armsman asked carefully.

"Given. I realise you are voluntarily stepping onto what you likely consider thin ice, Mister, and I respect and appreciate that. What is on your mind?" Hal asked.

"Allow me to start small and work up, Sir. Firstly, Mister Zupan screwed up, but he did so in a way that kept the matter 'in the family'. Regardless of how much he had or had not had to drink, if you are going to do something stupid like taking a swing at someone, I am the guy to do it at. Taking hits is my job, Sir. He got it out of his system, we got to keep the best Pilot-Navigator in the Fleet, and all I had to do was keep my mouth shut. Not that big a sacrifice, is it?" Christopher asked, sounding a bit more adversarial than he had intended.

"So you like Mister Zupan enough to take a couple of hits for free?"

"No, sir. I *respect* him enough, and that is an entirely different statement. Nor were they 'free'," Christopher replied with a snort.

"Bluntly sir, I do not *like* most people. But *respect* is a real thing with me; it is a valuable currency. I do not have to like someone to respect them and the skills they bring to the table. Mister Zupan has earned my respect with his skills in the Pilot's chair, and his discretion in keeping his personal drama from marring the *Sheerah's* good name."

"So that is it with you? Be good at your job, and do not screw up ashore so badly that it reflects on the ship?" Hal asked with a raised eyebrow.

"It is a start, at least, Sir. I am not a tea and crumpets socials kind of guy," Christopher remarked dryly. "I know an awful lot of 'likeable' people that I would never trust my life to. I know more than a few people who are 'unlikeable', but get the damn job done every time, dependable as a clockwork," the Chief Armsman said, punctuating the statement by a double-tap of a finger onto the control station beside him.

"Besides, let us be honest, Sir, 'unlikable' by who, exactly?" Christopher continued in a scathing tone. "That path is madness. It is shallow judgments, it is clique actions, it values appearances over effectiveness, it is praised unworthies and missed heroes. It is the start of a mob mentality. I will take respect every damn day for a man or woman over some mythical 'likeable' quality. I can *quantify* the things that are worth respect. It has nothing to do with the colour of my bowtie, or if I wear one, or if I smile at the right people while it is on."

Hal looked at him thoughtfully for a long moment, tapping a finger slowly against his cheek, before anything else was said. "You know, Mister Olivier, you suddenly make a lot more sense. You do not trust me because you think I worry about likability more than I am worried about earning respect." There was no accusation in Hal Lum's voice; there was no challenge. It was a statement.

Christopher hesitated for a moment, but given recent events, he felt Hal had earned the truth. "Correct. Until about three days ago, I was getting the impression you were running a popularity contest, Sir. The problem with popularity contests is that as soon as the luck runs out or the hard work comes in, it usually turns out there is not a lot there behind it. Lights, cameras, sound, but no action or product," Christopher answered coolly.

Hal nodded. He visibly did not like the answer, but he was apparently going to stay adult about it for now. The dark-skinned RSAV Captain looked out the Comm windows into the foggy night as the *Sheerah*'s bow broke a wave, showering the armoured glass with spray.

"The firefight earlier, you did a very good job, Mister Olivier. I bet my life on your abilities," Hal said.

"I know, Sir."

"If you do not trust me, why did you follow me out there into the middle of that?"

Christopher paused at the question. He had asked himself the same thing a couple of times since it happened. The answer was there, regardless of if he liked it.

"Over the past couple of days, from the dressing down in the O-Room, to the crisis management, to you standing watches for eighteen hours at a go to ensure everyone else could heal or do their jobs, to the moment you made it clear that what Soumerville is, what the *Sheerah* is, that those values and the ideals behind them was worth taking a bullet for, well," Christopher shook his head and sighed. Crow tasted terrible. "That is the kind of thing that earns my respect, Sir."

"So, tell me, Mister, when the Ironclad leader came riding at us out of the smoke, when you shot that man, what were you thinking?"

"Honestly, Sir, I was hoping not to hurt the horse," the Armsman replied tersely.

"Really? You are hitting a man in the face with the force of a blacksmith's hammer, and you were worried about hurting an animal?" Hal questioned, raising an eyebrow at him.

"Yessir. That magnificent creature did not request to get ridden into trouble by a jack-ass," the Chief Armsman replied flatly, running a hand through his dark and close-cropped hair.

The unsaid truth was there was no good reason for Christopher to have dialled up the grudge on the rifle as he had done. He did not know if Hal had seen him do it or not, but Christopher was very aware that it was an unprofessional act on his part. He would have to do better in the future.

Hal chuckled and nodded, apparently satisfied by the answer. He had a bite of his sandwich, followed by a mouthful from his flask, looking thoughtful all the while. Christopher did the same, his mind whirling. This was pretty much the exact conversation he had expected to never have with Hal Lum. The entire scene was almost unsettling.

Hal rubbed at his chin for a moment and then nodded before speaking. "Do you know why you are aboard this ship, Mister?"

"Well, my Service Record speaks for itself, Sir. I graduated at the top of my class; I organised the recovery and rescue of the survivors of the *De Lancy* in spite of being wounded in the incident; the Detail passed our last operational readiness check with top marks ..."

Hal held up a hand, turning his gaze out the window, resting his chin on the balled knuckles of the other hand. He shook his head. "No, Mister Olivier. Those are the reasons you were nearly transferred *off* this ship. *I* am the reason you are on this vessel."

Christopher did a double-take, and set his coffee and half-eaten sandwich down. "Pardon, Sir?" he asked, fairly sure he had either misheard or misunderstood.

"Before we set sail on this cruise, Mister, your name came across my desk on a set of Personnel Transfer Orders. You were being pulled off the ship, and sent to Fleet Training. Your exemplary Service Record makes you too good for the job of *just* being the Chief Armsman of my ship, apparently. You were going to be an instructor for the next two years, at least. You were destined to be shaping the skills and training program of the entire organisation. An exciting life of writing standards and procedures manuals, training regimes and testing sets," Hal said quietly, and then looked over at him.

"I infer you objected, Sir?" Christopher asked, suddenly nearly feeling sick at the prospect of being moved off the *Sheerah*. He would have been chained to a forsaken desk, away from all the things that mattered to him.

Hal nodded at him. "You could say that, Mister," he replied dryly. "I am sure that Mission Services Mistress Alodia Holt would have described it as closer to 'gross insubordination' and 'disrespectful conduct'. I bulldozed my way into her office and pitched a fit."

"You ... did?"

Hal nodded at him. "I told her she either reassigned you *back* to the *Sheerah* with me right there watching her sign the paperwork, or she could transfer someone *else* to the Big Chair of this ship. With the mission profile I had just been handed, there was no damn way I was sailing without the best Chief Armsman in the Fleet."

Christopher did his best to keep his jaw from dropping. Hal Lum had *fought with* and *threatened* the legendary Alodia Holt to keep him here?

"It turns out that you and I are not that dissimilar, Mister Olivier. I value respect an awful lot myself. It is also my job to take hits for the team; mine just involve India ink more than blood. There was no Spirits-forsaken way I was going to let you wither and fade at some desk for the next two years. That would have been the end of you, one way or another. Over the past couple of years you, Mister, have earned my respect. I might not like you much some days, but I do respect you."

"I ... thank-you, Sir." Christopher said slowly. Flabbergasted did not begin to describe his mental condition.

"I would appreciate if you would keep an open mind on the issue of trust with me. As well as with your level of respect for Salvage Leader Baasch; she disobeyed a direct order to the point of technical mutiny to pull our backsides out of the fire yesterday. I specifically told her to hold the ship at the beach, before I left. She might cut corners on the Book from time to time, but please *also* look at the results; that is your own metric, after all."

# CHAPTER FIFTEEN
*The Long Way Home*

## Veerhulm
**18h18 SST,**
**Monday, May 2nd**
**Vicinity of 43.2N, 66.1W**
**20C, Light rain, Winds 34 kph SSW**

Things in his adopted-him home were not going well, he mused. While he did not speak their language, the conversations with the Elder Marlon, as well as the body language of those around him told him enough of the story. Sickness had come aboard this remarkable underwater ship. Sickness from *his* home.

"Scale Back", as the disease was known to his people, was something apparently Elder Marlon's people had never encountered before. Once he had glimpsed the telltale rash on the spine of one man, he had told Elder Marlon what it was. Almost immediately, "Doctor Émile" had been peppering him with questions, via Elder Marlon's translation.

Unfortunately, Veerhulm was "just" a Seer; that was bad enough, let alone being a Medicine Man. He told the apparently excitable Doctor Émile what he knew in as much detail as he could about what he knew of how a Medicine Man might treat it, with ample caveats.

Where Veerhulm was from, it killed about once percent of children before age five, and crippled another two percent. It was almost unheard of amongst adults. Both Elder Marlon and Doctor Émile had been aghast at the idea that children died of a common and recognizable malady.

His leg was healing well. "Doctor", from what Elder Marlon had explained to him, was the equivalent of being *both* a Faith Healer *and* a Medicine Man, as paradoxical as that was. In addition, unlike the usual hostile view most of his kin would take to a Medicine Man, that type of healing practice was encouraged, cultivated and respected in Elder Marlon's culture, much as being a Faith Healer was in Veerhulm's.

What possibly would have been a lost limb where Veerhulm came from, was an hour's worth of patch-up work by Doctor Émile and a couple spoonfuls of something vile in taste each day. He could already walk on the injury, albeit with a cane. If it was not for the current Verdict by Doctor Émile against leaving the Sick House, he would be easily able to go for short walks.

He sighed, trying to contain the noise as well as any outward show of emotion. He flexed his injured leg slowly, and shook his head. This is what his people had given up.

The very pretty, if exotic-looking, "Nurse Ji-Hye" stopped at the end of his bed. Her eyes were angled compared to his, and her skin was like a late season sunflower in tone. Veerhulm had never seen anything quite like her.

"*Kiel vi sentas hodiaŭ?*" she asked him. Of course, they both knew he would not understand her, but as a Seer he could tell that she was being both kind and inquiring about something. He looked over at Elder Marlon, in the bed adjacent to him.

"She asked you how you were feeling today," Marlon explained, speaking to him in Veerhulm's own language.

"Thank-you. Please thank her and let her know I am without complaint, beyond wishing I could help you all in some way," Veerhulm replied.

Marlon nodded and looked towards Nurse Ji-Hye. *"Li sentas bone kaj deziras, ke li povus helpi nin iel,"* he told her.

*"Diru al li, ke li estas helpo. La Doktoro opinias, ke li estas proksima al efika traktado bazita sur kio nia nova amiko rakontis al ni,"* she replied with an attractive grin, and patted Veerhulm's foot before continuing on to another patient's bed.

"She said that you have helped. From what you have told Doctor Émile, he may have an effective treatment soon. I agree with her; if your willingness to volunteer information saves lives, or at least stops some of our crew from being crippled for the rest of their lives, then yes, my good man, you have most certainly helped," Marlon concluded firmly.

Veerhulm nodded, and adjusted the pillow behind his back, sitting up more fully. He gestured at the empty tray beside his bed. "Do you and your people always eat so well?" he asked.

Marlon chuckled. "Yes and no. When we are at home, yes. When we are at sea on a mission, normally no. We never go hungry, and the food is always filling, but the quality of tastes on this particular outing are well above normal. Counsellor Koolen and Captain Lum argued for the better food based on the possible dangers of the trip."

Veerhulm nodded. They had been stuffing him since he had woken up in his bed in the Sick House. He was used to two meals a day, with perhaps a snack in between. As Middle Class, that was fairly average. Apparently the normal for Elder Marlon's people was three full meals a day, plus two snacks. This was the sort of thing that would get anyone below Very Upper Class accused of Gluttony, he thought in amusement.

Even more surreal was that the portions were apparently identical irrespective of trade, job, skin colour or even gender.

Counsellor Koolen, he had learned, was Elder Marlon's equivalent of a Seer. So, beyond the fact of their radically different skin colours and genders, they were similar people. Except for the part where in her society, that sounded so odd to his sensibilities to think or say, she was a respected and powerful professional. As opposed to him, by contrast, being a Convict and Exile in his society.

"Do you mind some more questions, Veerhulm?" Marlon inquired politely.

They had been taking turns bombarding each other with questions, and learning a lot about both cultures in the process. Both men were often left blinking in disbelief at the assertions of the other.

For example, it turned out that Elder Marlon was a scholar. He was not a religious scholar, but rather surprisingly, a *historian*. This, as well, was taking some getting used to. History was the firm domicile of the Priests where he was from; they managed both its recording and its recounting. The idea that Elder Marlon was a part-time independent historian of some kind was rather interesting to Veerhulm. He was going to have to ask Elder Marlon how, if no central authority managed the study of history, it would be kept safe from being used against society to advance unsavoury or immoral agendas.

Veerhulm shook his head. "No, I do not mind at all. I rather enjoy these discussions. It keeps the mind engaged."

# Cordelia
## 18h56 SST

Cordelia leaned over the pilot station, checking the autopilot track. They were well past the tidal effects of Force Bay, and now near "Ghost Point"; the nickname Jonas had given for the location where he had first heard Veerhulm's clear-voice radio call over the RATT-net. This was, coincidentally, the extreme edge of RATT-net range for a direct connection to Soumerville. Hal Lum had asked her to essentially spend the entire four hours she was on watch here, focusing on trying to get a message back to 45N50W.

With Marlon, her usual Watch partner, still in Emm-and-Que due to actual honest-to-Spirit's quarantine measures being in effect, Hal was filling in for him. Or, should be. He was exhausted from being in the Comm for almost two days straight. He had shown up at the start of the watch to ensure everything was going as expected and then had left her instructions to call him in his cabin anytime she needed to step out of the Comm, had questions, or needed company. Otherwise, he was going to be getting some food and a quick nap.

Ise Koolen had been the previous Watch Officer, and while she was reasonably capable from Cordelia's perspective, Ship Ops were not a core competency for any Spirit and Morale Guide. So, Hal had felt obligated to stand that entire Watch with her. It was also the Salvage and Dive Leader's quiet personal opinion that spending more than about half an hour with the Spirit and Morale Guide was exhausting, so Hal had Cordelia's complete sympathy when he had headed for his cabin.

She made a couple of minor adjustments to the autopilot via the knobs and dials on the brass and wood surface of the device. So far, allowing for wind and waves, the autopilot was getting the job done. There had been some concern that the blast from the mine in Black Stone Harbour might have disoriented any of the trio of gyroscopes that the ship depended upon, but thus far everything seemed in good order.

Starting tomorrow, Jonas would be standing watch rotations alongside Ise, and that would improve a lot of things for the Command Crew in short order. She was considering suggesting to Hal to switch the Watch rotations around so that she would change spots with Ise. That would put Marlon working with Ise, which would be a good set of temperaments, and her working with Jonas. That would be fun for both of them, she figured. His quirky, humour-filled optimism was such a pleasure to have around; he was doing wonders for her personal morale.

"Okay," she said aloud to herself. "Time to work a miracle. Drop speed to five and stream the antenna," she said, narrating her actions. She moved over to her own crew station. "Warm-up procedure on the RATT-net transmitters started, with maximum transmission power selected. Come on, I want to hear you squeal like a cheap sex worker on his first day," she chuckled at her own bawdy humor while flipping the switches and slowly turning the dials to tune the RATT-net radios. They were in listen-only mode right now; it was pointless to transmit if they could not hear Soumerville's signal. She made a few more adjustments; the monitor speaker remained silent.

She sighed and flopped into her crew chair, twisting against the seat back in a vain attempt to both pout in frustration and be comfortable while doing so. "We are still too far away," she said to herself quietly, pulling a knee up against her chest and resting her chin on it. "Too damn far away."

# Jonas
## 03h05 SST
## Tuesday, May 3rd
## Vicinity of 43.2N, 64.9W
## 15C, Light rain and Fog, Winds 19 kph WSW

"Got it!" Jonas cheered, and punched the air in triumph. It was an action he immediately regretted, however, from the shot of pain that went through his chest. He winced for a moment, but the expression was rapidly replaced by a grin. "Cordie and the Skipper are going to be relieved" he said, pressing the "TRANSMIT" button on the AMTAC player for the RATT-net system. The trio of "sending, waiting, receiving" lights blinked back and forth in a high-speed ping-pong rally, and the tape drive whirred quietly. The collection of situation reports and condition updates, accumulated over the past three days, were now being beepity-beeped over the airwaves to Dockyard Operations at Soumerville.

Ise Koolen applauded. "Well done, Jonas! I marvel at your and Miz Baasch's ability to get that ridiculous contraption to do anything. I have never gotten it to work."

"It is very fiddly," Jonas nodded, turning back to where Ise was sitting in Christopher's chair. As he made his way back to his own crew chair, he said "Cordie is an absolute mistress with that thing. I have learned everything from watching her."

"I doubt that was your primary motivation for your observations, particularly from that angle," Koolen replied with a teasing giggle.

"Ise!" Zupan squawked, flushing red.

"I hear protests, but no denials," she replied mirthfully.

Ise was right of course, but he was mortified to hear her announce it like that. He was exceedingly glad that they were the only two in the Comm right now. He did the only safe thing he could think of; he went back to the original topic.

"No matter what else happens, Soumerville will know what we found at Black Stone Harbour now," he said, trying to ignore the heat in his cheeks and the mischievous smile on the Spirit and Morale Counsellor's face. "I would really hate for anyone else to blunder into that bunch of goons from the Ironclad Kingdom," he scowled.

"They are quite the bunch of uneducated barbarians," Ise answered quietly, apparently willing to put at least a temporary pause to her good-natured teasing. "Marlon has been using the Emm-and-Que's 'Quarantine Type Relay' to write reports about his conversations with Veerhulm. Hal has been passing them to me after he is done reading them. They seem to live by an absolutely delusional world-view that is so internally contradictory in its principles that I cannot understand anyone smarter than a daft dolphin being able to reconcile it."

"What did he do, anyway? He is an exiled criminal, right?" Jonas asked.

Ise laughed. "As far as can be determined, his crime is that he is not willing to go along with their culture without asking questions. If he had been born amongst us, he would likely be doing the kind of work I do. But, where he comes from, questioning authority and trying to reduce emotional costs within society will get you killed, apparently."

"Did he really have an argument with Damiano about getting an injection?" Jonas asked, while fine-tuning the settings on the autopilot.

"That is what Marlon reported, yes. Medical injections of any kind are banned in the Kingdom, according to Veerhulm. Something about them being against the will of their religious figure, and causing 'corruption'. To reinforce the notion, the only time they inject you with anything in the Kingdom is for an execution. I gather it was about a forty-five minute philosophical debate, involving the Doctor, the Nurse, Mister Pryce and Veerhulm before they could convince him that we start doing injections within a month of being born. Suffice to say that Damiano is appalled at the idea they do not do vaccinations of any kind," Ise chuckled.

Jonas laughed. "I would imagine so. Doctor Émile is very proud of his work and its value. He is always reading up on the latest news in medicine." Jonas liked Damiano for a long list of reasons, but near the top was just how smart a doctor he was. If you were going to get sick or hurt, there were fewer better places to be treated than the *Sheerah's* Emm-and-Que.

A comfortable silence arrived in the Comm as the pair tended to a handful of tasks involving paper, switches and dials that needed to be done at the start of every Watch. It was well past sunset, with rain squalls and swirling fog rendering the view beyond the brass-rimmed armoured window less interesting than the usual view twenty metres below the waves. The only thing currently visible outside were a trio of seabirds roosting on the forward deck, somehow managing to ignore the periodic waves that crested the bow and rushed over the flat steel expanse they were blissfully napping on.

"So, how is Jonas these days?" Ise asked a while later, sipping from a flask of hot tea.

Jonas rubbed at his forehead a moment before answering. "Well, better, I think. This trip has been hard on everyone, so I feel kind of funny about complaining about any of that. But, all those things I was worried about a couple of weeks ago just seem to have not mattered. It … it is kind of weird, actually. It all seemed so huge then. Now, I am not sure anyone cares about any of it, including me."

"'Funny' indeed, Jonas," Ise said with a smile. "One of those things I learned as part of my training is that often the things that we are sure are sea monsters turn out to be flat fish. Worrying about them is about as useful as snapping fingers to solve an algebra problem. The real troubles are the sorts of things that blindside us on a quiet Tuesday afternoon on our Second. If you can actually *see* the problem coming, it is rarely a problem you cannot solve."

"I suppose that is true," Jonas said thoughtfully. "I mean, that is the story of Soumerville and her sisters in a seashell, is it not? The Founders saw the Collapse of the Precursor world coming long before it arrived, and they came up with a solution. That was literally an 'end-of-the-world' kind of problem they were dealing with."

Ise nodded. "And here we are a couple of hundred years later; aboard a multi-hundred tonne amphibious rover limping home after hitting an anti-ship mine that nearly nobody saw. The one person who saw the problem figured it out as it happened, and we all came out okay."

"A metaphor for every occasion, Miz Koolen?" Jonas said with a laugh.

"More like a lesson *in* every occasion, Mister Zupan," she countered with a grin. "The philosophy of the Spirits is that is how we do better in, and with, the world around us. We are compelled to look at what happens, make notes about it, compare it to what we have seen before, and draw experience and lessons from the body of knowledge. Someone far more sage than I once observed that life is far too short for us to each be do-it-alls. Yet, to be able to live our lives to the fullest, we each have to be know-it-alls. The only way to bridge that chasm is by learning from what everyone else has seen and done, and keeping that body of knowledge up to date with our own experiences."

"It is a hard way to live, sometimes, Ise. You cannot just hide from the stuff you do not like, that way," Jonas said quietly.

"That is true," she said with a nod, and a sip of tea. "But when you were young, how many games of hide-and-seek did you ever win as one of the children *hiding*? Eventually, if the game goes long enough, everyone gets found. Hiding does not avoid the reckoning associated with being found; it just leaves you badly prepared for it. That includes anti-ship mines, unfamiliar diseases, and attractive torch singers," she concluded pointedly.

He stuck his tongue out at her as about the only relevant defence he could muster.

# Alodia
## 09h42 SST
## Soumerville

The ringing red, ebony, and silver phone on her bedside table woke Alodia Holt just before dawn. She scrabbled it out of the cradle before its horrific din woke her slightly snoring husband. Another part of the

266

urgency was that this was not the "house phone"; that was still silent out in the sitting room. This was the "work phone", and it rarely rang with good news.

"Mistress Holt", she said quietly into the receiver.

"Good morning, Mistress. This is Duty Signals Chief Charlize Amadi at the Fleet Message Centre. I apologize for the early hour of the call, but you had asked to be called if we heard from the *RSAV Sheerah*. We got a good RATT-net connection with them just after zero-three-hundred hours, Standard, Miz."

Alodia blinked at the phone. "I think you just made my week, Chief. Anything UNCLASS?"

"No, Miz. It is all flagged varying degrees of Sensitive, Confidential, Restricted or Secret; about half of it is flagged 'For Your Eyes Only', to your attention," the rich voice on the other end of the line answered, sounding apologetic.

"Chief, I hate to ask this, but can you jump those print jobs to the head of the line for me? I am going to get dressed and head to the office now," she said quietly, swinging her feet over the edge of the bed and sitting up. She shifted the receiver to the other ear, and untangled herself from the cord.

"Already done, Miz, and we have a fresh security bag with your name on it. I will walk the whole pile over myself, just to trim the 'Secure Messages and Materials Transfer' paper work down for you."

"Spirits bless you, Chief. Let me know what you drink, and I will have a bottle of it delivered as a thank-you," Alodia said with a chuckle. Her husband stirred slightly, and his light snoring changed tone a bit.

"My pleasure, Miz. I will see you in about an hour or so," Signals Chief Amadi answered.

Alodia hung up the phone and quietly left the bedroom, wrapping a house-gown around her as she went. She went to the study and quickly penned a note explaining that she had been called to work, and left it at her husband's place at the breakfast table. She then went to her dressing room and started getting her clothes together, her mind whirling.

Something had happened to the *Sheerah*. Something big, certainly. Captain Hal Lum was not the sort to frivolously tag trivial message traffic with security clearances, nor Fo-Yo-E-O restrictions. Given what had happened to the *Lanier* in the same area, Alodia found herself desperately hoping for nothing more serious than broken machinery. Gears, sprockets, pistons and pipes were all expendable, replaceable and consumable. The people were not.

She recalled that the RSAV *al-Jazari* was in port, and nearing the end of their ten-day. Alodia decided she would pre-emptively get the paperwork moving to have the *al-Jazari* rendezvous with the *Sheerah*. It would take a couple of hours as a minimum to sort through the reams of paper that Chief Amadi was going to hand-deliver, bless the woman; having the creation of all the sailing and supply orders running in parallel meant less time lost in getting the *al-Jazari* to sea. It was always much quicker to cancel a sailing order than to start one.

As she fussed with her corset, she muttered aloud, "With my luck, Lum has gone and started a war or something."

# Hal
## 10h56 SST

Right about now, Hal Lum figured, Mission Services Mistress Alodia Holt should be having a kitten. Jonas and Ise had gotten a RATT-net connection early this morning, and the accumulated outgoing message traffic of the past few days adventures and mishaps had been successfully sent over three connection sessions during their watch. From what Hal knew of the formidable Miz Holt, he had no doubt she would be carefully reading everything sent to her attention from the *Sheerah*.

Hopefully he would still be a Captain when they arrived home in Soumerville. He had his doubts. The summary of the *Sheerah* being a battle-damaged, partially flooded plague ship that initiated a shooting war with the first Top-Sider culture contacted in more than two generations, all under his "leadership", did not bode well for any future career review.

He was sitting in his chair in the Comm; he was taking over Chief Pryce's watch slot with Cordelia Baasch, since the Chief Engineer was still currently locked in Sick Bay. Miz Baasch was currently tinkering with the autopilot, based on some written instructions Jonas Zupan had left for her.

There were currently three additions to Emm-and-Que's population, all suffering from the Top-Sider disease. One of the Engineers already in Emm-and-Que was starting to show symptoms as well. From what Damiano and Marlon had learned from their Top-Sider refugee, Veerhulm, the disease crippled or even killed.

Cordelia glanced over at him. "You okay, Captain?"

"Hmmm? Oh, yes, I am fine, generally speaking."

"And specifically speaking?" his blonde Salvage Leader asked with a smile.

"You have been spending too much time in Councillor Koolen's company," Hal commented dryly. "I am just worried about the folks in Sick Bay. Mister Émile is a remarkably talented man, but there are limits to what he can do and what he has to work with."

Cordelia gave him a sympathetic smile. "Yeah, I worry too. About both us and him. I mean, if our passenger is a possible disease carrier I cannot imagine the Council agreeing to having him wandering loose around Soumerville. I would guess we will have to land him at one of the Food Forests with enough gear for him to set up and live comfortably, and that would be that."

"We do not give up that easily, Miz Baasch," Hal chided her in a good-natured tone. "For most of our history we have been bringing new people to our underwater world at their request. Veerhulm is no where near the first, and apparently we can now presume will not be the last. Sorting out imported sicknesses is nothing new. Once Doctor Émile can collaborate directly with his peers within Soumerville, I am sure our medical science folks will concoct both a cure and a vaccine. Then it just gets added to the list of things we are collectively protected against, across the globe. At worst we spend a month parked on the bottom in a holding pen a kilometre away from home, hooked up with supply tethers, while it all gets sorted out."

"I hope you are right, Captain," Cordelia said with a sigh. She leaned back in her chair, looking towards the deckhead. "I am finding this trip hard. I know that sounds stupid, of course it is hard, just look around, right? More what I mean is ..." she trailed off slowly. She sighed. "I do not know what I mean. Forget it."

"What you mean is since any of us joined the Service, things have gone so swimmingly well that up until now that it has been a stroll through a Forest Room. We have a remarkably talented and capable crew, and so none of us have had to deal with a real challenge. We are all used to being the top of our class, the top of our trade, the top of our lives, and we just all came to a sudden stop like an RSAV full-ahead into a breakwater. That sudden stop and the adjustments that we have been dealing with since are exhausting. That, I think, is what you mean. I know what you mean," Hal concluded quietly.

Cordelia looked visibly relieved. "So not just me? You too?"

Hal looked over at her and nodded. "Everyone, I think. But yes, myself as well. You are allowed to find this hard, Miz Baasch. As a leader, I understand that we both feel compelled to hide that from those people looking to us for assurance. Talk to Councillor Koolen. If you find Miz Koolen … *ahem* … somewhat overwhelming to talk to at times, talk to Mister Zupan; I know you two are friends. You can always talk to me, Cordelia. My door is always open; that has been my policy since I first sat in this chair."

The Salvage and Dive Leader blinked at him at the use of her first name. She was obviously surprised at the gesture of familiarity; Hal was fairly sure that other than Ise, he could count on two hands the number of times in three years he had used a crew-mate's first name.

"Thank-you, Hal," she answered quietly. "Who do you talk to?"

"Ise and Damiano," he replied, shifting his gaze out the windows. "I have to be careful, moreso than most, with what comes out of my mouth in front of who. I am aware there are a few crew who are convinced I am eventually going to get someone killed; that our current string of successes has more to do with good fortune than good leadership. Anything that I utter that might shake confidence or cause panic must be censored before it leaves my mouth."

"I could not do your job, Captain," Cordelia said. "I need to be able to throw my temper tantrums, and I need to have someone I can take orders from, on things I do not want to decide," she admitted.

Hal looked over at her. "Funny enough, I am not sure I could do your job, either, Chief. The hours you keep when we are ashore, the host of dangers and issues you casually work in the middle of, the keen eye for crucial items and how to make the most of limited resources … I can barely remember the right order for putting a set of dive tanks on, let alone the notion of keeping my nerve while running a cutting torch seven metres below surface in the middle of a ruins that might collapse on me if I cut the wrong thing," he said with a laugh. He glanced back over to her for a moment. "Do not sell yourself short, Miz. I consider myself damn fortunate to have you as my Salvage Leader."

271

# CHAPTER SIXTEEN
## *Down With All Hands*

**Ise**
**13h29 SST**
**Thursday, May 5th**
**18C, Clear & Sunny, Winds 6 kph WSW**

It had been a very long two weeks since the *Sheerah* had departed Soumerville on this fateful voyage, Ise Koolen reflected from where she sat in Christopher's crew chair. It was not over yet, either. The ship was about one hundred kilometres West-South-West of the southern side of the Great River Influence Zone. The weather today was blissfully nice; warm, sunny with only a mild breeze.

Yesterday had been like the inside of a washing machine with eight metre waves, black skies, a driving rain and howling winds. Under normal conditions, an RSAV would just bottom-roll during bad weather. However, damaged as she had been, the *Sheerah* was restricted to surface cruising only.

Reclaimer-Class RSAVs were notoriously bad sea-keepers in anything more than about a two-metre swell. By comparison, these walls of water had been four times that height. With most of her fuel tanks empty, and her cargo holds also largely empty, she did not have the mass to remain steady in the storm.

It had been a miserable, eleven hour-long ordeal. Even by sunrise this morning, parts of the ship still stank of vomit from the number of people who had been sea-sick. Fortunately, that was getting rapidly cleaned out, with the Salvage Techs and Engineers having rigged emergency ventilation. Additionally, but of no less value, the Armsmen were doing a yeoman's effort in working with the Stewards in cleaning and polishing everything to a dinner-table standard.

This morning, Hal had ordered Jonas to program the auto-pilot for station keeping. There was just eight hours of fuel remaining in the tanks now. The water was too deep to anchor, and so the remaining fuel was going to be used to keep the ship's nose into the wind, keeping her position relatively stationary. Under current conditions, that would stretch the fuel to sixteen hours. There was another six hours in the undamaged section of the batteries. After that, it would start getting cold, dark, and stale.

Ise's eyes flicked to the wall clock in the Command Compartment. The ship's reference time-piece informed her of two not very comforting facts; firstly, the RSAV *al-Jazari* was now over an hour and a half late for their *rendezvous*, and secondly, eleven minutes had gone by since the last time she checked.

A heavy metallic clang signalled someone coming into the Comm. Ise glanced in that direction to see Hal entering the compartment. It was as clear as the sky beyond the Comm windows he was not happy.

"Hello, Captain. I sense you have something on your mind," she said.

He nodded at her as he moved to his chair. "Good morning, Councillor. Yes, I do. Beyond the part where our saviour and escort is well past adrift, I just found out that Doctor Émile is now his own patient," he replied tersely as he sat down.

Ise blinked at Hal. "He has contracted the Top-Sider disease?" she asked.

"Yes," he answered sourly. A moment of silence was punctuated by his fist hammering down on the arm of his chair in frustration. This sort of display from Hal Lum was something Ise was unaccustomed to, and out of character.

"I am sure he will be fine, Captain," she offered, sounding reassuring. "As for the *al-Jazari*, for all we know she is surfacing as we speak. Daylight surface cruising is a no-no, under normal conditions. With the storm yesterday, she likely held position on the bottom and is just a couple of hours behind schedule. We have our short-range antenna up; as soon as she surfaces, I am sure we will hear from them."

Hal sighed and nodded. "You are quite right, of course, Councillor. We are less than sixty hours from home, under anything closer to normal conditions. Barely more than two days, and then we have the entire resources of Soumerville to help us take care of our sick and injured and replenish our larder and stores. But, until the *al-Jazari* makes her entrance, we are stranded here, waiting for the next turn of foul weather."

"Do not lose hope, Captain," Ise said encouragingly.

"Oh, I am full of hope, Councillor. I am also full of responsibility and contingency plans," he replied, getting up from his chair and moving to stand in front of a wall-mounted chart of the area. He tapped it with a finger. "If we do not hear from Captain Donovan Windsor of the *al-Jazari* in the next hour, we will head towards shore here. Between our remaining fuel and the batteries, we should be able to pull into a cove in that area. Before the batteries run out we will inform Dockyard Ops via RATT-net of where they can find us, and we will set up into long-term survival plans. We are coming into late spring, so as long as another Green Fog does not roll up the coast, we should be able to forage and live off the land and sea until a resupply mission reaches us."

Ise watched him as she listened. His voice was impassive; the unused hand folded behind his back. This was classic Hal Lum, attempting to be the cool and stoic leader despite being sick to death with worry. He looked over his shoulder at her, his features carefully neutral.

"A reasonable sounding plan, Captain," she answered. "What of the sick? With no power, we cannot run shipboard ventilation. They cannot stay locked in Sickbay."

Hal moved silently to stand in front of the windows of the Comm, gazing out through the armoured glass with his eyes on the horizon. "They will stay locked in Sickbay," he answered in a barely audible voice. "I have discussed the matter with Doctor Émile, and it is the only way to ensure the rest of us do not catch it, or inadvertently take it back home with us. On my orders, the ventilation to the compartment will be sealed, and the door will be caulked shut. When I give that order, Doctor Émile will pass out sleeping pills under false pretence to prevent panic or injury. They will all just drift off to sleep. The ensuing carbon dioxide poisoning will be a relatively merciful ending for them," he answered quietly.

Ise simply stared at Hal's back in horror.

"Please hurry, Donovan. For Spirit's sakes, please hurry," she heard him whisper aloud.

## Cordelia
### 15h04 SST

Cordelia had just gotten comfortably curled up in "her" chair in the O-Room and cracked open her current "bodice-ripper" romance novel when the intercom box came to life.

"All able hands to Replenishment Stations. All able hands to Replenishment Stations. We will be transferring solid goods and fuel from the *al-Jazari* in sixteen minutes," came Hal Lum's voice.

She glanced up at the wall clock and sighed with relief. A bit more than forty-five minutes ago, the *Sheerah* had turned Eastward, burning the last of her precious fuel reserves to get them to land. Cordelia had not yet given up hope, but it had been dwindling steadily up until Hal's broadcast message. Their escort would have everything they needed to get home, and would be ready to conduct a rescue if the *Sheerah* foundered. She snapped her book closed without a second thought, and headed towards the Comm.

She met Jonas in the hallway, still limping and leaning on a cane, but making his own progress towards the Command Compartment. He gave her a wave and a smile. "Just go on past me, Cordie. Let the Skipper know I am on my way. I am still not moving at full speed, so I will be there as quick as I can," he said, trying to hide that every step he took hurt. He was not managing to convince Cordelia, who had a pang of sympathy.

"No problem, Jonzie. I will let Hal know. Take your time and do not hurt yourself worse on that ladder. We cannot start without you, either way," she said and gave him what she hoped was an encouraging smile.

"Thanks, Cordie," he replied.

She made her way past him, being cautious not to jostle him. Jonas was noticeably shorter and slighter of mass than she was, and with the rolling motion of the *Sheerah* on the surface it would have been far too easy to carelessly bounce him into the steel walls of Salt Flats.

It did cross her mind to offer to help him along, but she was worried he might take offence or insult. He was making progress under his own steam, and she did not want to take that away from him.

Once she was up in the Comm, she greeted Hal. "I do not think I have been so happy to hear a Broadcast Message about an hour or so of upcoming hard work in a long time," she laughed.

"Oh, you have no idea," Ise Koolen said quietly.

Hal gave the Spirit and Morale Councillor an admonishing look that puzzled Cordelia. Generally speaking, from what Cordelia had seen, Ise Koolen could do very little wrong in Hal's eyes. Whatever it was the blonde Salvage Leader was missing out on, it was obvious that Ise had just stepped in something.

"So, Captain, I passed Mister Zupan about halfway down Salt Flats. He asked me to let you know he will be here in a few minutes," Cordelia said as she took her chair.

"Oh, thank-you, Miz. Once Jonas gets here, I will get him to start sorting out the approach course for the *al-Jazari*," Hal answered.

Cordelia nodded. "Once we are nose to the wind, I will get the hoist post up and the Salvage team will start rigging."

Hal glanced over at her. "I will feel much better when that first thousand litres of diesel is aboard."

Cordelia scratched something out on a piece of scrap paper. "We will need almost ten thousand litres to make it home, so just the fuel transfer is going to take a while," she replied. "But yes, just having that first three tanks on board will let me breathe easier, too."

"Heya, Skipper!" Jonas called as he came through the hatch door into the Comm. "I heard you needed some fancy steering stuff done, so I figured I would drop by in case you needed me."

Hal gave Jonas what could only be described as a scathing look and then shook his head. "No, not really, Mister Zupan. I am sure Counsellor Koolen could have managed just fine. However, since you dropped by, you might as well sit in your chair and do some work," Hal replied blandly.

Cordelia covered her mouth with her hand and turned towards the dials and gauges at her crew station. The idea of Ise Koolen steering the *Sheerah* doing eight kilometres per hour at a ten-metre separation from an other RSAV in a two-metre chop was nothing short of absurd to Cordelia. Ise Koolen was many things, but a skilled RSAV driver was not one of them.

Jonas grinned and hobbled over to his crew station and settled into his chair. "Good luck out there, Cordie!" he offered to her as she got up.

"Thanks, Jonzie. Keep her straight and steady for me. We cannot afford to split a line or drop someone over," she returned.

He gave her a jaunty salute, and set to prepping his station to take manual control of the RSAV. She glanced over at Hal to find him giving her an amused look. She felt herself flush slightly, and she was not even entirely sure why.

"*Miz* Baasch," he began, slightly emphasizing the salutation, "please call me on channel four when you get outside. The Armsmen will be providing the strong backs along Salt Flats as usual. Please do be careful out there; we are thin on manning right now. We cannot afford an injury."

"Will do, Captain," she replied and headed for the hatch.

# Christopher
## 15h12 SST

As a professional warrior in a culture that was designed from the ground up to promote peace, Christopher had come to understand that the triumphs and conquests in one's life were always to be found within. The greatest battlefield one could conquer was one's self.

A wise man, generations ago, had once remarked that "… *the basic difference between an ordinary man and a warrior is that a warrior takes everything as a challenge*". Sometimes, to truly be victorious, one needed to consider advancing in a different direction; that was his current challenge.

Thus it was that Christopher pulled himself up the forward deck hatch ladder onto the *Sheerah's* weather deck. The RSAV was forging along strongly, running with the direction of the waves. In spite of the light winds, the sea was still strong with the after-effects of yesterdays' storm. He felt the ship's bow drop slightly as it began to "surf" down a wave, being carried along with the crest even as she slightly outran it. Off to the right of the *Sheerah* was her sister-ship, the *al-Jazari*. The two ships were running a parallel course to each other, with the gap between them being less than the beam of either ship. He turned up his collar against the spray that greeted him as he looked forward towards Salvage Leader Cordelia Baasch.

"Helluva day for an RSAV drag-race, do you not agree, Chief?" she called to him as he made his way over to her on the constantly shifting deck. While her question seemed light hearted enough, the expression on her face, and on the faces of a couple of her Detail, was clearly wary.

He had earned that. He had let his pride speak instead of his actions, and its words had been both unprofessional and unkind.

"Indeed it is, Chief," he answered, trying to sound friendly. It was not something he was very good at, he reflected. "I know you are short a couple of people" he stated, opting to stick to what he was good at: pragmatic business.

"Yes, almost half my Detail is in Emm-and-Queue. Same as yours," she answered, sounding defensive.

"So put me to work," he stated. She blinked at him in disbelief. "I am here to help as part of your on-deck team. The able Armsmen, Stewards and Engineers have rigged an improvised trolley-tram down Salt Flats to maximize the people-power available. They do not need me micro-managing them. So, I have some muscle, wits and will to apply to the jobs at hand up here; just tell me what to do."

There was a moment of awkward silence as the two looked at each other; the sounds of the wind, the waves, more than six thousand kilowatts of roaring diesel engines, crew activity, and even sensations like the chill of a dash of spray, the smell of the ocean and the sound of a curious seabird were lost as he held her gaze quietly. She gave him a slight nod. "Thank-you, Chief. We can use the hands. Grab the signals helmet and vest, and get ready for them to pass us the pilot line. Once it is over, I will get you to work the lift line."

"I will be glad to, Chief," he answered. "This is your specialty, so I am working for you. Just tell me what you need as you need it," he reaffirmed. There was a moment where Baasch again just looked at him, but she then gave him a nod and something that was not quite a smile.

The next few minutes were a flurry of activity on the decks of both RSAVs. A hydraulic piston, mounted vertically in the bottom of the hull raised a telescoping steel mast up above the deck when a hatch door, roughly half way between the Comm Tower and the bow, was opened. The raised mast was a bit less than five metres tall, with blocks and pulleys at the top.

The deck crew of the *al-Jazari* used a compressed air launcher to toss a brightly coloured shuttle-dart over to the *Sheerah*. That shuttle-dart trailed a thin line behind it, barely capable of holding two hundred or so kilograms. That was used to pull a heavier line across the gap between the ships, and that second line was used to pull across a braided line nearly twenty millimetres thick. This third line, with a breaking weight of a couple dozen tonnes, was then anchored to the deck with a bolt and clevis. A "bight" of the line was passed through the mast block and tackle, which was then lifted to the top of the mast by hydraulics.

With that line under reasonable tension, leaving less than a metre of sag over the gap between the two RSAVs, with roaring water beneath, the first cargo sling was hooked on to it aboard the *al-Jazari*. Christopher could identify the contents of the sling from here; a steel-frame encasing a dark cylinder meant fuel.

Each cylinder contained three hundred and thirty-five litres of diesel, and massed a bit more than a quarter tonne. Using raw muscle-power, the sling was reeled across the gap on the suspended heavy line using a zip-line type pulley and lines on both ships.

Christopher knew that behind him, in the Comm, Jonas Zupan would be doing his remarkable best to hold the course of the *Sheerah* arrow-straight and bow-to-bow with the *al-Jazari*. If the two ships swerved apart, the line would snap with enough force to split a man in half and the cargo would be lost to the ocean. If the two ships swerved towards each other, the speed of the water rushing between them would suck them together, resulting in a disastrous collision.

Getting knocked over the side by a tightening line or a swinging cargo load meant better than unfortunately good odds of going through one of the trio of thrusters on that side of the ship. If somehow that did not happen, then the swirling turbulent stream of water between the two ships was likely to pull you under, roll you like a turtle in storm-surf, drive you several metres down and knock the wind out of you. You would be halfway to drowned before you realized you were in the water. If you were fortunate enough to miss *that* charming experience, then you got to watch your ship sailing away from you usually between twelve to eighteen kilometres an hour for at least the next few minutes while they tried to conduct an "emergency breakaway maneuver".

The speed of that process was tempered by the need to avoid injuring anyone else in the haste to save your sorry backside. Then they needed to turn the two ships around, and start the process of trying to find you.

Replenishment At Sea Operations, or "RAS Ops", were not for the low of skill or faint of heart. Nothing but exactly right would do.

Nothing less than excellence would prevent injury, or worse.

As he hand-over-handed the wet and cold traveller line with the members of Miz Baasch's team, Christopher quietly watched the fierce work and clear pride that the Salvage Techs around him displayed. While he was yet again reminded of his dislike for the taste of fresh corvid, his own personal quest for excellence meant that if he had been wrong, then he needed to learn better and do better.

The bow of the two RSAVs simultaneously broke through the crest of the wave ahead of them, sheeting a thin salt spray into the air. With a final, forceful effort on the traveller-line, the container reached the *Sheerah*. It was swiftly lowered to the deck, and directly onto a cart running along grooves set into the RSAVs deck. To everyone else's apparent surprise, Christopher single handedly pushed the cart back along the inverted railway.

It was heavy work, to be sure, particularly since he was effectively pushing uphill for part of it as the ship rode down the slope of a wave. However, it was nothing he could not manage. Besides, he knew there was a ratchet-type mechanism that would stop the thing rolling back on him, so all he had to worry about was it surging forward. Even that risk was mitigated by the squeeze-bar that had to be held down to get the friction brakes on the wheels to let go.

The rails led to a side-door in the structure that housed the Command Compartment. This was a dumb-waiter type system that lowered the cart down to Salt Flats. From there, the cart would be moved to the cargo bays for temporary storage and unloading. A new cart came up a few moments later, and Christopher ran it back forward, and the process was repeated.

Over the next hour and a half the two ships transferred over seventy-six hundred kilos of fuel, and another five hundred kilograms of food and medical supplies, in roughly quarter-tonne bundles. Then, the block and tackle were lowered from the top of the mast, the block opened, and the heavy line allowed to run free and slip over the side to be reeled in by the crew on the *al-Jazari*.

Wet weather over-clothes or not, by the time the two RSAVs began steering a safely diverting course away to normal team-cruising distance, cold brine had wicked into all of his clothing. He was soaked to the bone; the only good news was the seawater was above freezing at this time of year.

Miz Baasch waved him over. "Thank-you, Chief. You did a great job, and your hard work is appreciated," she offered over the roar of the ships engines, the whistle of the wind, and the sea around them.

"You are most welcome, Chief. You run a good team and a smart operation. I am sorry I did not fully appreciate that before now. Let me know if there is anything you need person-power for, and I will do my best to keep Armsmen available to help you out."

Miz Baasch tilted her head to look at him, and she pulled her weather hood back. Like him, her hair was soaked, her skin was reddened with the combination of wind and chill, and a rivulet of saltwater stung at an eye. She nodded to him. "Thank-you, Chief. I know what your standards are, so that means a lot to me."

She offered her hand to shake, and he did not hesitate in accepting the gesture. His mother had long ago taught him that the taste of crow could usually be improved by avoiding adding sour grapes or bitter salt to the meal.

# Jonas
## 17h01 SST

"Mister Zupan, you have been wrestling with the Old Girl for a while now. Are you comfortable enough to be able to get us down?" Hal Lum asked him. Jonas lied and nodded with a smile and a thumbs-up.

It was about an hour after noon, and the RAS Ops were wrapped up successfully and without unexpected problems. It had been a gruelling process for Jonas; with partial power available, they could only move half as fast as they normally would, making them more susceptible to the influence of the energetic ocean. In addition, the *Sheerah* was asymmetrical in her thruster output; the forward port thruster had been destroyed by the mine detonation, and the middle port thruster only generated about sixty percent its usual output. That meant that the RSAV wanted to veer to the left constantly; without perpetual care and adjustment, they would have snapped the twenty-millimetre braided carrier line between the ships like it was candy floss.

Jonas hurt. Getting down Salt Flats from his bunk, hurt. Getting up the ladder into the Comm, hurt. Sitting in his chair, hurt. Battling the willful sea and injured RSAV for almost a hundred minutes straight, hurt.

But there was one more thing that they still had to do. They needed to submerge and make their way to the bottom. Jonas had full confidence in Marlon's people and that the repair work on the cargo ramp-door had been completed to the best of their ability. Still, if that jury-rigged seal let go, he wanted to be the one at the controls for the emergency surge to the surface. If the forward cargo hold flooded, getting the *Sheerah* and all his friends back to the surface before she was too heavy to do so was something he was trusting to no one else.

Ise Koolen had called him the "*Chief Navigational Miracle Worker*" that evening so long ago in the Forest Room. He was not sure he bought that, but in case she was right he was going to be at the helm. He had promised her he would do everything he could to be here for his friends and crew-mates. He was not going back on that promise now.

Hal looked at him skeptically from his position at the Comm windows. Cordelia, her pale skin still wind-and-chill rosy, was visibly looking at him from her crew station at the edge of his vision. She sort of looked concerned to Jonas, but he was more worried about Hal Lum.

"Mister Zupan, are you avoiding answering my questions verbally so I do not hear the extent of the pain in your voice?" Hal asked him casually.

Jonas lied and shook his head, offering Hal his best attempt at a winning smile. Cordelia snickered.

"That is what I thought," he said dryly. "Miz Baasch, please inform the *al-Jazari* that we are ready for a team dive. We are changing to underwater telephone now. Mister Zupan, once I have the *al-Jazari* on the line, prepare to dive at ten degrees down angle and ten percent negative buoyancy."

"Aye-aye, Skipper," Jonas replied, trying to sound cheerful. Based on the look Cordelia shot his way, he was not sure it was working. If Hal noticed, he declined to comment on it, instead moving to Christopher's crew station and picking up the handset for the underwater telephone.

After a couple of minutes of back and forth with the other RSAV, Hal glanced over at Cordelia. "You have comms with the forward cargo bay, Miz Baasch?"

"Yes, Captain," Cordelia replied tersely and gave a slight nod. "When I asked for volunteers, First-Class Tech Anna Longo forbade anyone else raise their hand, and *she* volunteered," the Salvage Leader said.

Jonas suddenly had a lump in his throat. Anna was good people, and a dear friend of Cordie's. Jonas rather liked her as a crew mate. She was in the forward cargo hold, with the door locked behind her, to watch the seal on the cargo ramp-door.

Her job was to report if she saw any evidence of a leak as they went the eighty or so metres to the seafloor. Of course, that meant that if the leak was severe, Miz Longo was on the wet side of a locked door with no way out.

"Noted," was Hal's only reply. He paused, looked out the windows at the horizon and took a deep breath. "Take us down, Mister Zupan. Make your depth ten metres."

"Aye, Skipper, make my depth ten metres," Jonas replied formally and eased the control yoke forward.

Water rushed forward over the bow, racing along the deck and against the Command Compartment's armoured windows. Jonas glanced at his depth gauge, watching it steadily spiral from right to left. It measured from the bottom of the hull; ten metres down, meant about three metres of water over the top of the Comm. The pressure on the cargo ramp-door would be an additional eighty-percent of a full atmosphere now.

Less than a dozen seconds later, Jonas levelled the *Sheerah* out, glancing pensively at his variety of displays and gauges. He glanced over at Cordelia who was listening intently on her phone. Jonas guessed that Anna was giving a narrated inspection of the seal for the ramp-door.

Hal was waiting quietly at Christopher's crew station, one ear listening to the underwater telephone, the rest of his attention on Cordelia. Jonas could not begin to guess at the stress that Hal must be feeling right now.

Cordelia exhaled in relief. "We are good. Seal is holding and no sign of ingress."

"Thank Spirits," Hal answered. "Mister Zupan, take us down to twenty-five metres, please."

"Aye, Skipper, set depth twenty-five; ten degrees dive, negative ten buoyancy."

"If we can hold at twenty-five metres for twenty-five minutes without problem," Hal began thoughtfully, "then I will be confident enough to take us across the Great River Influence Zone. After that, it is straight on to home."

"Heya, Cordie?" Jonas asked, trying to sound casual.

"What is up, Jonzie?" she answered.

"When we get home, are you up for listening to some music with me one evening?" he blurted.

Cordelia blinked and turned in her chair towards him. "Did you just ask me on a *date*?" she asked, sounding surprised.

"If he did," Hal said sternly, "he is going to have to wait for the answer because I need you two focusing on us not breaking an RSAV under three atmospheres of pressure."

"Yessir" they both answered at the same time, sounding like a pair guilty teenagers.

Hal face-palmed and the two erupted in nervous snickering. "Come on, people," Hal growled. "I do not care what you two do in your off time, but right now, let us remain on the task at hand."

Jonas and Cordelia both nodded. Jonas felt well into the category of stupid right now. What Hull-Flooded Hell had possessed him to blurt like that? So much for being suave and non-threatening; he rubbed at his forehead, conscious of his embarrassment. He was surprised she had not just verbally sent him packing, he thought with an audible sigh.

"Depth now twenty-five metres, Skipper," Jonas announced. He shifted in his chair, trying to find something closer to a comfortable position to sit in. All he succeeded in doing was changing where it hurt, and by how much.

"Thank-you, Mister Zupan. Hold steady course and depth. Miz Baash, how is the brave Miz Longo fairing?" Every twelve metres of water equalled a weight of the entire world above, from ground level to the edge of space. A full two atmospheres of pressure was trying to push the sea into every crack and crevice in the emergency seal material around the ramp-door. Under those pressures, the flow of water would be like an acid; it would erode any leak it could find into a progressively worsening stream.

Any leak that Anna spotted would be dire news. There were not very many long-term survival options for a plague ship that could not park on the bottom and be supplied via tethers from Soumerville. That bottom, around Soumerville, was one hundred and four metres down; a full eleven atmospheres of pressure.

Cordelia offered a thumbs-up before speaking. "Still good. Seal is holding. No sign of ingress."

Half an hour later, the seal was still holding tight and dry against the hydraulic pressure of the ocean beyond the door. Hal keyed the underwater telephone.

"Donovan, we are going to step down to forty metres; that is most of the way to the bottom here. I intend to cross the Zone at this depth. We will start actually rolling when we get to the other side and the seafloor comes back up."

Jonas looked at his array of instruments. There was a total of around fifty metres of water here. The silt-laden Great River Influence Zone, which they were approaching was a three-fold problem to the injured *Sheerah*. It was deep, it was dirty and it was moving.

The surrounding shelves and banks were anywhere between thirty and sixty metres below sea-level, but when you reached the Influence Zone the bottom rapidly plunged nearly half a kilometre at a rate in excess of a seventy-degree slope. The pressures at a third that depth would crumple a healthy Mk.III Reclaimer like a cheap soup can. From what Hal had said, Jonas guessed the plan was to avoid touching bottom until they were across, so that there was no risk of driving off a proverbial cliff and losing control.

The Zone was also a massive conveyor belt of silt and sediment nearly three thousand kilometres long, before it even reached the ocean. Such a monstrous volume of water and material moved along with it that, over thousands of years, it had dug a trench from the river mouth, through the Great River Gulf, and out to the edge of the continental shelf.

The water was visibly a different colour; the mixing of chilled sea water, warm river water, rich organic sediments and brilliant sunlight meant that plankton bloomed constantly there. It also meant that the hull and thrusters would be coating in all of that; normally, fouling was a *non-sequitur*, but with the restrictions on power, it would slightly slow the RSAV.

Lastly, it was an inexorable force, pushing to the South-East at a constant five kilometres per hour. Normally, this would not be a problem. However, right now, the injured *Sheerah* could only manage three better than that. Shave five or ten percent of that margin off due to fouling, and getting across the Zone started to become an untenable process.

Hal looked towards Jonas. "Mister Zupan, make your depth forty metres."

"Aye, Skipper, make my depth forty metres. Cross your fingers," he suggested as he eased forward on the yoke, sending the RSAV deeper into the ocean. He watched his depth gauge dropping steadily, and levelled the ship out. "Depth now forty metres," he announced.

"Ramp-door holding; seal seems to be just fine. Zero evidence of ingress," Cordelia announced after a moment of discussion with Anna with the phone-set.

Hal nodded. He keyed the intercom to the Engine Room. "Eng, this is Comm. We are at forty metres by our dials up here. How are we doing back there?"

"Reading forty-two here, Skipper," came Dasia Lagounov's voice. "The aft emergency hatch is still leak-free, and all other notables are green. It looks like we are fine to hold this depth."

"Very good news. We are going to be reaching the Great River Influence Zone in a little while. We are going to need all the amps and clicks you can spare us."

"Understood, Captain. We can clear to ten kilometres per hour for one hour. Check back with us at that point and we will see if we can give you an extension."

"Very good. Thank-you, Eng. Comm out," Hal said and turned the intercom off. "Mister Zupan, start your timer, one hour. Set speed ten, please."

"Aye Skipper, set speed ten, one hour run, starting now."

"Pilot, take us home. Best course across the Zone, and then best course for home," Hal said quietly.

"With pleasure, Skipper," Jonas replied with a smile and then a wince.

"Miz Baasch, please go get Miz Longo out of that compartment. Give her my heartfelt thanks for her bravery."

"With pleasure, Captain," Cordelia answered and flashed a wink at Jonas as she headed for the hatch.

# CHAPTER SEVENTEEN
## *The Council of Seven*

### Hal
### 13h21 SST
### Wednesday, June 1st
### Soumerville
### 16C, Light rain and Fog, Winds 21 kph W

"I think that is easily one of the most extraordinary stories I have heard in all my years aboard or in charge of RSAVs, Captain Lum," Alodia Holt said to him as she leaned forward in her chair to set the thick report folder on her desk. "Thank-you for bringing the *Sheerah* and her crew home safely, in spite of all of that."

"It was my job and my duty, Miz. I am glad I could do it," he answered, his mouth a bit dry, and his face carefully neutral.

Nearly a month had gone by since they had gone under the waves alongside the *al-Jazari*. They had made it home, and immediately been parked for quarantine. The RSAV had been connected for air, power and communications like she was a work-shack, and sealed bundles of stores had been brought by dolphin train to a dive-lock.

A trio of doctors with a veritable pile of gear had come aboard as well to assist Doctor Émile in dealing with the Top-Sider disease and ensuring that the rest of the crew were in good health. In Hal's eyes, that trio were remarkable heroes, literally betting their lives that their science and skill could defeat a disease that the Ironclad Kingdom had been scourged by for dozens of years, before it crippled or killed them as well.

That had been three long weeks, sometimes sixteen hours a day for them, but finally, they had concocted a cure and a vaccine. Finally, the *Sheerah* had been allowed to completely come home.

She had not gone to a moon-pool; she had been ordered straight to the graving dock alongside the *Emilia Lanier*. Hal had walked off his beloved ship just three days ago, fully anticipating never seeing her again.

It was expected be at least four months to fully repair the damage done by the blast that had crippled her under his command. Work on the *Lanier* had discovered a myriad of hull cracks, pipe fractures and such that had not been initially detected when she first came in. The Mk.III Reclaimers were sturdy ships, to be sure, but they were never designed to withstand that kind of violence.

The most likely thing to happen, presuming the Mission Services Mistress was feeling benevolent, was that he would be given a desk job where his screw-ups would not imperil any other RSAV crews. Even in the most ideal of worlds, the best outcome he could hope for would be to be given another ship; likely one of the long-range passenger-merchants.

Ise Koolen, ever the encouraging optimist, had told him not to lose hope. She had been cheerfully certain that the entire crew would be back together in just a couple of short months, and the *Sheerah* would be taking them all off on their next adventure together. Hal had not had the heart to tell her she was likely delusional and in need of some time off.

Alodia Holt eyed him critically across the expansive applewood-inlaid oak desk. "As you might imagine, given the gravity of the events that unfolded on the *Sheerah*'s cruise, the Council wishes to speak with you directly. That will be Friday morning, fourteen-hundred hours SST. You will report here in your best bib and tucker, and we will head up to the Council Chamber together."

"… And that would be that", he thought with a sinking feeling in his gut.

"In the meantime, you and your crew are effectively on four-and-two Seconds for the next forty-five days, minimum. As you know, the damage to the *Lanier* has proven remarkably extensive, and we are just presuming until proven otherwise that the same holds true for the *Sheerah*."

"Of course, Miz. Those are prudent precautions," he said, trying to sound as neutral and professional as he could manage.

"I encourage you to make the most of your time off, Captain Lum. You have earned the rest, and given current events, I expect you will be a busy man in the near future. Dismissed."

"Thank-you, Miz. I will see you Friday," he replied. He stood, bowed, and left her office.

# Ise
## 14h17 SST

As she gazed up through the kaleidoscope of sea-filtered sunlight, streaming down through the cerami-glass dome and the spreading canopy of leaves, Ise Koolen exhaled deeply. It had been a remarkable journey, in so many contexts; there and back again. When modern RSAV crews joked about living a life of adventure, most were indulging in self-congratulatory hyperbole, born of an unavoidable envy of the heroes from the stories of the first half of the history of Soumerville and her under-sea sister towns.

This second half of history, that she, her family, and friends were all living through, was a far more staid and predictable time. Or so Ise had thought, until the past cruise.

She took a bite from an apple she had just picked, and settled down against the trunk of a tree. A small bird bounced onto the tip of her foot, chirped at her merrily, and then bounded away. Ise giggled in surprise, and waved in delight after the departing bird.

She wondered how Hal was doing. When she had last seen him, he had been so sure of his doom that he could not see his triumph. The good news was that she was fairly certain that Alodia Holt would grab him by the ear as required on the matter. The Mission Services Mistress was famous for having a, *ahem*, knack for getting people to listen to her. Ise had done a bit of prompting in that direction, professionally.

Hal; Ise sighed and shook her head. When the *Sheerah* had finally been secured in the graving dock, and the hatches had been opened, the crew had been greeted by cheers of adoration and tears of joy from family, friends, and supporters. Everyone, of course, but Hal. None of his family had been there. Ise had insisted that he meet her parents, and her father had not missed a second in thanking Hal for bringing Ise home safe, and congratulating him on the extraordinary achievement that this moment in history represented.

In a moment of self-righteous fury, which admittedly involved the fourth glass of wine at dinner with her parents and siblings later that evening, Ise had considered calling Hal's father and forcefully disassembling his ego for him. However, she well knew that would not solve anything. Hal had to solve this, if it could be solved. Anything else was a temporary solution that would heal nothing.

"The Letter" had arrived. She had skimmed it over yesterday while having a lazy brunch. She recognized none of the names, which made things equally more simple and more awkward at the same time. However, she had plenty of free time ahead of her in the evenings;

anywhere between three to six months if rumours were to be believed. Spirit's could only guess at what that whole process would be like. Her mother had been giddy with excitement for her; her father had just rolled his eyes at his wife. Ise was somewhere between the two ends of that spectrum. However, like anything else in her life, Ise had decided to have fun with the entire thing, and see where it took her.

She wondered how Veerhulm was doing. He had literally stepped into an alien world, one he openly admitted was so bizarre to him that he had to keep checking with "Elder Marlon" if he was really understanding correctly what he was seeing and hearing. He would have a long process of adjustment ahead of him. He was a fascinating individual, and Ise hoped that one day she could speak with him directly, that they could compare notes on their respective approaches to their common trade.

She sighed, and stretched. Time to get back to work. She had a few fruit trees to prune, and some compost-mulch to spread. It was going to be a good day.

# Marlon
## 13h14 SST
## Thursday, June 2nd

"So, are you sure about this?" Annabelle asked him in the dim quiet of their bedroom. She was curled up against him, the sheets in no particular order, with her cheek and hair against his shoulder, and a hand on the bare skin of his hip. He toyed with a lock of her hair in the gap of silence before he spoke.

"I am, dearest. When I was locked in that Sickbay, watching young people around me get sick, and get scarred and start to die, I realized I was done. I got very lucky with that wound. I got very lucky with that disease. I am well past where 'lucky' is enough. I will be delivering my retirement papers on Monday."

She nodded, and kissed at a bare patch of his skin. "I cannot truthfully tell you I am against the idea. I have spent more than twenty years waiting for the sea to take you away from me, forever. I will not miss that feeling at all."

He ruffled her hair affectionately, quiet comfort in response to the sensation of a tear tumbling onto his bare chest. "I will still be busy, as Veerhulm's Sponsor, but it will all be here, home, in Soumerville."

She exhaled a quiet sigh of relief. "He seems like a nice enough sort; certainly very striking in appearance. He is keen to fit in?" she asked, splaying a hand over his chest, and settling her chin on it as they chatted.

"Hmmm? Oh, yes, he is very keen to fit in. Very keen, indeed. We spent a sizeable amount of the time we were both shut-ins starting to teach him our language and the culture. So, the official Petition to the Council will be next week, and then it is formal classes and such. He will have a year and a day, as is the usual with this sort of thing, to be able to pass the citizenship tests, and take his STADE," Marlon replied.

"It is going to require a tremendous amount of commitment and work on his part," Annabelle noted thoughtfully. "Some of your commitment and time, as well."

"Yes. About four hours a week from me. Well worth it, I think; giving someone a new start on life? I thought we might even plan a trip for he and our family to an other town in a few months; a learning vacation, as it were."

"Oh, that sounds marvellous," Annabelle replied. "Would you be amendable to having Mahomet along?"

"Well, yes, of course. I think that is a capital idea. It would be good for Veerhulm, as well as an excellent chance for us all to get to know our daughter's fellow better. However, that is a bit of putting the shuttle before the dolphin, my dear. You can turn your instinct for meticulous social over-planning loose upon that unsuspecting pair once our newest resident can actually speak in full sentences," he chuckled.

She gave him a playfully sour look. "I do not 'over-plan'," she said with laughing mock indignance.

"To the minute and since I met you, dearest. You always have, and always will," he replied in visible amusement.

"Cad!" she replied. A playfully aimed swat by her was intercepted by a hand from him, and the ensuing wrestling and giggling between the two occupied the next few minutes until Annabelle kissed him soundly. "I think you are about to find out what I have 'planned' for you for this morning, right now," she said with a wicked grin.

# Hal
## 14h02 SST,
## Friday, June 3rd
## Soumerville

"Introducing Reclamation Services Mission Services Mistress Alodia Holt and Reclamation Services Amphibious Vehicle Captain Hal Lum to the Guiding Council of Soumerville," the burly Herald of Arms called as the pair entered the ornately decorated formal chambers. The floors were a stained hardwood of some kind with inlaid geometric patterns of lighter softwoods, all waxed and polished to a glow. The walls were done in bright frescoes of the surroundings of Soumerville, on some calm and sunny day, giving the oil-color faux-illusion of the Council Chamber being just a floor and domed ceiling in the ocean. The ceiling was alternating dark and light hardwood panels, lit by recessed and indirect lights, as well as a substantial crystal chandelier that looked to Hal's eyes like all of the stars of the night sky hung in single glittering array.

The entry to the chamber was from the South. The North of the chamber was a raised dais, with seven substantial chairs; one per member of the Council. The Council was four women and three men, chosen from prior Generations for their dedication and contribution to Soumerville's success and survival. The decisions made here had the power to change the course of history for the people who lived in this undersea town.

Ostensibly, being called to the Council's Chamber was a rare privilege. In this particular case, however, Hal was expecting a relatively unpleasant visit. He and Alodia stopped in the middle of the floor where a couple of Chamber staff held chairs for them, at a table facing the Council members.

Alodia was resplendent in a long-skirted suit, a deep burgundy ensemble trimmed with silver accents. The gown and coat were clearly custom-tailored to her. Her choice of jewelry echoed the mighty chandelier in crystal and silver. A smart little half-sized top-hat sat upon her impeccably dressed hair, combining the colours of both her clothes and her jewelry. On the walk over here, Hal had mused that there were a number of women half Miz Holt's age that would have been thrilled to possess half her style.

Hal, for his part, was wearing his formal service uniform including the double-breasted jacket with the half-length duck tails. The colours were two deep blue tones, lifted from the summer midnight sky, with bright red-gold accents and a white shirt. The look, like everything else about the Service, had been decided upon during Generation One, and had been fixed ever since.

Hal waited for Alodia to be seated before he took his own seat. The Chamber staff then poured them each a glass of ice water before stepping away.

One of the women, at centre of the arc of imposing chairs and accompanying writing tables, rose. Each of the Council members was dressed in deep grey robes of a loose fit, trimmed with red. The simple looking attire was a pronounced counter-point to the decor of the room, Hal thought.

"I am Council Mistress Anastasia MacPherson.  Please allow me to begin by introducing my colleagues.  This is Council Master Estanislau Albecki, Council Mistress Eleanor Mach, Council Master Walter Dratel, Council Mistress Courtney Guri, Council Master Zheng Huang and Council Mistress Fatsani Temitope," she concluded.  As she spoke, she gestured to each one in turn, and they rose, gave a polite demi-bow, and then sat down again.

"Welcome to the Chambers of the Guiding Council, Mistress and Captain," Council Mistress Anastasia said, sounding genuine in her words to Hal.  Whatever her original hair colour had been was completely replaced by the passage of time with silver, but her dark eyes were still bright and keen, he thought.  From what he could see, while he might be the youngest in the room by twenty years, he was hardly guaranteed to be in the top half of the sharpest witted.

"We thank-you for the invitation," Alodia responded.  Hal nodded, trying to be as attentive as possible, in spite of the nagging feeling of attending the verbal firing squad for his career.

"Captain Lum," Council Mistress Fatsani began, "I would like to start by thanking you for your remarkable service and dedication to the Reclamation Service.  We of the Council are aware that you could have chosen a more, shall we say, family-agreed-upon career by the way of a ridiculous piece of legislation I personally feel has outlived its usefulness."

Hal blinked, but otherwise tried to retain his composure.  They *knew* his father had tried to pressure him into the Foundry by the "Inheritance Clause"?  How?  Like the Spirit and Morale Counsellors, there was a certain reputation for a seemingly preternatural awareness that went with the so-called Council of Seven.  Even so, this was almost shocking.

Alodia nudged him politely. "You are allowed to reply," she offered quietly.

He blinked sideways at Alodia and then turned towards Council Mistress Fatsani. "Oh, it has entirely been my pleasure, Mistress. I am very lucky to have had the opportunities and experiences the Service have provided me," he answered, trying to sound sincere and absent of panic.

Council Master Walter spoke up, "Captain Lum, as someone who has been personally affected by the existence of the Inheritance Clause of the Assignment Articles of the Standardised Aptitude Determination Exams, I would be very interested in hearing what you think of it."

Hal bit his lip and hesitated. "I, ah, have personal reservations about the value of the Clause, Sir."

The various members of the Council glanced at each other. Hal was given the impression there was some amusement in the air, but he was not entirely sure about what.

Council Mistress Anastasia offered him a warm smile. "Captain Lum, I believe this your first visit before the Council, am I correct?"

"Beyond a grade-school visit to the Chambers, yes, Mistress," he answered, sounding rather meek, even to himself.

"Please, Captain, be at ease here. Speak your mind. We need to know and to understand what goes on in the lives of nearly fifteen thousand people. The decisions made here, in this Chamber, affect not only ourselves, but our children, and their children, and beyond. Soumerville will be undertaking its greatest achievement soon, the construction of a new '*Mare Oppidum*', like our home here. We need to know, from people like you who have been affected by decisions made by our forebears, how those decisions hold up in the modern world. The last thing we need to do is pass forward the mistakes of our past to the settlers of a new future."

Hal did about the only thing he could think was reasonable right now, and had mouthful of the iced water from the glass before him. What he *wanted* to do was explode, and tell them all about the lost nights of sleep, the anger and hurt of never seeing his father at the dock, the guilt of having let his family down, all caused by that damned stupid loophole. He took a deep breath.

"The kindest thing I can say, Mistress, is that my own experience would have been indescribably better if my father had never heard of that 'Clause'. I stand by my decision to support the purpose of the Exams, and my decision to put the needs of my fellow Citizens ahead of my father's patriarchal need to have a legacy. However, that decision continues to come at a noticeable cost to me, and so I am compelled to ask you all to spare anyone else this ... unpleasant side effect."

Beside him, to his utter shock, Alodia very quietly cheered. Before he had dealt with that, Council Mistress Fatsani openly applauded him. "Well said, Captain," she offered with a clear nod of approval.

A round of "here-here" passed amongst the other Council members. Council Mistress Anastasia glanced at her cohort and nodded. "I will table a motion at our next legislative meeting to terminate that Clause, effective immediately, then," she informed the room.

Hal was rapidly starting to feel like he was swimming at the edge of a riptide. So far, none of what had happened resembled anything he had expected or imagined in the two days since Alodia had informed him of the meeting.

"The next thing we, of the Council, would like to discuss with you, Captain is the recent events of your last mission," Council Mistress Fatsani said. "We have all been briefed by Mission Service Mistress Holt as to the details and timeline of what happened. While I know Mistress Holt well enough to know she has already thanked you for your extraordinary efforts in this genuinely remarkable circumstance, please allow me to convey to you my own personal thanks. The Service is near and dear to me, and so are the people in it, even if I only watch from afar and live your adventures vicariously via printed paper now. Thank-you so very much for being part of getting the *Emilia Lanier* home, and for everything you had to do and plan for in getting the *Sheerah* and her crew home."

Hal had to put his water glass down to avoid dropping it. He could feel mist at the edge of his eyes, and was not entirely certain what to do about that, or anything else right now.

Beside him, Alodia Holt whispered an amused "Steady on, Captain. They are not done with you yet."

Council Master Zheng offered Hal a friendly smile. "As my esteemed colleague alluded to just a few minutes ago," he said, gesturing to Council Mistress Anastasia, "Soumerville is very close to the point where we must make more room for our citizens. That will involve beginning the massive undertaking of building an entire new undersea town, just like ours here. I cannot begin, Captain Lum, to describe to you the logistical effort this will involve. It will be the *magnum opus* of Soumerville's Generation Seven; *your* Generation. What do you think of that idea, Captain?"

So, the rumours were true, he thought. The *Mare Oppidum* design was for '*a population of ten to twelve thousand, under optimal living conditions*'. It was very close to common knowledge that as of the peak of Generation Seven, Soumerville's numbers were beyond that by at least ten percent. Council Mistress Anastasia had just said it was nearly fifteen thousand, by the Council's reckoning.

But why would they care what he thought of all this? What did any of that have to do with Black Stone Harbour?

"Well, Sir," he began carefully, "I think it is remarkable that I will get to see that happen in my lifetime."

Council Master Zheng nodded. "I think we all feel the same, Captain. However, this discovery you have made at 'Black Stone Harbour', as well as the damage done to two of its RSAVs, means that the Council has some adjustments to make in our plans."

Hal nodded, listening carefully. He had no idea where any of this was going right now, but there was no mistaking the gravity of what he was hearing.

Council Mistress Fatsani spoke up, after a sip from her glass of water. "The initial repair estimates for your ship, the *Sheerah*, Captain, are better than expected. However, we cannot afford to have the area around Black Stone Harbour unmonitored for over a hundred days, and we cannot afford to have anyone unfamiliar with the culture and the area undertake the surveillance."

"We need to know everything we can glean about this Ironclad Kingdom, Captain," she continued. "Their borders, their capabilities, and their culture. The last thing we want is to be infringing into their areas and endangering our crews and ships. You and your crew are our experts, Captain."

Hal did his best to keep his jaw from hitting the table.

"The problem of course, as was said, is your ship will be out of action far longer than we can spare. Are you familiar with the *RSAV Grand Hermine*?" Council Mistress Anastasia asked him.

Hal wracked his brain. He was sure he had heard the name before. "Do ... do you mean the Mark One that established Soumerville?" he asked, his eyes wide in astonishment.

"Yes, that ship, precisely," Council Mistress Anastasia replied. "She has been sitting in 'active mothball' for ... oh, just call it 'quite a while'. By 'active mothball' I mean that as resources have been available, she has had her systems upgraded to keep her inline with the capabilities of the Mark Threes, but otherwise has had her internal atmosphere nothing but nitrogen and her hull painted in anti-rust primer. In thirty days, you will be taking command of the *RSAV Grand Hermine*, and will personally hand-pick your crew. You will work directly with Mistress Holt, and your specific, singular mission will be to use the noticeably more combat-worthy characteristics of the Mark One Reclaimer to surveil and monitor the Ironclad Kingdom, and if required, defend us against them."

Hal could do nothing else but sit back in his chair in shock.

"With due respect, Mistress Anastasia," Mistress Holt suggested from her chair beside him, "I would suggest you give Captain Lum a chance to process this. I suspect he is feeling a bit overwhelmed by the scope of what he was just told."

"Oh, I imagine he is, yes," Council Master Estanislau's deep voice rumbled. "Do not fret, Captain, it is a common reaction to occupying the chair you are currently seated in," he chortled.

Alodia covered her mouth with a flick of her silver fan and a glance away from Hal. She was clearly amused at Estanislau's commentary. Hal, for his part was still mentally churning through the adjustment of his world view. Unless he had completely heard wrong, he was being given command of the closest thing in over a Generation to a combat mission for an RSAV crew. A crew *he* would choose; he could assemble whatever dream-team he wanted, possibly from across the entire fleet, to crew a legendary ship on a history-making mission.

It occurred to him this was no effort at all. It was not the hull that mattered, he realized; it was the people. He knew which people he wanted. He wanted the crew from the *Sheerah;* all of them.

"Excuse me for the question, Mistresses and Masters, but … do I understand correctly that the Ironclad Kingdom are considered at least as likely opponents?"

Mistress Anastasia nodded at him before she answered. "Yes. With two RSAVs heavily damaged and subsequently several of your crew injured in direct combat, for now, we are treating contact with them with the utmost caution."

Hal nodded. "Mistress, may I bring forward an item of business?" he asked carefully. He was being possibly far too bold, but it was the right thing to do. He had to try.

Alodia glanced aside at him, but made no comment. Several members of the Council glanced at each other, but likewise remained silent.

"Of course, Captain Lum. What is on your mind?" Anastasia MacPherson answered smoothly.

"It is my understanding that the refugee that the *Sheerah* brought home, Veerhulm Klientan, will be putting forward a Sponsored Petition to become a Citizen. I wish it understood by the Council that while he may be from the Ironclad Kingdom, he is no enemy of ours. He did everything he could to assist the doctors and crew aboard the *Sheerah*, and has been a fountain of information about his former home. He is our friend, not our foe," Hal reiterated firmly.

"Noted, Captain, and thank-you," Mistress Anastasia replied with a warm smile. "The Council had heard of the impending Petition, and we are well predisposed towards it. Your assurances are valuable to us." She paused for a moment, clearly considering the young Captain sitting at the literal centre of attention.

"Captain Lum, in your report to Mission Services Mistress Holt, you specifically cited several individuals worthy of commendation due to the extremity of the situation they were in and the valour and courage with which they conducted themselves."

"Yes, Miz. I felt and still feel very strongly that without their

305

individual acts of courage or initiative, the *Sheerah* and her crew would have just vanished into the history books as another missing RSAV," Hal replied somewhat defensively.

Alodia cleared her throat while giving Hal a sidelong glance. "I do not believe that the Council has declared a disagreement with your recommendations, Captain Lum," she said pointedly.

Hal flushed slightly, smarting from the verbal cuff to the ego that the Mission Services Mistress had just issued him. "My apologies for my tone, Mistress," he answered, trying to sound like he still owned some dignity, somewhere.

Council Mistress Eleanor Mach lightly waved her hand and offered a kind smile to Hal. "It is quite all right, Captain. As the Mission Services Mistress herself pointed out," she noted dryly, "this entire meeting must be a tad overwhelming for you."

Alodia muttered something that sounded rather uncharitable, while still managing a polite smile and a deferring nod. Her precise words exactly escaped Hal's ears.

"I have the list of your recommendations here," Mistress Eleanor continued, gesturing to a sheet of paper on her writing desk. "Council Mistress Anastasia, with your permission?"

"Oh, yes, of course, Council Mistress Eleanor, please do."

Mistress Eleanor picked up a sheet of paper before her, and adjusted the spectacles she wore. "The following individuals shall have their Service Records updated, effective as of this reading, with the following commendations from the Guiding Council of Soumerville.

"Pilot-Navigator Jonas Zupan, Conspicuous Gallantry Under Adversity;

"Salvage and Dive Leader Cordelia Baasch, Ysande Szwedko Award for Leadership;

"Chief Armsman Christopher Olivier, Conspicuous Gallantry Under Adversity;

"Salvage and Dive Tech, First-Class, Anna Longo, Conspicuous Gallantry Under Adversity and the Virgil Stringer Award for Remarkable Dedication;

"Security & Weapons Tech, Third-Class, André Lindo, Conspicuous Gallantry Under Adversity;

"Additionally, the *RSAV Sheerah* herself will be awarded a Mark of Distinction, a Mark of Conspicuous Service, and an Augment of Battle Honours. She is now one of only a handful of Mark Threes in the world to hold that Augment," Mistress Eleanor noted as she concluded. She returned the sheet of paper to her writing desk, and laid her spectacles atop it.

"With all due respect to my esteemed Council colleague," Council Mistress Fatsani began, with a smile playing at the corner of her mouth, "I do believe you missed one."

"Oh?" Mistress Anastasia interjected, sounding entirely too innocuous.

"Yes. Suffice to say that Council Mistress Courtney Guri dumped the best part of a mail satchel on my desk a few days ago. The contents were a compelling set of recommendations. If I may?" Mistress Fatsani asked politely.

"Please do."

Council Mistress Fatsani looked at Hal, then picked up a sheet of paper on her writing desk. Holding it at arms length, she read aloud "Reclamation Services Amphibious Vehicle Captain Hal Lum, Meritorious Gallantry Under Adversity, the Ysande Szwedko Award for

Leadership, the Virgil Stringer Award for Remarkable Dedication, and the Fatsani Temitope Citation for Exceptional Action In Command."

Hal blinked, absolutely stunned to silence by what he had just heard.

"I told you they were not done with you just then," Alodia quietly offered in a bland tone.

The exceedingly petite Council Mistress Courtney Guri gestured to get Hal's attention. He blinked at her wordlessly, still in shock. "Those letters were testimony from each and every member of your crew, Captain. They made it amply clear, even from a few of your detractors, that your dedication, skill, encouragement, praise, and stubborn determination was what brought your ship home."

After a moment of silence, Council Mistress Anastasia spoke up. "Well, it is going to be quite a parade, I would suppose."

"Parade?" Hal asked, still trying to get his mental machinery working again.

"Yes, a parade, Captain," Council Master Estanislau boomed jovially. "Between the crews of the *Lanier* and the *Sheerah*, the Council has passed out more medals in the past thirty days than in the past thirty months. The Council believes that both crews should have their extraordinary events and awards well displayed before the public of Soumerville. So, in two weeks time, we will be having a one-day civic holiday declared, and the two ship's companies will be part of a parade of honour."

"Everybody loves a parade," Alodia commented amusedly.

# Epilogue

*... And thus concludes our story. Of course, with the benefit of twenty-twenty hindsight from here within the Eighth Generation, we know that Captain Lum did almost fully reassemble his original crew. We know that he and his crew did a remarkable job over the next two years in the face of continued escalating aggression in keeping both Soumerville as well as our home of Baslaurent safe from the Ironclad Kingdom. Even during the brief and tragic period of actual war between the two cultures, Captain Lum and those who served with him proved time and time again to be modern-day heroes here, and to many more around the globe.*

*Spirit And Morale Counsellor Ise Koolen eventually married, and subsequently accepted a titled teaching position at the Vniuersitatis Sub Mari where both she and her wife teach. Her principled and eloquent anti-war stance strongly influenced both Soumerville and Baslaurent's policies of avoidance and passive containment. If you have a chance to audit her lecture series on 'The Costs and Ethics of War', I strongly suggest you do so.*

*Pilot-Navigator Jonas Zupan and Salvage and Dive Detail Leader Cordelia Baasch went on to be leading authorities in their respective trades. Additionally, for those of you that enjoy a happy, romantic, story ending, they did eventually marry and have thus far, as the saying goes, have 'lived happily to the here and now'.*

*As a side note, "Samantha Shameless" also did several notable vocal performances with the "Jon Zee Clark Project" over the following decade, most of which were smash hits in dance halls and music parlours around the globe.*

*Chief Engineering Artificer Marlon Pryce did retire as he intended, and was not part of the crew of the Grand Hermine. The Chief Engineering Artificer of the Grand Hermine was instead Miz Dasia Lagounov, at Chief Pryce's own recommendation.*

*Marlon Pryce continued teaching and expanding our knowledge of Precursor Studies, and many of his insights are now foundations for the entire field. Unfortunately, Marlon Pryce is no longer with us, having passed on to the Summerlands peacefully in his sleep two years ago.*

*Chief Armsman Christopher Olivier, as I am sure many of you know, was killed in action during the War, at the Battle of Salted Wind Marsh. He was critically injured while protecting a group of refugees who were awaiting pickup by the RSAV Hedy Lamarr. He ordered his unit to leave him behind, and single-handedly stalled the enemy advance for nearly ten minutes before his position was overrun.*

*His remarkable last stand was crucial in ensuring that both refugees and fellow Service Members were able to escape with little harm. His book, 'On Excellence, Leadership and Devotion', is considered required reading by the Reclamation Service Command College.*

*Doctor Damiano Émile has become the foremost expert on Top-Sider diseases, and has published some twenty-one research papers on the subject, and assisted in the diagnosis and cure of nearly a dozen more unique maladies. In addition, Doctor Émile serves as Chief Medical Advisor and Diplomatic Consul for our Liason Services work with the Interior First Peoples Collective.*

*Hal Lum is now retired, and lives with his wife Anna Longo in Soumerville. He is a well-established historical fiction writer, with a trio of five-star works to his name. His wife Anna is also retired and works as a painter. She will have a gallery tour visiting us here in Baslaurent starting in early summer and running until fall.*

*As for myself, as I am sure you might have guessed, I did pass my Citizenship Exam and did eventually learn to speak in complete sentences. At Marlon and Anabelle's suggestion, I spent the first three years touring the 'dozen dozen' undersea towns that comprise this remarkable culture we are all part of.*

*As a result of my STADE exams, I subsequently became a professional educator, and amateur historian. When the construction of our collective home here began, I volunteered to be part of it, and have lived here since its original occupation.*

*To the ladies and gentlemen of the Baslaurent Historical Culture Society, please accept my sincere thanks for this remarkable chance to share my story with each of you. Best wishes to you all for a bright future, and good night.*

## *About the Author*

Michel R. Vaillancourt is a 24 year-old with 24 years experience living on the North Shore of Morell, Prince Edward Island, Canada. When he's not dreaming of airships and submarines, brass and leather, he is usually running a business, Twitch.tv streaming examples of how not to play video games, shaking his head on Twitter, playing Dungeons & Dragons, fighting with swords, and sharing life and laughter with his family.

You can catch up with Michel via his "About Me" page:

https://about.me/michel.vaillancourt

## *Other Novels By This Author*

**The Sauder Diaries:  By Any Other Name (book 1, amzn.to/tsdbyanyothername)**

**The Sauder Diaries:  A Bloodier Rose (book 2, bit.ly/tsdabloodierrose)**